Photographic
Memory

Also by Bill Schubart:
The Lamoille Stories (2008) ISBN 978-0-9897121-0-1
Fat People (2010) ISBN 978-1-615-39751-1
Panhead (2012) ISBN 978-0-09834852-6-1
I am Baybie (2013) ISBN 978-0-9834852-9-2

Photographic Memory © 2014 Bill Schubart
www.schubart.com

Published May 2014 by Magic Hill Press LLC,
144 Magic Hill Rd, Hinesburg, VT 05461
ISBN 978-0-9834852-8-5
Book Design by Alex Ching
Cover Photography by Peter Miller

MSRP: $15.00 PB // $9.99 EB

Publisher's Cataloging-in-Publication
(Provided by Quality Books, Inc.)

Schubart, Bill, 1945-
Photographic Memory / by Bill Schubart.
p. cm.
Includes index.
LCCN 2012916148
ISBN 978-0-9834852-8-5

1. Families--Fiction. 2. Country life--Fiction.
3. City and town life--Fiction. 4. Bildungsromans,
American. 5. Domestic fiction, American. I. Title.

PS3619.C467P46 2013   813'.6
      QBI13-600004

Library of Congress: 2012916148

Acknowledgements:
Special thanks to my editor, Hope Matthiessen, who helped greatly in the
shaping of this work; and to Ruth Sylvester and Jane Milizia, who enhanced
and corrected copy. Blessings on Alex Ching, who realized the work
graphically. I am grateful to my candid critical readers: Denise Shekerjian,
Miciah Gault, Kate, Anna. Thanks also to Gilbert, Betsy, and Michael Perlman,
sage advisers in this time of change in the publishing world. And finally
to my families, living and dead, who are disguised in this book.

Author's note:
Four of the chapters in this work were extracted earlier and appear
in *The Lamoille Stories* as short stories.

Foreword

Photographic Memory is about the impact of photographs on memory. Are the photographs themselves the memory or do they merely record it?

The question haunts me. I look back into my childhood and see images. Some are recalled images of people and places; others are recalled photographs. So then, is memory the repository of my past or are the photographs ... or both?

A shutter opens, exposes film to fragmentary images. My eyelids open; transduce an image into impulses I store in tissue. Is the image's longevity imprinted by the accompanying emotion? Is my later recall triggered by mnemonic cue or resonance?

Images exposed and edited by people I never met inhabit memory. Their photographs fade and curl in dusty albums. Who caught the sepia image of my unknown father, grandfather? Is he a character in *Photographic Memory*? He made so many choices I must live with.

And what of dreams? Are they projections sleeping memory makes of all these stills?

These questions haunt me. I am a fabulist, distilling stories from these photographic images and cinematic dreams. Will I ever know the difference? Does it matter?

Who are these people who took this century of photographs that haunt my memory? Are they just phantoms in my story?

Photographic Memory is wholly a work of fiction but, like all fiction, has its genesis in reality.

— Bill Schubart 2014

A Marriage, Death, and Birth

He doesn't know who he is. Family photographs confuse his sense of who he is in time and place; infuse his fervid childish memory with the malaise of unknown faces. They gaze at him, caught in silver halide, albumen and salt print memory, these relatives with their sad, dark eyes and sepia surroundings, Fragonard backdrops ... and the reticence of hands.

Fiorello LaGuardia signs his birth certificate. You may recognize LaGuardia from a Broadway musical or a busy airport, but the short, stocky, dark-haired man who loved to read to children, is the Mayor of the City of New York in 1945, the year David is born. It may be a slow day in the mayor's office, or the rubber stamp bearing his signature may have gone missing, but for unknown reasons, the Mayor signs the small certificate in his own hand with a broad-nib fountain pen.

David's visual memories are of faded sepia photographs around which his memory rallies to imbue the faces of family members and friends with events and emotions that may or may not be real–but it hardly matters, does it? We're all left a rich compost of loss. Do our photographs record the real fragments of experience or do their images just compel our fictions?

The only time David's mother brings him back to New York to spend two months alone with his grandparents he is almost four. He remembers having German measles and a German governess. He has his own bedroom across the hall from his grandfather's bedroom and office and adjacent to his grandmother's bedroom with its twin Biedermeier bed set, smoke-bordered mirror dressing table and brass-muntin glass doors that open out onto her balcony and Manhattan's bustling Upper East Side. His *pox,* as it is called by his grandmother and his governess, lasts ten days, during which he is confined to his spacious room. A lesser symptom of German measles is photosensitivity, so even the modest cheer of sunlight filtering through soot-stained panes is blocked by drawn curtains.

His governess speaks little English, so he is left to amuse himself during his quarantine in the company of a glazed ceramic grey fox curled up so its nose nuzzles its tail, and a small Stieff bear from F.A.O. Schwarz. He is too young to read and is dependent on the kindness of others for a story, which comes only at nighttime if he is still awake when his grandfather returns from his busy days on post-war Wall Street.

David shares his grandmother's bathroom where he often spends time alone entranced by the arrays of English tortoise shell combs, Kent boar-bristle brushes, Provençal bath oils, Oriental dentifrice powders, French alabaster-lidded bowls containing face powder and billowy puffs, natural sponges from the Aegean, and Erté perfume flasks with their abraded glass stoppers, which he removes, sniffs, and carefully replaces. The expansive tub seems like a pond to him. On its green-veined, white marble shore are arranged an assortment of pumice stones of varying granularities for exfoliating a corn or callus. Next to the tub, a white pedestal sink that he cannot reach without his pine stepstool rises up like a monumental altar from the polished, black marble floor with its fine white veins. The room is redolent of Chanel No. 5, his grandmother's signature scent that persists in her vacant spaces even after her death, exhaled by her favorite chair and shawl and the designer dresses that hang lifeless in her long closet.

The bath fascinates him to such a degree that he often ignores his nascent sense of propriety and walks in on his grandmother to find her nude or seminude performing her *soins* before the smoke-edged mirror above the sink. She never seems to mind and, in fact, occasionally turns fully to acknowledge his quiet presence, whereupon he affects little or no interest in her impressive manifestations of femininity. She keeps herself well and her nakedness only adds majesty and mystique to their shared room.

Many years later, David wonders why his grandparents didn't share a bed like his own parents. Their lives intersected rarely outside of dinnertime, social commitments, or their annual vacations abroad, from which his grandfather always returned early for business reasons. He wonders if the apparent indifference with which his grandfather greets his wife's presence and their separate living quarters emboldened her immodesty.

During the two months David is to know his grandfather, he is elusive, not by choice but because of a demanding career in international banking and post-war finance. His own very private room is but a *pied à terre* in his busy life rather than a place in which to enjoy the company of his family. Although Howard rarely seeks out his wife's company other than to resolve practical household issues or to clarify impending social obligations, he evinces joy on the few occasions when he has time alone with his young grandson.

His grandfather's adjoining bathroom is sparse and holds none of the allure of his grandmother's. The medications and palliatives his grandfather takes for persistent stomach pains and digestive ills lie behind a mirrored medicine chest door over the sink. Below the sink a sheet-metal door bearing many coats of white paint hides a puzzling array of vials, rubber tubes, and a cracked white rubber bag with a red rubber stopper. Next to it a vaporizer smelling strongly of menthol and eucalyptus may offer relief from the frequent whistling and congestion in his lungs. He is a steady smoker of *Balkan Sobranie* Turkish cigarettes and *Amphora* loose tobacco in the briar pipes standing upright in a black walnut pipe rack on the mantel in the library. Like the pervasive scent of Chanel No. #5 in his grandmother's quarters, his grandfather's room exudes the rich and piquant smell of Turkish tobacco – the same tobacco that will choke off his life in a precipitous, malignant decline when his grandson is eight. His grandfather will die slowly in his own room in a Lethe of morphia administered by a private nurse engaged by Dr. Leopold Stieglitz, his mother's brother. Over the ensuing four days he will gradually concede the struggle to breathe amid hushed whispers and restrained tears behind the closed door.

His bedroom, too, is spare but his few objects are of the finest quality. David will later be told that the tiger-eye maple chest-on-chest of drawers and the early American walnut highboy desk are now displayed together in a museum of such things and that he must promise to visit them as if they were relatives. He sleeps on a single daybed that is made up into a couch during the day. David never sees the intimate moments of his grandfather's life since he grooms, dresses, and works behind a closed door, only receiving visitors in his room when interrupted at his desk.

From the day three months before his grandson's birth, on which his only son's remains sink slowly into the murky depths of Leyte Gulf after his ship takes a direct hit from a Japanese torpedo, the few photographic portraits of David's grandfather convey an eerie dissonance between the studio convention that demands a smile and the gun-metal gray melancholia lurking in the kohl-black recesses of his heavy-lidded eyes.

Even after his grandfather's death, when David makes his second visit alone by train to visit his grieving grandmother, he is not allowed in his grandfather's room, nor does he ever sneak into it until many years later when the door is left open by movers. He peers in on the rare occasion when the maid is dusting surfaces in there, or when the door is opened briefly as someone passes in or out.

〜〜〜

With Hiroshima and Nagasaki less than a year away, an official U.S. Navy telegram arrives, followed shortly by a personal condolence letter signed by President Roosevelt. The grieving father turns to what he knows best, takes matters in hand, and installs his son's distraught and pregnant widow in an apartment in the Plaza Hotel to nourish her grief during her confinement.

Before the full-dress naval wedding in the same hotel five months earlier, Helen had only met her fiancé's parents three times. From those encounters, her future in-laws gradually warmed to their son's choice of a wife, even though it was not their own. But their son's death at sea and their own grief soon cool their affection and Howard and Dorothy fall back on the familiar social conventions, forgetting perhaps that their new daughter-in-law has lost her husband and the father of their grandson.

Two months later, David Schumann is born to muted joy. The same nurse who will attend his grandfather's dying is engaged to help Helen with the rigors of first-time motherhood. Helen's grief and sense of emotional "confinement" before the birth continue postpartum. The claustrophobia of a single room with only a nurse and suckling infant for company soon overwhelms her.

Not long after the war in the Pacific theater is brought to a close by twin holocausts, Helen flees the formalities of the Plaza, the nurse, and her new in-laws, booking a berth on the overnight *Montrealer* to Waterbury, Vermont, a town she picks at random from the station list. She knows only that she must leave the oppression of her in-laws' imposed mourning and solitude.

His New Family

Prior to meeting and marrying her husband, Helen's happiest memories are as a young girl in Vermont at the Putney School. Putney in those days was a relatively new boarding academy inspired by the educational philosophy of John Dewey. It was run by an eccentric but dedicated woman named Carmelita Hinton who for all practical purposes espoused the philosophy of communism. She would later emigrate to China to join the great experiment and raise her own family there through the Cultural Revolution and the murderous ascendancy of the Red Guard.

At Putney, her students "learned by doing," participating in all aspects of their community, raising their own food, heating their own buildings and, as needed, erecting them. His mother's few life-long friends would hail from this brief respite of happiness in an otherwise accelerated childhood.

The young widow installs herself and her son in a light-filled, high-ceilinged apartment on the second floor of a large house in Morrisville with lots of lawn, a massive rock outcrop with moss and small alpine plants growing on it and a wooded pasture in which one sheep grazes. Her newborn son gets the smaller of the two rooms, accommodating only a crib and a child's bed and a small chest of drawers. His few toys are in a painted wooden box under the bed. A single window opens onto the roof of the landlord's apartment below.

The house is owned by Bob and Ruby Nassau, two of the many warm people in the small town of Morrisville who welcome the war widow and her young son. Ruby, with her wandering left eye, at which she often catches him staring, cares for him while his mother goes off skiing or exploring with her new beau, Alain. A seamstress by avocation, Ruby has retired from the hospitality business and the motel she and Bob once owned. As David grows older, he often sees Ruby with her one eye intent on her intricate needlework and the other seeming to follow him around the room.

When he is five, his mother and Alain become engaged. Alain René Ferland is a kind man, born into a Québécois family, well-educated and reared with the discipline and curiosity that typify many immigrant families for whom a good education or the priesthood are the only alternative to another generation of grinding farm work.

Alain's father and mother, Clovis and Eugénie, own the jitney bus that runs regularly on Route 100 from Morrisville to Stowe, and on to the train station in Waterbury where he and his mother disembarked. Most of its passengers are locals going to work at the new Mount Mansfield Company in Stowe, the State Hospital for the Insane in Waterbury, or the Atlas Plywood mill in Morrisville.

It also meets eager down-country skiers clambering off the northbound *Montrealer* with their unwieldy skis and, less frequently, Quebeckers emerging from the southbound *Washingtonian* to visit relatives who have come down to farm or work in the Eden asbestos mines or the plywood plant.

Clovis and Eugénie also operate a local taxi service and four school buses. They have been awarded the town contract to "roll" rural roads in winter, compacting the deep back-country snow with a large wood-stave roller; the driver controls the team of horses from his plank seat over the roller. This makes winter travel possible for wagons and sleighs on rural roads that could never be reached by the new municipal plows.

Alain was educated at Peoples Academy in Morrisville and the Sacré Coeur convent school in the Canadian border town of Newport before entering the war and flying C-41 transport missions into Abadan, Iran, before peace was declared in the European theater. When Alain meets the newcomers to Morrisville, he has just joined the newly formed Sepp Ruschp Ski School in Stowe and is teaching one of his two passions to the many tourists visiting Stowe. His other passion, flying, has, for the time being, been sated in the war.

Perhaps the handsome ski instructor with black, wavy hair is struck by the beauty of the young woman with her brownish-blond hair and sad smile, for she is beautiful, both in her grief and in her search for a renewed sense of intimacy and security. Or maybe he is struck by her vulnerability, as she sits on the ski slope where she has fallen when her borrowed wooden skis cross in a snowplow at the Toll House rope tow.

In an early photograph of Alain, he wears an off-white cable-knit sweater over a white oxford shirt with the collar nestled neatly in the V-neck. The black, visored ski hat with tied-up ear flaps rests far back on his head, showing the natural wave of his black hair. He holds his head high and looks away from his camera-obsessed girlfriend. He is not used to having his picture taken. In Morrisville, the rare photograph, usually taken at a portrait studio, is formal and often associated with a sacrament like baptism, marriage, first communion, or extreme unction.

He must have been embarrassed by his beautiful girlfriend from the city who was constantly snapping pictures of him and his friends. The black and white print is yellowed now and shows emulsion spots through the paper. The window frame of a convertible is visible just behind him.

His new girlfriend, Helen, was born of the marriage of a hard-bitten intellectual and aesthete named Hilaire Sooysmith and a gentle artist named Edward Clarence Dean. They live in Greenwich, Connecticut, and in Coconut Grove, Florida, on wealth acquired by previous generations of architects and bridge builders.

Around the turn of the century Clarence, as he was known, attended *L'Ecole des Beaux-Arts* in Paris as a student of architecture. With little need to sustain himself, however, he is soon drawn into the fine arts, which he pursues through the rest of his short life, leaving a rich legacy of landscape and still life oils, watercolor and pen and ink drawings.

His remote and fiercely judgmental wife, Hilaire, fluent in five languages, pursues exotic cultures and literature and seems happier in the company of mannish women than with her soft-spoken and retiring husband. She often spends time alone or traveling on the Indian subcontinent, maintaining a lifelong friendship with the Hindi novelist Guptil Mukerjee. She also reads religiously the poetry and fiction of Rabindranath Tagore.

In midlife, polio reduces her travels to occasional excursions from her bed to a bathroom or, on rare occasions, the living room where she sits uncomfortably on a couch supported by heavy and complex iron braces. She is attended to by Rosa, a lanky, irascible and wholly irreverent Cuban woman "of a certain age" who follows the revolutionary politics of Cuba. "Venga la revolución," she often says, as she dreams of her homeland's future. In 1958, she will return to join her hero, "La Barba," deep in the Sierra Madre Mountains to expel the "Battista poison" from her homeland.

Clarence adores his only daughter. Away from the scrutiny of his stern wife, father and daughter shelter in a studio he has built for himself in a covert of palms far back on their Florida property. There they cook delicacies forbidden in the main house by Hilaire, who follows a strict Hindu diet of grains and vegetables. They ramble for hours in the family's wild coastal preserve, known as Panther Hammock. Their property abuts the eight acres of his friend David Fairchild, a botanist and amateur herpetologist who introduces Clarence and his daughter to the elusive and deadly coral snake, native to the area. Fairchild's property, which he calls *The Kampong,* is home to a bewildering variety of transplants he has collected in voyages to Polynesia and Southeast Asia, including mangos, papayas, and breadfruit.

Clarence offers Helen the only haven of warmth and affection in the stark home life prescribed by his ascetic wife. But only three years after his recently widowed daughter and grandson resettle in Vermont, Clarence succumbs to coronary disease. Helen, again bereft, becomes even more dependent on her new family. Hilaire, to whom the emotional aspects of maternity are alien, drifts into mental incompetence and finishes her life in front of a nursing home's TV set as she puzzles out the mysteries of a soap opera.

Helen's distant older brother, distracted with the rearing of his own family and growing his medical practice, can offer little more than an addictive stream of narcotic prescriptions to his grieving sister.

The sepia photographs of Helen as a young girl in Florida convey a sense of childish wonder. Rarely is she photographed in any clothing. In one haunting photo, she is a girl of about ten, sitting naked in the sand in a palm-shaded clearing with her legs extended in front of her. Her hands are by her side, palms down in the sand. She watches intently as a yard-long black snake winds its way across both of her legs. She appears at once curious and frightened. The photographer is suggested only by a shadow in the sand next to her. The black snake is not poisonous, but is known for its virulent bite.

The last formal portraits taken of her are in New York soon after her brief marriage. They are taken by her artist cousin, Georgia Engelhard, and convey the same penumbra of grief visible in the last portraits of her father-in-law, but over a faintly sensual smile.

The only images of David's mother and father are formal wedding photographs in poses prescribed by the wedding photographer. They offer him no glimpse into their brief time together and he is old enough to understand that his father would never have seen him. He is not old enough, though, to take on the task of trying to comfort his mother or relieve her melancholy. Unlike Helen, David has not experienced his father's death and finds it impossible to muster empathy he does not feel. He is also busy and distracted getting to know his stepfather and the kids in his neighborhood.

Helen and Alain are married by Father Lefèvre in a Catholic ceremony at Holy Family church in Morrisville attended by Alain's large family and his many friends from the ski school. No one from his fiancée's family makes the journey to the small town in Vermont. Perhaps Morrisville seems too remote, or perhaps they are put off by the idea of their son's widow taking a new husband.

Shortly after the wedding and against the advice of Helen's Wall Street former father-in-law, Alain begins building a house for his new family on an acre carved out of Volney Farr's hayfield along a dirt road leading from town toward Elmore Mountain. To conserve some of the money his father and mother lent him, Alain signs on with the builder as a framing carpenter.

Three days a week in the winter months, David rides with his stepfather on his way to work at the Mountain Company in Stowe to Mrs. Jaquith's nursery school. It is just off the Mountain Road in Stowe, atop a steep hill. In summer, when his stepfather works for the Trapp Family as a chauffeur, he is sent to Mrs. Mudgett's kindergarten on the other side of Morrisville near the Holy Family church. He likes both kindergartens, but favors the one in his hometown for its motley collection of kids with whom he plays and learns to roughhouse.

Blodgett Falls

David's favorite outing is Blodgett Falls. Often during the warmest summer months, Alain will forgo his lunch hour and leave work a half-hour early. In phoning Helen and asking her to put up a picnic supper, he will have tipped his hand and, when he arrives home at five, his new family will be standing in the driveway waiting for him, picnic basket and towels in hand. Helen and David clamber into the 1941 Plymouth Alain's father gave him as a wedding present and they set off through town and up into the hills leading to their favorite swimming hole.

At its source, Sterling Brook bubbles out of Sterling Mountain, meandering down through the largely uninhabited valley and picking up new waters from the small tributaries and rivulets that flow into it. At points, it deepens as it passes through several narrow and inaccessible gorges and then cascades over waterfalls, gouging out the moraine to make popular swimming holes before flowing placidly into the neighboring resort town of Stowe.

Blodgett Falls is about half-way up the road that dead-ends at two hill farms huddled at the base of Sterling Mountain. The falls here lack the drama of those further downstream. The water here spills several feet over moss-covered rock into a small basin just deep enough to swim and wade in but not deep enough for the dramatic dives that are popular among the teenagers who frequent the deeper swimming holes below.

Alain parks his sedan in a small turn-off large enough for two cars and the family piles out and picks their way down a narrow path to the water.

"I hear it, I hear it," says David looking back at his mother behind him. "I can hear the waterfall."

"Watch your step. Be careful," urges Alain as the family emerges onto a large flat rock.

Helen sets down the picnic basket and spreads out a white and blue checked tablecloth she has brought. Alain sets down the three folded bath towels and David rushes to the water's edge, squats down and sets his little wooden boat in the water. The rock shelf retains the warmth it absorbs from the plentiful sunlight filtering through the birches that line the brook. Unlike many of the swimming holes, Blodgett Falls gets a full day's exposure to the sun. On clear days, it is warm and full of light. The large flat rock gives way to several feet of sandy gravel that line the water's edge. Helen loves this place because her son can wade into the shallow water without her worrying about strong currents or him getting in over his head. Only under the falls does the water get more than several feet deep.

Helen spreads herself out on the warm rock in a self-conscious pose and Alain pops open Carling Black Label beers for himself and his new wife.

Alain is proud of his ready-made family. He and Helen plan to have more children, although Alain has embraced the widow's son as his very own. Helen never talks of her former life or husband, perhaps out of fear that Alain might imagine that she is harboring a comparison or that he might worry that she loves him less than her dead husband, whom she had barely come to know beyond the initial social encounters, subsequent dates, and finally nights spent together at borrowed apartments. Then followed the urgent call of naval redeployment and the discovery that Helen was pregnant, pressing them into a hasty but happy marriage.

David loves to dig out a little harbor for his wooden boat in the gravel. The boat is a gift from his Uncle Maurice, Alain's brother. It is a flat piece of shellacked pine with a V- shaped prow. Two wood slats protrude symmetrically from the stern, between which is mounted a four-finned paddle wheel, suspended in a rubber band. Maurice taught David how to counter-wind the paddle wheel until it was taut and then set the boat down in water and let it go. David loved the gift from his new uncle and brought it everywhere they went where there was water.

Helen and Alain lie back on their elbows facing one another and sipping from the brown bottles of beer as they watch David play in the shallows. Occasionally, he looks back and sees his stepfather being tender with his mother, caressing her cheek and is grateful to see her happy again. He is not jealous, only glad that he now has a father like his other friends and that his mother appears again to be happy.

Alain springs to his feet and comes to the water's edge. He asks David if he would like to see the waterfall up close. David looks back at his mother and she nods a smiling assent. Alain takes David's hand and they wade into the deeper water toward the falls. When the water gets above David's trunks, Alain scoops him up and puts him on his shoulders and they continue wading out into the deep. Under the waterfall, the water is only about four feet deep. Alain turns around to face Helen on the shore and urges his son to wave to his mother. He does so and she reciprocates. Alain backs slowly in under the waterfall which falls on David. The rush and power of the falling water almost knocks him off but he clings to Alain's forehead and begins squealing with joy at the feel of the powerful water. Alain moves in and out of the waterfall several times and then steps away. David yells "Again, Alain, again. Do it once more." And so begins the repetitive plea of the child entranced by his parent's novel entertainments.

Back on shore, Helen has spread out their picnic. Alain has opened two more beers and Helen hands out the tomato and chicken sandwiches she has prepared from last night's leftover broiler hen. Each is wrapped in wax paper and held together with a piece of scotch tape.

The three bask in the sun munching on their sandwiches and sour pickles, and then take turns with the one fork, finishing a leftover quadrant of pumpkin pie Alain's mother, Eugénie, left off the day before.

Alain opens the last two beers. David goes back to the water's edge and plays with his boat. Looking back once, he catches his mother and new father kissing. They see him looking at them and are embarrassed. Helen waves to him and smiles. David plays with his boat and thinks of the many times his mother has kissed and been tender with him. He associates her tenderness with bedtime and bath time so the tenderness he sees between Alain and his mother seems only natural in this evening place of water.

When the time comes to go home, David doesn't protest. The light is fading and he is feeling sleepy. His lips are quivering and bluish from the chilling night air. Helen wraps him in her own towel, rubbing briskly him to generate warmth. The towel is dry as she didn't swim, preferring to sun herself on the warm rock and leave Alain time to play with his new stepson.

Fanny Fancher

It is his second day in first grade and his first time walking home alone from school. Maple Street is a half-mile long, one of several streets in town canopied with fountain-like elms. Try as he will, he can't count the houses on both sides as he walks home from school. He loses track as his eyes dart from left to right and the sum vanishes.

Just below the hospital, Maple Street merges into Washington Highway, which leads east out of town toward the hill farms in the shadow of Elmore Mountain. The street's lofty name belies its washboard gravel surface and cavernous potholes after prolonged rainfalls. His Uncle Benoit tried to teach him the French term for *pothole*. "Nid de poule, nid de poule," he'd repeat, pronouncing only two of the three syllables. David's whispered "nipple" elicited gales of laughter from his uncle who would start in again. Though the French term's pronunciation eludes him, the expression's literal English meaning, "hen's nest" stays with him and each time he sees a pothole he envisages one of Mrs. Farr's hens sitting stoically in the pothole on a clutch of eggs, looking nervously about for passing cars or bikes. His house lies just beyond the hospital and within the town limits, which disqualifies him from riding on the school bus run by Alain's parents.

His neighborhood includes the three-story, wood-frame Copley Hospital, girded with a rocker-filled white verandah and surrounded by tall white pines. Farther up lives Dr. Foss, the town dentist, and Adrian Morris, the president of the bank. Across from his own house is the Collette's, with an attached small engine shop. Beyond lies Volney and Gladys Farr's farm, the Ned and Lyle Stewart farm, Mrs. Roleau's tenant house attached to the Stewart farm, the town dump, and, farther up the road, Greaves Dairy.

His first-grade teacher, Mrs. Fancher, is a warm woman, exuding sympathy for her students' trials as they tackle the first steps of learning. Her occasional efforts at being strict invariably fall victim to the enjoyment she gets from her charges' antics.

Her generous, heaving bosom draws the attention of many of the boys in the large classroom except when Mrs. Fancher looks straight at the ogler. Alain also had her as a teacher and confides to his stepson that when he was little, her bosom was referred to as a *balcon* in the French his friends spoke among themselves, "Like the mezzanine in the Bijou Theater downtown," he laughs.

She is too heavy to genuflect next to the desks in her classroom so she leans over in order to assist a first-grader. Her generous décolletage then becomes the child's entire horizon. One can look up into her kindly face, down at the work in question or straight ahead into the cleft between her abundant breasts.

The tall, small-paned windows in the corner classroom flood the square room with light. Silver-painted cast-iron radiators, noisy in winter, cling to the dark maple wainscot below the windows. The many applications of shellac on the scuffed maple floors are evident only in the un-trafficked nooks and crannies along the walls or where the black cast-iron desk mounts are screwed to the floor. The aisles between the desks are worn down by the endless scuffing of small leather shoes laden with playground grit. David's desk is near the middle, three rows back and, on overcast early winter mornings, it will be mid-morning before the warmth from the radiators reaches him.

Five times daily, the class is marched single-file down to morning *basement*, morning recess, lunch recess, afternoon *basement* and school dismissal. Going to the bathroom is called "going to the basement" and is highly regimented. The school has no kitchen facilities, so the basement is dedicated to boys' and girls' toilet facilities, janitorial services and a massive asbestos-clad coal furnace visible only when the janitor's door is ajar. The basement is painted a pale institutional yellow. Students are admonished to hold onto the shellacked railings as they make their way down the stairs and, on reaching the lowest level, girls divert to the right and boys to the left.

Five minutes are allotted for *basement duty* and a vigorous hand-washing with yellow soap. Students then reassemble at the foot of the stairs for a single-file ascent back to class. Mrs. Fancher brooks no horseplay. She listens discreetly from outside the labyrinthine entrance to the boy's basement for the sounds of running water indicating *proper ablutions* and oversees this directly on the girls' side.

To the confusion of David and his classmates, a plumbing innovation has been installed at some point to ensure toilets are flushed. The toilet seats are spring-loaded, so that when left, the seat rises slightly and activates the flushing mechanism. Since neither David nor any but two of his first-grade colleagues are heavy enough to depress the toilet seat and activate the valve, they must "do their duty" perched at a precipitous incline, hanging on to the side walls to maintain balance.

During his second day of school, David is in the basement with the other boys and, mindful of the five-minute rule, he hastily pulls up the troublesome metal zipper on his cotton pants and catches what is left of his tiny foreskin in the mechanism. The pain takes his breath away and he cries out. Most of the other boys have left to reassemble. The room begins to distort through the tears welling up from pain and fear and he can't see who is left. Any effort to move or even touch the zipper is excruciating so he simply stands by a porcelain sink crying.

The five minutes are up and Mrs. Fancher is tallying her brood. David's absence is noted and she calls in through the doorway, "Time's up. Boys reassemble." The two remaining boys, noting his predicament, leave. Neither reports David's circumstance to Mrs. Fancher as her demands for his exit become more adamant. The segregation of boys and girls extends as well to adults, so Mrs. Fancher has to enlist Roland, the janitor, to enforce David's exit from the boys' basement.

Roland is a kind and simple man and sees the problem immediately. A practical man as well, he knows there is one fix and it is not medical. He tells Mrs. Fancher to go ahead, that he will bring her student up shortly and explain later. Then he cautions him to hold his breath and without preamble reopens the zipper quickly. David gasps and cries out.

He then leads David by the hand into his utility room next to the silo-sized furnace that generates steam heat for the cranky radiators in the eight classrooms above. From a drawer in his tool bench, he removes a brown vial of mercurochrome and daubs a bit with a tissue onto the torn and bleeding glans, assuring him that the pain will subside soon. He then gives him a minute to compose himself and leads him by his hand back up to the classroom. There was no school nurse in those days. Roland speaks quietly with Mrs. Fancher, whose sudden intake of breath makes clear to the class that he has revealed to her the reason for her student's tardiness. She says nothing, but gives David a look of understanding and forgiveness.

Later that afternoon, Phyllis Dempsey wets herself. She often has a hard time "holding her water," as Mrs. Fancher confides to her nervous mother. She sits in front and across from David and he is the first to notice the trickle of pale fluid making its way down her tan brown leg and into her white socks. She cradles her head in her folded arms on her desk and sobs silently. David can only imagine her terror. Mrs. Fancher soon gathers from the snickers of the Forcier twins what has happened and, after threatening them with loss of recess privileges, ushers Phyllis into the cloakroom, where she offers some gentle admonishment and tells her to go to the basement and clean herself up as best she can. He cannot imagine coming back into the classroom after such ignominy. After some time has passed and Phyllis has not returned, Mrs. Fancher leaves the class *on honor* and goes to find Phyllis, who is still in the cloakroom where she is trying in vain to hide among the small coats, crying and afraid to return. Mrs. Fancher comforts her and gradually convinces her to return to her desk, while glaring furiously at the smirking Forcier boys.

The event elicits both fear and empathy in much of the class and deflects attention from the zipper incident in the boys' room. Unfortunately, it also fuels the Forcier twins and the clique of boys who curry their favor. They withheld their taunts until recess and then make Phyllis' life miserable by broadcasting the event to the kids in the higher grades in an effort to impress them.

When the lunch recess bell rings, boys and girls gather the books and papers they are working on, stow them in the lift-top desks, rise together, and file into the adjacent cloakroom. This is a long, narrow room with a window at one end and numbered black cast-iron hooks screwed into the dark wainscoting a yard above the floor to accommodate a six-year-old's height. From there, everyone files down the stairs and out the heavy front door held open by Mrs. Fancher onto the dirt playground with its swings, teeter-totter, and "go-round" all occupied and dominated by bigger kids.

First-graders huddle together in defensive cliques in case they are approached by older kids. Eventually they let down their guard and swap wax paper-wrapped sandwiches and begin to dig small *pots* with their heels against the building to play marbles with one another as the second-graders do.

At three in the afternoon a loud electric bell rings throughout the school signaling dismissal. Children living within a mile of the school, in the village or on the outskirts of town, walk home. Those who live on the hill farms farther out queue up near the yellow buses lined up beside the playground.

Four crosswalks exit the triangular school playground, each managed by a sixth-grade patrol. Patrols wear white belts that encircle the waist and cross the chest diagonally, all held together with a brass buckle. On these is pinned a chrome-plated badge larger than David's hand. To his astonishment, the patrols can stop cars coming in either direction, although patrols are trained not to interrupt the flow of cars but to wait until there are none in sight and then lead kids across, stopping any cars that approach while they are between the curbs by simply holding up a hand like Moses parting the Red Sea. David, like his classmates, aspires one day to be a patrol.

Crazy Chase

It is a cool late summer day and everything is still green, but fall is in the air as David walks along Maple Street alone as there are no other first- or second-graders in that neighborhood. He tries to imagine what it will be like walking home in the winter and being confined to snowbank-lined sidewalks.

Having abandoned the distraction of counting houses, he's acutely aware of car, bike, and foot traffic on his new route. He stops to look at play sets, peers discreetly into houses, and keeps his eyes peeled for others coming or going on the sidewalk. The concrete squares that make up the sidewalk have heaved into odd angles either from frost or the growth of elm roots underneath. This means looking down as much as up in order not to trip. It also means that the fourth-graders who can ride their bikes to school ride in the street instead of on the sidewalks, slaloming among the potholes.

During an up-glance he notices a grownup striding toward him on the same side of the street. The purposeful gait and hunched shoulders indicate an older man. The black dangling purse indicates a woman. An encounter means his upbringing will call on him to greet the person and perhaps even carry on a polite conversation as his stepfather so often does. It seems to him that Alain knows everyone. He himself knows few people beyond the neighbors his own age and their mothers. He dares not stop, but glances down and keeps walking toward the curious person striding toward him.

Still a block away, David glances up again to better read the approaching figure. He is worried that the person notices him as well but keeps up his gait and the downward cant of his vision. He doesn't know why he thinks this person is a "he" because the figure is wearing a light gray cotton dress with white lace around the collar, black women's shoes with a low heel and a nondescript pillbox hat perched precariously on a profusion of gray hair. David quickly glances back at the pavement, determined not to make eye contact as the person approaches.

Still a house away and fingering the 51 cent coin in his pocket he has brought to school for "show and tell," he dares another glance and is unnerved by what he sees. He is convinced by the approaching figure's stature and stride that he is a man, but everything else indicates an elderly lady. The mass of gray hair is done up carelessly into a bun, above which perches the dark brown pillbox hat, held in place by bobby pins. The face is stubbled with hair even more extensive than Mrs. Rider's, whose depilatory failures are a frequent topic among her fourth-graders. His left hand clutches a large black cotton purse with wooden clasp handles. But he doesn't carry it high and close like Mrs. Farr; it hangs low from his loose grip like a plumber's tool bag.

David determines to walk the rest of the way home without looking up except to be sure to make the turn onto Washington Highway. Curiosity overwhelms fear, however, and without moving his head he glances sideways as the figure strides by on his left. The gender ambiguity is evident in the person's calves, which show the curved musculature and hair of a man but are covered in heavy textured nylon stockings rolled into a doughnut below the knobby knees. His gray dress covers the rest.

David knows that to be sure he will have to see the person's chest. In a strained glance up without moving his head, he catches a glimpse of the torso. The person lacks breasts or any pretense of them. The limp darts of the dress under-hang a hairy male décolletage decked with a large ivory-colored brooch.

His glance returns to the safety of the sidewalk as the man-woman strides past, leaving a masculine scent in his wake. There is no perfume, only a slightly acrid and distinctly male smell, tinged with a faint scent of camphor or mothballs, the same smell he'd noticed when he opened his father's suitcase to pack for his trip to his grandmother's or opened his mother's trunk in the attic.

David hears the click of heels as the man lopes by. He does not see the expression on his face but imagines that he is angry and perhaps in a hurry to castigate someone for something they have done to him or have not done for him, and he wonders what that might be.

He puts three houses between himself and the enigmatic person before looking back over his shoulder to ensure that the man's stride continues to distance them and that he hasn't changed his mind and turned around. A car passes heading toward town and David wonders if the young woman driving sees what he has seen and experiences the same confusion.

As he turns left onto Washington Highway below the hospital, he sees in the distance that his mother is waiting for him in the front yard and he runs the rest of the way home. Perhaps because she is anxious to hear about his second day at school and there is so much to tell, he doesn't tell her what he has just seen. But later that night lying in bed he details the encounter to Alain, whose smile he can see by the light of his nightlight.

"Sounds like you met Crazy Chase," he laughs.

David does not press him on details. He fleetingly reviews in his own mind the experience in the school basement of the day before and then falls into a deep sleep.

The next day at school is filled with new "learnings," as his grandmother Eugénie calls them. During recess, David wins an agate while playing marbles and masters riding a two-wheeler on the playground.

His second walk home is uneventful. He keeps a wary eye out along Maple Street and its few side streets, but sees no sign of Crazy Chase. His stepfather's jovial tone reassured him that he had little to fear and everything to be curious about when next he encountered the man.

As the final days of summer pass and the chill nights of autumn set in, the town begins its preparations for the fall firehouse dance, an annual event that brings the eager and the disapproving together in a social truce. At the gathering, the few who disapprove of dancing or pretend to because they have no one to dance with busy themselves with the laying-out of casseroles, baked goods, and drinks, and, when the dancing begins, continue to fuss about, tasting goodies, comparing recipes and commenting on the culinary successes and failures of others.

A bandstand has been cobbled together out of two-by-sixes in front of the firehouse, along with a primitive PA system wired up from the public-address horns borrowed from the electronic carillon in the steeple of the Puffer Methodists, a dented Western Electric broadcast mike borrowed from WDEV, and a livid, static-emitting brace of vacuum tubes borrowed from Henry Fogg, the town's radio and TV repairman.

When the platform is finished and tested, the womenfolk of the Order of the Eastern Star take over, decorating it with bunting and newly harvested Hubbard squash, pumpkins, cornstalks, and apples. For the last few years, the dance has been used to raise money for the "pumper fund" and each year brings the town closer to owning a refurbished LaFrance fire truck.

The afternoon of the dance has some locals struggling to get an upright piano borrowed from the activity room of the elementary school across the street up onto the bandstand. Champ, lionized locally for his appearance on the Ed Sullivan Show as the drummer in the U.S. Navy Jazz Band, unpacks and sets up his flashy new chrome and mother-of-pearl drum set.

For the dance, the fire trucks are brought out and lined up on the street at the ready in case a barn fire should break out during the dance. Fall and early winter are the times for spontaneous barn fires, as a few farmers will risk putting up wet hay when the weather doesn't cooperate during late cuttings. Lying dormant and airless, damp hay heats slowly to the flashpoint and then combusts spontaneously, burning the barn to the ground, killing livestock, and, occasionally, spreading to the nearby farmhouse.

Six folding tables with ironed, white cotton tablecloths laden with comestibles line the walls of the empty firehouse. The men folk have set up a number of straight-back kitchen chairs brought in from various homes in the backs of pickups for elderly singles who come to watch, but also to dance if asked. The final touch is a tiara of clear light bulbs dangling from a pair of wires with frayed cotton insulation tracing the perimeter of the square macadam entrance that will, that evening, fill with dancers.

As the muted fall light fades in mid-afternoon and the temperature drops in earnest, preparations for the dance continued. The black and chrome Prussian General inside the firehouse is stoked until the sheet metal body glows a faint red near the base and its heat radiates throughout the building.

The Ladies Firehouse Auxiliary arrives, aided by the Ladies of the Eastern Star and the Uplift Club, all bearing baked goods. They vie for position on the tables, moving others' goods to the rear and placing their own out front where they can both be admired and sampled. An empty pie tin or cake pan is the prize. Leftovers provide an excuse for slighting commiseration on how much of their contribution has gone uneaten.

"I knew there was too little sugar in Rena's apple turnovers. Look how many's left!"

Marge Brown, the pianist, is also the town's lone piano tuner and has her tuning key deep in the cabinet of the old Kimball upright, fussing the metal pegs back and forth in the cracked soundboard until she's satisfied. Champ has his drum key out and tunes his drum set with evident pride, sticking the drum head and tightening or loosening the chrome pegs around the perimeter of the drums until he too is satisfied with the sound.

It's pitch dark at 6:30. Throughout Lamoille County, the white ironstone dinner plates are washed, dried, and put away, cows are in their stanchions, biddies in their roosts, and folks are gussied up and headed to town. Pickups, farm flatbeds, sedans, and even a few buggies pull up and park along Elmore Street across from the firehouse. Vehicles are parked facing the firehouse, often to hide the alcoholic arrays in the back. Drink ranges from home brew and hard cider to Canadian whiskey smuggled across during a full moon on logging roads late at night without benefit of headlights. And there is always local *screech*, a rum-like spirit distilled from whatever is handy. In all cases discretion is required, as one's prospects of a proper marriage might be ruined by offending the church ladies, who remain steadfastly alert to improper behavior

The degree of eagerness of womenfolk to engage someone of the opposite sex in conversation, dancing, or more can be read in their outfits. The flouncy, western-fringed, full-skirted cowgirl look indicates a willingness to be entertained. The trussed-up, black-and-white, floor-length outfit with flattened bosom and indeterminate waistline conveys a general distrust of men and an unwavering commitment to chastity. The young girls, as yet unsure about their nascent desires, wear plain cotton dresses and patent leather shoes and huddle in the corners giggling and pointing at the swains as they arrive.

It is not a school night and kids of all ages are welcome, even on the dance floor, but only the girls dance. The boys, as yet unsure of their dance steps and confounded by puberty, disdain dancing and huddle together talking of the upcoming deer season, the fall tractor pulls, or car engines they hope someday to rebuild. Girls from French families step-dance side-by-side, often five or six at a time, while the Protestant girls sashay one another like Western swing dancers, each imagining the other to be a handsome boy.

David arrives with his parents but soon leaves to seek out their long-time friend, Ron Terrill, who owns the local Texaco station. Ron is watching the proceedings with amusement and keeps up a running commentary about who was doing what with whom. Having no children of his own, Ron speaks to kids as he does to adults, except in his more reproving role as a side judge in the County Court in Hyde Park.

The dance begins when Marge Brown starts pounding out chords and Champ seeks a rhythm with his bass drum and snare. Across the dance floor, Crazy Chase, still an object of curiosity to David, but no longer of fear, climbs the platform with his wooden violin case and his purse. He sets the purse on the piano, opens the case, and takes out his fiddle, which he tunes in a few strokes of his horsehair bow before launching into a town favorite, *La Bastringue*. The piano and Champ adjust their rhythm to Crazy Chase's fiddle. The dance floor fills quickly and the evening is under way.

After a few rousing reels, polkas, and two-steps that bring much of the crowd to their feet, the pace slows and Crazy Chase guides his bow into a lilting waltz tune. Marge Brown's heavy left hand soon finds and sets the low end of the waltz rhythm, while Champ sits out the waltz, leaning back on his padded chrome stool, and enjoying a Lucky Strike. Crazy Chase plays the lilting waltz melody as if fronting a symphony orchestra, bending forward into the first beat and then sweeping back for the second and third.

Across the room David sees his mother leading a reluctant Alain on to the dance floor as she whispers in his ear. Alain is uncomfortable with such displays and often looks down at his feet, which David notices do not always move with the rhythm. Later, Helen notices David watching and smiles, although she seems far away. The music picks up again and Alain and Helen retreat to the tables.

Ron smiles and taps his foot. He is not a dancer and seems indifferent to female attractions, although he has many women friends, including David's mother.

Without looking down at him, Ron says, "Your Dad tells me you met Crazy Chase."

David nods. Ron asks him what he thinks.

"Dunno," he replies. "Is he a man or a woman?"

"He's a man who dresses like a woman," Ron responds.

"Why?" he puzzles.

"Dunno. I suppose he just wants to. What do you think of that?"

"Dunno," he echoes.

There is silence for a minute and Ron continues, "Arthur's eccentric. He didn't always dress like a woman. He grew up in Middlesex, oddly enough. I knew him when he was younger."

"Did he dress like a woman then?" David ventures.

"No," Ron answers, "he dressed like a man."

"Why did he change?" David asks over the music.

"Hard to say," Ron answers, still looking straight ahead. "One never knows about these things, but he's dressed that way ever since he came to town twenty years ago; buys his bloomers at Adrian's Dry Goods just like the minister's wife."

"Don't people tease and make fun of him?" David persists.

"The boys do sometimes, but a few whacks with his purse usually puts an end to it," Ron says, looking down with a smile at David.

The music ends but the floor doesn't clear. A Canadian reel called *Le reel du pendu* follows. David recalls his Uncle Benoit trying to impart to him and his other nieces and nephews, who spoke no French, bits of Québécois language and culture, explaining to him once at a family outing that the song was called "The Reel of the Hanged Man" because the steps recall the dancing movement of the feet of a man who has just been dropped from a gallows. Many years later, David hears the true legend from Louis Beaudoin, one of the great Québécois *violoneux*. A man condemned to die by hanging asks for a violin and, while in his cell, learns to play so well that, when he takes out his fiddle on the scaffold and plays the reel he has composed, he is set free.

Like a marionetteer's crossbars, Crazy Chase's bow moves the townfolk around the dance floor ... Jack, the dark-suited mortgage foreclosure and his wife, and Ned and Hilda Fournier, the failing Hyde Park farmers still smelling of fresh manure and falling further and further behind in their payments; Ray, the dark-eyed Rexall drugstore owner, standing next to his daughter who shoplifts his cosmetics; Dora, the 16-year-old mother and her seemingly shy uncle and unwanted lover, Alfred; Corrinne, with no visible means of support other than the coterie of brilliantined men orbiting her; Reverend Pease, the sober Methodist deacon and his wife, who hides port bottles in the parsonage, all dance to his music, seeing nothing except one another when the music ends.

Crazy Chase's repertoire of reels, jigs, hornpipes, two-steps and waltzes bring strangers together and for others sow the seeds of separations to come. When he stops, they, too, stop and look anxiously around for him to start up again. His pillbox hat, faded cotton dress, and heavy, rolled-up stockings no longer seem out of place as he plays.

A Promised Visit

David is in third grade. He lies sprawled on the kitchen floor playing with his Matchbox farm toys—a tractor with manure spreader and hay-lift attachments. The phone rings. It's the familiar "two longs" that signal a call to the Ferland number on their four-party line. His mother answers. He senses from her words and tone it is his New York grandmother calling. Like animals before a storm, children perceive impending conflict well beyond the understanding of the parents, who try to camouflage it. But the child intuits discord and, in the absence of a reason, assumes they are the cause.

On this occasion, his mother's language is clipped, her responses cryptic. She looks out the window as she speaks into the receiver. He is indeed the center of an argument between the two women. At issue is an earlier informal understanding that he will spend time with his grandmother, perhaps to fill the gap left by the loss of her husband and son. Except for his first visit alone when he was just turning four, his mother's exodus to Vermont has left the commitment unmet. The two women finally agree that he will go to New York alone to be with his grandmother for the week of Thanksgiving recess. To avoid more disagreement, the details will be worked out between his grandmother and Alain.

Later, after the supper dishes are cleared, Alain turns to him and confirms the plan with a smile, "You're gonna have to pack your scratchy clothes."

David goes into the living room and sits down next to the cat on the long section of the L-shaped couch. His feet don't yet touch the floor so he tucks his legs under him and stares at the new black cat his mother has named *Bagheera*, a literary allusion to Kipling's *Jungle Book* lost on Alain and David. Bagheera has done nothing specific to earn his distrust, but is new to the family and so, like a recently arrived sibling about whom the older child is ambivalent, has yet to find its place in the family.

David recalls his grandmother's familiar perfume and sees her naked in her bath. He imagines her getting ready for dinner at her glass-covered dressing table with its matching smoke-edged mirror, applying mascara, rouge and lipstick and asking his help with his small, agile fingers to clasp a pearl necklace under the fall of her long hair. He can see his grandmother dressed formally for dinner and presiding over the oval Empire table with her bare arms. He imagines the duplex apartment's nooks and crannies he has explored and where he has hidden from Margaret, the maid. Once a source of wonder to him, the sensual memories of his grandmother feel now like a betrayal of his mother.

The next day, after school, he climbs the two lower shelves behind the bar of hanging clothes in his closet and pulls from the top shelf a varnished, hard-shell, herring-bone valise with his father's initials between the two spring-loaded brass clasps. It's one of the many quotidian things bearing the initials he shares with his dead father that he has inherited.

When condoled by people in his new hometown about the loss of his father, David is polite but blasé. Any sense of his father comes from photographs and, to a lesser degree, from anecdotes or the little he might infer from the things solemnly passed on to him. These mementos usually bear his father's name, likeness, or initials and include a blue book of letters written home during his service in the Pacific. David never knew the man people refer to with such sympathy, only that he and his ship sank in the war. Before long he abandons any pretense of sadness for this man of whom his mother never speaks.

In his room, there is a simply framed photograph of his father in his Navy lieutenant's uniform, taken on the white-painted iron steps leading up to the bridge of his ship. It conveys little beyond a likeness, although one can see the nervous bravado of a young man who must appear belligerent. A surviving officer on board the *U.S.S. MacDougal* assured both grieving widow and parents in a letter sent after the war that "he would never have known what hit him that day in the engine room."

The small suitcase is redolent of smells that David cannot identify but that call up his grandmother's apartment, starchy smells of stiff and scratchy clothes infused with lavender. Pulling back the buckled straps, he carefully lays out his white underwear, rolled socks, two pairs of thin corduroy school pants, a pair of blue cotton shorts, and two thin-striped shirts. He then folds on top the dreaded pair of black wool slacks that feel like steel wool on his skinny legs and a starched, white dress shirt that hangs like a sandwich board on him. Finally, he carefully folds a navy-blue wool blazer with a gold crest of generic genealogy. It is too big for him, having been passed on to his mother from Ruby Nassau when a customer never claimed it. His stepfather insists he pack it so he can dress properly for dinner. He also lends him a narrow tie that is as long as David is tall, assuring him that his grandmother will help him tie it should the need arise. He has never worn a tie before, not for Sunday Mass or for the funeral of his stepfather's Uncle Alcide several months earlier.

When everything on Alain's list is packed, the suitcase is still not full, so he leaves it on the floor at the foot of his bed and goes outdoors

to see if any of the neighbor kids are playing and receptive to his joining them.

Stevie Stewart, Petey Foss and Cécile Collette are riding their bikes
up and down the gravel road. David watches from the John Deere pedal
tractor his new grandfather, Clovis, has refurbished for him. The cast-
iron tractor is hard for him to drive, as the pedals are connected directly
to the small front wheel and the lack of any gearing makes it difficult to
pedal except on a smooth flat or downward-sloping surface. He uses it
as a perch from which to watch the older kids pump their bikes up the
hill to Mr. Farr's white farmhouse, make a wobbly U-turn in the middle
of the road and then careen down the gravel hill past him and on down
past the Foss house. At full speed, Stevie Stewart lets go of the handle-
bars and throws his arms out to his sides in a bravura show of daring
and balance. David imagines that someday he will do the same if he
stays in Vermont and isn't made to live with his grandmother where
there are no bikes or hills, just kids on slow-moving tricycles supervised
by nannies in a park.

At 4:30, his mother calls him in. The November days have shortened noticeably and she wants him to have a bath before supper. The
following night he and his stepfather will drive to Waterbury to board
the *Washingtonian* that will take him to New York.

Next to his bed and Mr. Farr's dairy barn at dusk, the bath is his
favorite place. The shared bathroom is just large enough to enclose a
tub running lengthwise and a small corner-fitted sink without a counter.
The toilet is in a niche beyond the tub.

His mother makes a game of keeping him from hopping into the
filling tub until she has adjusted the water temperature to her liking. He
likes sitting in the tub with the warm water running on his feet. Perhaps
the sound of flowing water, the diffuse light from a recessed fixture in the
ceiling, the warmth of the off-white tub and roseate tile colors suggest to
David the breathless, fluid, prenatal warmth inside the woman adjusting
the water's warmth.

When his mother leaves to make supper, he can hear but not understand his parents discussing the logistics of his departure. His mother

returns occasionally to add hot water and swirl it around.

He stays in the tub until the last water forms a gurgling eddy and disappears down the drain. Then he stands up and is wrapped in a large towel warmed on the wall radiator and vigorously dried from head to foot in the warm and abrasive cotton.

There is little talk during supper. His mother rarely looks up from the food she has prepared. He senses that his parents have been arguing about his trip. Alain forces conversation about the interesting people he meets on the Stowe ski slopes. The newsman Ed Murrow is in town and has booked a week of private lessons. Mr. Ruschp has chosen Alain as the tyro's instructor because of his patient and relaxed teaching style.

David pokes nervously at what his mother calls her "salmon pea wiggle," while his parents exchange sidewise glances. Each seems to be urging the other to begin the conversation in which the details of his New York visit will be explained in ways he can understand and hear without tears.

His stepfather begins, explaining why he must spend time with his New York grandmother. She is getting on in years and deserves the company and companionship of her only grandson. The trip down will be a "piece of cake."

David stares at the remains of the chocolate cake his mother made the day before that has reappeared for this evening's dessert. Neither Alain's smile nor the dried-out cake conveys any reassurance about his trip.

Helen covers her face and begins to cry quietly over her plate. Alain suggests they check over the things he has packed and then read a story from his favorite book, an elegantly illustrated copy of *East of the Sun, West of the Moon*–one of the few things Helen had been given by her own mother.

His stepfather reads as if he were back in his elocution class at Sacré Coeur, reciting in the same way his mother, Eugénie, read to him as a child. She believed stories told themselves and wouldn't want a reader to feign emotion or assume the role of a story's character. In

Alain's childhood, the rare reading of a nighttime story was women's work and was followed by a solemn recitation on one's knees of the *Our Father* and *Hail Mary* in French. By the time Alain went to bed, even on a school night, his own father, Clovis, would have long since retired in anticipation of a 4:00 A.M. breakfast or an emergency call to clear the back country roads of a new snowfall.

David lies awake with his "puff" pulled up to his chin and his head deep in his pillow. He tries to imagine riding on a train alone. Alain has assured him that his grandmother will meet him at the station in New York. His thoughts turn to worries of what might go wrong, but having no memory of his first train trip, lying curled up to his mother in a lower berth, he can give no shape to his fears. His first memory of his arrival in Vermont is of sitting in a car with strangers driving on a country road and seeing cows grazing in a foggy landscape.

He can hear his mother crying and talking quietly in the next room. His stepfather is trying to comfort and cheer her, an effort that will replay itself many times. His concern for his mother's sadness overwhelms his own anxiety about the impending trip, a pattern that will also recur.

In the morning, Alain reminds him to be ready when he comes home from work, as they must leave promptly for Waterbury to meet the train. His mother is still in bed and his stepfather suggests he go "cheer her up," a task to which he has often aspired and only much later comes to understand is not within his ability, as he notices the pill bottles next to her bed.

The shortened November day passes quickly. Alain arrives home as it is getting dark around 4:30. David is sitting in the living room on the couch with his packed bag on the floor between his ankles, tentatively scratching the impassive black cat between the ears.

The Washingtonian

Helen sits expressionless on the couch, watching the preparations for David's departure, her knees pressed together and her hair cascading around her downcast face. David can't tell if she is sad about his leaving or merely angry at the ease with which his stepfather has acquiesced to his grandmother. Alain busies himself in an effort to distract his stepson and keep Helen's tears at bay. Alain had grown up in a family in which the display of emotion was rare, unless disinhibited and fueled by alcohol. His Catholic faith has both forewarned him of life's pain and assuaged it with the promise of an ecstatic afterlife, so long as he adheres to its earthly tenets. Eugénie, the sole woman in a family of men, maintained a stoic and practiced calm in the face of her family's occasional calamities. Alain's brother, Marcel, had died in a car accident when Alain was only twelve and Clovis' occasional alcoholic misadventures with the slatterns of Rue Ste.-Catherine in Montreal were quickly forgiven but never forgotten.

In the driveway, Helen's eyes fill again with tears as David stretches up to kiss her good-by. He looks at his stepfather who, smiling, nods toward the taxi borrowed from Clovis. David climbs onto the passenger seat and waves to his mother from behind the window into the darkness of a late afternoon as they drive off down Elmore Road.

Traces of opalescent light emblazon the western horizon as they drive south along Route 100 with the car radio tuned to WDEV. The evening edition of the *Trading Post*, a kind of radio lawn sale, keeps them both absorbed. A jovial announcer details the items offered: a freshened Guernsey – a PTO pulp saw, "needs a new drive belt" – an *International Cub* tractor with belly mower "runs good" – a hundred-odd bales of dry timothy "best offer" – a *Maytag* wringer-washer with stainless tub "like new"–an Emerson floor model radio ... "needs a rectifier tube" –two *American Flyer* sleds ... "faster 'n a Ford–a 450-pound sow ... "good mother, good breeder, eatcha outta house and barn, best offer, will trade." The list of animals, tools, vehicles, appliances and produce drones on as they near Waterbury and the three blinking towers from which the broadcast emanates on Blush Hill. David tries but fails to relate the towers to the glowing radio dial and the sound of the announcer's voice coming out of the chrome grill on the dashboard.

Alain drives through the well-lit downtown. On the right is an array of drab brick buildings. A yellowish light emanates faintly from within. Occasionally, he catches sight of shadowy figures moving behind barred windows. His stepfather explains that this is the Waterbury State Hospital for the Insane, about which David has heard from the older boys who liked to call up lurid stories about the "Insane Asylum" in Waterbury and the "Weeks School," a reformatory for boys in Vergennes. Censorious adults would often threaten fractious youngsters by raising the specter of incarceration in either of these feared institutions. He recalls the dark descriptions he'd heard from Billy Sparks who had accompanied his mother to the Insane Asylum to visit his alcoholic father undergoing treatment. Billy's dad had been apprehended by his wife during a period of enforced sobriety sneaking brandy out of the larder in their stately Victorian home on Congress Street. Billy described people in dank cages with enlarged and pointed heads clinging to bars and staring mournfully at visitors. The Methodist minister, Pastor Pease, was also known to invoke both destinations as "hells on earth" to which "errant lads" might be confined at the will of their parents, or at his suggestion, prior to God's final damnation and their eventual descent into the fires of hell. For a few of the boys under his pastoral charge, these allusions temporarily induce improved behavior but, for the more inured, only a dubious smirk.

Alain parks next to the pale red brick station; turns off the ignition and leaves the key. To most inhabitants of a small town, ignitions are just rotary switches to be turned on and off rather than security devices to discourage theft. Most men and boys can hotwire a car in minutes anyway, should they need to. He reaches over and pats his stepson's knee several times, saying nothing but offering tactile comfort.

They step out into the cold night air. David glances around uneasily and waits as his stepfather grabs his suitcase, pats his right rear pocket to ensure that he has his wallet, and then takes David's hand. They climb the freshly painted but rotting wooden steps into the cavernous warmth of the station.

David's apprehension doesn't overwhelm his curiosity and, still holding Alain's hand, he surveys the station's interior. A pot-bellied Prussian General woodstove, topped with a chromed oak leaf cluster, sits in a corner on the track-side of the station, radiating heat from the coal fire inside and creating a radiant cherry-red ring around its sheet metal girth. A full coal scuttle sits nearby. Alain chats with the station-master, whom he has known since he was first allowed to drive the family jitney. A Dutch door separates the stationmaster's office from the waiting room. The narrow shelf on the lower door functions as a ticket counter when the upper half is open. Inside the stationmaster's office a bay window juts out from the station onto the platform so that he can see either way down the express tracks and the siding without going outdoors. Several telegraph keys and sounding boxes sit on the tidy oak desk along with a black Bakelite phone.

The far wall is a wainscoted surface indexed with brass hooks from which a dozen oak clipboards hang, clutching sheaves of schedules and freight manifests. The only other enclosed spaces in the station are a cramped baggage and freight room piled neatly with red and white-labeled Railway Express parcels, wooden crates, and steamer trunks awaiting their consignees or outbound trains, and finally the men's and lady's toilets, separating the waiting room from the baggage room.

The waiting room has recently been painted off-white. The peeling plaster has simply been painted over, leaving the impression of frozen whitecaps on the walls and ceilings. Two varnished hardwood slat benches with concave seats on both sides dominate the center of the waiting room. Alain lifts David him onto the one nearest the ticket office. The heels of his leather shoes barely clear the edge of the bench. He sits there feeling stranded as he explores the station's interior from his perch.

The silence is interrupted by a burst of telegraphic clicks. The stationmaster sticks his head out to say that the train has just passed the Jonesville grade crossing and will arrive in fourteen minutes. His stepfather, who has been warming himself by the stove, beckons to David to follow him, winking at the stationmaster, who shakes his head in a gesture of disapproval. David follows Alain through the heavy oak station door back out into the cold. They walk toward the grade crossing at the west end of the concrete platform. This crossing connects the town proper to warehouses, a grain depot and a rambling carpentry shop that uses iron jigs and steam boilers to cut and shape the ash wood, steel-edged skis that are all the rage for the new sport.

At the end of the platform, his stepfather jumps down three feet, ignoring the stairs, and signals David to jump into his arms, one of his favorite things. David closes his eyes and leaps off the platform. They walk over to the tracks. His stepfather checks his watch and signals to his stepson to wait for a minute. While fumbling in his pockets, he explains the working of the tall semaphore signal that stands across the tracks as well as how the barrier and flashing lights descend to stop cars when the train is approaching about a mile down the tracks. David will recall Alain's explanation several days later as he surveys a vast train layout and watches the signals and barriers anticipate the arrival of the small trains on the second floor of F.A.O. Schwarz.

Alain glances anxiously at his watch again and then pulls a worn silver half dollar and a Lincoln penny from one pocket. From the other he retrieves a roll of white adhesive tape. Positioning the penny in the center of the half dollar and taping the whole to the railroad track, he turns to his stepson, "When you get back," he smiles, "I'll have your own 51-cent coin for you. You won't find many in town except the ones I made." Then, to his surprise, his stepfather takes his head firmly in his hands and gently forces his left ear onto the cold steel rail. "Hear anything?" he asks, "can you hear the train yet?" David waits uncomfortably with his ear pressed to the cold rail for several minutes and then suddenly his face lights up. "I hear it! I hear it!" he cries. The distant and rhythmic clickety-clack radiating from within the rails soon becomes distinct. His stepfather releases his grip but David continues listening to the mesmerizing rhythm as it retards and grows more pronounced.

Suddenly, in the far distance, a deep-throated train whistle roars through the night. "It's coming into town now," Alain says. "That's the Bolton Road crossing at the far end of town. C'mon, let's go."

"What about the coins?" David asks.

"You mean the coin. I'll get it for you after the train leaves. It'll be by your bed when you come home." This is the first David hears that he will be returning.

David follows Alain back to the platform. His stepfather bounds up the steps two at a time. Together they walk briskly into the warmth of the station to retrieve his suitcase. The stationmaster shakes his head and smiles, "I never should a taught you that as a young'un. Now look what you done. Mind the Missus don't find out, and take care he don't lose his head to the *Montrealer.*"

They re-emerge onto the cold platform in time to hear the slow, deep chuffing of a steam engine, but see nothing. "Which way will it come?" David ventures. "From down there," his stepfather indicates, pointing to the end of the platform where he had been listening to the rails. His eyes drill into the dark, but see nothing. Suddenly a blaze of vibrating white light sweeps out along the gentle curve of the tracks and the deep, toiling sound of the engine increases. Then, as the rhythmic chuff slows, a whistle blast rips through the night as the train nears the grade crossing where his stepfather taped the two coins to the rail.

Since the crossing is next to the station, cars wanting to cross must wait the 18 minutes allowed for passengers to disembark and board, for freight and mail to be unloaded, and for outbound freight to be stowed. Most drivers just leave their cars idling and join the activity on the platform, use the facilities, or chat with the stationmaster, warming themselves by the stove.

To David's astonishment, a conductor in a dark blue uniform steps off the still-moving train carrying an iron footstool. He drops it on the platform and runs into the station.

David is left looking straight into the moving undercarriage of the massive engine. A black-painted iron cylinder is plunged slowly by a shiny steel connecting rod linked to the perimeter of the still turning drive wheel, itself taller than David. A last stygian blast of escaping steam obliterates his view as the engineer applies the brakes and the massive engine comes to a stop. The steam condensing in the cold air envelopes everyone on the platform.

He looks anxiously at his stepfather; understanding for the first time that he is about to board a train alone and resume roaring through the dark countryside toward his grandmother's in New York.

Alain squeezes his hand and says, "This will really be fun. I wish I were going." In that moment, he believes his stepfather. Already in their short life together his new father has become a trusted friend.

The conductor returns with a sheaf of papers under his arm, aligns the footstool with the car's iron steps, and invites people to board. As he is about to step onto the stool, Alain lifts him under his arms and hands him up to the porter who sets him down. Alain climbs aboard and leads him through a heavy steel and glass door into the sleeper car. He notes that the dark-skinned porter's uniform is less ornate than the conductor's.

"My name is Mr. J. Wha's yer name?"

"David," he answers, never taking his eyes off the black face.

The porter intuits that his charge has never seen a Negro before. David retains a distant memory of having seeing black people, although his only image of them comes from the exaggerated facial features illustrated in *Little Black Sambo,* where a Negro boy watches from the safety of a palm tree as a pursuing tiger churns himself into butter chasing his tail around the base of the tree. The story left him with the impression that tigers contained cream since Mrs. Farr told him she made butter from cream. Similarly, he thinks that hay contains milk that cows extract as they chew their cuds.

On board, his stepfather hands Mr. J the ticket, which he pockets without a glance. Tickets are the purview of conductors and Mr. J will surrender it later on his charge's behalf when the conductor makes his ticket pass. Mr. J leads them along a corridor lined with heavy blue drapes. Brass number plates are riveted to the curtains near the top and bottom. At the end of the car, he pulls back the curtains to reveal a turned-down bed. He sets his new charge on the edge of the lower berth. For a minute, Mr. J and his stepfather converse in whispers. Alain then hands Mr. J a neatly folded piece of white paper and a dollar bill. He then kneels down next to the berth and in a clipped manner that indicates to David his stepfather's own anxiety, he repeats, "This will be fun. Do what Mr. J tells you and tomorrow you'll see your grandmother. You'll have fun there." That said, he kisses him on the cheek, stands, and leaves the train. David suddenly notices his own legs kicking in and out involuntarily as if he too were leaving.

Within a minute of his stepfather's departure, the engine issues two furious whistle blasts and then a loud chuff. The sleeping car lurches forward as the engine takes up the slack in the couplers. His vision blurs as the tears well up in his eyes. The train gradually picks up speed, accelerating along the dark Winooski River Valley east of town. David looks down at his legs still swinging in a walking motion over the side of his berth. His fear soon succumbs to curiosity and he rolls over onto his stomach on the tightly made bed and lies looking out the window. His feet, now in the air, keep moving in a waving motion.

The sconce light in his berth is off and his eyes adjust quickly to the moonlit countryside. The crisp night is lit by a three-quarter moon, emerging periodically from backlit banks of dark clouds to flood the landscape with a nacreous light. The train continues to pick up speed along the straight rail bed that follows the river and the rails of the adjacent track. He notices the river's occasional turbulence as its waters rush over rocky shallows and coruscate in the intermittent light of the moon.

In the meadows and swales that border the river, Holstein cows stand like cemetery statuary, their black and white patchwork evident in the moonlight. Here and there, the pale lights of a farmhouse glow in the distance. The distraction of the landscape through which the train rushes gradually diminishes his fear and he becomes attentive to its details. Mesmerized by the fleeting landscape and the rhythm of the train, at first he doesn't hear the deep voice of Mr. J in the corridor outside his berth calling to him.

"Time for you'se to getcher PJ's on and tuck in."

Mr. J's warm, glistening face appears between the curtains. He holds out a waxed paper cup of ginger ale. "Drink this first," he says, "This here'll settle ya up. Then puts on your PJ's," which he hands in neatly folded. He reaches in and flips a small toggle switch that flood the compact berth with a pale yellow light filtered through an etched, amber-colored glass sconce on the wall.

"Put your clothes 'bove in the net up there and be sure ta fold 'em nice so you looks good for your grandmamma. I'se gonna close your curtains for ya and ya'll stick yo head out when ye's done with your gin-ja-ale." With that he disappears behind the curtain.

David sips the sweet ginger ale and then sets it on a small fenced shelf above the bed. He considers the challenge of changing clothes while sitting down; then gets out of his pants, shirt and undershirt but leaves on his underwear in case anyone should look in. He wriggles into the pajamas, takes another swallow of ginger ale, folds his clothes carefully and stashes them in the black mesh netting above the window. He guesses the upper berth is empty as there is no noise from above. He hears the faint sound of someone snoring erratically somewhere in the sleeper car. He rolls over and looks out the window until he hears the curtains drawn back and Mr. J announcing, "Time for you to tuck in, boy, and rest up for ta see your grandmamma tomorrow brights and early. You wanna use the toilet before you tuck in?"

David follows him down the corridor of closed drapes to a gray-painted door. Mr. J pulls open the door so David can go in alone. He stares at the small porcelain sink, feeling more directly now the pulsing movement of the wheels clicking across rail joints. He goes into the bathroom and pees, standing on his toes to reach over the lip of the fixture. He doesn't flush the toilet as there seems to be no water in it like there is at home, just a dark hole in the bottom through which a dank unpleasant odor emerges. At the sink, he has to reach up to wash his hands with the small bar of Pullman soap. He dries his hands on a nearby cotton hand towel, also bearing the Pullman logo. It takes a considerable amount of strength and all his weight to force open the spring-loaded door. When he comes out into the corridor and looks back in the direction from which he came, he realizes he can't tell his berth from the others. Stymied, he stands stock still in the corridor until Mr. J appears, carrying a pile of folded fresh linens.

"C'mon, boy, don' jes stand there, le's tuck you's inta bed. Gettin' late and I be busy when we'se stops in Monspelier and take on mo' folks." He hustles him back to his berth.

David waits in the passageway, noting for the first time the various noises coming from behind the upper and lower echelons of closed drapes, while Mr. J pulls back the blanket and top sheet on his bed and signals him to climb in. He slides into the crisply ironed sheets and Mr. J, humming to himself, pulls the sheet and wool blanket up to his chin then reaches over and clicks off the yellowish light. He then lays his black hand with its pinkish brown underside on David's forehead; smoothes back his hair, and to his surprise, kisses him gently on the forehead, before closing the curtains.

Alone in the wide berth, he rolls over on his side so he can again watch the moonlit panorama scrolling by. The rails' persistent rhythm brings to mind his mother and he sees her face with its sadness and hurt as he approached to kiss her goodbye. Just then, he felt that somehow their roles had reversed. She needed him at the precise time when he needed her. An involuntary gulping begins to wrack his small chest, calming eventually to a whimper. He feels even more sharply now, not only that he has left his mother, but that he is alone in a train snaking through the dark countryside toward New York.

Penn Station

"We be here. Time to get dress, ya'll hear, David? Don' wanna keep grandmamma waitin' on the platform. We be there in 'bout 30 minims.

Getcherself dressed up good."

He opens his eyes and sits up. The train window is flooded with daylight and there are buildings as far as he can see. Cars make their way through littered streets as the train slows down through the industrial section of Queens toward Manhattan. He pulls off his pajamas and hurriedly pulls on his pants, shirt, and socks. When he opens his curtain and looks anxiously for Mr. J, he is nowhere in sight. He goes down to the bathroom only to find it occupied by a large man who is shaving at the sink. He edges by him into the toilet and, on leaving, is too shy to ask him to let him wash his hands. Back at his berth, the drapes are pulled back out of sight, the bed is gone and there are two large upholstered bench seats facing each other where his bed had been.

A neatly dressed young woman sits on one seat and he sits on the other, somewhat confused. Mr. J appears with his suitcase and sets it down next to him.

"Yo' PJ's inside," he said. "Sit here and keep this fine wimmen's company. I got lots to do. We's comin' into Penn Station in 'bouts fifteen minims. I'll be back for you when we'se here."

"Where did the bed go?" he asks Mr. J, who is helping a woman across the aisle. Without turning around, Mr. J points high up to a handle sticking out of the curved metal ceiling.

"Iss all folded up in 'ere, neat as yo grandmamma's house gwine be."

He looks up, unable to imagine how the two berths have become two seats.

"Hello," he says to the woman across from him. He has been taught by his stepfather to greet everyone he meets politely. She looks at him quizzically, as if he has asked her for something she doesn't have, nods, and then looks anxiously out the window. He turns his attention to the city, oblivious to the walking motion of his legs.

The train approaches New York from high on a rail trestle and David can look down into the streets below full of people, cars, and a few dogs. There are many more people like Mr. J.

From time to time, he glances at the woman sharing the compartment, but she seems distracted and appears not to notice his presence at all. He glances up at her and sees that she is not looking at the cars or the people, the street-level shops, or the red brick warehouses or tenements, but seemingly at nothing or at something far away that he cannot make out. He thinks fleetingly of his mother and imagines her still in her nightgown, making coffee and toast in the kitchen for his stepfather.

The elevated train wends its way slowly in a straight line between dreary brick buildings. In the streets there are no white people at all. He stares at the people going about their business in the streets. A large black woman waddles ponderously on the sidewalk, her bulk shifting heavily from side to side as she walks, clutching a little girl's hand as she might a purse. He wonders how this huge woman can cuddle her daughter. She seems more like a piece of furniture. Some men wearing open suits walk purposefully, while others sit on stoops gesticulating and talking to one another. One tries to attract the attention of a wary dog with something in his hand, but the dog will not come close enough for the man to touch him. Other men talk quietly among themselves as if their work is finished. It strikes him as strange that there are no farms or fields.

Suddenly the street scene disappears in darkness. There is nothing but the small space inside the coach, himself, and the woman who still stares out into the dark as if nothing has changed outside. In the Bijou Theater, he remembers the projector arc burning out during a western movie and the audience being plunged into darkness while Alfred, the projectionist, ticket taker, and bouncer replaced the carbon arc amidst the catcalls and howls of the young audience. Each time this happened, the theater's owner, Blanche, would have to abandon the candy counter and run upstairs to see what was wrong. The Forcier boys would then take advantage of her absence to steal nickel candy bars, always leaving enough stock so that their thefts would go unnoticed.

The darkness in the tunnel is interrupted periodically by the sudden appearance of a pallid light bulb burning against a stone wall, lighting small sections of the dark tunnel through which the train slowly moves. Having recently learned his numbers up to 1,000, David takes an interest in counting things while walking or riding in a car – pavement joints, houses, power poles, billboards. Under the ninth light bulb an old man sits in a shabby suit with oversize shoes fumbling in a paper bag for something he seems to have misplaced. To his surprise, the man doesn't look up as the train rumbles by but keeps fumbling in the bag. The intermittent lights flash slowly by for several more minutes and then, with a burst of bright light, the train emerges into the maze of tracks and platforms that signals their arrival in Penn Station.

Mr. J appears. "We's here," he announces, grabbing David's suitcase with one hand and David with the other. David says good-bye to the woman on the opposite bench. She glances at him but doesn't seem to see him. Her gaze returns to the platform.

He and Mr. J now stand in the passageway between cars as the train slows. Suddenly with a loud burst of steam and a shriek of iron brake shoes, the train comes to an abrupt stop and people carrying their luggage jostle one another in the small passageway. Mr. J, who is being questioned now by several people, holds firmly to David's hand.

"Mind yes don' slip down the crack," he says with a smile as they step carefully over the space between the train and the concrete platform. "We'se gonna fine yo grandmamma."

A tall Germanic woman with a wry smile approaches them and introduces herself as Paula. "Und dis muss be young David," she notes in a clipped accent that is at once familiar and strange. He doesn't remember his grandmother looking or sounding like this.

"This here's David from Ver-mont. Y'all mus' be his granny," Mr. J replies, surrendering him to the stranger.

"I am Paula. I cook for his grandmother. She sanks you fur your kindness." With that, she hands Mr. J a pale blue envelope.

"His Daddy already tooks care of me," Mr. J says.

"Ziss can be sumzing extra for your fam-a-lee," answers Paula, grasping her charge's hand firmly and leading him away.

He turns to look as Mr. J waves goodbye. "See ya's next time ya come. Y'all be kind to yer granny," he says, returning to the still-emptying sleeping car.

David doesn't know this stranger who clutches his hand too firmly. She says nothing to him as they walk down the seemingly endless platform. There are trains everywhere, some still moving slowly. The platforms teem with people, some getting off recently arrived trains, and others clutching their bags and looking anxiously at tickets and track number as they tried to find the right train or coach.

He struggles to keep up with the striding woman holding his free hand. The suitcase, which weighed so little before, now seems heavy and keeps banging his right knee painfully. He can't shift it to the other hand that is gripped tightly in Paula's dry, cool hand. He wonders if the train he has just left is going back home with Mr. J and he feels his eyes welling again with tears. He thinks for a second about wrenching free and running back to Mr. J and his berth and going home. The train, however, is still southbound and Paula keeps a tight grip on his hand.

They leave the murky underground maze of tracks and emerge into the light-filled great hall of Penn Station. His eyes climb the wall to the vaulted glass ceiling high above the swarm of travelers. The highest enclosed space he remembers seeing is inside Mr. Farr's barn where, standing in the middle where the hay wagons are unloaded and looking straight up, he can see the sunlight coming in from the high opening at the end of the loft wall, its rays lighting up cones of hay dust and making them seem almost solid. A barn owl perches on the iron hayfork hanging from its single track.

In the station, the vast expanse of glass distracts him to such a degree that he bumps into an elderly lady making her way across the marble floor. Paula gives his wrist a tug and his gaze returns to the welter of rushing travelers.

A yellow Checker cab whisks them out of the station and nudges its way onto Eighth Avenue. He wonders if the old man rummaging in his paper bag in the tunnel found what he was looking for.

Dorothy

All the traffic lights on Park Avenue change from red to green at the same time, so the black limousines and yellow cabs accelerate together, trying to cover as much ground as the interval allows. The sudden changes in momentum make it hard to maintain his perch on the Checker's cracked leather seat. The cab veers west on 71st Street and discharges them at the first awning on the left. A large, ruddy-faced man, whom Paula addresses as Oskar, wearing a black uniform with white piping and brocade and a chrome whistle dangling from a cord around his neck, smiles at them both, helps Paula out of the cab, and then takes the luggage, greeting David with a pat on the top of his head and an avuncular, "This must be young Master Schumann."

Paula settles with the cab driver and with her gloved hand counts over the change he returns.

David has little memory of elevators and doesn't know what to expect when yet another uniformed man pulls a large lever, closing the door on the lobby, and then draws a second folding grillwork door shut inside the cab. He feels the upward rise in his knees and in the rush of warm air moving around him. He begins to silently mouth the numbers stenciled in white just below the landing of each passing floor that are visible through the brass grillwork door. "How come there is no thirteenth floor?" he asks of no one in particular. The uniformed man smiles at Paula, who does not return his smile, but notes in her clipped accent that "Nobody vould liff on a zurteenz floor, so zere aren't any." David thinks about her response but can make no sense of it. It seems to him that he is importuning her each time he speaks to her, so he asks no further questions although many occur to him.

As they arrive at the 18th floor, he notices that there was no 17th floor, no door or number "17," only a blank space. When he asks the elevator man why, he explains to him that his grandmother lives in a "duplex." He does not know what that means but chooses not to pursue the question since the elevator man is busy moving a walnut handle connected to a large brass disk back and forth in an effort to align the floor of the elevator cab with the 18th floor landing. Flustered and sensing Paula's impatience, he lets the handle come to rest, leaving a significant step up to the floor and withdraws first the grillwork door and then the outer door.

"Mind your step," says Paula, looking with displeasure at the elevator man. David looks carefully down and steps up three inches into the reception area. In the narrow space between the misaligned floors, he looks down into the deep chasm of the elevator shaft, and remembers the time he and Jimmy Greaves climbed the wooden rungs up to the top of Mr. Farr's corn silo and looked down into the deep wooden cylinder, almost empty of silage at the time. He feels a frisson of danger, and suddenly wonders if his stepfather remembered his coin.

"Why does everyone in New York wear gloves?" he asks. But Paula seems not to hear this question as she touches the doorbell and a raspy buzz goes off somewhere inside the apartment. She then unlocks the door and they step into an unlit foyer with a large side table and a mirror. The base of the table is the head and breast of a large eagle in gold ormolu. The eagle's beak is even with David's chin and its talons clutch a gold ball on the floor. The tall mirror above the table is framed in ornate gold gesso and reflects only Paula. An arrangement of dried cattails fills a clear vase on the table with a cast iron frog in the bottom holding the stems so the brown catkins fan out evenly as they emerge from the vase. He wonders why Paula rang the doorbell when she has a key.

Once inside, he notices the familiar smell of his grandmother's perfume and suddenly recalls his old bedroom and their shared bath. She sweeps into the hall smiling and wearing her gold dressing gown with loose, low-hanging sleeves that remind him of Father Lefèvre's vestments. Her brown hair is done up in a tight bun.

"Come give me a kiss."

Paula relinquishes his hand and he walks over to his grandmother, who kneels down and gives him a long hug as he stares at the gilded snail-shell earring clipped to her right earlobe. Finally, she releases him. "Come with me," she says with a wink, "you must be hungry."

He isn't. At his age, the call to a meal invariably interrupts something more fun and presents questions for which answers are often difficult. He is, however, wondering what people in cities eat.

"But first, we must put away your things and you must wash up."

After his grandfather died, most of the evidence of his existence was parceled out to museums, doormen, and a few work colleagues. His grandmother then sublet the lower floor of her duplex to her niece, Ruth; she lives there with her young daughter Terry. David's early memories of the lower floor, where his and his grandparents' bedrooms and baths were come back to him, but that is now "off limits." So he now becomes more acquainted with the main floor.

Formerly, he knew little beyond the library and dining room. The formal living room with its baby grand Steinway piano remains closed off. Behind the kitchen and pantry he finds a rabbit warren of tiny servants' bedrooms sharing a rudimentary bathroom. Since his grandmother retains only Paula and Margaret as "live-ins," he is installed in the vacant room adjoining his grandmother's. It was originally intended for a valet or personal maid. Instead of sharing Paula and Margaret's bath, however, his grandmother tells him that he is to again share her bath between his room and her own.

The master bath is larger than her former one on the floor below, but the landscape of it is familiar. Artfully arranged on the expanse of white porcelain are the tortoiseshell combs, pumices and sponges, wood-handled brushes, amber bottles and perfume flasks he remembers. His white-painted pine stepstool sits under the sink.

Paula helps him unpack and put away his few clothes on the shelves in the closet. Its interior, like the other surfaces in the apartment, bear many layers of cream-colored paint, looking more like his grandmother's evening application of cold cream than paint. He wonders if people in the city paint every year as he watches Margaret lay out his underwear, socks, pants and pullover shirt on a low shelf well within his reach and hang up his starched shirts, scratchy pants, and blazer beyond his reach.

He hears his grandmother call from her room for him "to freshen up." He doesn't know what this means and his quizzical look conveys this, as Paula whispers, "You muss vash your hands effry time you come in und special before you eat. The city iss a filthy place."

He withdraws his stepstool and climbs up. The stool brings his chest several inches above the porcelain edge of the sink and he leans forward as far as he can to turn on the nickel silver and porcelain cold water handle. Water gushes out under great pressure and he immediately closes the valve, somewhat shaken by the rush of splashing water. He eases the four-pronged handle again until a more modest flow of water emerges and grabs a perfumed bar of soap that is larger than both his hands together.

"You must always use hot water to wash your hands," explains his grandmother. He doesn't see her come up behind him as he is below the mirror's image. She turns on the left handle and adjusts the two knobs until the water is pleasantly hot then lathers his hands with the fragrant soap and washes his small hands within her own. He can see her varicose veins beneath the lather and is reminded of the web of bas-relief tunnels burrowed by moles in their front lawn when the snow melts in the spring. She rinses their hands together and dries his with an abrasive hand towel bearing her monogram: DOS. He steps down from the stool, replaces it under the sink, and follows her into her bedroom.

As they pass through her room, she explains to him how they will share her bathroom. If the door connecting his room and the bath are shut, he is to knock before entering and she will do the same. The toilet and a bidet are within the bathroom and unlike, her former bathroom downstairs, the toilet does not have a space of its own behind a closed door. He nods his understanding. Her bedroom on the main floor is smaller but still accommodates the Biedermeier twin bedroom set, the French glass dressing table, a Victorian fainting récamier and a tall but narrow walnut chest of drawers for lingerie. A deep walk-in closet is accessible from one corner of her room, and a balcony looking north up Park Avenue is evident behind double brass-framed glass doors. He follows her down the corridor toward the formal dining room where they will have breakfast.

The Empire chestnut table forms an oval at which eight can sit comfortably. The luster of its finish looks to him like standing water. His grandmother sits at the head with her back to the pantry entrance and he on her right. He hears her slipper moving under the table in search of what, on later exploration, he finds is an electric button that rings a buzzer in the pantry. This is how she signals to Margaret and Paula that she and her guests are ready to be served. Before the sound fades, Margaret enters, wearing a black dress with a decorative lace apron that matches the white tatting on her cuffs and collar. She places in front of them blue-bordered China-trade plates that bear an unfamiliar sliced fruit. He doesn't ask what it is but spears a slice and brings it to his nose to sniff discreetly to see if he recognizes the scent. It is unfamiliar, but he enjoys the sweet tang. It has the consistency of a peach, but tastes different and the slices are longer and spear-shaped. It is like nothing he has eaten.

"I see you like mango?" his grandmother queries.

"I do, yes, very much," he returns with an urbanity that surprises him.

Some minutes later, the buzzer again clatters behind the swinging pantry door and Margaret arrives to retrieve the fruit plates. She returns shortly with larger plates of the same oriental design, but this time covered with matching china domes with a small handle on the top. She sets his grandmother's down first and removes the dome, then does the same at his place. This time he is relieved to find familiar food and gives Margaret a grateful smile. She retreats to the pantry with the two domes. He and his grandmother are left to their unsteady conversation, scrambled eggs, buttered pumpernickel slices, and a meat that he doesn't recognize. He picks at and eats the familiar eggs, but as inconspicuously as he can, edges the alien meat to the side of his plate. His grandmother notices and begins a discourse on the nutritional value of chicken liver. It contributes to good health and growth by adding iron to the blood, she says while demonstratively eating her own. His understanding of iron extends only to the material from which farm implements, hand tools, bikes, and jungle gyms are made and he tries to imagine how this metal might get into and flow in his bloodstream were he to eat the oily, brownish lumps on his plate. There follows a reprieve and a caveat. He is absolved this time but will be expected to eat it next time it is served. The meal ends after two more buzzes, one producing an ebony-handled silver coffee pot and the other signaling that they are finished.

His grandmother announces that she is going to her room to "prepare herself for the day" and that he can read in the library until she comes for him. Before leaving, however, she tells him the plan for the day; they'll walk over to the Park to visit the animals in the zoo and then he will pay a visit to his great-grandmother Selma – Granny Sis to her family – and to have lunch with her at the hotel where she lives. He has only heard mention of "Granny Sis" and never in endearing terms, so, although he wants to visit the zoo, he's unnerved at the idea of meeting his great-grandmother alone.

Walking through the wide double doors into the library, he looks earnestly at the book spines on the shelves, but recognizes none of the legible titles. Closer to the floor, however, there are larger picture books and he withdraws one and carries it over to a couch. The chairs and couches he encounters, except for a child's chair upholstered like a pink seashell, require his climbing up and into them. He sets the book down on the couch, clambers up onto the cushion and then puts the heavy book onto his knees to leaf through it.

The artist's picture on the folio page betrays a devilish leer and the longest horizontal moustache he has ever seen. The artist is dressed like a dandy. His hair is heavily oiled and he wields his cane like a weapon. The pictures at the beginning of the book remind David of ones in his missal at home. The later ones, however, are distorted and show misshapen people, often with crutches or wooden limbs. One picture shows a droopy watch, broken people and leafless tree limbs near a beach. Near the end of the book, a soft-edged painting of a blue Madonna looks down at the baby Jesus she cradles in her arms, recalling a similar image of the Virgin Mary in his missal. The serene yet tender look of the mother comforts and stays with him.

His reverie is interrupted by his grandmother's entrance. She is dressed in a fur coat with a matching muff and a curious animal-like hat. He wonders if the three articles of clothing are in fact one animal or several. He closes the cover of his book, but not before his grandmother glimpses the page he's been looking at.

"Do you like Dali's work?" she asks.

"I don't know," he answers, "I picked the book out of the shelf and was just looking at the pictures. Some of them are strange."

"I shall have a surprise for you when we return. But we must go now. Selma takes it as an insult if I'm late. Surprising, as she takes so little pleasure in my company," she adds, not quite under her breath.

Sliding the book carefully back into its space so the spine lines up with the others, and noticing that there is dust on the tops of all the books, he follows his grandmother into the foyer where they wait silently after his grandmother pushed the lower of the two black buttons embedded in a polished brass plate. He hears a door close far below and feels the gentle whoosh of warm air from the gaps around the elevator door as the cab rises in the shaft.

"Do they ever fall?" he asks.

"Does what ever fall?" his grandmother asks, caught off guard.

"The elevator," he answers.

"Never that I've ever heard of and certainly not in our building."

Much of his time in elevators during the trip will be spent daydreaming about how they work. He imagines a heavy hemp rope and tackle block like the one in Mr. Farr's barn used to lift the massive iron fork full of hay off the wagon and transport it high up into the rafters, where it is then pulled laterally with another rope to a side loft. A pull on a trip rope opens the fork's prongs, dropping the hay. He also thinks of Mr. Collette's small engine repair shop in the barn across the street from his house with its perpetual smell of blue two-cycle exhaust and oil, the scattered array of engine blocks with their shiny pistons capable of gliding smoothly inside them. He wonders if the cab is a piston and the shaft a cylinder. He doesn't know the elevator man well enough to ask him how it works, but since the elevator man never seems to be able to land them level with their floor, perhaps he isn't the right person to ask. He also is coming to understand his grandmother's low tolerance for questions that she cannot answer. He wonders if other passengers know how elevators work. The driver, with his white-gloved hand on the mahogany knob, breaks the silence, "And how long will you be visiting your grandmother?"

"A week," his grandmother answers dryly as if she has been interrupted.

The elevator man tries unsuccessfully to align the floor of the cab with the lobby floor and then opens the two doors into the marbled lobby with its Oriental carpet runners, formal furniture, silk floral arrangements, and uniformed doormen.

Oskar is stationed out front under the awning and greets David and his grandmother with an exaggerated and formal "Gut morning, Mrs. Schumann," after which he turns to David and gives him a conspiratorial wink.

His grandmother retaliates with a stiff, "Good morning, Oskar. We'll be needing a taxi when we return at half past eleven. My grandson is going to the Delmonico to have lunch with his great-grandmother and she will expect him to be prompt."

"Certainly, Mrs. Schumann, we'll have one waiting when you come back," he continues in his Norwegian accent.

Selma

They walk west across Madison to Fifth. David must skip or run to stay abreast of his grandmother who, soon after they leave, gives up holding his hand so she can maintain her own brisk pace. Seventy-First Street dead-ends at a stone wall behind which grow thick foliage of a kind he has not seen since he left Vermont. They walk south to the zoo entrance where they enter past an ivy-covered administration building that looks to him like a castle he has seen in one of his books. The zoo makes him sad almost as soon as they enter. Cramped iron cages flecked with rust and peeling black paint enclose the listless animals. The bottom of the bars are worn clear of paint where the large cats and other mammals have rubbed themselves raw. They pay no attention to the stream of parents and children trying to attract their attention.

A boy somewhat taller than David and dressed in a wool tweed coat and matching cap stands at an adjacent cage making noises to get the attention of the lone zebra lying in the dust staring into space. Seemingly annoyed at the zebra's lack of response, he picks up a bottle cap off the pavement and throws it at the zebra, but it bounces off the zebra's scarred buttock and elicits no response. The dark-skinned woman in a nurse's uniform accompanying him seems as oblivious to her charge's presence as to the zebra's. David's grandmother, sensing his lack of enthusiasm for the zebra, hastens them along to the polar bear exhibit that has just re-opened and is said to offer its occupants a more salubrious environment than the cages they previously occupied.

The bears do seem animated in the cool fall air. Their sculptured concrete habitat has two large pools and a fake-looking ice cap, but it seems to offer more room to roam and to imagine that they are not living in the middle of one of the world's largest cities.

David's mind has drifted to home, however, and he tries to imagine what the neighborhood kids are up to this morning. Recently, they had all been gathering at a fallen-down tree deep in the woods behind the Collettes' ramshackle house to plan their day's adventures. They thought of it as a kind of clubhouse, which lent stature and formality to their decisions.

"Do you like the polar bears?" his grandmother asks, apparently for the second time.

"I do, very much," he answers, snapping back from the conclave at the fallen-down tree.

"Well, that's enough for today. We must be on time."

She takes his hand and heads off at a stiff pace he cannot sustain, so he pulls his hand loose and skips alongside her.

When he and his grandmother appear at the end of the block, Oskar blows his chrome whistle dangling from a chain around his neck and a cab appears at the curb.

Oskar holds open the door for his grandmother and David follows. Once Oskar has closed the door, he taps twice on the driver's window to signal that they are ready to leave. Sometime later as they become more acquainted, and often when David is waiting for his grandmother, Oskar takes the time to explain things to him that are not of interest to his grandmother, as he has done with the two odd little jump seats that flip down behind the driver's bench seat in the taxi. There are no Checkers in Morrisville, where a taxi can only be distinguished from a family car by recognizing the driver.

David and his grandmother are whisked off into the brisk flow of traffic on Park Avenue and head south toward the Delmonico Hotel. Sitting on the jump seat with his hands gripped tightly underneath to maintain his balance, he thinks of the polar bears which remind him of the piles of *National Geographic* magazines lying in a corner of the attic at home. At Jackie Collette's suggestion, they had foraged through all of them looking, as Jackie said, for "bare titties." The local librarian had put some issues of *National Geographic* on the "restricted shelf" for their photographs of women young and old after some boys showed an absorbing interest in African and Micronesian cultures. Word of this off-limits, titillating trove had spread rapidly at school. This led David's older neighbor Jackie to press him into a census of the issues in their attic. David rapidly lost interest in the search, however, and was distracted by an article about animals on the Serengeti. He now imagines these caged animals as they were in the pictures of the African veldts and along the watercourses that form their natural habitat and again feels homesick.

Suddenly the taxi pulls up sharply in front of a blue and gold awning. The door is opened abruptly by a liveried doorman almost before they come to a halt. David folds back the seat so his grandmother can get by and follows her onto the sidewalk. Her gloved hand discreetly passes a folded bill to the doorman so that he can pay the driver.

The elevator ride to his great-grandmother's apartment on the fourth floor is too short for him to see the elevator cab's ornate details. The hand control for the elevator is similar to the one at his grandmother's, but the operator is experienced at aligning the cab with the landing and does so on the first try.

His grandmother takes his hand as they walk slowly down a rather gloomy corridor. He imagines people listening behind each door as they pass. His grandmother explains in a hushed voice that she will see him to the door and push the buzzer but will then leave him to meet his great-grandmother by himself. She offers no explanation other than to say that she will meet him in the lobby downstairs at four o'clock. He is distracted by the apartment doors. They are all deeply convex, swelling outward like pods containing something inside. He resolves to ask Oskar next time he sees him about these curious doors.

After she pushes the buzzer, his grandmother turns and walks back to the elevator bank.

David waits, shifting his weight from one leg to the other, until he hears the lock turn. The door swings open and an old woman, dressed entirely in black except for the white lace handkerchief tucked into her left sleeve and the ivory amulet resting on her substantial bosom stands there smiling. An aureole of fine white hair radiates from the off-center bun on her head. "You must be young David," she says.

"Yes."

"Come in," she offers.

He steps into a narrow hallway and then into a modest sitting room crowded with oversized furniture. Granny Sis moves slowly, using a silver-topped black walking stick. She makes her way to a large chaise in the corner and lowers herself stiffly into the lavender upholstery. Uncomfortable in his scratchy wool pants and stiff white shirt, he scans the cluttered room. The off-white plastered wall is a mosaic of framed photographic portraits. One of them in which a short, stocky man in an ill-fitting clown costume is poised to strike a large bass drum strikes David's eye.

The subject is holding a large, felt-topped baton poised in his right hand near the drum's head as if awaiting a cue. The dark features below his macassared black hair betray a sadness at odds with the oversized clown costume with its large dots and frilly collar. David wonders if the man in the picture has been caught off-guard by the camera or is about to perform, but awaits an off-camera cue. David can't read the Italian inscription but recognizes his great-grandmother's name in the florid letters scratched into the negative before the photo was printed.

With some effort and the help of her hands Granny Sis lifts her legs up onto the chaise where she lies back in a recumbent position. "My good friend Caruso," she exhales.

"Enrico Caruso, the great tenor of my time," she adds, looking at the photograph and smiling. "He was a dear friend and I miss him every day. I still see his wife, Dorothy, but I miss him terribly. *Pagliacci* means "clowns" in Italian, the language of all great opera. "Do you know Italian?" she inquires.

"No, I don't," he answers.

"The French and German languages clash with opera's great leitmotifs," she continues.

"Yes," he answers to be polite.

"The picture was taken at the Met on January 26th at a Saturday matinee of Leoni's *L'Oraculo* and Leoncavallo's *I Pagliacci*. I was in the audience and went backstage after the almost endless curtain calls. Muzio was not in voice and Enrico had to carry the whole drama in his own magnificent voice. The house had been sold out for weeks. The Family Circle was full of Italian carters and drivers who had simply left their drays and hansom cabs on Broadway. Traffic was impossible. When the audience finally left, my brother Leopold, who had treated Caruso for his pulmonary problems – he smoked constantly, you know – took me backstage to meet him and so began our friendship. We had dinner whenever he was in New York and from then until his untimely death three years later, wherever he sang in the world, the sixth row center seat in the opera house was reserved for me. Of course it remained empty most of the times as I could never maintain his travel schedule."

Sighing, she indicates a black casting of a sculpture on the side table. It is the torso of the man in the clown costume. "He gave me this bust he sculpted of himself. He was such a talented man and the great voice of this century. Do you know his voice?"

"I don't," David replies, now looking at another photograph, the subject of which is a heavyset mannish woman.

"Gertrude Stein, a really loathsome woman. She cast my horoscope when I was in Paris, but I didn't like what it said so I hid it away, and I certainly never went back again for a consultation. She did not understand my first book of poems. I suspect she found them too erotic, which is saying a lot for Gertrude. We did not get on well from our first meeting. Her salons were brilliant, though. I will give her that." He tries to remember *loathsome, horoscope, erotic* and *salon* to look up when he returns to his grandmother's apartment, but the words fades as the conversation gallops on.

David can barely make out his great-grandmother's whispered words as his eyes flit from photograph to photograph. Following his glance, she narrates the stories behind the framed images.

"Is that your little girl?" he asks.

"That is your grandfather," she answers with a faint smile.

"Why is he dressed like a girl?" David asks.

"Little boys wore dresses until they were three or four."

"Oh," he replies, neither understanding nor pursuing the matter.

A large color photograph catches his attention.

It is his great-grandmother as a young woman. She is seated in a straight-back chair with arms, her large hands in her lap and her fingers interlaced. She is wearing a diaphanous white lace over-dress with short sleeves. She holds her head high and stares comfortably into the camera as if accustomed to being photographed. Dark thick eyebrows curve gracefully over her intent eyes and her chin juts slightly forward. Her hair falls in straight tresses from a part over her left eye, creating an arch in which her strong features are framed. She looks as if she is waiting for her brother, the renowned photographer Alfred Stieglitz, to ask something of her before he exposes the plate.

"I was thirty-four when Alfred took that picture. It is so me. I am no longer beautiful, but you can see I was once. Men adored me," she smiles. "It was one of my brother's first color photographs, an "autochrome lumière." They were very new in those days. This one appeared in *Look Magazine*.

"You must be hungry. What do you like to eat?"

He isn't hungry but agrees that he must be by nodding his head. Chicken salad is the most familiar, and all that comes to mind so he mentions it, still intent on the wall of black and white photographs. She picks up the heavy Bakelite receiver from the phone next to her. He notices that it has no dial.

"Get me Oscar in the kitchen." David hears the name and wonders if Oskar works here as well.

He noticed earlier that there were turtles placed about the room and he begins to count them. As is often the case, he loses track of what he has already counted and has to start over, moving as methodically as he can around the room. There are ceramic turtles, brass turtles and silver and glass turtles. They are placed on shelves and side tables. Several larger ones are in out-of-the-way corners on the Aubusson carpet.

"Oscar, this is Madame Schumann. My great-grandson is visiting and he will have a chicken salad. I will have my usual lunch and please have your boys remember to peel the cucumbers. Adieu." She returns the receiver to its base and carefully wipes her hands with a lace handkerchief then tucks it back into the sleeve of her dress.

"I have Coca-Cola," she continues. "You do drink Coca-Cola, I suspect. All young people seem to. Even I like it."

"I like Coke," he answers, losing his turtle count again. "Why do you have so many turtles?"

"I've always loved them," she answers. "I collected them when I was a little girl. At Oak Lawn we'd find them sunning themselves on the rocks and in the brooks feeding into Lake George. Father would help me and one year for Christmas he gave me that little green ceramic one over there on the stand. It's still my favorite. Would you like to have one?"

"I would, very much," he answers.

"You must pick one out for yourself."

After he picks out a lifelike painted turtle, a little smaller than his own hand and puts it in his pocket, his great-grandmother invites him to sit in the wooden chair next to her so they can talk.

He climbs into the chair and, to avoid her penetrating gaze, begins looking again over the many photographs around the room. He notices that, although there are no bookshelves, books are stacked against the walls. Many are large books like the ones he saw at his grandmother's. Others are reading books with dark spines and faded print titles. There are also piles of magazines and journals.

His gaze returns to the woman in the chaise. The errant wisps of white hair around her head remind him of halos in the pictures of saints in his missal at home. He also sees her pink scalp beneath the thinning white hairs.

"What do you want to be when you grow up?" she asks, smiling at him.

"An astronomer," he answers promptly.

"Perhaps you will cast my horoscope someday," she suggests.

"What does it mean to cast a horoscope?" he asks.

"You observe the heavens and the alignment of the planets to better understand their influence on the course of our lives," she whispers.

David knows that the stars and planets are the subject of astronomy. One night, when the temperature was 27 degrees below zero and the night sky was at its brightest; Alain took David into the back yard to look for a promised display of northern lights. Finding none that night, Alain salvaged the adventure for his stepson by identifying the major constellations visible in the night sky. Unlike his great-grandmother, though, Alain said nothing about the stars' and planets' ability to influence one's life or provide a basis for predicting the future.

The astronomy-astrology misunderstanding persists in David's conversation with his great-grandmother. It will be several years before David's fifth-grade teacher explains the difference between the science and the belief system and, until then, David will continue to believe that the positioning of stars and planets will influence his future life.

He notices that the apartment has a musty smell and that the only window has been painted shut. Only when he sits near his great-grandmother is the smell masked by the lavender scent dominating the space around her. She is on to another subject, leaving him free to look more closely at the bewildering array of objects in the room.

His spots an unframed tintype propped up on the shelf behind her.

It is corroded around the perimeter where the emulsion is blistered. The image is of two young girls, eight and ten he guesses. They are sitting partially in the lap of their father, who sits on the ground on a wooded hillside and looks off-camera. His expression is stern. He has a bushy moustache below an aquiline nose and pronounced cheekbones. He wears a black, broad-brimmed, high fedora and appears not to notice the two daughters sitting uncomfortably on either leg. He has on a black wool chesterfield greatcoat and his arms are crossed on his chest. A stiff white collar frames his neck but lies open in the front with no cravat, perhaps because they are in the woods. The older daughter looks angry and stares in the opposite direction from her father. A slight pout is evident and her jaw is set low. She wears a dark skirt over thick, dark wool stockings. She is wearing a doublet with large shiny buttons and, under that, a sort of waistcoat with an oversize white collar and large black bow. Her sister, wearing an identical outfit, looks vacantly off to the left. Her mouth is open. She looks asthmatic. The older sister has wavy, dark brown hair that tumbles down to her waist while the other girl's lighter brown hair comes only to her shoulders. It strikes David as strange that the father and his children seem unaware of one another.

"I'm the younger one. Wasn't I pretty as a young girl? Aggie never had my beauty." His great-grandmother is more animated now.

"You look sad, Granny Selma."

This is the first time David addresses his great-grandmother directly and uses her family name.

The buzzer interrupts them.

"Could you get the door? These old bones don't get up and down that easily," Selma asks.

He slides off the chair and walks to the door. It isn't locked and swings open easily. Given its apparent mass, he assumes it will be hard to open, but it opens easily and in the dimly lit entryway he confronts a formally set dining room table rolling toward him. Two places are set on a starched, white tablecloth and between them is an etched-glass budvase containing two white roses. Two scratched and dented nickel-silver domes with handles cover the china plates. An older man in a starched white jacket and pants propels the rolling table forward. David moves aside, edging into a niche in the entryway that he realizes is also a tiny kitchen. The table rolls past him and into the living room where the waiter parks it near his great-grandmother and locks the casters.

"Good day, Louis," says his great-grandmother, handing him a bill she seems to have withdrawn from her ample bosom. Louis nods deferentially and then, without saying a word leaves, closing the door quietly behind him.

"Well, well...here we are...one of the few enjoyments left to me in old age. I never planned on being this old. My only pleasures in this *oubliette* are the occasional visitors like you, my books, my pictures, and my food, which still gives me great pleasure though I eat much less than I used to. What appetites we used to have. All kinds, I might add," she says with a wink. "All these dusty pictures remind me of the past. I think about taking them down, but then I worry that I will forget who I was."

She removes the dome with a flourish. On the blue and gold-rimmed china plate is a pale brown crab the size of her hand and next to it, a thin slice of white bread spread with mayonnaise on which cucumber slices are laid out and mottled with a red seasoning. He tries not to stare at the unfamiliar food, but watches intently as his great-grandmother cuts into the crab and begins to eat it shell and all. He remembers watching his mother and stepfather eat lobsters once, but they removed the meat from the bright red claws and fantail shell with metal picks. His great-grandmother seems to relish the still-armored crab.

When he lifts the dome from his own plate, he is relieved to find a mound of chicken salad in a bowl of iceberg lettuce leaves. But on closer inspection he is dismayed to find walnuts, celery, and raisins mixed in with the chicken. He likes none of these foods and begins carefully to segregate them with his fork into small piles on the edge of his plate. The large cuts of chicken make his job easier.

They talk little while they eat. Selma takes occasional small sips from a wine glass filled with Coke. He follows suit, being careful to hold the unfamiliar glassware by the narrow stem as she does. He eats while watching his great-grandmother alternate between her crab and her cucumber sandwich with evident relish.

As she dabs her lips with the large starched napkin, she muses, "Food is indeed one of the last great pleasures, don't you agree?"

"I do, Granny," he agrees without looking up. "May I go to the bathroom?"

"Of course. Never mind the mess. It is on the left through my bedroom."

He leaves the table and walks through a passageway into his great-grandmother's bedroom, spotting another door ajar on the left. Even in the dark of the bedroom with its single drawn shade, he notices mounds of books everywhere. In fact, most of the floor space is covered with vertical piles of books, some reaching to his waist. There is an open space around the bed and near the window, but the rest of the floor is like a cityscape seen from above with tenements of books rising from the ground separated by narrow avenues and side streets too small to walk through. The walls in her room are hung with more paintings than photographs but the images are hard for him to make out in the low light.

He goes into the bathroom and reaches for the light switch. Two square porcelain fixtures with bare bulbs on either side of a large mirror over the sink flood the small space with harsh light. The fixtures seem to grow out of and match the tiles that make up the bottom two thirds of the walls. There are no pictures anywhere, but the paraphernalia of old age lies everywhere. There are coiled white rubber tubes and a pink bag, a wooden shower stool, vials of lotions and medicines covering the mirrored glass shelf over the sink. A chipped white enamel cylinder with graduated increments etched in its side sits next to the toilet.

A bristle brush with a long handle coated with soap scum leans against the corner of the built-in tub. A toilet brush and a cracked pair of white rubber gloves lie on the floor next to the toilet. There is an acrid smell of cleaning agents. David lifts the toilet seat gingerly and stands on tiptoe to pee over the rim of the bowl. A dark rust-colored ring marks the toilet's waterline. When he has hiked his trousers back up and re-buckled his belt, he goes around to the side to reach the low flushing lever. The sudden burst of noise made by the release of water under high pressure unnerves him and he leaves the room without washing his hands or lowering the toilet seat as he has been taught. The loud noise embarrasses him and he lowers his eyes on coming back into the living room.

"Did you find everything?"

"I did, yes."

"Did you wash your hands?"

"No, I forgot, but I will, though."

He goes back into the bathroom. The light is still on. He moves the wood stool near the sink and steps up to wash his hands, drying them on the liner of his pants pocket rather than disturbing the neatly folded, monogrammed towels hanging on the rack. Then he carefully replaces the stool, lowers the toilet seat and extinguishes the light before returning to his great-grandmother, who is again recumbent in her chaise.

She has a small lavender book in her hand. He cannot make out the title.

"Would like to hear one of my stories?"

"I would, Granny."

"I'll read you one of my favorites. It is from my book of story poems called "Nothing New" It is called simply "My Fantasy."

Before He Came

She anticipated his coming with delight. For he made her laugh. And she loved to laugh. His wit was keen. Stimulating, like champagne that went to her head; or bright and sharp–a blade, to be parried. Now and then a home thrust, but so light, one hardly felt the prick of the point.

*She pictured to herself the few hours they would spend together.
Pictured them as though sauntering over a meadow. Trackless. Field
flowers peeping through the green grass. Golden sunshine. A deep
blue sky, fleecy clouds chasing each other. Spring air. Crisp and clear,
with a promise of early summer. They would walk. Slowly. Delightfully
planless, with much silence. A smiling silence–restful, understanding.
Perhaps they would pluck a few flowers.*

*That was her waking dream as she watched the smoke of her
cigarette unfurling fantastic shapes.*

As It Was

*There had been no green meadow. No sunshine, only glaring artificial
light. No smiling silence. Nothing but words. Words without end.*

*She heard herself saying things which should have remained unsaid.
Memories locked away, gently laid aside – their sting gone–all that
remained, the aroma of faded roses. Yellow roses. She seemed to be led on
by a vague dread of being misunderstood. And the more she talked, the
more she realized the futility of words. And their power.*

*He flung question after question at her. Probing as a clumsy surgeon
might. She wanted to beg for mercy. But went on talking as if possessed.
She knew he didn't believe a word she said. He told her so. Why couldn't she
lie to him? All men believe lies. Why should she care whether he believed
her or not? He was nothing to her.*

*She must be crazy. It did not follow that because they had laughed
together he would take her through the sunny meadows of her fancy.
He never laughed–but smiled and smiled.*

That was infinitely worse.

His face was like a mask–the mask of a satyr.

*Suddenly she felt herself gliding down as if into a pit muddy and deep.
At the bottom of which a huge wall seemed to rise with every word she
spoke. Each word an added stone– brown in color. When he left her she*

felt as if she had been beaten. She wept. Tears of rage. To have bared
her soul thus. To such as he. Better had it been her body.

That was the language he understood. He talked of women as if he
had handled them (like a dealer his wares) all his life. He needed no
keys to their doors. The secret password, the "Open Sesame," was his.
To women–stacks of women. He never had time for a woman. The woman.

Where were the trackless meadows? The smiling silence? Turned
into a bottomless pit of mud, a wall of brown bricks, rising high –
insurmountable....

Selma's narrative trails off. He looks up from the brown leather shoes his stepfather had shined for him, now scuffed from the perpetual involuntary walking movement that scratches the sides of them as they brush together. He has difficulty following much of her story. She is looking away at a photograph on the wall. It is of a dashing man with a tall black hat. He has a moustache and looks like the photograph of her father on whom she and her sister sit as young girls in the other portrait. The eyes are those of a different person, however.

"Is that the man in your story?" he asks.

"Yes, it is," she answers, "He was dashing, but I came to dislike him intensely. He did not like women. He married my sister, but it didn't last. She never recovered from the marriage. It was only a dream, poetic license, not to be taken too seriously. You will understand someday."

David doesn't understand what she is reading to him. She called it a story, but it seems to him more like a dream.

He notices a small color photo on the wall.

Its colors are faded. It's the only other color photograph he has seen in the apartment, a view of the peony garden in bloom at Oak Lawn, the family's summer estate on Lake George. A woman stands among the profusion of white flowers looking at the photographer. She wears an ankle-length, black-and-white vertical-striped skirt and white blouse under an open blond sweater jacket. A wide black belt that accentuates her shapeless bosom encircles her waist. A narrow-brimmed summer hat shades her features. In the background is the great house, three stories of stone, dark timbers, and small diamond-shaped leaded windows. The scene could have been photographed in the Swabian Alb or the Black Forest to its east, though the family had long since migrated from southern Germany to New York. The veranda wall above the garden is consumed in ivy, leaving no trace of the stone architecture other than a suggestion of its imposing height. The woman is not looking at the camera as his great-grandmother always seems to do.

He guesses it is someone else who looks like her.

"I don't like that picture," she exhales. "It's Alfred's friend Laura Gilpin. I've kept it because it's the only picture of the old house at Lake George. Father sold it to pay for his affairs, I suppose. It's also one of the earlier color lumières. They're quite rare, you know."

Selma's heavy eyelids close slowly. He thinks she is asleep and he asks her if she is. She responds with a humming sound from deep in her breast. Her head inclines forward and her chin pleats onto her bosom. Tentatively, he slides off his chair, all the while looking at her eyes to see if they open. He begins to explore the apartment.

The stacks of books that make up the cityscape on her bedroom floor are mostly large format photography books. He opens one at random and finds photographs of American Indians. At first he thinks they are natives from another country like those in the *National Geographic* magazines at home. There is little resemblance to the Indians he sees in Westerns at the Bijou Theater on Saturdays or to their landscape, tepees and headdresses. He remembers his stepfather telling him about movies and actors and he remembers seeing a newsreel about how Westerns are made, in which a white man is being made up to look like an Indian.

He comes to understand that he is looking at real Indians photographed as they lived in the Plains and far West. Their bronze skin and Mongol features bear no resemblance to the painted pallor of the movie Indians he recalls. The subjects are formally posed in native dress. Some stare into the camera, others are in profile. Their features are of a race he has never seen before. Occasionally, there is a long shot of a cluster of Indian hogans near a river, but then there are no people in the view.

These haunted and sparse images will often come back to him as he watches with his friends the serial Westerns on the Bijou Theater's silver screen at home with its many small tears that distract him from the set piece dramas.

He opens another book. It contains naked photographs of a woman from different perspectives. Her nakedness reminds him of his grandmother, though the camera subject is more slender and considerably younger. He sits down on the floor and looks all the way through the book. Some pictures are close-ups of the woman's body and appear more like landscapes. There is one in which the gentle curve of her thigh looks like a sand dune and her pubis an oasis.

His great-grandmother seems to be sleeping peacefully. But after several more minutes, her telephone rings. He rises quickly, replaces the book in its stack and hurries into the other room. His great-grandmother is on the phone saying, "Oh, my. Oh, my. Yes, he'll be right down."

"Our visit is over. I am sorry I fell asleep on you. I hope you amused yourself while I dozed. I usually nap after lunch. You must hurry down to the lobby where your grandmother is waiting for you. She doesn't appreciate being kept waiting. She doesn't seem to appreciate much, including me. You must be off." The evident pain of rising to her feet inflects her speech as she walks him slowly to the door.

"Goodbye, Granny Selma. Can I come again?" he asks as he opens the door.

"Of course, we shall count on it." The door closes behind him, leaving him in the dimly lit corridor. David wonders who the other person might be, as his Granny Selma was the only person there.

He walks to the elevator bank and pushes the lower of the two buttons at his eye level. The elevator comes promptly and, after a brief descent, deposits him in the lobby. To his surprise it is again Paula who meets him. She says only that her mistress does not like to come to her mother-in-law's hotel.

The silent taxi ride back up Park Avenue affords him an uninterrupted opportunity to see his grandmother's neighborhood. The buildings are similar, though there are subtle differences in the color of the stone façades, and each canopied building entrance has its own liveried door-man standing at alert, either by the door or by the curb. Some blow whis-tles and hail cabs. Others chat with maintenance men or delivery boys.

Suddenly on his right, there appears a large red armory with crenellated fortress walls and towers with parapets at the corners. He crouches low in his seat to look up to the ramparts to see if there are any armed guards, but he can't see any. A sagging cloth banner over the entrance on the side street indicates that there is an art show there. As the cab stops for a red light on the avenue, he is able to read most of the sign in spite of the oblique angle.

Oskar is off-duty when they arrive and his grandmother has gone out to do errands, so he goes to his room and lies down. He doesn't fall asleep right away but lies there thinking about the afternoon. He thinks how out of place the doormen, the domestics and the formality would be at home. He hopes his neighborhood friends won't ask him where he has been and what it's like, as he wouldn't know what to say.

Rose among the Fragonards

His grandmother wakes him for dinner and reminds him to wash his hands. He is still in his itchy wool pants and stiff white shirt. He asks if it would be all right to change. She tells him he looks handsome and that he can put on his pajamas and a robe after dinner. He doesn't remember packing or for that matter having a robe and worries about it.

Dinner is a quiet affair. Margaret serves without a word or a sound other than the clink of the silver serving spoon against the blue and white serving dishes. His grandmother depresses the foot button under the table to summon Margaret only once, as she seems to know instinc-tively when to appear with more food or to remove empty dishes. David watches his grandmother out of the corner of his eye and mimics her ways of eating and placing her implements. In this way he learns to lay his knife and fork across his plate horizontally when he is finished eating and to spread out his napkin at the beginning of the meal in his lap, though it invariably falls to the floor, so that he must get off his chair to retrieve it.

"Did you have a good time at Selma's?" his grandmother asks, without looking up.

"I did."

This produces no response and they continue to eat in silence.

When the plates are cleared, his grandmother announces that Saturday they will dine at Louis Sherry's before seeing the opera *Aida* at the Met. The role of Aida will be sung by Maria Callas, and his grandmother's friend in the membership office has arranged for them to go backstage to meet the diva after the performance.

The following morning, however, he will be meeting his Aunt Rose for lunch at Reubens and then a visit to F.A.O. Schwarz next door, where it is her intent to have him select his own Christmas present. He remembers hearing from his mother that his grandmother's sister Rose was a bit "batty and forgetful." She was a great beauty as a young girl, but never married and now lives alone.

He tries to imagine what "The Met" and "Aida" are and what the woman whose name he has not retained will sing. Neither does he know what Reubens and F.A.O. Schwarz are. He understands the idea of selecting his Christmas present and imagines all the playthings that his neighbor Jackie Collette has – mostly old tools or things cobbled together from expended parts salvaged from his father's repair business. From a lawn mower engine, some lumber, and four salvaged wheels, Jackie made a small "doodle buggy" go-kart that he drives around the yard. It has a chain drive and is always hard to start. Jackie doesn't let anyone else drive it, although he freely shares his collection of toy tractors and trucks rescued from the dump and repaired. He hammers out small dents, replaces lost wheels, and repaints them in his father's shop, which is the envy of the neighborhood boys.

Supper is much later in the city than at home and, after David has gotten into his pajamas, brushed his teeth, and washed his hands again, he is sleepy. He lies down on his bed. His grandmother knocks on the door, entering only after he answers. This is unfamiliar to him. At home, people come and go as they please except in the bathroom. She comes in and asks if he would like her to read him a story. He thanks her, but declines, telling her that he is tired and that Granny Selma read him a story.

"One she wrote herself, no doubt," his grandmother notes stiffly.

"I think so," he answers.

"I hope it was not inappropriate," she sniffs.

"I don't know. I didn't understand much of it," he whispers.

"I suspect not," she answers. "Few, other than her, do. Good night and sleep well."

"I will," he whispers and promptly falls asleep.

He wakes to the sound of running water in the bathroom next door. He lies there for a moment recalling where he is. The cool night air has filled his room from the partially open window and he pulls the covers up to his chin. He listens to the sound of water running in the bath and his eyes well up with tears as he imagines himself in the tub at home with his mother in the next room. He wonders if she is still sad. She promised to call while he is away but has not done so yet. He is never sure when Helen promises something if she will follow through, whereas he has always been able to count on Alain. He drifts off to sleep again and is awakened by his grandmother's knock on the door saying, "Breakfast in ten," from which he assumes ten minutes.

He jumps out of bed and pulls on his comfortable corduroys, a cotton pullover shirt with a small embroidered kangaroo near where the pocket should be. The bathroom door is ajar, which means his grandmother has completed her "soins" as she calls them. He goes in, climbs up on his stool and splashes his face with cold water as Alain has taught him to do. He brushes his teeth and combs his hair with a tortoise-shell comb that he first holds under cold running water. He still doesn't understand why one must brush one's teeth again in the morning, not having eaten anything during the night. After tying his shoes, he stands up and pulls his bed clothes together as best he can with one side of the bed against a wall.

In the dining room, his grandmother is already seated at the head of the table in her dressing gown, sipping a cup of black coffee and holding the *Herald Tribune* aloft in her other hand, her glasses on the very tip of her nose. She glances down at him and tells him that her allegiance to newspapers shifts essentially between two cousins, one who owns the *New York Times* and another who is the music critic for the *Herald Tribune*. She used to get both papers, but soon found she had time to read only one, so she alternates subscriptions. Like much she tells him, this information means nothing to him.

Breakfast is familiar. He eats the bacon and eggs with relish, but skips the grapefruit juice after a tentative sip. He finds it bitter, even though his grandmother urges it on him as being "fresh squeezed" and a source of something he will need to grow "straight and tall."

After breakfast his grandmother adjourns with another cup of coffee to her bedroom to get dressed for the day and to place Margaret's weekly grocery order. Having nothing else to do, he goes to the library to look at books again.

At 10:45, a buzzer rings in the back of the apartment and he hears his grandmother approach the front door and greet her sister. David gets up and replaces the large book of Edward Steichen's World War II naval and aerial photographs in its place on the lower shelf. It is the first time he has seen photographs of the war that killed his father. He looks up at the oil portrait of his father over the fireplace. It was commissioned after his death in the Philippines and was painted from the same studio photograph he has at home.

His father is seated at a table. His arms are crossed. His left hand holds the visor of his lieutenant's hat at an angle and his right hand rests on the two gold officer's stripes on his left sleeve. This is the image the son retains of his father. He sees a difference in his father's mien between the painted portrait and the black and white photograph in a monogrammed silver frame in his room at home, though he cannot put it into words.

The photographic demeanor is markedly different, self-satisfied, almost arrogant, his features illumined by a broad smile, challenging the viewer to an engagement of some kind. The photograph was taken after his graduation from Yale and induction into the Navy but before he saw combat.

In the painted portrait, the remains of a smile linger, almost as if he sat for the portrait after having learned of his own death. The surprise of death is absent, as is his former juvenile arrogance. He appears to express sympathy for the survivors. It is a sad portrait, even though his pose matches exactly the one in the earlier photograph.

His grandmother speaks rarely about her sister, whom David calls "Aunt Rose," though she is, in fact, his great aunt, except to tell him that she never married any of the attentive suitors who sought her company as a young woman. As her lovely, fragile body aged and the noted beauty of her clear, pale skin deteriorated behind increasing applications of face powder and rouge, her circle of attendants diminished as well. Now it is limited to the gentleman gays who moth about the older female patrons attending the Metropolitan Opera on 39th and Broadway. Rose has friends within the Opera as well. She counts Schwarzkopf, Gueden, and Ghiurov as "chers amis." In her later years, her younger sister treats her to an effete and inexpensive escort named Cliff from Bow, New Hampshire. Cliff deftly and swiftly adapts himself to her circle's social protocols, even managing to pronounce the names of opera roles, singers, and arias with a continental flair.

The double doors to the library open and his grandmother enters with a frail woman on her right arm.

"This is your Aunt Rose," she offers, smiling as if introducing him to a child his own age.

"Good to meet you," David says.

"Come, let me see you. You look so much like your father when he was your age. How wonderful. Do you have a dog?" Rose inquires.

"No," he answers, "but I would like to have one."

"We'll have to see about that," she smiles.

"Now, Rose, dear, don't be going off and buying a dog for David. His parents will want some say in the matter and besides, how would he take it home on the train?" his grandmother chides her sister.

"I didn't mean today," she answers, looking hurt.

"Let's start our adventure," Rose says taking him by the hand. They leave the apartment, promising to be back by four o'clock.

Many years later, as David sorts through boxes of family photographs, he finds there is only one photograph of Rose as a woman. There are posed family portraits in which she appears as a little girl with her mother and two sisters, but she seems an afterthought—an extra, perhaps. Her father does not appear in these childhood pictures. The young girl with dark tight curls is clearly distracted and defies the photographer's admonition to look into the camera.

In the lone photograph of her as a grown woman Rose appears to be crying or anxious to the point of tears. She is standing just in front of a stone archway leading to an obscure interior, perhaps to a courtyard or a warren of apartment hovels. The iron grillwork doors are swung back into the obscurity. She is not framed by the archway, but rather stands off center. The setting could be in Southern France or Italy or Spain. It is a tourist snapshot, perhaps taken by her sister or her father. Though she is the subject of the photograph, she appears surprised in the background. A girl chasing a boy on a bicycle bursts into the foreground of the camera's range. The girl, in a white dress, looks angry at the boy as he pedals to get away from her. They are not tourists, but locals. They consume all the energy in the picture, leaving Rose as an afterthought. Perhaps the photographer was distracted by the incursion of the boy and girl into his camera's field of vision. The depth of field favors Rose, but the foreground is what we notice.

Her shapeless coat lies over her shoulders. Her left arm hangs inside the coat and her right arm emerges from it to draw it closed at the waist as if she is cold. She wears a hat that an Italian cleric might wear. It is out of place. Her large purse peeks out from the coat's folds near her knees. Her feet are close together and her shoes are not the shoes of a seasoned traveler. She looks at the camera as if asking for help of some kind.

The descent in the elevator is swift. David feels in his knees the controlled fall and the breeze of displaced air swirling about the elevator cab. Oskar's hand is on the mahogany control knob and the cab lands exactly at the level of the lobby floor. David again feels his weight in his knees. The three leave with Oskar in the lead as he is covering for the elevator man during his break.

Rose suggests a visit to the Frick. David doesn't know what the Frick is, but assents with an earnest nod. They walk over to Fifth Avenue, where again he sees the woods of Central Park, and down another block to the Frick Museum. He thinks it looks more like a rich person's home than a museum and asks his Aunt Rose about it. She explains that it was indeed Henry Frick's New York residence and that, when he died, it became a museum to house and display his art collection.

Rose is recognized as a member and does not need to pay for herself or her guest. They simply walk past the security guard, who doffs his hat to her as they continued on into the atrium. There they both sit down on a white marble bench at the edge of the shallow pool that mirrors the atrium above and reflects its flood of warm sunlight. The pool is surrounded by several graceful areca palms in marble pots, giving the impression of an oasis.

"This is my favorite place in New York," Rose confides to her charge, staring across the water at a painting hanging on a far wall. It is of St. Francis in the desert with wild animals in the foreground.

"If I believed in God, I would want to pray to St. Francis," Rose observes with a smile.

"You don't believe in God?" her nephew asks surprised.

"I don't believe in Him or not believe in Him. I don't know Him and I find it hard to believe in things or people I don't know," she answers gently, aware that she has contravened her companion's beliefs.

"Tell me what you do," she says, changing the subject.

"Mostly I go to school or play with my friends. I like to read my books," he answers.

"What books do you like to read?" she continues.

"I like *Monarch the Big Bear, Animal Heroes, Heidi, Sidsel Longskirt and Solve Suntrap*, and picture books of animals."

"You like the outdoors."

"I do," he answers, staring at the pennies collected on the bottom of the pool.

"What do you do outdoors?"

"Lots of things. It depends on who is playing that day, I guess."

"Who are your friends?" she asks.

"Petey, Annie, Cecile, Jackie, Gail and Glenn, and sometimes Stevie."

The questions about home animate him and he begins to tell his aunt of the many adventures he and his friends contrive while exploring the woods in Mr. Farr's pasture or sneaking into his barn, or just riding their bikes in the neighborhood.

Unlike his grandmother, Rose is enthusiastic about his accounts of adventures with his friends. She seems wistful as he tells her of their adventures in and around the neighboring farms and woodlands. Only his stepfather seems to enjoy his adventures with equal interest. He thinks Alain would like his Aunt Rose.

Rose asks him to tell her about the cows in Mr. Farr's barn and he tells her in great detail how, after morning milking, they leave in single file at daybreak and return at night to be milked and usually go straight to their stanchions by themselves. Sometimes "the girls" get confused, however, and go to the wrong stanchion, which means that they all back up until someone comes to help them figure out which one is their own.

He also tells her about their latest adventure sneaking into the Fishers' fallen-down barn behind their house.

"It's a little scary. If it's windy outside when we're in there, it creaks and groans and we get afraid parts of it may fall down on us. Billy Kinsey got hurt badly in there once when he fell through a trap door covered with hay in the loft and landed on the concrete gutter below. He cracked his head and was unconscious for a long time. They say he's mostly okay now, but I don't know him so I couldn't say. Mr. Stewart gets really angry if he catches us in there and he has a shotgun. He shot someone once for looking for their dog in his cornfield, but didn't kill him. He shot him with salt instead of bullets."

"How's that?" asks Aunt Rose.

"I don't really know. That's what Jackie Collette told us," he answers.

"Salt doesn't kill you but he said it hurts more."

"That's awful," she responds, "Was he arrested?"

"I don't think so. He's still there, but he doesn't milk no more 'cause the bank sold his cows."

"*Any more.* If you're going to be in the city, you must speak properly. You can imagine what my sister would say if she heard you talk like that. She'd have a conniption and we don't want that."

"What's a conniption?"

"It's a fit," she answers with a smile.

He isn't sure he understands this, either. Since he has been in the city, he has heard many different words that he doesn't understand. Then, when asked about the meaning, people use more strange words to explain. Alain has taught him to use the dictionary, but its use is predicated on knowing how to spell the word, which he doesn't always know unless the word appears in a book or he intuits it correctly from the sound.

"We also have a clubhouse at the fallen-down tree with a secret password. I can't tell you the password, but if you come up I could take you to the clubhouse and you could see it. You have to walk across the fallen-down tree to get there. We broke off most of the branches, but we left a few to hold on to so you don't fall. The bark all came off, so it is slippery, especially when it rains, but I know you could do it. We built the clubhouse at the end of the tree, or Petey and Jackie built most of it, 'cause they know how and we used a lot of Jackie's father's tools. His father lets him use them." David is breathless.

"I'd like that very much," Rose says, and he believes her.

Rose then gets to her feet and says, "I want you to see my favorite picture here. I'm not much on paintings really. The Frick is my summer camp. It's where I come to rest and gather my thoughts when my head gets muddled, which it sometimes does. My sister has no doubt told you."

"She hasn't, but my mother has," he answers.

"She would know. She was a nurse, wasn't she?" she adds, smiling.

"I think she was."

They rise from the bench and he follows her into the inner rooms of the Frick. They wander through several rooms with dark walls and paintings lit by small lamps like the one he had seen at his grandmother's over his father's portrait. Some of the white plaster walls are edged with gold and polychrome moldings. In others, the walls are covered with dark red fabric. He has never seen cloth-covered walls before. He surveys the odd-looking furniture, trying to guess its purpose ... tables, desks, dressers or bookshelves? Most are fenced off from closer examination by brass stands connected by red cording. The ornate and uncomfortable-looking chairs have ribbons across them to prevent visitors from sitting in them.

As they pass through several rooms, uniformed docents acknowledge them with a nod and occasionally offer a "Good morning, Miss Rose." On those occasions, she stops and chats with them, asking after their health or the well-being of a family member she seems to know.

They come into a large room, flooded with light from floor-to-ceiling windows that look out into the park across Fifth Avenue. Rose stops and looks around, as if relieved to have arrived. She sets her large purse down on the parquet floor without ever looking down.

"This is my room," she announces. "This is where I was raised when I was a young girl. When I could not be here, I would often come here in my daydreams. Isn't it beautiful?"

"It is," he answers, "I like it."

She walks over to a large mural on the wall. "This is my favorite. It is called *The Pursuit*."

"The paintings look alike," he observes.

"They are all by a Frenchman named Fragonard. He painted about 150 years ago. These were painted for Mme. DuBarry, but were moved here by Mr. Frick. He had so much money, you know. Some feel they are overly sentimental, but I don't. They are beautiful to me and show how life ought to be."

He approaches the painting to see what his aunt so likes about it, but soon realizes he can only see it if he steps back to where she is standing. He looks up at her for a clue and sees her wistful smile. He turns again to the large painting to try to see what she is seeing.

His first impression is of deep green trees that seem to erupt like fountains from the landscape and dominate a garden scene. In their midst is a massive stone outcrop with two cherubs wryly observing the scene below. Three people are in a stone niche on the periphery of a formal garden. A foppish young man offers a small bouquet to a woman who looks askance at him, perhaps put out by his persistent attentions. A demure young girl between them seems distracted by something on the ground and misses or ignores her mistress's distress. A sensuous energy pervades the painting, but the logic of the action is elusive, suggesting little beyond the young man's pursuit of the young woman. David sees the paintings as if they were images in a children's book but, without text to inform the story, he loses interest.

"Do you like it?" his aunt asks.

"I do," he responds.

"What does it say to you?" she asks him.

"I'm not sure," he replies. "The boy seems to want the girl to like him, but she seems frightened by him. What do you see, Aunt Rose?"

"There is so much in the painting. I myself was once pursued by a young man but I did not acknowledge his attentions. He followed me everywhere, invited me to the opera, to his family's summer home on Lake Placid, to concerts, but I wasn't sure I liked him and didn't want to hurt him. He was so nice, but I never got to know him." She stares at the painting, no longer smiling.

"You could still call him," David suggests, noticing the change in her demeanor.

"No. He died in France after the War. He wrote to me several times, but I didn't respond to his letters."

Suddenly, with a slight tremor, she picks up her purse and asks, "How about some lunch?"

"I'd like that," he says, wondering what unfamiliar food he will encounter.

Caviar and Champagne

David and his Aunt Rose leave the museum and walk farther down Fifth Avenue to 58th Street. There, they enter a restaurant with a large red neon sign that says only *Reubens*. A barrel-chested doorman in red livery beckons them into a revolving door. David has seen these wonders before but has never entered one. Somewhat confused, he follows behind his Aunt Rose and must tiptoe his way through to avoid stepping on her heels or having his own heels hit by the glass partition sweeping along behind him. Once inside, and to the amusement of the maitre d', Rose explains to him that only one person goes into each quadrant at a time, and the woman always goes first. He knows about women going first.

Inside, he finds himself facing a large sandwich counter and to his left a circular, red, silver, and black bar that is higher than he was tall. As his eyes adjust to the darkness, he sees over the bar a sign that says, "Friendship is Life's Most Wondrous Treasure" and another, "Gather Ye All Here Who Have Forsaken Gloom." The restaurant itself is farther in to the right. The interior is furnished with crimson leather banquette seating, walnut paneling on the walls, and gold-leaf trim on the ceiling, and features a dusty array of game-fish taxidermies, model sailboats and yachts on the walls above the booths.

David approaches the sandwich counter to see what food they serve. He recognizes nothing except some small, dark pancakes. Displayed in the glass refrigerated case are duck with red cabbage, apple pancakes, chopped liver, pitchers of borscht, chow mein, and cheesecake along with slabs of planked red fish and whitefish and porcelain tubs of caviar.

They are ushered to a booth near the front. He slides in on one side and Rose on the other. David begins to worry about what he will be offered to eat.

"After lunch, we'll go upstairs. You'll like that. I'm sure," Rose announces.

"What's upstairs?" he asks tentatively, imagining even stranger food.

"It will be a surprise. I'm certain you will enjoy it. Did you like the Frick?"

"I did."

"What did you most like there?"

"I liked the room with the pool with the pennies in it and the window in the ceiling. Do people ever go into the pool?

"If they did, they would be asked to leave, I'm sure," his aunt laughs. "But I've often had the very same thought, especially after I have walked a long way to get there and my poor feet are swollen up from these awful shoes I wear. Next time we go, we must try. I could distract the guard and you could take off your shoes and wade in. I'd whistle if he comes."

He smiles. "That would be fun. Do you think we'd get caught?" he asks in earnest.

"I doubt they would do much. I'm a patron, you know."

"What's a patron?"

"Someone who gives them money."

"So that is why we didn't pay but the other people did?"

"Precisely."

A large waiter with a black, bushy moustache appears. His tuxedo sports grease marks on the sleeves and lapels. He places two very large menus on top of each place setting and leaves without a word.

"They are not very polite here but the food is very good. You'll see," Rose says, rooting in her purse for a pair of reading glasses.

He tries to read the giant menu, but the sandwiches are only a long list of people's names followed by words he has never seen.

"What do you like to eat?" she asks him.

"I like chicken," he answers promptly.

"Then you shall have the Anna Maria Alberghetti," she advises, "I always have the same thing each time I come here."

Again, when the waiter arrives he says nothing, but holds a pad and pencil poised on his ample belly. He peers through large, black-framed glasses whose lenses look as if they've been polished on his greasy sleeve.

"My nephew will have the Anna Maria Alberghetti 'number 26' and a glass of Coke, and I will have blinis with Sevruga and white wine."

"I'm sorry, Madame," he announces brusquely in an accent David has never heard, "We are saving all the Sevruga for a large wedding party tonight. I can offer you Osetra for the same price," he continues without looking up from his pad.

"That will do," Rose nods.

The waiter turns abruptly and leaves.

"Not all Jews are that rude," Rose says softly.

"What's a Jew?" David asks.

"We are all Jews in a sense," she answers cryptically.

He doesn't pursue the matter, sensing her discomfort.

Within minutes, the waiter returns. He takes from his forearm a fragile dish of translucent blue and white china and sets it down in front of Rose. An opalescent oyster shell filled with what looks to David like black BB's in oil rests on one quadrant of the plate and a ramekin filled with sour cream in the adjacent quadrant. The other half of the plate is filled with small, thin pancakes. The waiter then plunks down in front of David a scratched, white ironstone platter with a sandwich the length of the waiter's forearm. A large pickle slice and an ice cream scoop of cole-slaw sit next to it. A pale tomato slice on a leaf of iceberg lettuce adjoins the giant sandwich.

Again, the waiter leaves without a word. David wonders about the Coke, but the waiter returns with a Coke in a scratched Coca-Cola glass, an empty wine glass, and a bottle of white wine with a towel around it. He fills the glass halfway and sets it in front of Rose and leaves.

"Why didn't he fill your glass?" David asks his aunt.

"Good question. They never do by convention. I guess it's so one must order another," she answers, smiling.

He peels back the bread to see what's in his sandwich. There is both chicken salad and slices of white breast meat. He doesn't recognize the bread but notices its many seeds. He lets the piece of bread fall back onto the chicken and begins to watch his aunt, curious as to how she will eat what she has ordered.

"What is in the shell?" he inquires.

"It's caviar, fish roe."

"I don't know what that is. It doesn't look like fish."

"It isn't fish properly. It's their eggs."

"I didn't know fish laid eggs," he answers.

"They do, delicious ones. This is sturgeon caviar from Russia," she adds.

He watches his aunt take a dollop of sour cream and spread it delicately on the small pancake. She then takes a small spoon made out of horn and ladles a spoonful of the fish eggs onto the sour cream and spreads them around. With her fork, she pierces the whole and slides it into her mouth.

"Are they good?" he asks.

"Delicious. Would you like to try one?"

"No, thank you. I wouldn't," he answers.

Then he folds back the thick slab of bread, like a surgeon opening up a patient and eats slowly from the sandwich with his fork, as if the bread itself were merely a platter. The chicken is to his liking, both the salad and the cuts of fresh white chicken. He sips unsteadily from the glass of Coke, all the while observing Rose eating the fish eggs.

The closest thing he has seen to caviar is at the frog pond in the cemetery below the Fosses' house. He and his friends often go there in the spring to catch pollywogs in Mason jars and bring them home or to school to watch them change into tiny frogs. Last spring, they had gone down early, at Jackie Collette's suggestion, and found only gelatinous clusters of frog eggs in the murky shallows along the shore. Jackie's mother worked part time at Paine's Restaurant and often brought home empty gallon mayonnaise or condiment jars for her husband, who used them on the shelf over his workbench to store small engine parts and other hardware. Jackie brought two jars with him, which they filled with frog's eggs and brought home. Jackie, whose age and experience with natural phenomenon had dulled his own interest, gave a jar to David with his promise to return the jar when the eggs hatched into pollywogs and then frogs. His stepfather had been delighted with the experiment and helped him periodically change the water in the jar using a colander. Alain explained that the gelatinous mass surrounding the small dark eggs was in fact their food supply and that they would eat their way out into the world. He compared it to the white of a chicken's egg, explaining that the tiny blood spot on the yolk would become the chick, which would nourish itself on the egg until it had enough strength to break out through the shell with its tiny beak. He promised to take David up to Mr. Farr's to watch the chicks hatching later in the spring. Although the details of their gestation reduced David's enthusiasm for eating eggs for a while, his taste for his mother's buttery scrambled eggs eventually overcame the phenomenon of how they become chickens.

They eat together in silence for a while, each lost in thought. Rose seems very far away as she ceremoniously prepares and feeds herself the small hosts laden with sour cream and caviar. He eats through all of the chicken on one half of his sandwich leaves one half and the garnishes untouched. Nor can he finish the large Coke.

The waiter breaks their reverie when he returns and pours Rose another half glass of wine.

"Any dessert or coffee?" he asks in a deep bass voice. "Shall I wrap the young lad's sandwich?"

"No, save it for Virginia, please," she answers.

The waiter takes his platter and leaves.

"Who's Virginia?" David asks.

"She's a lady who sings religious songs every morning on the corner of Fifth and 58th. She plays a small button accordion and sits on a folding stool, the kind you see at Saratoga during the race season. She's a lovely person. I often stop and talk with her between songs. She's blind, but she can sing for eight hours and never repeat a song. She lives in the old Markwell Hotel in the West 40s. Her rent is paid by the Lighthouse where I volunteer. Much to the dismay of my sister, I go visit her occasionally. It is a sad apartment, but she is so kind and she makes one feel as if she lives in splendor.

"At the end of each day, she comes to the back door here and Mintz, the maitre d' we saw coming in, gives her a bag of uneaten food for herself and her friend Baybie Hoover, who also sings, but is wheelchair-bound now and cannot always come out. When they're together on the street, they sing lovely duets. I don't recognize the songs, as I'm not religious, but they sound very sweet together."

"Do people give them money?" he asks his aunt.

"They do. It's right near Bloomingdale's, so there's lots of money to be had on that corner. They seem to get along all right," she adds, while ferreting in her purse again. She removes a money clip and counts out four crisp bills which she hands to the waiter, who again disappears without a word.

"My sister makes me bank at the Bank of New York. I am not so fond of them. They're very stuffy there and they have no office in my neighborhood, but they only give you uncirculated bills and the city is such a dirty place. It was founded by Alexander Hamilton, you know. Have you ever heard of him?"

"No," he answers as they leave the restaurant into the bright light of 58th Street. It is his first solo passage through a revolving door.

Train Layout

F.A.O. Schwarz is next door to Reubens. David follows his aunt inside. Immediately on his left there is a display of Stieff bears like the small one he still has from his early childhood. A few bears are arranged in a Tyrolean kitchen tableau. They are seated at a table near a woodstove. They seem to be eating and drinking. The smallest bears are playing some game on the floor. The male bears, with their alpine hats with a small arched feather jutting out the side and loden-cloth capes, sit at a rough-hewn table with small plates and steins. The female bears wear dirndls and fuss around the kitchen stove and a nearby woodpile of tiny logs fashioned from sticks.

David has never been in a toy store before. He's been to the local five-and-dime store at home where a few toys are displayed and sold in a small section, but never imagined that toys would warrant their own store, or that there might be enough toys to fill a store, especially one as large as this. Most of the toys on the ground floor are stuffed animals of all sizes: giraffes, zebras, bears, monkeys, and even domestic farm animals. A large display on the right features dolls and doll houses and these attract Rose's interest. One of the doll houses is as tall as David and has electric wiring that lights miniature chandeliers and candelabra on the walls. Some of the furniture reminds him of what he has seen in the darker rooms at the Frick.

"What I brought you here to see is upstairs. Let's go up," says Rose.

They climb the broad marble staircase with its gleaming brass banister in the back of the store, and enter a space with less décor but many more toys. He stops to look at an elaborate trestle bridge made from an Erector set, tin cavalry soldiers in blue in a fortress made from Lincoln Logs, and a circus midway. The rides are made entirely from Tinker Toys. David never imagined there could be so many toys. The few toys he has seen at Annie Foss's or owned himself gave no clue to the universe of toys that he sees here. Many of his friends, like Jackie, have no store-bought toys but instead make do with old tools, made-up things, or items salvaged and refurbished from the dump.

In the corner by the windows overlooking Fifth Avenue and 58th Street is a landscape on multiple tabletops. It fills a space as large as the library in his grandmother's apartment and about a quarter of the second floor. He lets go of his aunt's hand and rushes over to see.

It is a vast model train layout that mixes the large "O gauge" Lionel model trains with the smaller "S gauge" American Flyers. The layout compresses what seems like an entire country into a sprawling landscape that includes a small city and a farming community. Logging, farming, coal mining, and passenger service are all part of an active tableau indicated by the many specialty rail cars coupled to the dozen or so small engines either parked at railheads or chuffing through the landscape.

At various points on the layout's perimeter observation platforms have been built for children and David clambers up the several steps onto one where there are no other kids. The height enables him to take in most of the panorama except for what lies beyond the papier mâché mountains to his right.

His eye goes first to a black steam engine with four passenger cars slowing down in front of a red brick station in the village. Magically the crossing gates lower as the train approaches the grade crossing and pulls into the station. Tiny lights on the barrier gate flash. He can see the backlit silhouettes of the passengers through the translucent train windows. It almost seems as if they are moving within the car. He sees the paddles on the semaphore signal change and wonders at the miraculous logic driving all this tiny reality. He thinks again of the coin his stepfather will have for him when he returns and how it was made.

He notices a balding man sitting across from him on a roped-off platform. Then he sees that the man is surrounded by control transformers with black and red Bakelite levers. There is a black console with two horizontal rows of miniature toggle switches, each bordered by green and red indicator lights. He watches the man controlling the tableau of trains, a municipal trolley, people, cars, and trucks. He thinks how much his neighbor Jackie would enjoy this with his knowledge of mechanical and electrical devices gleaned from his father. He wonders if Jackie will ever see such a miracle as this or if, in fact, he ever leaves Vermont to go to a city. He doubts that his friends would believe him if he tried to describe what he sees when he returns home.

His eyes return to the station platform. He sees himself there, jumping off the platform into his stepfather's arms and then taping the coins to the rail. He feels again the icy chill of the rail as he lays his ear against it to listen for the approaching train and marvels again at how he could hear it even when it was still a mile away. His eyes fill as he realizes how much he misses his home and friends. He tries to imagine what his mother and stepfather might be doing. He knows his stepfather will be at work, but with school still on Thanksgiving recess, he wonders what the neighborhood kids are up to. He wonders if they think about him or if they are too distracted by their own fun to even think of him. He wonders if he will be welcome when he gets back. He wonders how much he will tell them when they ask what he did in the city.

He watches a logging train with flatbed cars filled with Lincoln Logs disappear car by car into a tunnel in the mountain. He jumps down and runs around to the other side and up onto another platform where he can see the train emerging from the mountain. He can see the approaching headlight of the steam engine as it comes into view at the mouth of the tunnel. Real smoke comes out its black stack. It crosses an iron trestle bridge spanning a river at the base of the mountain. He looks down at the painted water. Around the trestle's high abutments the river's turbulent waters are flecked with the whitecaps of an artist's brush. From there the river enters a dark flume and the waters turn from blue to brown. As the river emerges from the chasm, it widens again, meandering through farm fields, and ends abruptly at the end of the layout.

A switching engine waits at a mine siding for its retinue of empty hopper cars to be loaded with coal for a factory in the nearby city. A diagonal conveyer is poised over one of the hopper cars waiting only for its operator to begin the loading process. A larger engine hauls flatcars with milk cans and livestock cars loaded with silhouetted cattle through the countryside. He is distracted by movement everywhere, racing from platform to platform to try to see it all, each time discovering some new activity.

Finally, he goes over and stands behind and below the balding man who peers over his wire spectacles at the controls. David can see the vast array of switches and throttles and wonders how the man keeps it all straight. Then he sees that a scaled-down diagram of all the tracks on the layout have been etched into the control panel in front of him and at each place where tracks converge is a toggle switch. He coughs a couple of times, hoping to get the man's attention, but the bald operator is focused on his console and the layout beyond it.

He hears Rose calling him from across the room, where she has become interested in a large display of board games arranged in a fan like a peacock's tail.

"Do you like Parcheesi?" she asks.

"I don't know what that is," he answers.

"It's an Indian game and lots of fun. Would you like me to get us one?"

He has only heard of American Indians and tries to imagine what their game might be like but he doesn't like board games in general and says, "No, thank you."

"Is there anything you would like?" she persists.

"I would like a model railroad someday," he says earnestly.

"Perhaps for Christmas," she answers.

"That would be nice," he says looking down and feeling that perhaps he had asked for too much.

"We must get back to your grandmother's. She disapproves when I'm late. I brought my watch today, but I never wear it. It isn't wound. Are you ready to go?"

"I am," he replies, casting one last glance at the trains going about their work.

"You liked that train layout, didn't you? I knew you would," she observes.

"I did like it, very much," he answers, resigned to their leaving.

They descend to the main floor. Rose detours them again through the doll section as they walk toward the exit but his attention is still absorbed by the train layout above, wondering both at its realism and how the bald man with spectacles keeps it all working. He wonders if that is his job. They leave F.A.O. Schwarz and walk up Fifth Avenue toward 71st Street.

When they arrive home, his grandmother smiles as she greet them but he senses that she is annoyed. He can smell dinner being prepared and hears the clink of dishes far back in what he now knows to be the "servant's quarters." After thanking his aunt, he goes to his room, while his grandmother and her sister exchange quiet words. He soon dozes off and begins to dream of the train layout.

In his dream he, too, is "O gauge," able to take the train from the city to the model village and to explore the different hives of commercial activity in the manmade terrain. He dreams he is the engineer in the cab of the steam engine waving to Jackie and Petey as he roars past them on their bikes and they pump furiously trying to keep up with his train. His engine hauls Mr. Farr's and Mr. Greaves' milk cans and some of their cows through the countryside. He wonders if Mr. Farr's cows have ever been on a train. He thinks the heavily tinned milk cans that Mr. Farr wrestles every morning out to the end of his dirt road, each later to be loaded onto a flatbed truck, might well end up on the Waterbury train bound for New York, though that is not, in fact, the case. He dreams the coal conveyer to life, conveying loose coal from the mine shaft up its diagonal incline and dropping it into the hopper cars below, as he advances the train slowly when each hopper car is full.

Folk Medicine

Margaret wakes him up from his dream and tells him his grandmother is "at table" and that he should wash his hands quickly and join her. It is the second time she has tried to rouse him. As he heads into the bathroom, he notices on his nightstand a blue book with gold embossed titles next to his father's photograph that was not there when he fell asleep. He doesn't stop to look at it as he is late to dinner. He splashes water on his hands, skipping the soap, and rushes to the table, withdrawing his chair noisily.

"You aunt is teaching you bad habits," his grandmother observes with a wry smile. "We serve dinner at seven and we are all at table when it is served."

"Sorry, I fell asleep," he answers, looking down at his empty plate.

Margaret arrives and quietly fills their plates from a silvered serving dish, first with what looked to him like a small chicken or large bird and second with asparagus and parsley roast potatoes. She holds the platter with one hand and, holding a silver fork and serving spoon with the other, clasps a portion of food and sets it on each plate.

"Is this chicken?" he asks his grandmother.

"It's squab," she answers drily. "Do you like squab?"

"I don't know what it is," he answers tentatively.

"It is a young pigeon," she answers as she slices into the small breast.

"Oh."

David tries to mimic her movements.

It tastes to him like chicken, but in his mind is the flock of pigeons he and his aunt sat watching outside the Plaza Hotel across from Reubens as an elderly couple with two white bakery bags fed them breadcrumbs. His aunt said only, "Flying rats. How can they feed them?"

"We saw lots of pigeons today," he observes, trying to sustain the conversation.

"These are not the same," she replies firmly.

"Oh," he answers, wondering what the difference is.

His grandmother bears the burden of conversation after that and inquires in detail about his day. He goes into as much detail as he can, but she seems uninterested in his description of the model train layout.

"I don't understand her obsession with Fragonard," his grandmother interrupts. "He is such a minor presence in a minor era. But my sister is a romantic and always will be so," she says rather crossly, resuming the intricate surgery on the small fowl.

Worried that he might somehow trouble his grandmother, he changes the subject and asks, "Rose said you had another sister. Do you see her very much?"

"Ann is a complex character. She is an intellect and a bohemian at heart and conducts her life that way. We see little of each other and are probably both happier for it. She is always raising money for this and that cause and, as I am lucky enough to have some, she is constantly soliciting me and trying to elicit my sympathy for one or another of them," she answers, not looking at him.

"Like Father Lefèvre at church?" he inquires.

"I don't know your Father Lefèvre but I suspect so. She is currently on a mission to better the living conditions of the Städtle Jews living in the Bowery and tells me dismal tales of their cold-water flats. She even has some photographs that she trots out. I am sympathetic, but find it all depressing. I don't know how she does it, but she does and I pay for it." The tone of her voice indicates that this line of discussion has ended.

At his grandmother's suggestion, dinner is followed by time together in the library where twice she asks him to stop the walking motion of his legs. She points out various family objects to him, explaining their importance and where they came from. She identifies relatives and friends in paintings and photographs, including a smiling middle-aged woman with blond hair who is his "godmother," although she now lives in Texas. He doesn't know what a "godmother" is and makes a note to ask his mother. The photograph looks like those he's seen in magazines of movie celebrities where the shallow depth-of-field makes all but the facial features blurry while light scintillates from the subject's hair and aqueous eyes. He doesn't remember ever meeting her.

His grandmother senses his lack of interest and, rather than send him to bed, simply turns around in her chair to tackle a small pile of letters on her highboy desk and begins writing with a marbled-green fountain pen. David can hear the nib scratching on the stationery and wonders why she doesn't use a pencil.

After what seems to him like a long time, he asks if he might go and get ready for bed.

"It's early for bed," his grandmother observes without turning around, "but I suppose in the country you retire early. I'll have Margaret run you a tub and then you can tuck in. Tomorrow we're going to the opera. I left a gift by your bed from your father. It is a collection of his letters to Howard and me, your aunt, and your mother from overseas before he was lost. You must read them when you can. You will come to know him for the lovely person he was. I am sure Alain is a lovely man, but you must know your father as well." Her voice cracks and trails off.

"Run along now and get ready for your bath. Margaret will meet you in my bathroom," she adds, when she has composed herself.

The next morning he gets up early and dresses. The door to the bathroom is ajar, so he enters and pees. He doesn't flush as he worries that the loud rush of water will awaken his grandmother and the water in the toilet bowl is barely discolored. He pulls on his comfortable clothes and leaves by the other door in his bedroom that leads into the corridor adjoining Margaret and Paula's rooms.

He continues on to find a small dining space almost filled with a pale pink, enameled metal dining table and two matching metal chairs. On the table is a small pot of blooming red geraniums. He guesses this is where Margaret and Paula eat their meals, as he has never seen them at the large table in the dining room. The small room with its simple furnishings reminds him of home.

From there he enters a spacious kitchen with a high ceiling and cabinets filled with cooking utensils and china rising well beyond the reach of most grownups clear to the plaster ceiling. The space is dominated by an eight-burner black enamel restaurant range with two ovens and a warming oven in between. A nickel-silver pipe runs along the front interspersed with ten white porcelain handles; large black sheet-metal shelves overhang the array of burners. A small loaf of bread wrapped in a white dishtowel rests on one of the shelves.

Margaret is at a large porcelain pot sink, filling a tea kettle with water. Paula is kneading a mound of yeasty dough on an adjacent deal table.

"Guten Morgen," says Paula with the first smile he has seen from her.

"Good morning," he responds.

He looks around the kitchen while the women bustle about. He soon smells the aroma of coffee, and shortly after, of bread toasting. On one counter a trestle tray is set up on its legs with a formal place setting on it. A wineglass sits in one corner and a tall silver coffee pot with an ebony handle in the other. Margaret is turning lemon halves over a porcelain juicer. When she finishes, she tossed the empty rinds into a trash can and pours the juice into the wine glass. She then removes what looks to him like a large pill and drops it into the wineglass with the lemon juice.

"Is that a pill?" he asks.

"It iss garlic," Margaret answers with a smile.

Anticipating his confusion, Margaret explains to him that his grandmother is an avid follower of "Herr Doktor Jarvis."

"You must know him, he iss from Vermont," she adds.

"No, I don't," he answers.

"He wrote a buch called Volk Medicine, and your Grammy follows it, at least at breakfast. She has lemon juice and garlic. It iss supposed to clean the blut," she continues, still smiling.

"Is it like lemonade?" he asks.

"Zer iss no zugar," she answers. "Would you like to taste it?"

Paula interrupts, "Don't make him drink zat awful schtuff."

"No, thank you," he answers, missing the lightness of their exchange.

He goes into the next room which is like a smaller kitchen. It has no stove, only two sinks and more cabinets that extend to the ceiling, though these are filled with glassware, china, and serving dishes. Two more doors confront him. One is a swinging door with no doorknob, the other a conventional door. He chooses the conventional door and enters a room one end of which has a floor-to-ceiling wooden rack with green bottles lying on their sides. The other end has more glass-faced cabinets, but these are filled with folded table linens. A mangle sits beneath the lone window like the one Mrs. Foss keeps in her basement where he and Annie often play dress-up together.

Finding little else of interest, he returns to the pantry and pushes open the swinging door to find himself in the dining room. He now understands that he has come full circle on this floor of the duplex apartment.

He passes through the dining room into the main foyer and down to the end where his grandmother's bedroom door is now ajar. As he approaches, he hears her ask, "Is that you? Do come in."

He pushes the door open into his grandmother's bedroom. She is lying in one of her two beds, with a pale silk bedcover pulled up over her knees. A paper lies folded in half by her legs.

She looks up and smiles. "Do you know *Aida*?" she asks.

"I don't think so," he allows. "Does she work with Paula and Margaret?"

His grandmother laughs and answers, *"Aida* is the opera we are going to see this afternoon. Come. Let me tell you the story."

Aida

"Aida is a slave girl," she begins. "The story takes place in Egypt in ancient times. When I am up and properly dressed, we will go to the library and I will show you pictures of the pyramids. Aida is a young Ethiopian girl who, unbeknownst to the Egyptians, is the daughter of the King of Ethiopia. She is enslaved in Egypt and an Egyptian army captain named Radames has fallen in love with her. When he is chosen to lead the Egyptian armies to defend Egypt from an attack by the Ethiopians, he is torn between his love for Aida and fighting the armies of her homeland. The plot thickens when the Egyptian king's daughter whose name I can never remember—it sounds like "memory," or some such—declares her love for Radames. It is a classic love triangle with all the tragic consequences."

"What is a love triangle?" he asks, remembering both the shape in his second-grade workbook and the musical instrument Petey played in the Junior High band as a drummer.

"It is when one person loves another, but someone else loves them, too."

"Like you and Mom and me?" he asks.

"Not at all," she answers sharply but clearly taken aback. "We are three people and that is a triangle, but we all love each other. Your mother and I both love you very much," she continues.

"Do you love my mother?" he asks.

"Very much. I do not always agree with her and sometimes we have our *contretemps*, but I will always love her as my son did."

"You mean my real father?" he asks, not knowing what *contretemps* were.

"Yes, that's right," she says with finality.

"The curtain goes up at two and we're having lunch at Louis Sherry's on the Grand Tier. If I remember correctly, Mr. Sherry was from Vermont as well. Now you go clean up. I will meet you in the dining room in 15 minutes and we will see what Paula and Margaret have made for our breakfast. I'm hungry. How about you?"

"I am, too," he replies, as Margaret enters the room with the tray he saw in the kitchen. David wants to stay and see his grandmother drink the lemon juice, but sensing that he has been excused, he leaves by the bathroom door, which he closes behind him as instructed.

In the foyer, David hears the loud click of the minute hand advance in the grandfather clock case. It's a Colonial era antique with a hand-painted pine case. The door covering the movement's interior works is cracked enough from its two centuries in heated homes so that if one peers up close, one can see the polished brass pendulum swinging inside. While peeking through the crack, David holds onto the edges of the case. He has been told by Margaret and his grandmother not to touch the clock but is convinced that he is alone in the foyer. Margaret spots him on her way from the dining room to the pantry. She sets down the two pewter porringers she's carrying off to be polished and comes over and takes him by the ear.

"Vollow me," she says in her heavily accented English.

Margaret came into the family at the war's outbreak and was a refugee from Germany although not Jewish. She leads him by the ear into the large kitchen behind the pantry.

"You haff been told never to put your hands on zee grandfazzer clock."

She lets go of his ear and opens the newly painted GE refrigerator with its large white condenser coil humming on top. He is surprised how few foodstuffs are inside the cavernous interior with its ripple-glass shelves. From the top shelf Margaret removes a small masonry crock of mustard with a pendant silver spoon. She scoops out a spoonful of mustard and puts it to his lips.

Although he has been punished before, it is usually with words and, only once in his life, with a single hand slap to his rear. His curiosity at this odd punishment makes it difficult to repress a smile. He swallows the pale mustard. It is unusually hot, unlike the yellow mustard he dollops on to hotdogs at the summer patrol picnics. He promises Margaret never to touch the clock again and returns to the library, where he retrieves the Steichen book of World War II battle photographs. His grandmother leaves it out for him as Steichen had been a student and friend of his great-uncle, whose more famous photographs hang about the apartment.

There is a Steichen portrait of his grandmother as a young woman in the entry hall. She is leaning forward and embracing the black Bakelite steering wheel of a large touring car. She is photographed from the driver's-side window. Perhaps the door is open, as the window frame is not evident. Her two hands meet on the upper left side of the steering wheel. Her right arm is draped over the top of the steering wheel and her right elbow points to the rear view mirror above. Her straight black hair, parted in the middle, cascades over her right arm, obscuring part of it. She is wearing a light wool overcoat with a wide, open collar that obscures her neck and into which her hair on that side disappears. The knot of a white neck scarf hangs below her chin. A severe part in her hair looks like an aerial view of a river flowing out into the sea of her forehead. She is a young woman, uncomfortable in this sensuous pose, not yet convinced of her beauty. She stares at the camera intently, as if she wants to ask the viewer for affirmation of some sort. Although her mouth is closed, her lips do not quite meet. She seems to whisper a question to the viewer, "Am I beautiful?"

That afternoon, he is again bothered by the chafe of his wool pants as he and his grandmother climb the carpeted steps in the Metropolitan Opera House to the Grand Tier and the entrance to the posh restaurant whose founder had run a greasy spoon in St. Albans, Vermont, although the restaurant looks like nothing he has ever seen in Vermont. The walls are covered with red velour punctuated with full-length and larger-than-life paintings of opera stars in costume, and baroque sconce lights designed to look like candelabra. The floor is a veined white marble, the inverse of the marble in his grandmother's former bath.

They're ushered to a table in the middle of the dining room. An elderly, slightly stooped waiter approaches them swiftly with a broad smile. His long, still-dark, wavy hair is combed back behind his ears, and a large aquiline nose supporting black-framed glasses defines his face. He wears the formal black attire of all the waiters David has seen in New York and his order pad is tucked into his cummerbund.

David's grandmother greets the waiter warmly and introduces her grandson. To David's surprise, the waiter shakes hands with him and bows slightly, explaining in heavily accented English that he knew and waited on his father when he was "your age."

He leaves with their order as his grandmother explains that Juan Davido used to write Spanish verse. "He was very kind to your father, whom he knew well before he went away to school, as we used to come here often when he was little. He is a very cultivated and thoughtful man and used to give us copies of his poems hand-written in Spanish, though, unfortunately, we could not read them."

Neither of them is hungry so they share a fruit salad plate and pastries. A three-tone gong sounds outside in the corridor. He can hear it moving through the horseshoe outside the restaurant as a uniformed usher passes by the entrance. Juan Davido bids his grandmother an effusive farewell in broken English, conveying again his sympathy for her son's death in the war, and smiles gently to her grandson as he shakes his hand.

They return to the lobby and enter the orchestra section. Their seats are in the sixth row. His grandmother hands him a program. He leafs through it looking at the pictures. Suddenly the lights dim and loud applause begins as the conductor makes his way through the crowded orchestra pit to his place on the podium in front. He bows to the audience and bids the orchestra to arise to further applause. He then reaches down to his left and shakes hands with the concertmaster. After opening the score on his elevated music stand, his arms rise slowly and hold their place as he scans the attentive musicians around him. His hands then drop suddenly and the overture begins.

David has never heard a live orchestra before. He has heard classical music only from the five-inch speaker in his Motorola radio with its Bakelite case and gold-painted dial and knobs. Live music performance at home is confined to summer band concerts on the green, with the town or school marching band, or dances at the firehouse with either a local western swing group or pick-up ensembles convened to enhance the fiddling of Crazy Chase.

As the sonorous voices of the celli and double basses decay in the cavernous hall, the curtain rises suddenly on a palatial scene with a desert background. The sheer scale of the set causes him to draw in his breath. He doesn't see his grandmother watching him rather than the stage.

He tries to recall the unfolding plot his grandmother explained to him earlier, but is distracted by the splendor of the sets and the detailed exoticism of the costumes. The narrative interplay of martial and amorous arias eludes him as he is more interested in the conductor, who seems to be paying the most attention to the violin section on his left. Dressed like the waiter who served them lunch, the diminutive man lunges at the orchestra in great dips as he draws circles in the air with his baton. Occasionally, he stands straight back, thrusts his torso out to the orchestra, and slowly raises his arms, eliciting a crescendo. In appearance and stature, he reminds David of the man controlling the railroad landscape. But the conductor is elegantly dressed and in constant movement. In his more animated gestures toward the orchestra, his shock of silver hair flies forward over his forehead and eyes, and he must push it back with an impatient gesture.

The languorous rise and fall of the strings, woodwinds, and brass fill the cavernous space in the opera house above him. He turns and looks at the balconies rising up behind the orchestra section – the private boxes and the people standing in their everyday clothes at the very top – until his grandmother taps him on the shoulder to draw his attention back to the stage. He notices for the first time that the desert backdrop is a painted cloth the size of the whole stage and that a breeze from somewhere offstage riffles it periodically.

"She's a bit too emotive for me," whispers his grandmother into his ear, "but then she is Callas."

He doesn't know the meaning of "emotive" and remembers that "Callas" is the woman playing Aida.

When the curtain falls on the last act and they ready themselves to leave, he again feels the discomfort of his wool pants and stiff shirt and looks forward to being home and changing into the knee-length blue cotton shorts he is allowed to wear in the apartment when there are no guests present or expected. He's taken aback by the burst of applause and the raucous shouts of the audience, who up to this point, have only expressed their enthusiasm after an aria with applause and frequent shouts of "Brava!" The house soon loses its prior composure with shouts of "La Divina," as the woman singing the role of Aida appears on stage alone. Armfuls of flowers are heaped at her feet as she curtsies with wide-spread arms repeatedly and blows kisses to the frenzied crowd.

"We are not going to fight the crowds backstage. You'll have to meet Callas another time," his grandmother announces to David.

It is another twenty minutes before the house begins to calm down, the curtain calls end and people begin to gather their belongings and spill into the aisles. His grandmother takes his hand and they make their way slowly to the lobby. He is relieved when they finally emerge into the daylight and cool air of Broadway.

"We'll have to walk over to Madison to get a cab," his grandmother says and they begin to walk east at a brisk pace. His short stride has him skipping again every few steps to keep up with his grandmother who occasionally turns around to see that he is still with her. She seems anxious to get home, as the sky had darkened considerably and ominous rain clouds lower above the city.

"If it should start to rain, we'll have to call for a car, as we will never get a cab here."

But his grandmother flags down a Checker headed up Sixth Avenue and they clamber in.

"730 Park," she announces. "Just off Park. The entrance is on 71st."

There is no response from the cabbie, who accelerates in silence.

"How did you like it?" his grandmother asks, inclining her head toward him and smiling.

"I did very much. Will you tell me the story again when we get home?" he asks.

"I will indeed," she says, as the cab approaches 71st and veers left to the awning.

At dinner that evening they are joined by his aunt Rose and his grandmother's friend Sylvia. He sees that the table is set with more china and silver than when he and his grandmother eat alone. The tall silver candlesticks sitting on mirrored-glass leaves are lit. The doors to the Colonial-era corner cabinet are open and the cabinet's interior lights illuminate the array of antique pewter pieces like those he had seen in the movie "Billy Budd." The table centerpiece is a shellacked wooden trencher filled with dried artichoke blossoms spray-painted gold. His grandmother is wearing a necklace of white jade beads, each of which is carved in shapes too small for him to make out. It hangs low on her black evening dress. His Aunt Rose looks as she did when they had their "adventure," wearing a mauve cotton dress with shoulder straps and an open pink sweater. In contrast to both, Sylvia is awhirl in a flamboyant floral-pattern dress with white background. Her lacquered black hair glistens in the candlelight and when she emits her tenor laugh and tosses her head her sculpted hair moves like an object rather than a mass of hair.

Margaret serves boned leg of lamb slices with green mint jelly from a red and white china platter, and then passes a matching bowl of small roasted potatoes and finally cold white asparagus with salad dressing on a square silver tray. David has never seen white asparagus before.

Sylvia's apparent enthusiasm for her friend's grandson leads to a rapid-fire interrogation about his home, his new stepfather, his school, his church, and his friends. Keeping an eye on his grandmother, whose facial expressions signal to him her pleasure or displeasure with his responses, he answers the questions, careful not to digress into the "country matters that are of little interest to city people."

After a moment of silence, he seizes the opportunity to ask his grandmother why Aida and Radames are buried alive in the sealed tomb at the end of the opera.

"Perhaps your Aunt Rose, who is an expert in matters operatic, can tell you," his grandmother answers.

"I will want to hear this, too," Sylvia puts in.

After an awkward silence, Rose speaks up softly.

"Radames is condemned to death for treason, for choosing a slave girl over the love of his King's daughter, Amneris, who is jealous of his love for Aida. The King is caught in a tragic conflict between his love for his daughter and his gratitude to Radames, the hero who has just saved his country. Tragically, the King chooses the rule of law as expressed by his high priest Ramfis over his love for Radames and orders him buried alive. Once in the tomb, Radames discovers that Aida has hidden herself in there to die with him. It is very romantic. You heard my good friend Mario del Monaco singing Radames. He is a lovely man and a perfect match for Callas' theatrics."

"I am sure we've all heard enough about tragic operas for one night," his grandmother announces. "Sylvia, do tell us how Ed's new show is coming." Sylvia launches into a long story about the challenges her husband, Ed Sullivan, is having with his television variety show and the hard work of finding suitable talent for his expanding audience.

Rose and David pick at their plates. David notices lamb fat congealing on the side of his plate and turns to the asparagus which he likes, remembering to slice each spear to a length that will fit in his mouth rather than eating it with his fingers as he is allowed to do at home.

At the sound of the buzzer, Margaret appears and clears the plates. She returns shortly with smaller plates holding green glass bowls filled with water and a slice of lemon. He wonders if this is a new dessert or another cure like his grandmother drank in the morning. When in doubt about table manners, his mother taught him to watch his grandmother and simply follow her lead. This advice serves him well. When his grandmother squeezes the juice from her lemon into the water and immerses her fingers in the bowl, rubs them together, and then dries them on the napkin in her lap, David does the same, watching his Aunt Rose who offers him a furtive smile.

"Do you use finger bowls at home?" his grandmother asks.

"We don't," he says. "But maybe we could. I'll ask Mom."

"I don't suppose it's a country habit," she answers, pressing the buzzer again with her foot.

After a dessert of poached pears, they retire to the library for further conversation and for Sylvia to have a cigarette. It is evident to the women that David's attention is drifting from their conversation and that he is struggling to stay awake. His grandmother excuses him to "prepare for bed," after exacting from him cheek kisses for all present.

The Fallen-down Tree

David glances again at the book on his bedstead, noticing his name is the same as the author's, and then remembers that the book is by or about his father. But his fatigue overwhelms his interest and he climbs into bed.

He dreams he is walking through a covert of mixed-growth young poplars and white birch trees behind the Collettes' house along the path that leads to their clubhouse in the fallen-down tree. The sunshine is lost in cloud cover, yet it's still light between the dark clouds. The contrasts are infused with yellows and dark grays as if a storm is imminent. Mosses growing on the north sides of the slender tree trunks catch his eye, emanating flashes of color that seem to oscillate between emerald green and dark gold as he walks by. He enters the cooler wood of old-growth pines and a few dying oaks whose canopies have starved the undergrowth. He soon finds himself at the fallen-down tree. He sits for a minute on the recumbent trunk and looks up at the pale light filtering through the pine boughs.

Out of the corner of his eye, he notices a slow-moving object and looks down to his right. A long freight train with several dozen boxcars and half as many flatcars winds its way across the forest floor drawn by two steam engines. There are lights in both engines and the red caboose and figures seem to be moving inside. Puffs of steam emerge from both engines as the long freight makes its way along the tracks and disappears around the base of a pine several yards away. He jumps up to follow the disappearing train, but then sees that the forest floor has tracks leading in every direction. Picking his way through the maze of rail beds, he follows several to the points where they disappear into the hollows of trees or tunnels without egress. His peripheral vision catches more and more movement on the forest floor as his glance jumps from train to train. A silver train with ten passenger cars makes its way around a long, curving track that follows the base of an oak tree and vanishes into the darkness beyond. The last car has a rounded tail with a small platform where two familiar men are leaning on the railing and staring back at him. To his left he notices a small brick station with a crowd of people waiting on the platform, their valises at their sides. Some are conversing while others just peer down the empty track. He hears the steady clang of a bell and sees a crossing gate lower slowly across a dirt road and then sees the light of a steam engine approaching the station pulling a mixed lot of freight and passenger cars. The train slows to a crawl as it approaches the station and a conductor jumps off. Now he is on the platform in scale with the other passengers. He's holding his stepfather's hand as they say goodbye to his mother. She is crying again and looks imploringly at him as she turns on the Pullman's platform to look at him and wave good-bye. He starts toward her from the station platform to reassure her but, in a burst of steam, the train gathers speed and leaves him and his stepfather behind. Alain grips his hand and they watch the last car disappear around a long curve.

Later in the dream, he picks his way through the dead branches of the fallen tree up the gentle incline to where they built their clubhouse. He remembers the secret password although no one is there to ask him for it. "Grange," he says to himself, and draws open the hinged plywood door that Jackie rescued from his father's junk pile. Inside he is confronted with a vivid array of multi-colored indicator lights, bat-handled toggle switches, and black plastic transformer throttles, behind which is a spider web diagram of train tracks. There is no one in the clubhouse. He sits down in the wooden office chair they dragged down from the dump. He looks at the array of lights. Although he touches none of the controls, lights change color as he watches. He rises and goes back outside to see if the trains are still there.

In the forest he sees again the rail beds leading off into darker parts of the woods with their slow-moving rolling stock, but as his eyes follow the disappearing trains he notices the quiet presence of animals in the forest. They are of his scale and seem not to notice the bustle of activity at their feet. Instead they seem to be watching him intently. A doe with two fawns stands near a gnarled pine trunk, looking at him warily as her white tail twitches. A distracted raccoon trundles back and forth near the base of the fallen-down tree. It appears to be searching for something and stops periodically to paw at the ground. A red fox lies curled up on a bed of moss several yards away looking intently at him, its nose buried in its bushy red tail. He recognizes its sly smile.

To his left, he notices a person taller than himself duck behind a tree. He's afraid for the first time and sits down on the stump of the fallen tree to try to get his bearings. A tall, heavy-set man emerges from behind the tree and walks toward him. It's his grandfather, although he looks younger than he remembers him. He is wearing a dark suit of an indeterminate color and his dark tie is centered neatly in the collar of his white shirt. His face has no expression. He sits down next to his grandson and begins to tell him a story. There is no book.

The Train to China

At breakfast his grandmother asks him if he got a good night's sleep.

"I did," he answers, still groggy, "But I had a dream and Pappy was in it."

His grandmother looks at him with renewed interest. "How interesting ... tell me more," she says.

He pauses. "He was about to tell me a story."

"A Snoodlepussy story, I'll bet."

"Yes, it was," he answers, although he wasn't sure since the story hadn't begun in his dream.

"I miss your grandfather every day. He was a kind man. He worked himself so hard, especially after the war started. I saw so little of him. After your father died and the war ended, I felt I was widowed twice and then, of course, I was. I had hoped that I would be able to reinvigorate him, but the loss of your father seemed to sap what little life was left in him. I could see him dying day by day. He and O'Keeffe were close and I would have been happy if she had been able to bring him back, but it wasn't to be."

Her voice trails off and they finish breakfast in silence. When he looks up at his grandmother, she looks away as if to avoid his glance. David has never heard his grandmother speak this way and is surprised at the sadness in her voice.

Later that day, David is excited to hear that he is to see his Aunt Rose again before returning home. After David's trip was confirmed, his grandmother declined an invitation to an opening at the Museum of the City of New York. Patrons were always invited and initially she planned to take David, but then thought better of it, deciding that the show of Lower East Side immigrant art would be even less interesting to him than to her. The director of the museum's curatorial department had, however, called personally to invite her because of the several gloomy Swabian landscapes she had donated and she now felt compelled to attend.

Rose comes for David around 4:30 and they walk several blocks east to Lexington Avenue.

"Where are we having supper?" David asks.

"I thought we'd eat in China," she answers cryptically. "It's a long way from here and we'll have to take a train to get there."

David's first thought is to ask what kind of food Chinese people eat. He has seen so many new and exotic foods during his visit that he has no idea what to expect.

"I thought China was on the other side of the ocean," he says, looking up at his smiling aunt.

"Oh, it is, but there's a Chinatown here in New York."

David makes no sense of her answer, thinking China is a country, but he is accustomed to enigmatic answers from his aunt, so he just walks alongside her, taking care to step on each expansion gap between the concrete sidewalk squares.

Soon they come to a set of downward steps surrounded by a cast-iron fence. Rose pauses and looks around as if confused, then grabs the handrail and starts down the steps. David follows.

"Where are we going?" he asks.

"To get the express train to Chinatown," Rose answers.

"Just stay close by me and hold my hand when we get down into the subway. It's not always a safe place."

David grasped his aunt's hand as he steps off the last step onto the concrete landing. He thinks again of the old man clutching the paper bag he saw by the tracks and wonders if they are entering the same tunnel.

He follows his aunt to a ticket booth that looks like one of the birdcages at the zoo. He wonders why the Negro man selling tickets is in a cage, as he looks harmless and says nothing as he scoops up the small change that David's aunt tenders and pushes four little coins back through a gap in his cage.

"I hardly ever take the subway so I never have tokens in my purse. I bought us two round-trips and if we take a cab home, then I'll have two extras. I prefer to walk and if it's too far, I take a bus or taxi. I hardly ever ride the subway unless I'm going to Brooklyn to see my other sister."

David remembers his mother telling him with great fondness of Ann. He remembers seeing another girl in the sepia photo on his grandmother's desk. He wonders why he has never met this other aunt.

"Your grandmother would never forgive me if she knew I brought you down here. She doesn't approve of or use the subway. She says it's dirty and dangerous. I'm not sure she's ever been down here. Thousands of working people ride it every day and not much happens. It is filthy though."

"Why is he locked in there?" David asks his aunt as they leave the iron booth.

"The bars are to protect him from burglars who might want to steal the money people pay to get subway tokens," his aunt responds as she counts her change and hands a token to David.

"Are there burglars down here?" David asks.

"Sometimes, but not now," his aunt answers distractedly. David looks around for people who might be burglars.

David suspects there is more than one train, because people are walking around in every direction. Some mill around, avoiding eye contact; one woman is sitting on the platform and holds out a hand as if asking for something.

His aunt slips her token into a slot and pushes her way through an oak turnstile. David does the same, but has a hard time pushing until the man behind him helps him and he walks through. He could have easily ducked down and walked underneath. His Aunt Rose turns and takes his hand again, explaining that they will have to go down another staircase through a tunnel to get to the express train, as the local takes forever to get to Chinatown. They descend another set of ironclad concrete steps. The white-tiled walls look like walls he has seen in public bathrooms. At the bottom they turn right and walk through a tunnel only to arrive at another staircase, which they go up and onto a platform between two sets of tracks. His aunt pauses at the top to catch her breath.

"I forgot how many stairs there are," she pants. "Maybe I'm just too old for the subway. We should have taken a taxi, but Chinatown is so far downtown that I hate to spend that much money on the fare. Unlike my sister, I must watch my expenses."

"There are lots of old people down here," David answers encouragingly as he leans out over the track and peers into the dark tunnels in both directions.

"Don't cross the white line," Rose warns.

David steps back and again takes his aunt's hand.

Soon David feels a rush of warm, fetid air coming from the tunnel. Loose wrappers in the tracks began to swirl in the onrush. David spots a rat skulking along the far rail. It look bigger than the ones he remembers seeing at the dump. He wonders if kids are ever allowed to "pop" rats in the subway like they are at home after the dump closes. He doesn't ask Rose, as he doesn't think she'll know.

Soon he hears the screech of steel- against- steel and leans out as far as he can over the white line. He sees the train's headlights. They are not as bright as the single light on the steam engine he saw with his father when he left. The train comes into view and whooshes by the people waiting as they begin to jostle for positions closest to where they think the doors will be when the train stops.

Aunt Rose tells him to push his way in and hold a seat for her, as it is a long ride downtown and her balance isn't good enough for her to stand all the way. He's one of the first into the car and takes an open twin seat near the end of the car. He sees his aunt making her way through the crowded aisle down to him when a large man sits down in the seat next to him.

"Excuse me sir, but I was saving this seat for my aunt. It's hard for her to stand on a train," David says. The man looks quizzically at him and turns away. When his aunt has made her way to where David is sitting, he looks again at the man who avoids his gaze, so David gets up and offers his seat to his aunt who drops into it, clutching the vertical post as if she has yet to recover her balance. David clings to the post as the train accelerates. The ride is smooth, but the train occasionally veers sidewise as it switches tracks.

Half of the people in the car are "colored" as he hears his grandmother say, though he has learned the term "Negro" in school. He now understands why his grandmother never takes the subway. He doesn't see any people with whom she associates, nor are the subway riders dressed the way his grandmother's friends dress.

Occasionally, the car is pitched into darkness and the lights flicker back on just as suddenly. Knowing nothing about the third rail supplying the car with electricity, David imagines one of the many standing passengers leaning against the light switch as his mother did once at home.

The express train speeds by regular bursts of exterior light, indicating a local station but stops only at express stops. Blue tile letters in the local platform's white-tiled walls indicate the fleeting street addresses and remind David of his first elevator trip.

Rose tells him that their stop is Canal Street as he tries to make sense of the large subway map across from where he is standing, but he can't relate the colored lines to where they are. Then he hears a conductor say, "Next stop... Canal," and he whispers to Rose that they're coming into the station, as she has drifted off, her head cradled in her forearm clinging to the pole. He recalls his grandmother telling him that Rose has low blood pressure and sometimes nods off.

When the train stops, Rose pulls herself up and, clutching her purse to her breast, follows David off the train onto the platform. The train ride to Chinatown took less time than he had inferred from his aunt it would.

"I have to walk up the stairs slowly," she whispers to David. "It's early and we're not in a hurry." David follows his aunt up two long flights of stairs. Halfway up the last flight he can see the early evening sky above. It is a late fall afternoon and it will soon be dark. He can smell the sudden downpour that has left the upper steps glistening with water. He turns around to warn his aunt.

As he crests the last steps onto the wet asphalt sidewalk, already glistening with the reflections of red and yellow Chinese paper lanterns swinging from storefront awnings and strings of small light bulbs strung between lampposts, David recognizes the strong smell of fish. He is surrounded by Chinese people, swarming both ways on the sidewalk.

Looking at his aunt leaning against the cast-iron barricade around the subways stairs as she catches her breath, he asks, "Is this China?"

"It is," she answers. "Isn't it fun?"

David looks wide-eyed at the block-long row of wooden tables set up along the sidewalk. The first he sees holds shallow crates with drifts of crushed ice on which lay a display of fish – shellfish and crustaceans he has never seen before. On a stand behind the table stands a large aquarium filled with brown eels, their narrow dorsal fins rippling in the brackish water.

While Rose catches her breath and recovers her energy, David runs from sight to sight. He recalls the smell of newly eviscerated fish from having helped his stepfather clean a bucket of perch pulled from below the ice on Lake Elmore in winter or a creel of brookies after a day on the Lamoille, but he has never seen fish as large and alien as those splayed out at eye level on the ice. He spots several fish the size of a man's leg nestled in the ice.

Further down the block, tilted crates hold neatly arranged vegetables and fruits David has never seen before. Girls and women stand behind the crates, holding out a fruit or vegetable and calling to passersby what David presumes to be the names of the produce they're selling. David doesn't whether they're speaking Chinese or English.

"Take my hand," he hears his Aunt Rose say behind him. "We must stay together. Your grandmother will never forgive me for bringing you down here, especially if I lose you. This is not her idea of a suitable outing. She doesn't frequent the ethnic neighborhoods, though I have always found them exciting."

Hand-in-hand they run a gauntlet of food vendors thrusting produce at them. At the end of the second block, the outdoor market tapers off with a few spice sellers and several tables of small toys selling for five and ten cents. Curious, David picks up and looks at a small gong. The old woman behind the counter springs to her slippered feet and says to David, "You like? You like? I give three for two. You like?"

Curious about what toys Chinese kids play with and unaware that he has initiated a haggle by picking up the small object when he only wanted to see it up close in the poor light, David demurs, replacing the gong in the cardboard box.

"I give two for 50 cents," he hears behind him as he and Rose continue along the wet sidewalk.

"I have one more thing to show you before we eat," his aunt whispers to him as they walk. "We must visit a Chinese apothecary. After we eat, we'll visit my favorite teashop and buy some tea. I'm almost out of tea and the Chinese have such lovely teas. My sister makes such a fuss of buying her tea at Fortnum & Mason in London, but of course they just buy it from the Chinese. I just go to the source and save money to boot."

"You mean it's the same and she must pay more?" David asks.

"In New York, where one shops makes a difference," his aunt answers brusquely.

Aunt Rose turns into a narrow nondescript shop with a dirty display window facing the street. As they walk in David looks at the dust-covered objects lying on the shelf of the display window. He recognizes nothing but a few leaves and some pieces of bark. Three shriveled objects that look to David like desiccated small animal organs are arranged among the objects. A faded Chinese paper sign is tacked to the back wall.

Inside, the musty smell reminds him of being deep in the woods behind the Collette's house where the fallen-down tree is. The small man who owns the shop is busy sorting a collection of roots and leaves on the counter. Several wooden apothecary drawers behind and above him are open. David stands on his tiptoes to see onto the counter, but can make no sense of the objects the man is dicing and sorting. The man looks down at him through thick spectacles and smiles. David looks away, feigning interest elsewhere in the cramped shop. Nothing is said as he and his aunt leave and the spring-mounted bell above the door again tinkles.

"Do they sell pills there too?" David asks as they walk down the street.

"I suspect they do sell a few, but I don't know. Most Chinese medicine is composed of various leaves, roots, and animal parts. They are dried out and then compiled according to the doctor's prescription into tea bags and the patient drinks the tea. My dear friend Ellie only goes to Chinese doctors and I came with her once when she was not feeling well. Her doctor lives and works out of a two-story walk-up apartment somewhere in this neighborhood. She brings his prescription here to be filled. The prescription itself is a work of art and she gave me one to keep, which I will show you someday."

"How did the doctor know what was making her sick?" David asks his Aunt and thinking of his mother.

"He looked at her tongue, took her pulse, looked into her eyes, and then felt her kidneys from what I could see. That was all."

"Mom was a nurse," David mentions. "I wonder if she knows about these things."

"I expect not. Our medicine is very different from Chinese medicine."

David and Rose have dinner in a small noodle shop that Rose frequented in earlier days, although the proprietor did not seem to remember her.

"The food here is very good. Everything is very fresh and the kitchen is clean," she notes as they walk by a display of cooked ducks hanging by their feet.

Rose orders for David who can make no sense of the menu's English.

"Do you like it?" his Aunt Rose asks.

"I do, very much," David answers as he picks at his plate of still crisp vegetables and beef strips in black bean sauce. Relieved to have recognized the components of the dish his aunt ordered, he eats with gusto. He soon notices that the few other diners are eating with sticks rather than forks and spoons and he asks his aunt if that is how Chinese people eat.

"Chopsticks," she notes. "Chinese people use chopsticks. I don't know how they do it. I tried them once. I held the food with one and tried to stab it with the other, but I looked so foolish, I finally had to ask for a fork."

They both laugh at the image of his aunt trying to stab her food with a chopstick and David makes a note to tell his stepfather about her experience with them.

Rose settles the bill. They leave and walk several blocks back toward the subway. The tea shop is closed.

"That's a mystery. I hope Mr. Lee isn't ill. I have never come here, night or day, when he wasn't open."

They peer in the window. There is no light inside the shop, but the reflection of the streetlight allows David to see shelves extending from the floor to the ceiling, all with identical tin canisters labeled with Chinese ideograms.

"We'll come back another time. You will enjoy Mr. Lee. I do hope he's okay."

There are plenty of seats on the subway riding back uptown and, again, his aunt dozes peacefully on her forearm while David scans the different faces in the car.

The Montrealer

Paula wakes him the next morning with a glass of fresh-squeezed orange juice and a "Ziss iss ze day ven you vill go home to your mutter und vatter," but gets no response.

He is still among the images in his dream and can make no sense of the stream of foreign-sounding words. He rolls over and rubs his eyes. Paula is smiling at him and places the juice glass on the table beside him.

"Your grandmutter iss vaiting inzite for you. Comen as zoon as you vash up."

When Paula leaves, he wants to pull the covers up and re-enter the fading dream, but instead throws them back and goes into his grandmother's bathroom to get ready for breakfast.

Settled into his chair at the table, he is again confronted by the dreaded chicken livers of his first day. "Good morning," his grandmother says, looking up from her coffee. "Did you sleep well?

"I did," he answers.

"Did you and Rose have a nice dinner last night?"

"We did," David answers, afraid his grandmother will ask where they went and what they ate.

But his grandmother questions him no further.

"Today, we have no plans as you must get ready for your journey home tonight on the *Montrealer.* Margaret will help you pack."

David eats his scrambled eggs and a slice of toast but leaves the chicken livers in their yellowish puddle of grease on the side of the plate. His grandmother does not press him on the issue.

That evening, after a day with his grandmother looking at family albums and stories about the behavior of certain family members from a generation or two before him, David gets ready for Paula to take him to Penn Station where she will see him onto the train.

Before he leaves, his grandmother kneels and draws him to her with a hug, whispering into his ear, "You must come again soon."

"I will," he replies. "I like to come here."

"Tell your mother that I think of her often and hope to see her one day again. And don't forget to read the book that I packed in your valise."

"I won't," he nods. "I mean, I will tell my mother," he clarifies.

With that the elevator door opens and he and Paula step inside. He likes counting the floor numbers backward and has grown accustomed to going from fourteen to twelve, a habit he will later find himself trying to break when he is "it" in a game of hide-and-seek.

Oskar has a yellow Checker waiting at the end of the awning for them. He takes David's suitcase from him and ushers Paula in first. Then he helps him up onto the floor of the taxi and slides the suitcase in next to him. He pokes his head in afterward and says to David, "You must come to visit us again. I knew your father so well. Please give my best wishes to your lovely mother."

"I will," he replies gratefully, adding, "See you next time I come to New York."

On platform sixteen, bustling travelers wrestle their baggage along the cement platform as they look for passenger car numbers posted in windows near their entrances. An elderly man and a young boy walk side-by-side linked by a heavily decaled, brown steamer trunk at a precarious angle, reflecting the differences in their height. The elderly man is nearsighted, as they keep setting down the trunk so he can approach each car and read the coach number.

Paula walks at a brisk pace, with her charge trailing behind her carrying his small suitcase with both hands so it again bangs his knees. She stops seven cars down from the platform entrance and waits for him to catch up. He notices they need no iron stepstool as the platform is at the same height as the entrance to the car. He follows Paula in and they walks down the long corridor of curtained berths.

"9A," Paula announces, as she unbutton and draws back the heavy drapes of his berth.

It is identical to the berth he had coming south. This time, however, there is no porter nearby, so Paula helps him into the lower berth and lifts up his suitcase. She removes his pajamas which they had packed on top. She then snaps the valise shut and tucks it under the bunk.

"Your mutter will meet you in Fermont," she says crisply.

"Who will wake me up?' he asks.

"I vill zee to it," Paula answers. "I am leafing now, ready yourself for bed. Ze train leafs in zeven minutes."

David says, "Good bye," and to his surprise, Paula gives him a hug and kisses him on both cheeks before turning abruptly and leaving the car.

David turns toward the window and realizes the shade is down. With both hands he slides it up its metal tracks so he can see the activity on the platform outside. But he is on the wrong side and sees only the grimy façade of an adjacent train that also has its interior lights on. He rolls over and lies on his back, feeling the starched linen pillowcase on the back of his neck.

After several minutes, he hears a low-pitched whistle reverberate through the underground station followed by another a few minutes later and then he feels the tug of the engine and hears the clank of the couplers engaging. On boarding, he looked down the platform to see how many cars were on the train, but beyond the fifth coach, they disappeared around the gentle curve of the tracks into the darkness beyond.

The train moves slowly now and David rises on his right elbow to look out. The vacant, dimly lit coach interiors on the adjacent track scroll past slowly. In a sleeping car, he sees a Negro porter carrying a stack of folded sheets along the corridor. All the drawing room doors are open. David wonders how the engineer gets the engine from the front of the train to the back again or if he simply backs the train out through the vast web of tunnels through which it entered. He has seen engines coupled together in tandem pulling freight cars loaded with lumber through the center of Morrisville.

His thoughts turn to home and he wonder if his mother or his step-father will meet him when he gets off in Waterbury. Then he begins to worry that he might not wake up and will travel too far, remembering that the train goes beyond Waterbury to another country where Alain's relatives live.

The train moves at a crawl through the tunnel. He remembers the slow passage into the station and the man seated under the light fussing with his paper bag. They soon leave behind the train on the adjacent track and he can see again the maze of tracks and switches. He feels the sideways tug each time the train passes over a switch onto a different track. Each time they pass the light of a bare yellow bulb he looks for the man, but he doesn't see him.

The train soon leaves behind the underground yards and moves faster along a straight track with only one additional track visible from his side. As the train picks up speed, it suddenly emerges into the glittering light of the nighttime city. It climbs the gentle incline onto an elevated track and on the horizon to the west between the blocks of tenements he can see a luminous dusk. He rolls over on his stomach and lies watching the night city like a movie spooling by on an endless panoramic screen.

No one brings him a ginger ale or comes to help him with his pajamas. As he watches the rapid successions of light and darkness and the nightlife below, he wonders if Mr. J knows he is on the train. The train suddenly passes close to a long row of tenement buildings. He can see people moving about inside their apartments. He sees a Negro woman slumped forward at her kitchen table with her head in her arms. He thinks perhaps she is asleep or resting. An old man squats on a fire escape by an open window, smoking and looking straight at the train. His eyes begin to ache watching the fast-moving foreground until the train veers away from the buildings and continues along the trestle above a wide avenue with endless storefronts and kids navigating their bikes along sidewalks and through a littered playground. The train rides high over the evening city and he has to prop himself up on his elbows to see down onto the street life below.

The rhythm of the rail trucks passing over joints in the rail bed make a *du-dun, du-dun* sound similar to the prenatal sound of his mother's heartbeat that leaves him blinking to stay awake. He soon gives up trying to follow the fast-moving foreground and looks out instead at the city's skyline, where the occasional billboard mounted on top of a building, touts a shaving product or the success of a Broadway show. Red lights on towers blink miles away and the last light of a late autumn dusk fades, leaving the city an evanescence of small lights in a black sky.

<hr>

As the train leaves behind the lights of the city, David dreams of Mr. Farr's pasture. He is with two boys who seem familiar. Annie Foss is also with them. Annie is dressed all in white – shorts, sneakers and a cotton blouse. Ringlets of tumbled pale blond hair frame her earnest face. Perhaps she looks serious because she is in the company of boys who are planning to dam up the small brook in Mr. Farr's pasture, creating a pool big enough to wade in. One carries a claw hammer, a small hatchet, and a can of rusty, mixed-size nails, the other a round-headed shovel he uses for balance as they pick their way straight down the steep ravine criss-crossed with narrow cow paths. In the lower pasture a rill flows from a spring in the gravel detritus below the ravine. No trees grow on the steep wall of the former gravel pit. David senses he is with them in the pasture, but doesn't see himself in the dream as he watches them make their way down to the brook. The brook is joined farther down by another coming in from a dark stand of balsam on an adjacent hill.

The boy with the hatchet leads the way. They arrive at a grassy knoll next to the stream and under the shadow of a tall red pine. Annie is distracted by some wild strawberries growing on the other side of the brook and gets down on her hands and knees and begins picking the pearl-sized berries with one hand and cradling what she picks in the other.

No one talks, but the two boys set immediately to work. David is conscious of watching and wondering if the others know he is there. The boy with the shovel begins hauling up loaf-sized stones he finds lower down in the brook and placing them in a straight line across the water's flow. The boy with the hatchet disappears into a low-growing stand of cedars, returning with an armload of thin cedar posts that he begins to lay upstream of the stones across the brook's flow. Almost immediately, the water begins to overflow its banks and the boy who gathering stones picks up his shovel and begins digging away at the side of the brook's bank above the impromptu dam. He cuts mounds of turf from both banks and tosses them against the horizontal poles to reduce the leakage. The basin behind the dam fills rapidly even as the backed-up water begins to find new pathways over and around the dam.

After a while, they sit down to rest. Annie passes the berries around. The boys roll up their corduroys and Annie removes her white sneakers and socks and lays them near where she's been picking straw-berries. A watery-eyed Jersey cow wanders into the clearing and slurp up silty water from the small pond as the waders pause and watch.

The tableau changes and the pond becomes Lake Elmore. They

are all splashing waist-deep in the waters far offshore. Annie is lying on the water's edge. Glenn Roleau splashes water at his younger brother, Pudge, with his cupped hands. Their mother is shouting at him from the shore and then begins to cry inconsolably, her craggy face buried in her cracked hands. Time passes and Glenn hasn't returned on his bike from swimming. His body is later recovered by police divers from the muddy bottom of Lake Elmore. David wakes up suddenly recalling the actual incident.

The train is moving swiftly through a river valley, following the curve of the streambed. By flattening his face against the window, David can see to the last car which, to his surprise, is not a caboose but another passenger car. He counts fourteen cars in all, including the two engines in the front. A lowering silver sky caps the verdant hills beyond the river. It looks as though it rained in the night, as the trackside glistens with moisture. He hears two sharp whistle blasts from up ahead and the train begins to slow as it passes a grade crossing and a small wood-framed station needing paint. A flaking white sign with black letters reads "Northfield." The train doesn't stop but gradually resumes its former speed.

He hears a voice in the aisle outside his curtain say, "Montpelier Junction, Waterbury, Essex Junction, St. Albans, and Montreal. Montpelier 12 minutes, Waterbury 28. Please be on the platform with your baggage. If you require help, ring the porter."

When he pulls off the starched linen top sheet and blue and gray wool blanket with the Pullman logo, he realizes that he's slept in his clothes and, sometime during the night, worked his way under the covers. He collects his shoes from the netting above and puts them on, tying the laces to the length his stepfather showed him. He then opens the curtains and jumps down into the aisle. He goes to the toilet at the end of the corridor and when he returns a porter he doesn't know is closing the upper bunk into the ceiling. The lower bunk splits in the center, folding into the side walls of the compartment and leaving two bench seats facing each other. He chooses the forward-facing seat this time so he can see as they approach a station. When the porter finishes, he asks David where he's getting off. He answers, "Waterbury Station, sir." The Negro porter smiles and asks to see his ticket. David produces his ticket after checking both pockets. The porter puts on the steel-rim glasses he pulls from inside his red uniform jacket and scrutinizes the ticket, "Waterbury it is. Y'all come up ta the front of the car when's ya hears the conductors callin' out "Waterbury" and I'll help you wit your things. Don' ferget yer luggages now. I'll sees you in a bit." With that he leaves.

David looks again out the window at the river. At times the train travels close to the bank so he can see the brownish rocks and wavy green algae over which the slow-moving water flows. Then the train meanders away from the riverbank and a hayfield intervenes. He can see hayfields on both sides of the river as the train winds its way through the loamy bottom land. The browning hay has recently been cut and raked into parallel ridges the length of the field. David remembers watching Mr. Farr and recalls the next harvest steps, in which horses or a tractor pulling a haylift will come and load the hay onto a flatbed wagon to be stowed in the barn.

The heavy glass and steel door at the front of the car suddenly swings open and there is a rush of cold air and track noise. He hears someone shout, "Montpelier Junction, four minutes, Waterbury, eighteen. On the platform, please."

Looking again out the window, he sees signs of a town ahead. Farms give way to houses and then tree-lined streets with rows of houses. A cemetery occupies much of the hillside behind the houses. Unlike the cemetery in his neighborhood in Morrisville with its familiar rectangular granite and older marble gravestones, the monuments in this cemetery are intermingled with ornate statuary, carved angels with wings, odd steles and obelisks, and carved bas-relief tableaux. There are small stone buildings with cast bronze doors. He wonders if there are dead people inside or if they are just shelters or tool sheds.

Suddenly the houses are gone, replaced by another track running alongside with flatcars loaded with timber and hopper cars heaped with coal glistening from the recent rain. When he looks up at the two brick warehouses in the background with most of their clerestory windows broken out or in shards, he realizes the cars are stationary and unattached to an engine.

The *Montrealer* slows again. The whistle sounds twice and the voice he heard before shouts, "Montpelier Junction, Montpelier, Vermont. Please move to the platform." He hears the shrill whine of the brakes as steel shoes make contact with the engine's drive wheels. The train lurches to a stop. He jumps down off the seat and crosses the aisle to the other side of the train. There is no one in the seat across and he wants to see the station activity and people getting on and off. A man in gray coveralls jumps off the train, carrying a gray canvas sack to the side of the brick station where he drops it under the overhanging eave, picks up another and returns to the train. He and a colleague then unload half a dozen boxes and two steamer trunks and then re-board. He hears a hand whistle blow and, looking forward toward the engine, sees the conductor wave his right arm forward to the engineer as he jumps up onto the lower step, still holding the iron stepstool and the train lurches forward again. David estimates the stop at little more than five minutes, which makes him anxious about being ready when his stop comes next.

The train picks up speed for several minutes and then shortly begins again to slow down. The conductor's voice calls "Waterbury. Next stop Waterbury." David grabs his valise, looks around the compartment to see if he's left anything, as his stepfather taught him, and then works his way through the empty aisle to the large steel and glass door. He sets his bag down and tries to open the door but can't. The conductor, already on the passageway between cars with another couple, sees him behind the glass, and opens the door. David steps out, feels the rush of cold morning air, and hears the familiar track noise that, nestled in his berth, seemed more like a lullaby than the fearsome mechanical clatter he now hears. His view of the passing landscape is now framed in the open upper half of a Dutch door on the iron steps.

As the train slows further, another whistle sounds. The conductor steps down and opens the bottom half of the Dutch door. David can now see the town of Waterbury scrolling by at the speed of a man walking. He again hears the screech of brakes and the slowing rhythm of the engine's chuffs. The train slows to a stop on the station platform where he jumped into his stepfather's arms. An iron-framed, wood-planked Railway Express baggage cart sits on the platform. The stationmaster stands in the doorway checking his silver pocket watch. David sees his mother in the open frame of the doorway. The conductor jumps down with his steel stool, positions it below the lower step of the Pullman's stair and holds out a hand to assist the disembarking couple. Grasping his valise with both hands, David follows them down onto the platform and looks up to see his mother walking toward him with a broad smile on her face.

First Death

Increasingly, David notices the sadness in his mother's eyes. Her early flashes of animation and enthusiasm for their new life in Morrisville seem to fade just as his sense of discovery is heightened by daily events and new friends. She spends more time in her bedroom, sleeps later and retires earlier or doesn't get up at all. After the brief joy and pain of his half-sister Juliette's birth at the hospital down the street, he begins again to notice the profusion of pill bottles on her night table.

"Are you sick, Mom?" he asks.

"No, but I have to take some pills to get better. It was a hard birth. I'll be fine."

He takes his mother at her word, as he has always done.

One night he kisses his mother goodnight as she nurses his new sister and then follows his stepfather into his room for a story. He notices his stepfather holding a familiar blue book. There is no picture on the cover.

Much as his own mother did to encourage his reading when he

was young, Alain begins by asking David to read the first few pages of whatever storybook he has chosen, saying that he, too, likes to be read to and "it is only fair." This night, however, his stepfather simply starts reading from the book he recognizes as the one his grandmother left on the nightstand in his room. The book contains letters from his own father to his mother and parents, written while he was on naval patrol in the Pacific. They were compiled and edited by a teacher and mentor of his father's from the boarding school he attended and were published "In memoriam" for family and friends.

After listening for a while to Alain reading his dead father's reports of events from the Philippines war zone and expressions of affection for his wife and enthusiasm for the imminent birth of their child and then realizing that there is no story, he asks Alain to stop reading. Surprised at the tone in his stepson's voice, Alain stops in mid-sentence.

"You don't want to hear about your father?" Alain asks.

"No, not now," he answers. "I'm sleepy."

His stepfather closes the book and together they say an "Our Father" and a "Hail Mary." Laying his hand on his forehead, Alain tucks him in, pulls his puff up to his chin, kisses him goodnight and leaves the room, turning off his bedside light and leaving the hall light on and the bedroom door ajar.

Lying there, David tries to make sense of his birth father's chatty tone detailing a skirmish with a Japanese destroyer, but soon falls asleep trying to untangle the two paternities.

David dreams he is driving Lester Collette's doodle buggy into the birch forest toward the fallen tree but never seems to arrive there. The woods thin out eventually into a cornfield and he realizes with panic that he is running down Ned Stewart's cornstalks. He remembers that Ned once shot at two boys with 12-gauge rock salt loads as they chased their dog through his cornfield. He wakes in a cold sweat, goes to the bathroom and returns to his bed and a night of dreams he doesn't remember.

David hears the familiar "two longs" and answers, as his stepfather has taught him to do, "Hello, this is the Ferland residence."

"This is your grandma. I'm sorry to tell you your Granny Selma died yesterday."

Not knowing what to say to his grandmother, he hands the receiver to his mother who is standing nearby. A brief and chilly exchange follows and his mother hangs up. She puts her arm around him, saying only, "I loved Granny, for all her strangeness. I hope your grandmother didn't let her die alone." David doesn't feel like crying, only wonders what will happen to all her turtles, books, and pictures.

"Nobody dies of cancer in a day. Why didn't she call and tell us, so we could be with her before she died?" his mother blurts out through new tears. "I had no idea Granny had cancer."

Having spent time in nursing school before meeting and marrying David's father, Helen would know about dying of cancer. David has no answers for his mother who always speaks affectionately of Granny Selma. He wonders if his mother and grandmother will ever be able to resolve their differences.

Dorothy attends quietly to her mother-in-law's removal and interment. She convenes no funeral or memorial for friends and family to gather and mourn her death. Perhaps her own childhood memories of keening Jewish women in babushkas and black-hatted men mourning and clutching beards seem far away from the world she now inhabits, where Jews behave like Anglo-Saxons and attend services at the Ethical Culture Society. Within a few days of Selma's death, the two-room apartment in the Delmonico Hotel is emptied by strangers.

David wonders what her death was like. He wonders what will happen to all the turtles and looks over at his shelf to see the turtle she gave him. He wonders if people move when they die or whether they just close their eyes as they do in the movies. He wonders if any of her famous friends in the photographs were with her. She seemed so lonely to him when he was there, reclining among the memories evoked by the photographic portraits surrounding her.

Although he and his mother occasionally talk of his great-grandmother's death, it never again surfaces during the terse and strained phone conversations that occur several times a year between Helen and her mother-in-law. More often than not, if Alain is home, Helen simply hands the phone to him, saying, "It's her. Can you take it?" David suspects that he is the reason for the anger in his mother's voice, the long silences, and the inevitable tears after she or Alain hangs up.

Uncle Benoit

Two years later, his Uncle Benoit dies in a spectacular late night car crash. Uncle Ben, as he is called by the kids, or "Mon Onc'," as he's called by the elder family Francophones, is Alain's uncle on his father's side. Alain's mother, Eugénie, married Clovis Ferland, acquiring Benoit as a "beau-frère." Clovis died several years earlier in a grueling descent into stomach cancer. Another brother, Arnaud, took Holy Orders and become an Edmundite missionary in Venezuela among the rain forest people.

Uncle Benoit and his wife Colette have a dairy farm on Route 100 in North Hyde Park on the way to Eden. Several hundred acres and as many Holsteins and Guernseys produce thousands of pounds of cream-rich milk each day and a good living for Benoit and Colette's growing family. Every few years Benoit wins a "Green Pastures" awards from the Vermont Department of Agriculture for his model dairy. Over years of hard work, he has built a modern dairy barn and farm equipment shed behind the house and another smaller barn to the south for poultry.

The "viewing" is to be a two-day affair at the farm to accommodate the relatives already making their way from the logging camps of northern Maine, the convents of Quebec, and the trailer parks of western Florida. Massey's Funeral Home couldn't dedicate two days to the event or feed and house the stream of relatives already en route to North Hyde Park.

Ben's surviving brother, Père Arnaud, was notified by telegraph and native runner and is already aboard the first of three flights from Caracas to Burlington.

News of Uncle Ben's death spreads rapidly through the community by word of mouth, overheard party-line conversations, a lengthy notice in the *News and Citizen*, and from pulpit announcements around Lamoille County and beyond.

For the wake, Alain wears one of his two charcoal-grey wool suits. David, now eleven, is again wearing scratchy worsted wool pants and a starched white dress shirt. His half-brother Paul twists uncomfortably in David's hand-me-down woolen pants and white oxford shirt with one of Alain's ties. The tie is knotted to allow the right length in front, so a large amount of unused tie is stuffed uncomfortably into his shirt below the first button, leaving a curious bulge. His half-sister, Juliette, looks like a fleur-de-lys in her First Communion dress, She holds David's hand.

Alain knocks slowly and firmly on the front door of the farmhouse, an indication that this is to be a solemn affair. Only traveling salesmen and "State boys," knock on the front door of a farmhouse. Daily comings and goings are through a back door, usually sheltered by an attached wood-storage area housing boots, barn coats, and a still working refrigerator or chest freezer. This leads into the kitchen. Living rooms or parlors are reserved for large gatherings and sacramental occasions when their costly formal furniture and additional space are needed to welcome and accommodate guests.

During winter, most rural families live in the kitchen near the woodstove, retiring in the evening to cold bedrooms under heavy wool blankets and patchwork quilts. Summer days are mostly lived outdoors.

The door is opened by Bruno and Yves who look both solemn and pleased to see their cousins. After a brief expression of sympathy in French by Alain, the family is waved in and immediately to their left see

Uncle Ben laid out in a shiny wooden casket with four large brass handles. He seems very much alive, lying there in what is normally an anteroom, now cleared of coats and barn boots. A faint odor of manure persists beneath the pervasive scent of lilies cascading from vases behind the casket. A prie-dieu borrowed from Holy Family Catholic Church in Morrisville is in front of the casket. David keeps waiting for Uncle Ben to sit upright, smile and greet him from the white silk-cushioned coffin. David often came on him like this during his afternoon nap. Alain nudges them toward the prie-dieu. Following his example, David and Paul kneel on either side of their father on the padded kneeler and bow their heads while keeping a curious eye on Uncle Ben. Juliette remains standing behind them, as there is no room. The children have never seen a dead person before except in the movies.

Uncle Ben was a source of wonder to them all. The only family elder who seemed to enjoy children more than adults, he often erupted in laughter at their antics, taking them in turn on his knee and teaching them to count to ten or recite the Lord's Prayer in French, his breath smelling faintly of his home brew.

Kneeling there, David hears his stepfather begin under his breath, "Notre Père, qui est aux cieux, que votre nom soit béni." He remembers the words Uncle Ben taught him and can recite much of it, but always got tangled up with the "Donnez-nous aujourd'hui notre pain quotidien." The gutturals rattle around in his mouth like a dozen marbles and whatever comes out elicits gales of laughter from Uncle Ben and the surrounding audience of family or hired hands.

Aware of the solemnity of the occasion and anxious to observe the proprieties, David follows his stepfather's example, closing his eyes and bowing his head. Curiosity overwhelms decorum, though, and he squints at the dead man in front of him.

His thoughts drift and he remember sitting far back on the bench seat in the cab of a snowplow. It's dark and Uncle Ben is at the wheel of his sister-in-law's dump truck with its two rusty yellow plows on the right front, a curved plow that lifts the snow from the ground and then a deflector blade higher up that sends the snow aloft in a continuous white stream to the side of the road, burying the pasture fence.

The cab of the truck is filled with the smell of coffee. Two white porcelain cups and a brown paper bag permeated with grease, sweating from the hot doughnuts inside, sit on the seat between them. A plaid thermos is nestled in Uncle Ben's wadded-up, red-and-black-checked wool coat on the floor between the larger of the two stick shifts and the truck's torn bench seat. David is too short to see out the window, but his eyes are fixed on the endless stream of airborne snow lit by the high-mounted headlights.

Whenever he isn't talking, Uncle Ben hums to himself, jigs and reels the small boy next to him on the bench seat recalls from the firehouse dances where they were played by Crazy Chase and other fiddlers.

"Tabarnac! Look at dat snow, can' see nuthin' dere. Climb up 'ere and look at dis."

David scrambles to his knees and, kneeling on the truck seat, leans onto the warm dashboard, and peers out the windshield ahead. A faint morning light dawns over Elmore Mountain, enough to see the landscape taking shape ahead. They are careening down through a field under two feet of fresh snow, bluish in the predawn light, guided only by the fence posts lining either side of what was a road before the night's heavy snowfall.

"Weren't for dem posts, I'd no idee where dis road be," roars Uncle Ben. He glances over at his nephew, perched like a collie against the dash and again roars over the engine noise and the sound of the plow grating against gravel, "Pour some cafés when we hit de pavemins."

David sits back down and uncorks a thermos, carefully pouring out the muddy coffee, rich with fresh, raw cream and sugar, into the two steaming mugs until they are half full as he was taught.

"Don' be stingy," laughs Uncle Ben. "A little spill in dis truck only brighten 'er up," he roars again with laughter at his own humor. David pours a little extra into both cups and hands him the fuller one. He was told at home that coffee and hard drink were only for grown-ups, so sharing the sweetened beverage with Uncle Ben makes him feel as he did when he got his first patrol badge in middle school or when he first served Mass.

"Beignet," Uncle Ben shouts, slurping the hot coffee. "You dip in your café, mighty tasty!"

David pulls two warm brown doughnuts from the bag and hands one to his uncle who breaks it in two, dipping a half into his coffee and eating it in one bite, while never looking away from the expanse of white ahead. David does the same, but in smaller bites, as pieces of soggy doughnut fall back into his cup.

"Good to have m'assistan' wid me," he says, smiling. "Your Aunt Colette don' like bein' up in da middle of da night 'cept for da hanky's panky. I take my eyes off da road and whoosh, we be on our side in da ditch and Eugénie gets all h'angered."

Benoit is helping his sister-in-law Eugénie, who has kept up the business after Clovis's death. After a big storm, Eugénie calls and asks her brother-in-law to help with the plowing. In winter, there is little farm work to be done other than to oversee the milking by his sons and hired hands well before the school bus arrives at 6:30. Dropping bales down from the hayloft, graining chickens and pigs, mucking out cow stalls and gutters, and spreading manure when his tractor can get into the fields fill out the daily chores of winter. Ben looks forward to helping his sister-in-law after a storm.

Alain gets up and crosses himself, awakening David from his reverie. He and Paul follow suit, keeping an eye on Uncle Ben as they leave the ante-room. In the rarely used sitting room, a swarm of people have gathered to pay their respects to the family and to say goodbye to Benoit.

Aunt Colette holds court from an overstuffed chair in the corner. Her daughters, Nicole and Yvette, stand on either side, occasionally sitting down on the expansive armrests with their crocheted doilies. As visitors approach to express their condolences, Aunt Colette clutches her embroidered white handkerchief, bringing it to her mouth and sobbing, nodding all the while, accepting the expressions of grief and loss like a priest hearing the confessions of his parishioners. Between receiving condolences, Aunt Colette reverts to her role as châtelaine, smiling orders and requests to her children and the legion of women arriving with casseroles, pies, baked goods, and sandwich platters to help feed the several hundred people who will pay their respects over the next two days. Friends and relatives continue on into the dining room where hillocks of egg and ham salad sandwiches lie arranged on white ironstone platters and glass pitchers of home brew are being replenished from the milkshed.

The front door opens again and two large men wearing dark green woolen pants with leather suspenders and red flannel shirts burst in, waving a loud "bonjour" to Ben in the anteroom, but not pausing as is expected. They are followed by a very small woman in a black nun's habit with a white wimple and shawl.

David has heard tell of Sister St. Alphonse but has never met her. She trails behind her brothers, Rémy and René, loggers in the forests of northern Maine. They drove their pickup truck to Trois Rivières, Quebec, to pick up their sister and bring her to the wake and funeral of their second cousin Benoit. David tries to imagine this tiny woman wedged between these two giant men for the five-hour drive.

Eugénie, "Memère" to the family, told him about Sister St. Alphonse. When she was a young girl, both her parents died in the flu epidemic. Sylvie, her given name, nursed them as long as she could at the age of eight and sat with them as they died without palliatives. Mercifully, they died within two days of each other. Sylvie's older brothers, Rémy and René, were at a logging camp 60 miles away and did not learn of their parents' deaths until the spring log run ended in May and they returned home to rest with their meager savings. A Mi'kmaq neighbor who had helped young Sylvie bury her parents took her in in exchange for help with chores.

When the brothers returned and found the house empty, they set out for the nearest house, found their sister working as a domestic and learned of their parents' deaths. They sought the advice of the local priest, who suggested that the boys give their sister over to the care of the nuns across the border, as they often took in orphaned girls.

Sylvie was surrendered to the Carmelite nuns in Trois Rivières by her brother René in a farewell without tears and, later that spring, the boys returned to the logging camp near Presque Isle to support themselves and to send a modest stipend to the convent for the care of their sister.

Sylvie thrived under the strict but benevolent Carmelite sisters. She assumed the name of the saint that the abbess chose for her, St. Alphonsus Mary de Ligouri, and took vows of poverty, chastity, and silence at the age of 15. The latter vow had very little impact on her daily life as she had said very little as a child, except when required to recite at the one-room schoolhouse she attended in Quisibis until her parents died.

Sister St. Alphonse stops in the anteroom. She crosses herself with the hand holding her wooden rosary, kissed its cross, kneels down on the prie-dieu, and bows her head in prayer, pausing only occasionally to look up at her cousin and the wooden crucifix hanging amid the lilies above the casket.

Rémy and René make their way through the crowd nodding and greeting relatives in Québécois. Aunt Colette cannot suppress a smile at seeing them approach with their louche grins and loud greetings. She rises from her chair and receives their hugs, which lift her well off the floor. Rémy swings her around and sets her back down.

In the dining room, where David and Paul are chewing on egg salad sandwiches, Henri Landry unpacks his fiddle from its wooden case. A *violoneux* and distant cousin from Asbestos, Québec, Henri lives alone in a very small house on the Nicolet River. He has worked all his life in the Jeffrey Mine, the largest open-pit asbestos mine in the world. Unlike his father, he suffers no ill effects from his work and, in his retirement, has become a celebrated fiddler, known for his ability to play indefinitely without repeating a jig or reel. David and Paul watch as he takes out his dark sprucewood fiddle from its black velvet-lined case, rosins his bow, fits the luminous instrument between his chin and shoulder and begins to tune. Just as the music starts, David bites into an eggshell and then tries discreetly to extract the humid mass of chewed egg and bread from his mouth without being noticed.

"La valse fâchée," roars someone in the crowd, and the music begins. Toes tap everywhere and somber faces light up as Henri plays from his perch on a chrome and red vinyl chair, part of the matching dinette set that is dispersed to provide seating for the guests.

The table disappears like an altar under the steady stream of offerings from ladies in stained white aprons carrying heaping plates with white-bread sandwiches, carrot cake slices, casseroles and pies of every sort.

A French-Canadian pie crust can be home to any kind of filling. There are sugar pies, confected of various forms of molasses, maple, or penuche fudge melted and blended with Karo syrup into a gelatinous filling that spills out of the crust when served. Sugar pies always get a wistful look from the heavier ladies, who suffer from diabetes, known as "the sugar." Meat pies appear in several variations, some with pork fillings and others with minced venison. The pitchers full of home brew empty quickly and are replenished just as quickly by the ladies ferrying food and drink from the large kitchen.

Father Arnaud arrives looking pale and weary. His long trip from Venezuela to Hyde Park has taken its toll. He nods smiling to the guests and relatives who notice his arrival and then joins Sister St. Alphonse on the prie-dieu, staring intently at his dead brother. The resemblance between Arnaud and his brother is remarkable – crested shocks of black hair; deep-set eyes; short, thick noses; and prominent, furrowed foreheads. Arnaud wears glasses. His reposing brother doesn't.

Alain is lost in conversation with his cousin Yvette, the oldest of Ben's children. Yvette has the round face and warm skin tones of the Blessed Virgin Mary in the graphic renderings in David's Roman missal. A lambent sadness infuses Yvette's warm smile, because, according to Alain, of the earlier suicide of an admiring boyfriend.

Five years older, Alain developed an early friendship with his cousin. Yvette often talked to Alain of how, as a young girl, she imagined the course her life would take. She told Alain that in her dreams she did things that men did, like farming, opening a store, sitting behind a desk and managing something of significance. At twelve, Uncle Ben taught her to drive the red International tractor as he and Yves wrestled the hay bales extruded from the baler up onto the trailing flatbed truck driven by Bruno, only ten himself, but taller than Yvette.

Alain told David the rudiments of the story when it happened. He knew his young son would hear it on the playground in more gruesome detail. It shocked the community and changed Yvette forever. She had just turned 23. Five years earlier she had graduated near the top of her class but without more education her future choices were limited to marriage, holy orders – marriage of another sort – cook, counterperson, or counter sales, but Hyde Park, Johnson, and nearby Morrisville had precious few of even these jobs.

Yvette's would-be boyfriend, Rosaire, was a sallow boy with thin hair, a narrow face, aquiline features and an Ichabod-like frame. Hopelessly in love with Yvette since ninth grade, he was shy at first but declared his love the summer after their graduation. Yvette indulged his affection with occasional dates, demure occasions where both talked uncomfortably of events and people and then later, with somewhat more intimacy, of their aspirations. This proved fatal, as Rosaire's sole aspiration was to be the mechanic who maintained the diesel engine powering Stowe's single chairlift. Yvette's were higher.

One day, Yvette borrowed her father's Oldsmobile 98, resolving this time to tell her persistent suitor that she won't accept his proposal of marriage, that she likes him well enough but doesn't love him.

She later tells her father and the state policeman that they drove the back roads deep into Sterling Valley. After crossing Sterling Brook on the covered bridge, the road parallels the brook, meandering past Blodgett Falls and up toward the old Lapine Farm. At a pull-off, Yvette parked the car and the two walked down to a favorite trysting spot, a naturally formed basin in the brook where local people come to swim on hot summer days.

David's stepfather often took the family there for secluded picnics and a swim below the icy fall of water cascading down over moss-covered rocks. Brookies swiveted under the falls, agile shadows occasionally venturing out from the darker recesses into the sunlit parts of the basin, flashing their pale neon colors amidst the sparkle of quartz crystals embedded in the surrounding rock.

Yvette sat down on a boulder and stared into the water. She knew what was coming as Rosaire cleared his throat. She turned, smiled, pre-empting what was to come, explained in a few practiced sentences that, although she liked him, she would never marry him. To ease his pain, she added that she had decided not to marry anyone. Rosaire stared into the dark woods beyond the water as she spoke slowly and gently to him.

When she finished, Rosaire got up and walked back to the car alone. Yvette, waiting for his return, heard the gunshot, and began to sob. She left the car and Rosaire's body in the two-track turn-off and walked to the Levesque Farm two miles back down the road. They had no phone, but drove her home where her father called the police and told them in somber tones what had happened.

Rosaire's death marked Yvette. She confused his suicide with the Christian martyrdoms about which she had heard so much in her faith and struggled to sort out its meaning and her own role in his death. She considered again, as she had many times, joining one of the three orders of nuns in Burlington. A marriage to Christ would avoid the dark complexity of physical love. She could not speak of this with her mother, Colette, whose persistent joviality brooked no tears. She talked with her father, who consoled her and told her only that he loved her with all his heart. She refused all social invitations and worked hard on the farm. The only nun in the family, Sister St. Alphonse, spoke to no one but God and so could not even talk with Yvette about her decision to take holy orders.

~⁀~

In the living room, Yvette and Alain continue talking together in hushed tones.

David goes again into the kitchen where muscular ladies of great girth wrestle with heavy platters. The woodstove, warm and redolent of the meat pies inside, is the focal point of the busy room.

Father Arnaud and Sister St. Alphonse leave Uncle Ben to make room for the local parish priest, Father Lefèvre. Sister St. Alphonse smiles as she nibbled around the edges of a ham salad sandwich.

David and Paul talk about how it would be to go through life without ever being able to say a word to anyone.

"How'd you ask someone if you were in the toilet making number two and there was no toilet paper?" giggles Paul. David laughs at the thought but stifles his glee for fear they might be overheard laughing at a wake.

The fiddle strikes up again in the kitchen, the familiar *Reel du pendu*. The sound of the fiddle galvanizes the crowd. Conversation fades as people begin to tap their feet and nod their heads in time to the rhythm.

Yvette's younger sister Nicole steps forward, lifts the front of her black dress, and begins a lively step dance as everyone turns to watch. She is soon joined by three younger girls ranging in age from six to about ten, dancing slowly into a straight line. Uncle Didier grabs a pair of spoons from the table and begins to play them with his right hand and knee and Léon Dumas pulls up a chair sits down backward and begins mouthing the traditional yet wordless *musique à bouche*.

"*Deedideleedelumdeedideeumdedidelumde do*"

Then to the surprise of everyone in the room, including Aunt Colette, Sister St. Alphonse steps forward beaming from ear to ear, gently lifts the front of her black habit high above her ankles, exposing her dark heavy stockings and high black lace-up shoes and begins to step dance with a fluidity and grace that surprises everyone. Although there is no sound coming from her other than the hard click of her leather heels, her lips move silently as she follows the music and makes her own ecstatic form of mouth music. The younger girls and Nicole open a gap in their line for her, and she dances into the center keeping perfect time with the music.

Paul and David watch from the dining room as Sister St. Alphonse rises and falls in rhythm with the four girls. Nicole's well-developed breasts rise and fall inside her black high-collared dress in rhythm to the music, inviting the louche attention of the men clapping their hands and nodding their heads to one another in appreciation. Each time the reel speeds to a finale it begins again at a slightly faster pace. Hands, feet, and nodding heads begin again to chase the newly accelerated rhythm.

After a blazing finale, with lots of pizzicato and percussive bowing that calls to mind the twitching feet of the dying man dancing in the air below the gallows, Henri Landry brings the reel to a climactic close and the room falls silent for the first time since he arrived. A burst of applause follows.

Quiet conversations resume in French and in smaller enclaves of English as more and more people from town drop in to pay their respects, eat, and sample Uncle Ben's renowned home brew.

It's getting dark. Alain signals to the children that it it's time to say goodbye and head home. Paul and David say goodbye to anyone they know and wait by the door, peering occasionally into the anteroom to catch their last glimpse of a dead person.

Driving home, everyone is quiet. As they pull up to the house, David ventures a question.

"Why didn't mom come with us?"

"I don't know. You'll have to ask her. Maybe she's still sad about Granny Sis's death. She does not take death well, and I suspect she wasn't ready for another just yet."

He tries to visualize his great-grandmother reclining on her chaise in the cramped apartment and whispering stories of her many loves to him. He can hear her whisper and see her lips moving but can't make out the words, her wan smile framed by errant wisps of white hair. She looks as she had when she fell asleep during his visit.

Inside, the house is quiet and the lights are still off. It looks as if no one is home. The boys race to their room to rid themselves of their formal clothes and then return to the kitchen. Juliette, still rapt by the attention she received at the wake, seems in no rush to change out of her white dress.

"Where's Mom?" he asks.

"She must have gone to bed early," answers Alain, shaking his head. "She loved Mon Onc'. I don't know what's happening to her."

No one is hungry and each drifts off to spend the remainder of the evening on their own. David sneaks into his mother's bedroom to say good night, but sees only a mound of covers and notices again the array of pill vials on her side table. He goes to his room and reads himself to sleep.

Low Mass

The next morning his stepfather wakes David early. It's his day to serve the 7:00 A.M. daily Mass. Consistent with acolyte training, he must serve daily Mass six times before graduating to Sunday Mass and a full church of parishioners. He rises groggily from bed, washes, dresses, and goes downstairs, where his stepfather has left a bowl of breakfast cereal and a glass of apple cider on the counter.

"When will they put Uncle Benoit in the ground?" David asks as they drive through the gray morning light toward church.

"The burial will be day after tomorrow in Hyde Park," Alain answers, not looking away from the road. "Tomorrow, more people will come to the house to pay their respects. Mon Onc' knew a lot of people. Ron said the governor's coming tomorrow with the secretary of agriculture to pay their respects. Mon Onc' was greatly respected in the farming community."

It's cold in the vestry. Father Lefèvre is already in his vestments and sitting with his head bowed, his hands on his knees and his eyes closed. The maniple on his left arm touches the floor. He greets David with a nod when he comes in. David pulls his black cassock and white surplice from their hangers and dons them on in a hurry. As soon as he's ready, Father Lefèvre rises from his chair and nods again that he will begin Mass. David follows him into the sanctuary. He notices only three people in the pews: Gladys, the choir director, who never misses daily Mass except when ill, his stepfather, and a woman he doesn't know far back in the unlit nave near the entrance. Only the floodlights in the sanctuary are on, their light spilling out into the front pews. This is done to encourage the few attendees during the week to sit up front and to save electricity.

David has come to love the drama and ceremony of the Latin Mass, its choreography of celebrant and acolytes cued by the succession of familiar prayers, the Confiteor, Kyrie, Gloria, the Collects, Nicene Creed, the Offertory, and then the most sacred Sanctus, where he rings the bell three times as the priest transubstantiates bread and wine into the body and blood of Christ, then Communion and the final Benediction. During acolyte training David learned where he was to be in the sanctuary, when to stand and kneel, genuflect or sit, and how to approach the altar with the cruets of wine and water to be commingled in the gold-plated chalice touched only by the priest. In catechism class, he learned the significance of the ritual migration through the liturgical year from Advent into Christmas, Epiphany, Lent, Easter, Ascension, Pentecost and Ordinal Time, each with its own color of vestments and unique gospels and epistles. Saturday catechism classes not committed to the Ten Commandments or differentiating between mortal and venial sins are dedicated to studying *The Lives of the Saints*. Like *East of the Sun and West of the Moon, The Firebird,* and *Bulfinch's Mythology, The Lives of the Saints* often stirs his errant imagination and occasional dreams.

His stepfather waits for him in the idling car outside the church. Heavy snowflakes began to fall during Mass and a blue light spreads across the outline of Elmore Mountain to the East. An empty yellow school bus passes by as his stepfather pulls into the road.

The following Sunday marks his first service in a Sunday Mass. Altar boys are expected to take Communion, to have fasted, and to have avoided the temptations of the flesh, since one can only receive the sacrament in a state of grace. As such, those who have fallen prey to "self-abuse" must confess just prior to Sunday Mass, as Saturday afternoon confessions leave them subject to the temptations of a Saturday night and the interdiction against receiving Communion with a mortal sin on one's soul. An altar boy's failure to receive Communion is read as a public admission of sinfulness to Sunday morning's congregation.

Like most boys, David is uncomfortable with the sacrament of penance and he shifts from knee to knee inside the shadowy confessional causing the kneeler to creak, just as when he was younger and anxious, his legs would begin the involuntary walking motion that so annoyed his grandmother.

He saw Mrs. Bates enter on the other side just before he pulled back the curtain and went in. He can barely hear the sibilants in Father Lefèvre's whispered voice behind the screen, as he conveys words of comfort or approbation to Mrs. Bates. He wonders what sins his shy classmate's mother might have committed. On the few times David has been to their apartment over her beauty parlor, he envies Donny the warmth and comfort his widowed mother lends their modest home. He can make out an occasional word or sentence, but is distracted by his own rehearsal of the sins he plans to confess.

He has committed to memory some of the euphemisms for masturbation that he and the other Catholic boys share among themselves to minimize embarrassment in the confessional. "Pleasured myself" is in common use among the boys of David's age. The nuns in Saturday catechism are their main source: "self-abuse" and "self-touching," are also common. Sister Lamoureux can hardly broach the subject without blushing and losing her composure and her control over her rowdy charges, who aren't much younger than she. Sister Duchesne, however, is unequivocal about the damnation and physiological damage wrought by self-abuse. "Insanity and incarceration" are the inevitable result of a life of "evil stimulations" and "casting one's seed on dry sand."

The thin plywood slide moves back along its noisy track and he can see the dim outline of Father Lefèvre leaning forward in the armchair with his elbow on his knee and his forehead resting in his hand.

"Yes, my son?"

"Bless me, Father, for I have sinned. It has been a week since my last confession..."

"Did you make your proper penance?"

"I did, Father."

"And how have you sinned, my son?"

David lists a camouflage inventory of made-up lesser sins such as "failing to obey my father, being mean to my sister, and copying a homework assignment." Buried in this volley of venial sins he injects the mortal, "abusing myself three times."

"Do you pray to the Virgin Mother for purity of thought?"

"I do, Father," he answers, relieved at the mild response.

"You must say five Hail Marys now and every night before you fall asleep for your penance. Now, go in peace, my son."

"Thank you, Father," he answers as the slide closes and he rises to leave the confessional to get ready to serve the eight o'clock low Mass.

His friend and classmate Warren Wolfe is already in the sacristy. Warren is noted among the other altar boys for the little tricks he plays on Father Lefèvre during the celebration of the Mass. This day is no different and during the consecration of the sacred host when the priest genuflects once and then holds the chalice heavenward and genuflects again and the acolyte holds high the back edge of the outermost vestment so the celebrant doesn't step on it, Warren, with an expression of great piety, takes hold of and holds high the underlying black cassock so that Father Lefèvre's spindly, white legs with their web of blue varicose veins are visible to the entire congregation. This is greeted with knowing snickers among the other altar boys and some demure smiles in the pews.

On Sunday, high Mass is sung in Gregorian mode, and Warren sings the responsories along with the small choir and those congregants familiar with the Gregorian liturgy. As the Mass ends, Father Lefèvre intones, "Ite, missa est." This elicits the sung response, "Deo gratias." Singing along full-throated, Warren suddenly transposes the final monadic syllable into a rich major third, adding to the austere Gregorian response a lighter element of barbershop.

Hard of hearing, Father Lefèvre misses the amusement this produces, but the choirmaster frowns at Warren from the choir loft in the back of the church. The singing congregants smile and look down to hide their amusement. Father Lefèvre, oblivious to the fun, wishes his congregation well as they leave the church to return to the large breakfast spreads awaiting them at home. The fasting requirement prior to Communion means that the farm population, accustomed to a hearty breakfast well before sunrise, will be especially hungry on their way back from church.

Gloria

That afternoon, David has promised to help Mr. Farr gather the drying hay he tedded the day before. It's second cutting and the weather is not promising. At home, David sheds his church clothes, leaving them on his bed and climbs into a pair of old corduroys ripped in both knees and heads up the road to Mr. Farr's. He finds him in the lean-to shed tinkering with sparkplug wires coming out of the distributor cap on his Farmall A tractor.

"Confounded 'stributor cap's allus breakin', but I got me a spare. Just a sec while I put 'er on. Why'n chu go check th' air in th'haylift and wagon tires while I finish 'iss 'ere."

"Yes, Mr. Farr."

"I tell ya call me Volney! Don' know who Misser Farr is; never hee'rd of 'im."

"Yes, sir."

"Sir's army talk."

David runs off to check the air pressure in the haylift's tires, which prove to be fine. One of the four mismatched tires on the hay wagon, however, looks soft so he brings the hand pump and pumps it up. Both implements are parked near a rhubarb patch that feasts on the adjacent manure pile. The plants have not yet gone to seed so he breaks off a stalk at the root and begins to chew the stem, extracting the sour juice.

"Ready fer action, boy?" yells Mr. Farr over the accelerating putt-putt of the tractor.

Together they connect the haylift to the dragbar on the tractor and the wagon to the dragbar of the haylift with some linchpins Mr. Farr fishes out of his bib overalls. David grabs a fork and clambers onto the wagon while Mr. Farr steers the tractor, haylift, and wagon into the open field where the hay lies drying in parallel rows. Mr. Farr centers the haylift on the first windrow and starts down. The tines on the haylift grab the hay and claw it up the sheet metal incline, then drop it over the spillway into the front end of the trailing wagon. David's job is to fork it to the back of the wagon until the wagon is filled back-to-front.

Once begun, the work doesn't stop until the wagon is loaded to the very top of its slatted front and back. There are no sides. As the pile of hay mounts, it becomes increasingly difficult to make his way from the front of the pile to the back through the loose hay. When the hay nears the top, David climbs down the slatted front and runs forward to tell Mr. Farr that it's time to unload, since he can't see behind the haylift except when turning the tractor at the end of a windrow. David unhitches the wagon and the haylift. Mr. Farr drives the tractor around and David reconnects the wagon to the tractor directly, leaving the haylift behind in the field. He steps up on the dragbar behind the tractor seat. Mr. Farr shifts into second gear and the tractor and loaded hay wagon lurch off toward the barn.

Mr. Farr drives up the ramp of oak planks and into the center alley of the barn between two open haylofts. He kills the tractor engine and signals to David to uncleat the thick manila ropes holding a cast-iron hayfork with a six-foot grasp high above them. The rope feeds through two wooden pulley blocks, making the pull twice as long but twice as easy. Mr. Farr helps him with the ropes and maneuvers the fork along its trolley until it hangs directly above the wagon. Hand over hand they feed out the rope until the fork's open jaws settled onto the hay. Then they haul on the rope together to close the forks around the hay, drawing nearly half the wagon's load up through the dust-filled air above the wagon.

The south loft is almost empty, so when the hay is well above the wagon David climbs the wooden ladder up the wall of the loft while Mr.

Farr holds the rope. Once inside, he takes the rope from Mr. Farr and draws the fork along the iron trolley attached to the girts above until it is almost at the end of the barn, Mr. Farr pulls the release rope from below and the jaws of the fork open with a clank so that the hay showers down into the loft. David forks the hay around evenly and then climbs back out to reposition the fork on its trolley above the wagon to get another load. A pair of mourning doves nesting in the purlins above and some itinerant rafter pigeons coo their disapproval of the proceedings below.

The comings and goings continue until late in the afternoon. Gladys Farr shows up in the field midway through the afternoon with a quart Mason jar of ice-cold lemonade with the lemons still floating in it and a saucer of leftover ginger cookies she baked for the Grange meeting.

It's time to quit for evening milking. Mr. Farr tells David to get the cows while he puts away the tractor and implements. David lies down for a minute in the hay stubble and looks at the clouds massing over-head. Most of the hay is in. The rest will soon be drenched by a storm brewing in the west over Mount Mansfield. Lying on his side with his head on his hand and the lingering taste of ginger in his mouth, he can see the distant lightning strikes over Sterling Valley and hear the remote rumble of thunder.

To the south, he can see the sunlight filtering through a fabric of heavy rain. His Tante Lucienne told him when he was little that the steep staircase formed by slanted rays of sunlight after a rain means that someone has died and is being ushered up into heaven. The image reminds him of the light he sees while lying in Mr. Farr's hayloft when the upper hay door is still open and the sunlight filters through the hay dust hanging in the air, creating the same illusion of a staircase of light.

A heavy raindrop sends him scurrying to the pasture gate to the east where he knows the girls will be milling around waiting for their evening amble back to the barn. Mr. Farr enjoys making light of the recently introduced black fiberboard ear tags some farmers have started using to identify their cows. When asked if he's going to use them, he snorts, "I ain' tartin' up my girls wi' no earrin's. They look fine as they is." Volney and Gladys have 28 cows and know them by the names they have given them.

David pulls the loop wire off the gate posts and swings open the gate. Elda, the lead cow, leads the others back to the barn through the open field as David counts. When everyone has crowded through the gate, he is short one and runs ahead to recount. He knows the girls only by number, but confirms a missing cow, which he races back to report to Mr. Farr as he is leaving the equipment shed.

It is spot raining now, large intermittent drops. Mr. Farr joins David in the barn and they close the oak stanchions on the girls, who generally wander back to their own places. Occasionally, one gets addled, looking around in confusion until Mr. Farr or David leads her to her own place in the barn.

Mr. Farr stops to turn on the valve that fills the cast iron watering bowls in front of each stanchion and announces, "I'ss Gloria, she's still in the pastcha, due to freshen. Le's us go take a look, she's one o' my mos r'liable of my girls, somep'n' mus' be wrong. Birthin', I 'spect."

The heavy drops of rain continue, but the downpour has not begun although the sky is now black. David follows Mr. Farr back to the open pasture gate and down into the pasture. The pasture has steep sides like an amphitheater, as it was once a gravel pit. Water seeps from springs along the steep incline traversed by cow paths and flows down to the middle to form a rill that runs down into the flats where the cows usually spend their days chewing their cuds in the higher grass and nearby shade. From above, one can see most of the open pasture. A small covert of balsams and hemlocks grows on the east side of the pasture and an open grove of young sugar maples, the west. Mr. Farr's vision, like his hearing, has declined so he asks David what he sees.

"I don't see her yet; she must be in the woods," he responds.

"Th' girls hardly go in 'ere cause 'ere's no grass and the soil's all acid," Mr. Farr answers, "but bes' go take a look-see."

In a clearing among a cluster of hemlocks, Gloria's licking clean her new calf. The calf is struggling to get its gangly legs under itself amidst a stain of dark blood. The mother is licking off the placenta but in the pool of blood lies another dark membrane.

"She done cast 'er withers," Mr. Farr says, shaking his head and looking sad. "Naught for it but ta relieve her mis'ry. I'll get a rifle. Stay with 'er and make sure nothing gits ta her young'un. Keep an eye the calf keeps breathin'. If she don', ya slap 'er hard coupla times on the chest or the face." With that, Mr. Farr disappears into the hemlocks.

David stares at the calf. He looks at Gloria. Her glassy eyes are a mixture of dark brown, pale blues and greens and appear gauzy, as if life is already leaving her. He remembers Mr. Farr telling him when he was much younger that cows "don't complain when they'se dyin', they jess look sad. Only really bitch when their bags is full o' milk or when 'eys caked."

He sees the sadness in her darkening eyes. The calf continues to struggle to get to its feet. It manages to get its hind feet up, but can't seem to get its front feet under it. David looks away.

Mr. Farr returns with a single shot .30-06.

"Ya don' wanna watch 'iss," he growls, "why don'tcha wait inna woods. I'll need your help gittin' the calf back."

"I'll stay," he answers.

Mr. Farr moves the calf well away from the mother, who moans softly.

"No fix ta poor Gloria, sh' been a good girl, produced six calves and all's milked good fer me. She's Gladys' favorite."

He lowers the barrel and without hesitation fires a bullet into the cow's forehead. She falls and her hind legs kick erratically from a lying-down position. David imagines she is trying to run away. The running motion subsides to occasional trembles and finally stillness.

"I'll come back wi' th' tractor and git 'er. Jes 'elp me with th' calf." Mr. Farr hefts the calf to its legs. It stands for a moment and then its rear knees buckle and it again falls into the congealing blood.

"She'll be fine, jess like 'er ma," says Mr. Farr.

He looks at Gloria. Her head is cocked back in death as if she is mooing and her legs are stilled in a running motion. The gauzy look in her eyes now obscures the deep colors that reminded him of the prized green and blue marbles he won in third and fourth grade.

Mr. Farr hefts the bleating calf onto his shoulder and they leave the woods, climbing back up the steep hill to the upper field. Mr. Farr becomes winded halfway up and hands the new calf to David.

When they reach the top near the gate, David takes the calf's hind legs and rear and Mr. Farr cradles her head and forelegs. Clumsily, they make their way back to the barn where Mrs. Farr is ready with an old quilt to take the calf and clean her up.

"We'll keep 'er in the shed t'night so's no dogs gits after 'er," says Mr. Farr to his wife.

She nods as if she already knows. Mr. Farr starts up the tractor.

"Can I help?" David asks.

No; you g'won 'ome ta yer folks. Iss dinner toime and they'll be 'spectin' ya. I can haul 'er back with a rope. Bring 'er back 'ere and bury 'er tomorra with Cliff's digger. Thanks fer y'er work today. Gladys'll settle whicha next Sat'day afore the Bijou show," he says with a wink.

Walking home David remembers the photograph next to Mr. Farr's rocking chair in the sunlit kitchen. It stands on a high oak plant table next to a dusty Christmas cactus.

The black leather frame is cracked with age and peeling in an upper corner. A young woman looks confidently off camera. Her strong jaw is clenched and her lips are slightly pursed. Dark brown hair rides high on her head and is gathered in a loose bun in the back. Her left ear is centered in the image. She wears a tight, narrow neck-cloth tied in the back. Her creamy white dress has lacy edges at the shoulder and neckline. Her upper arms are bare. An unadorned straight pin hangs askew at the midpoint of her high collar. She looks resolute, perhaps impatient with whoever brought her to the photographer's studio. The picture lacks the finesse of a studio picture and may have been taken as a candid at a family gathering.

One day several years back when he was buying extra eggs for his mother who was in the midst of a brief flirtation with pastry baking, he asked Mr. Farr who the lady in the picture was. He answered, "Gladys," and added "afore we wuz married."

David cannot not relate the fierce young girl in the picture to the

Mrs. Farr he knows, hunched over her flattened breasts and clutching a large black purse as she walks around town taking orders for eggs, butter, and jam. Her features have lost their fullness. Her white hair is now wispy and thin. More notable, however, is the perpetual smile that brightens her aquiline features. Now, much nearer the end of her life than the beginning, she seems a happy woman to him, greeting neighbors with a smile and a pleasant exchange of words. Although David hasn't asked him, Alain told him the Farrs never had children, which was unusual for farm families.

O'Keeffe Nude

This fall will begin his last school year at home as the following fall he'll attend the "preparatory school" his dead father attended. Although he is a party to the decision when his grandmother calls to discuss the matter with Alain, he knows little of what it means and even less about whether he'll be happy there, and so he chooses not to think about it until the time comes.

Realizing her grandson's deepening enthusiasm for "country life," Dorothy accelerates her campaign for more time in New York. Her goal of exposing him to her more urbane acquaintances and all their opportune social connections becomes more urgent as she and Margaret age together among the many empty rooms in her apartment.

Furthermore, as time and the reality of her son's brief life gradually unravel, she is free to knit warmer memories of him and her own maternal role in his life, although according to Aunt Rose, David's father was reared largely by nannies. Like her own parents, Dorothy expected her son and daughter to behave like adults. Once they mastered toilet, hygiene, table etiquette, proper dress, and speaking in full sentences, they were treated as small adults. On an earlier outing to either the Frick or the Metropolitan, David remembers seeing the *Enfanta* paintings by Velasquez. He had a hard time differentiating the formally dressed adult dwarfs and court children in their scaled-down versions of what adults in the same painting wore; their disquieting features and expressions those of miniature grown-ups rather than of children.

When Dorothy's social friends are introduced to David and express their sympathies to him over his "terrible loss," he understands now that this is largely for his grandmother's benefit. As he spends more time with his Aunt Rose, he learns he can ask her anything about family members, friends, and domestics. Rose loves her young nephew, more for what he gets wrong than for his conformity to the social norms expected of him. She suggests with glee that, when younger, he was occasionally a source of embarrassment to her sister.

After another tense call between his mother and grandmother, during which his more dispassionate stepfather must take the receiver, it is agreed that David will again visit his grandmother for Thanksgiving recess.

David listens and accepts the verdict without testimony. He understands his filial obligation to his dead father, although absent the phone calls, Helen's tears, and Alain's efforts to maintain peace, he never thinks of his father.

School begins after Labor Day and the rapid cycling of wet and dry weather leaves many farmers anxious about getting dry hay into their barns. Most of David's friends are also pressed into farm work–family members out of a shared sense of survival and non-farming neighbors for a modest hourly wage. With fall coming on hard, many farmers are still waiting for a few days of sunshine to dry the hay lying in their fields. David is pressed into service to help Mr. Farr get in the last cutting.

Later that fall, David comes home one afternoon to find his mother planting daffodil bulbs. He is happy to see her outdoors and doing something she enjoys. When he was younger, she would tell him stories of garden projects that her father would first sketch on paper and then, together, they would sow in a chosen spot behind their sprawling house in Florida. Clarence's friendship with David Fairchild gave them access to a variety of bulbs, seedlings, and saplings from around the world that they would label and spade into the earth. When they were all done, the two would sit down on the sharp palmetto grass and compare their work with the landscape drawing Clarence had sketched, breaking into gales of laughter at the stark difference. Clarence would remind his attentive daughter that planting is only the beginning, and that feeding, watering, and pruning are also essential.

Helen has dug up a border section of the lawn and spaded in peat moss and bone meal and is arranging bulbs upright in random order in the flensed landscape. David offers to help but, as she points out, he has turned up for the work that is the most fun and she's happy to finish the project herself. She urges David to go in and make some iced tea for them.

David changes out of his school clothes and goes into the kitchen to boil water for the tea. Juliette and Paul have after-school play dates and won't be home until supper, as is often the case if they've completed their chores. David pulls the lever on an aluminum ice cube tray and releases the contents into a glass pitcher. He pours the hot tea onto the ice and listens to the break and crackle of the shrinking cubes. Helen taught him to squeeze half an orange into the mixture rather than the usual lemon. Both agree this is more to their liking than the sourness of a lemon amended with lots of sugar.

He hears his mother return, go into the bathroom, and run the shower for a few minutes and then nothing. He goes to the hallway leading to her room and calls in, telling her that the iced tea is ready. She asks him to wait a minute while she changes and then to bring the tea into her bedroom. David gets a tray, two tall glasses, and slices onto a saucer two pieces of the carrot cake Eugénie dropped off the day before. He goes to the bedroom and finds his mother in her house dress sitting up in bed. She is shaking capsules out of a brown vial and looks up surprised, saying, "all that digging irritates my arthritis."

"Did Doctor Phil say you had arthritis?" David asks.

"Well, you know, could be just aches and pains, but these help," she says, setting the medicine bottle back onto her bed table. She swallows two green capsules with a sip from the ice tea and complements David on the brew.

"Just the way I like it," she smiles.

David likes to please his mother but imagines she might just as well be referring to the green capsules as the ice tea.

David sits on his stepfather's side of the bed, as there is no room for a chair in the small bedroom. He must sit sideways to see his mother. They sip tea for a while and, finally, David asks his mother if his father ever talked about the school he went to, the one David will attend the following fall.

"Not that I remember," she answers. "He talked a lot about his years and friends at Yale. Why do you ask?"

"I just wondered," David answers. "I have no idea what it will be like."

"You're only going because your grandmother wants you to," his mother says, looking out the window by her bed. "I doubt you really want to go there."

David senses the ignition in her voice and is aware that he is alone this time, again on the tinder of her anger at his grandmother.

"She's always been jealous that I'm your mother and she isn't. She made idle threats when you were little about my fitness as a mother, but soon realized that she didn't have a leg to stand on and has had to content herself with meddling in your life ever since. Your father certainly understood her maternal shortcomings during his time at sea. You won't find very many letters from her to her son when he was fighting in the War. Ask her about that some day when she's carrying on about family and such."

David searches for an exit to the conversation.

"She called my brother once to ask about the prescriptions I depend on, but he wouldn't talk to her. She can be devious and you should remember that. She'll try and buy you with things that Alain and I can't afford. She already has."

"You're my mother, Alain is my father, and it was never my choice to go to New York, especially when I was little. You know that," David answers, surprised at the tone of his voice.

The room is silent.

His mother's speech is slower. "Granny Selma disliked her, too, you know. She made no effort to hide her feelings about her daughter-in-law. I suspect that's why Dorothy let her die alone in that cramped apartment."

David doesn't answer. Helen's speech is beginning to slur and he turns around to look at her. She's slumped down on her pillows. David feels a paroxysm of anger as he watches his mother's slow departure from reality.

"It's your choice now to go to there, though. You could stay right here with your own family and get a perfectly good education. All you'll learn there is to appreciate a bunch of things and people you'll never be able to afford. It's your choice."

"The decision's made. I'm going," David says quietly.

"So why'd you ask about it?" his mother returns.

"I just asked," he answers, getting up to leave.

"Go ahead, walk out."

"I will," he says.

<hr/>

The train to New York arrives at the Waterbury station seven minutes late. Its new diesel lacks the chuff and bluster of the livid black steam engine with its external mechanical parts: pistons, cylinders, drive wheels, steam tubing all on the boiler's exterior where the oilers and mechanics can quickly attend to them between runs. The diesel's mysteries lie hidden behind a louvered gray sheet metal body. The engine hums. Only the hiss of the airbrakes recalls the earlier steam engines.

David boards a sleeper car five cars behind the engine. The hustle and bustle of passengers boarding and exiting makes the progress to his berth difficult. He remembers the berth numbers of his earlier trips to New York as if they are the birthdays of siblings. The berths are all open and made up. He slides his father's suitcase under the bed and climbs in. Before the clutch of boarding passengers has settled into their drawing rooms, berths, or seats, the train resumes its slow journey south through Vermont. He notices that the familiar lurch of the engine starting and taking up the slack in the couplers is gone.

Still in his clothes, he lies on his side looking out the Pullman window at the countryside scrolling by. Heavy clouds weigh down the night sky and the waxing quarter moon emerges occasionally to cast a pale argentine light on the bottom-lands along the Winooski River.

He imagines with some anxiety the social events his grandmother will have planned with their precise formalities he has learned, and the friends she will have enlisted for him to meet. He falls asleep sometime after eleven. The last thing he remembers is passing an abandoned sugarhouse that reminds him of last spring's sugaring at Uncle Euclide's farm in St. Johnsbury.

At thirteen, he no longer needs to be met at the station, as he knows how to navigate his way from the arriving tracks to the cabstand on Lexington where he waits his turn in the cool morning air.

Several minutes later he's at his grandmother's building. Oskar greets him warmly, and tries to relieve him of his suitcase. He learned from his stepfather that one never lets an older person perform a physical task one can do oneself, and he declines reflexively with a "Thanks, but I can manage."

David has not yet come to understand the complex service relationships in this city of great wealth, nor has he seen the parts of the city not served by domestics and doormen, except from the elevated tracks as the *Washingtonian* enters the city through Queens and Harlem before its descent into tunnels.

His Aunt Rose later explains to him that to decline Oskar's proffered hand is to deprive him of the job he is paid to do and, just as he would be embarrassed to have the 60-year-old uniformed doorman carry his light suitcase for him, so too will Oskar be embarrassed entering the building with a visitor carrying his own luggage.

He is greeted in the eighteenth floor foyer by his grandmother, still in her dressing gown. He has come to understand how arriving guests are announced by intercom, allowing the host to greet the guest at the elevator door. He is not aware, though, of her anxiety at seeing him and comes to know of it only later from her sister, who has no compunctions about confiding her perceptions to him.

After leaving his suitcase in his room, he joins his grandmother in the dining room where he again confronts a plate of chicken livers. He is hungry and next to the small pile of livers finds a mound of buttery scrambled eggs with red paprika flakes. Margaret later brings out a side dish of fresh papaya and mango slices, which she remembers that he enjoyed on earlier visits. He again eats around the liver while answering his grandmother's perfunctory questions about his life in the country and his schoolwork. He remembers Rose explaining to him that her sister may question him on subjects to which she does not necessarily want full or truthful answers, and he has begun to discern which questions require subdued or dilatory responses. He talks less about his work on Mr. Farr's farm or his adventures with his friends and more about what he is learning in school or his fun skiing in nearby Stowe, where Alain still teaches on weekends to earn extra income and free skiing for his family.

As David expects, his grandmother announces that a few friends will join them for cocktails and hors d'oeuvres at six and that, in view of his long trip, they'll have a quiet dinner "in" and then retire earlier so as to be fresh in the morning for another "adventure." He nods and asks if he knows any of the people coming.

"Your cousin Terry; she's your age and I suspect you two will have much to talk about as she, too, lives in the country. Her father is a horticulturalist, a gardener really. They live in the Greenwich back country where he cares for the grounds of one of the estates on North Street, not that he needs to work with all that Harkness money in trust for him. They're in town for theater so I asked them to come by for drinks."

"Didn't they used to live downstairs," David asks.

"Yes, but only briefly," Dorothy answers. "Less than a year after they moved in, Terry was accepted at Greenwich Academy and Ruth began missing her husband or his money. Hard to say which she missed more. I suspect she realized she wasn't going to do any better here in the city and returned to Greenwich. They seem happy enough now. God knows it's easier to be happy when you have no money worries. Of course, great wealth can be a problem, too. Many of my wealthiest friends tell me they never know for sure whether they are truly appreciated for themselves or just for their money."

His grandmother sets down her coffee and, excusing herself, sweeps off to make herself ready for the day.

David is left alone in the large dining room with the chicken livers and the smell of his grandmother's unfinished coffee. Margaret clears the table and smiles as she removes his plate. "Zu ztill haff no taste for zee liffers."

He smiles and whispers, "Not yet," replacing his refolded napkin on the table. In the library, where he spends most of his time when visiting, he settles in to wait for his grandmother.

The room is rich with distractions: books, artwork and photographs. His grandfather's undisturbed office desk dominates the south end of the room with its red leather desk set and a brass lamp with three bulbs and a parchment shade. As an altar boy, he recognizes the lamp's former life as an altar candelabrum. The desk looks as if it has never been used and all the drawers are empty except one that contains photographs no longer bound by the dried rubber bands that have snapped and lie curled in the corner of the drawer. The only other contents are two sets of canasta cards still in their cellophane wrap.

His grandmother's highboy walnut desk sits against the east wall, the doors to its upper shelves closed except on the rare occasions when she is working there. The fold-down desk surface lies open with its pink blotter paper and behind that an array of small walnut-faced drawers.

On earlier visits, he loved to explore the contents of all the small niches and drawers, finding paper clips, erasers, small slide-drawer boxes containing photo mounting corners, adhesive labels, pencil leads, pen nibs, rubber bands, address labels, and a small cinnabar box filled with ornately-handled furniture keys.

David opens the tall doors, exposing a small silver canister that dispenses 5-cent postage stamps from the roll inside. The uppermost shelf is filled with bundles of letters tied together with lilac ribbon. The shelf below holds a box of stationery bearing his grandmother's monogram "DOS."

At home, he lost interest in his Boy Scout stamp-collecting project, but has remained enthralled with the stamp images. He thumbs through the envelopes bound in ribbon without untying them and finds stamps from France, Italy, England, and Germany. He says aloud to himself the names of the towns in the cancellations, trying out the various foreign accents he has heard on his visits to New York.

A large bundle of letters from Annecy, France, piques his curiosity, but he is afraid to untie the ribbons in case his grandmother should enter unannounced and find him reading her letters. The shelves also hold a collection of small wood and tarnished silver frames, people he has come to recognize as relatives photographed standing by touring cars, on steamer decks, descending gangplanks, picnicking near streams under trees, holding the reins of horses, and leaning toward the camera on verandah railings.

In a photo of his grandmother, perhaps in her late thirties, she stands demurely on a sand dune. Clumps of beach grass sprout around her. She is wearing a skirted bathing costume that covers her upper thighs. A tunic top creates the impression that there are two pieces when, in fact, there is one. The suit does not camouflage the effects of the births of the two children standing on either side of her. Her arms are resting on their shoulders. Her breasts drape within the loose top and there is a slight rise below her waist and above her pubis. As always, her hair is severely parted in the middle. She is looking down to her left at her son. A large signet ring stands out on the index finger of the hand that grasps her son's upper arm. He is about seven, and the girl on her right, is five. The girl's bathing suit almost exactly matches her mother's. Her knees are touching, but through her skinny thighs we see light. A long vertical crease in her bathing suit, rising to her waist, mocks the vaginal cleft. Her eyelids are partially closed. She may have blinked or perhaps she is squinting while attempting to smile, but the smile is inhibited by time or circumstance. Perhaps she is responding to the photographer's demand. The boy's insouciant smile conveys his confidence in his superior place as a male child. His mouth is open and we see his upper teeth as our perspective is looking up from below the dune. His bathing suit is black. The shoulder straps fit tightly around his neck, his chest is covered and the woolen leggings come almost to his knees. His open hand rests over his crotch. The trio's bare feet are buried in sand. David wonders who the girl is. Perhaps she is a cousin, but he notices a strong resemblance to the boy and to his grandmother. He makes a mental note to ask his grandmother.

A lower shelf in the desk displays a collection of Murano glass paperweights in *millefiori* and Bohemian designs. On an earlier visit he discovered this trove in his grandmother's desk as she was reviewing the dinner menu with Margaret still in her bedroom. The profusion of color trapped in smooth glass captivated him. At home, Mrs. Collette had shown him her collection of plastic liquid-filled snow toys with their microcosmic landscapes. She showed him how turning them upside down and back again produced a gentle snowfall, giving them novelty and grace. But David has never seen anything like the explosion of color trapped in these glass paperweights. He loves cupping them in his hands until their warmth matches his own. He tries to imagine how they are made. Are they indeed exotic flowers frozen in glass or are they just kaleidoscopic shards?

Closing the doors to the desk, he goes to a bookshelf and leans side-ways to read the spines displayed from floor to ceiling on either side of the black marble-faced fireplace centered in the north wall.

The large oil portrait of his father hangs above the fireplace. His father's eyes seem to follow him as he moves about the library. He is in his naval lieutenant's uniform and his arms are crossed in front of him. He holds his dress cap in his left hand. David is still troubled by the knowledge that the portrait was painted after his father had been dead for many months. The lamp cord of the brass light over the portrait emerges from behind the painting and trails off to the side of the mantelpiece to an outlet on the floor. It is partially hidden by a black walnut pipe rack holding his grandfather's briar pipes and a wooden amphora of dried-out tobacco that David has often held to his nose to savor the still pungent smell.

The books in this section are mostly treatises by German philosophers and economists. He recognizes neither titles nor authors and moves to the shelves on the left of the fireplace where, judging by their titles, novels are shelved, many still in the original dust jackets – still others with crumbling leather bindings and illegible titles ... D.H. Lawrence, Colette, Sappho, Kipling, T.E. Lawrence, Graham Greene, Fitzgerald ... Again, the author's names are unfamiliar. He notices a curious title, *You Can't Go Home Again*, but he doesn't withdraw the book.

A large couch upholstered with coarse, embroidered material occupies most of the west wall and to its left there is another freestanding bookcase, its shelves set higher to accommodate the many art and photography books.

Lying atop the books on the bottom shelf is a large folio tied with a narrow black ribbon, too tall to fit vertically in the shelf. He listens for footsteps and then unties the ribbon and opens it. The photographs inside are loose. He looks through them slowly. They are more nude photographs but not of the same woman he remembers from his great-grandmother, Selma's. This photographer's subject is a severe looking woman he will later recognize as his great-aunt. He recalls meeting her several years before in the apartment; although she seemed to look right through him when they were in the same room. His Aunt Rose said that the woman has a "checkered history" with his grandmother, although his grandmother has regaled him with tales of their many adventures together around her farm at Lake George, picnicking and painting together.

Alert for the sound of his grandmother's footsteps approaching on the black marble floor, he studies the photographs. Only a few show the subject full-length.

Most are close-ups, of her breasts, of the curve of a raised arm and a breast, the slight mound above the triangle of black hair obscuring her sex, of her upper thigh flexing toward the dune of a buttock, of the angle of a pointing foot. There is one close-up of her eyes and forehead with her black hair pulled back severely. These are corporal landscapes of a woman clearly proud of her body, framed by a conspiring photographer equally enamored of it. Several photographs show an articulating hand in various postures as if the subject is doing shadow puppets off-camera. In still more images her fingers splay and mimic curves in her torso. There are no backgrounds in the photographs.

Farther into the portfolio, the subject is photographed against a highly polished touring car that, like her body, is never seen in full. There is no written identification of either photographer or subject, though he recognizes both.

From his great-grandmother Selma, he recalls the scandalous tale of how her brother Alfred and O'Keeffe met. She detailed with gusto the details of the affair and how she, their mother Hedwig, and Alfred's wife Emmy once sat stone-faced at the dining room table while Alfred and his new protégé disported themselves a floor above. He remembers the photographer's portrait of his own absent father, Edward, in his great-grandmother's apartment in the Delmonico.

Hearing his grandmother's bedroom door close, he quickly reties and replaces the folio on its shelf then grabs a book and sits down on the nearby couch, opening it at random.

"It is no surprise to me that you are a Rockwell Kent fan," his grandmother observes as she sweeps into the room coiffed and dressed for the day ahead. "Your grandfather was, as well. Perhaps it's all that lusty farmer plowing his fields stuff ... lovely really. Are you ready to go?"

He thinks of Mr. Farr as he rises to join his grandmother. He remembers when he was very young Mr. Farr's team of horses tugging at the two-bottom, mouldboard plow. David marveled that the horses knew to walk so straight and at how smoothly the furrows rolled over on their sides as the team advanced across the field with Mr. Farr following behind the plow, the reins wrapped around his forearm and his hands on the plow. David wondered who was plowing.

David and his grandmother spend the day doing small errands together, getting cash at the Bank of New York, stopping by Rhinelander Florist to consult with Mr. Leitz about an arrangement for that evening, dropping by Gristedes to ensure the tomatoes and avocados are ripe, and finally meeting Sylvia Sullivan for lunch at the Russian Tea Room.

The Piano Lesson

As they arrive at the restaurant, David is still marveling at the price of the birch logs for sale at the florist shop and can't wait to tell Alain. To the left of the glass-fronted refrigeration units with their tubs of cut flowers was a large produce crate containing a dozen paper-birch fireplace logs of matching diameters and lengths. A hand-lettered sign indicated that they cost a dollar each. Back home, his neighbor Lester Collette sells mixed dry hardwoods for $11 a cord and white birch lowers the value of the cord, as it is not a choice wood for furnace or cookstove. During the walk down Fifth Avenue with its ornate hotel entrances, David tries to calculate the value of one of Lester's cords in New York. But he knows enough not to raise this question with his grandmother, who will not find the matter of interest. She speaks little on the walk down Fifth Avenue except to point out the Plaza Hotel where he and his widowed mother lived before they left the city for Vermont.

When they are seated with Sylvia, who arrived earlier, the waiter hands each of them a large, glossy menu adorned with the crest of the Russian royal family. Sylvia greets her friend warmly and then turns to David to ask if he is enjoying himself in the city. He knows to reserve his melancholy and responds, "Very much, I only just got here, but it's fun."

On his last visit when he first met Sylvia Sullivan, he was invited to her apartment, in the same hotel where his great-grandmother Selma lived and there met her famous husband, Ed. David had not seen the new television variety show but had overheard a friend's mother telling his own mother about it. The family had just acquired an Admiral Television set and was dispensing regular news of its marvels to their neighbors.

A photographer for the *New York Daily News,* in which Ed Sullivan had a regular column, met them at the apartment and took a picture of them. The photo ran the following week under the banner, "Ed Sullivan with admiring fan."

In the blitz of magnesium light glistening off the many awards and citations that serve as a backdrop for the photo, Mr. Sullivan is holding a bronze statue of Donald Duck mounted on a black Bakelite base, a gift to him from Walt Disney. He is showing the gift to his "admiring fan," who returns his enthusiastic smile. In the glossies sent by messenger the next day to his grandmother's apartment, his grandmother notices the beads of sweat on his nose and forehead from the overheated apartment and the woolen sport coat he is wearing.

The restaurant's menu again leaves him puzzled as he scans the unfamiliar list looking for recognizable choices. *Sevruga, Osetra* and *Beluga* appear in many of the descriptions. He asks his grandmother what *borscht* and *blinchiki* are.

Interrupting her banter with Sylvia, she turns to look at him and answers with a non sequitur, "I don't suppose you get much opportunity in Vermont to taste caviar." He sees from her conspiratorial smile that her observation is intended for Sylvia. He allows that he saw caviar once when he and his Aunt Rose had lunch at Reuben's and she ordered it. The two women again smile at each other and his grandmother expresses surprise that her sister can afford caviar on her modest remittance. He lets the matter drop with a nod and resumes his search for something familiar on the menu.

Occasionally, Sylvia senses his absence from the conversation; turns and asks about his life in Vermont. His responses are brief and to the point, as he cannot be sure that what interests him will be of interest to his grandmother's friend.

"I like history and reading the best," he answers to a question about his schoolwork.

"Oh yes, we ski every weekend. Dad,"– he corrects himself – "my stepfather is an instructor so we get to ski free, but even then it's still expensive. They want fifty-five cents for a ham and cheese sandwich at the Octagon, so we pack our own lunch and hide it in the base lodge for later."

"That doesn't seem so much for a sandwich if it's a good one," Sylvia responds, with a smile aimed at his grandmother, whose lotioned skin begins to gather at the corners of her mouth.

"Well, we won't be having any such sandwiches here," his grandmother pronounces, bringing the line of rural inquiry to a close as David again takes refuge behind the large menu.

The waiter returns and begins swanning about, rearranging salt cellars, pepper grinders, goblets, and the rosebud vase, evidently dissatisfied with their placements. With a feigned solicitude, he commits to memory the complex orders from Sylvia and his grandmother and then turns to David, saying in an accent similar to Margaret's, "and for ze young gentleman?"

The menu lists *"Anise Scented Center Cut Pork Chop, sour cherries in red wine with melted pearl onions, braised pork golubtzi, manka kasha, haricots verts, and braised mushroom."* David manages the only words familiar to him, "I'll have pork chops."

At Paine's restaurant, where his friend Warren Wolfe's mother often waits on them, he usually orders "pork chops with mixed and mashed." A few minutes later a heavy white china plate with two bright blue circular bands near its perimeter arrives with two thin pork chops, two ice cream scoop-dispensed mounds of mashed potato and a colorless and largely tasteless mix of canned vegetables, along with two slices of square white bread, two pats of butter and a glass of milk. He remembers Juliette when she was an infant sitting in her maple highchair at the end of the booth licking a pat of butter that he or his half-brother Paul would sneak to her while his parents ate their meals.

To his surprise and relief, the waiter congratulates him heartily on his selection, then bows and disappears, knowing there is no lucrative favor to be curried from a child. Some twenty minutes later, he returns with an artfully arranged plate in each hand and a third balanced on his forearm. He makes a great show of their placement, swirling them once in a wide arc before setting them down in front of each of his patrons.

As David stares down at his own heaping plate of unrecognizable food, he feels a sudden wave of nausea. He forks the two pork chops and green beans to the side and recovers enough to eat a chop and most of the beans, leaving the rest of the plate's alien landscape intact.

When the picked-over plates, still laden with food, are cleared by a dark-skinned man looking more like Aladdin's genie than a waiter, an elaborate tea service is brought, with a small brass samovar and glasses mounted in brass frames that make them into cups.

Sylvia again punctuates the dialogue with his grandmother with occasional questions to him about "living in the country" or his "visits to the city." She professes to know a lot about country living, explaining that she and her husband have a farm in Greenwich.

"How many cows do you have?" he asks to the obvious dismay of his grandmother.

"None," she answers with a sympathetic smile. "We have no cows, just a dog,"

"Do you have a tractor or horses?" he persists.

"No, we just go there on weekends. Rocco takes care of the place for us."

"Is he your hired hand?"

"Well, he's our gardener."

"Oh," David answers, eliciting a faint smile of finality from his grandmother at his good judgment in ending the colloquy.

The maître d' who seated them on their arrival returns and discreetly sets a gold-embossed, crimson leather wallet on the table, which his grandmother takes promptly and opens. She scrutinizes the handwritten bill inside, removes her own red wallet from her purse, licks her right thumb and index finger and counts out three of the uncirculated bills counted out similarly by the teller at The Bank of New York. The teller, however, wore a rubber thimble on his right index finger. She puts two crisp tens into the crimson wallet and sets it on the far edge of the table.

Sylvia thanks her for a "lovely meal and the opportunity to visit with David," reminding him to add his own thanks for the lunch.

The maitre d' returns and with a resplendent smile sets the wallet down and thanks everyone. He watches his grandmother again scan the bill and remove three ones from the tendered change, leaving two inside. She returns her wallet and removes a tortoise-shell compact from her purse, opens it and brings its lid close up to her face. Cocking her head from side to side, she surveys her features and, removes a pad nested inside, dabs ecru powder onto her high cheekbones, temples, and chin. "There, I'm ready to go," she says to her waiting guests, snapping the compact shut and returning it to her purse.

He is again left to his own devices as the two women walk ahead of him east on 57th Street chatting about mutual friends and, especially, the most recent scandals befalling the Baekeland family. A decade hence, Barbara will be stabbed to death by her son and occasional lover, but the scandal of the moment seems to be Brooks' latest affair in Ibiza.

David is distracted by a comparison of the cost of the lunch with Mr. Collette's asking price for a cord of dry firewood. He figured that the $18 meal would buy almost two cords, or 128 cubic feet, of cut, split and delivered wood. Two cords would take him and Jackie, working without breaks, five hours to stack. He doesn't know how long it takes Jackie's father to hew, buck, split, and haul the wood in a disabled manure spreader towed by his doodle buggy. He goes over again the wonders he will tell Alain in the long-distance call home he is permitted halfway through his visit.

His grandmother spends the afternoon at her desk "corresponding with acquaintances at Lake Placid, Lake George, and on the continent." David sits on the couch with an unabridged dictionary open on his knees. Again, hearing the familiar sound of the thin nib etching her florid script onto the pale-blue monogrammed stationery and dispensing a flow of the dark-blue ink that is familiar to her friends and family, David pauses his leafing through the Bible-paper pages. He imagines the trace of her lacquered cinnabar fountain pen. He knows her handwriting by sight, as she occasionally writes him in Vermont. Her letters always fit on one side of note page, just enough to accompany an enclosure such as a check or photo or her best wishes to him and his "new family." Perhaps she assumes that Helen will read the letters or she may have little to tell him, since in the few serious conversations they manage together, she seems to want to know more about his mother and stepfather than about him. He is drawn to the flourish and affectation of her elaborate script and loves to watch the ceremony with which she draws ink from the crystal inkwell into the pen's bladder and then wipes the nib with a tissue.

"Roe: the mass of eggs contained in the ovarian membrane of a fish."

In a dictionary he often uses to determine the meaning of the many new words he hears in New York, he verifies that the restaurant's signature offerings are fish eggs and, from that, assumes that the unrecognizable names adjacent to "caviar" on the menu describe fish he has never heard of.

He remembers fishing with Pete Trepanier on the Willoughby River one spring when the salmon – known as "lake trout" – were running. Pete taught him how to make bait, using scraps of cheesecloth tied around a clutch of pale red salmon eggs in their gelatinous goo, with a small treble hook in the center of the egg mass. He showed him how to cast the sachet far out into the river roiling with salmon returning through the St. Lawrence and Carillon rivers up the Willoughby to spawn. He thinks about his trip home in four days.

That evening, the first guests to arrive for cocktails are his grandfather's first cousin, Ruth, and her daughter, Terry. Terry is a tall girl. Her father is Scottish and her mother German like most of the blood family. The reception is to be held in the living room, now rarely used except for social functions. A bartender has been hired and Margaret will pass hors d'oeuvres hot as they came from Paula's oven.

He explored the living room once when Margaret and his grandmother were occupied in the kitchen. It is not locked, but the double doors are always closed. He was careful to open one door silently and to close it behind him in case his grandmother returned. Inside, he discovered over a couch the familiar painting he saw of the blue Madonna and child. He went back to the library and again took out the Dali book to be sure it was the same as the one he remembered from his first trip. "Enfon gegu et Ange, 1949," was the inscription under the book's full-page reproduction. He remembered the comfort he felt when he first saw the Madonna in the book full of otherwise strange and troubling images.

Now, with both doors opened wide for the party he again sees the familiar painting and the lacquered rosewood Steinway grand piano. The glossy instrument was personally chosen from Steinway Hall by his grandmother's friend George Copeland. According to his grandmother, Copeland's performing career ended in a repertoire disagreement with the Victor Recording Company. He had been a student and devotee of Nadia Boulanger and her composer sister Lilli. Nadia was active in the Paris music scene in the first half of the century. Her sister Lilli died a young woman. Copeland had known Debussy, Satie, and Albeniz but now, in his dotage, lived alone in a cramped apartment near the Armory on Park Avenue.

David remembers visiting Mr. Copeland with his grandmother when he was eight. At his grandmother's insistence and with her support, David began piano lessons at home and recently mastered "From a Wigwam" in the Beginner's John Thompson Piano Book, although he had not memorized it.

When David was ushered into the dark apartment, the eminent pianist inquired of him whether or not he played piano. Before David could answer, his grandmother allowed that he is taking lessons and suggests that her friend might consider giving her grandson a "brief master class," as they are only there for a short visit. The heavy, soft-fleshed man with cherubic features smiles kindly at him and with a gesture of his hand invites him to sit down at the Pleyel grand occupying most of his cluttered living room.

Aware that he might embarrass himself and his grandmother in the presence of the great pianist, David protests, detailing his lack of accomplishment. But he is urged on, by both the pianist's suasion, and his grandmother's forceful smile and nod toward the piano. He sits down and lays his hands out on the keys as Mrs. Burnside had taught him. When the right fingers are on the right keys, he looks up at the music stand hoping to find only a smattering of black dots on a white page. Instead he sees only a framed photograph of a woman. His grandmother cannot see what is on the music stand as she is perched on the edge of a love seat beyond the piano's open lid. He looks confusedly at the pianist, whose unfocused gaze seems to have left the room.

"It is not the musical notation to which you are accustomed," he whispers, "but nevertheless you must learn to play it."

The woman in the photograph is wearing elbow-length gloves of black lace and holds a closed fan between her right thumb and index finger. Her left hand lies in her lap. Sitting on a straight-back settee, she holds herself erect, neither leaning against its upholstered back nor sitting forward. A black lace mantilla cascades from her black hair down over her pale décolletage and into her lap. She is disengaged from her surroundings and stares only at the lens, neither smiling nor frowning, so that there is no way to tell what she is feeling. She seems infinitely patient with the process of having her picture taken. Two pendant gold earrings are her only adornments.

David can't see his grandmother, but senses that she is impatient for him to play. He remembers the first few bars from the first page of the Anna Magdalena Bach Book and attempts the opening theme, trailing off after a few notes.

The pianist smiles and sits down next to him. David slides over to make room for him. Without flourish, Copeland begins a slow piece. Looking up, David notices the pianist has no eyebrows. As the notes begin, his heavy-lidded eyes close and he seems to be straining. Then Copeland's head rises, his chins unfold, and his eyes open and look up, seeming to study the woman in the photograph. The pianissimo notes emerging from the piano are sad and stately, as if accompanying someone walking slowly with deliberate steps in a funeral cortege. He notices the pianist's lips forming silent words. Suddenly the notes end, even as they continue ringing deep within the piano's fruitwood case.

"Lovely, George, as usual. I am afraid my grandson has a way to go before he merits your attention. Perhaps next time he will have something prepared for you."

The room is silent. The pianist doesn't move from the bench or respond.

"We shall let ourselves out, George. Thank you for seeing us."

He and his grandmother leave the pianist sitting on the piano bench. Safely in the elevator descending to the lobby, his grandmother offers, "I am afraid dear old George is getting maudlin in his decline. I must say I expected better of him. You will forgive him, won't you? He was once a renowned concert pianist playing all the great halls."

"I will," David answers, but his mind is on the striking and enigmatic woman in the photograph.

The Quarry

The keyboard cover on the Steinway is always down, but on earlier furtive excursions he lifted it and examined the ebony and ivory keys, never touching them for fear of being discovered in the off-limits room. Smoked-glass mirrors covering one wall give the room an illusion of great depth. A small fireplace with an unadorned black marble façade and brass andirons dominate the room's center, creating a focal point for the satin-upholstered Empire furniture. The bartender has set up in a corner near the doors to the exterior balcony, now unlocked for the occasion, even though it's getting cold outside. He stands in his formal dinner wear, polishing highball glasses with a linen dish towel which is otherwise draped over his left arm.

Ruth and Terry are ushered into the room by David's grandmother and he follows. Terry looks back at him, broadcasting a curious smile. She looks a little older, but it's hard to know, as the girls he knows at home matured much faster than the boys. Many of his female class-mates evinced early signs of womanhood in fifth and sixth grades. A few of his eighth-grade pals have just begun to shave.

Terry is slightly taller than David. She wears a dark teal cardigan sweater over a white blouse, a green, knee-length skirt, and penny loaf-ers without socks. Titian hair cascades in ringlets over her full breasts. She walks straight to the bartender and asks for a rum and Coke, which the bartender makes by splashing some dark rum into a tall glass of Coca Cola and ice. He winks at her and she wink back, as if they know each other or share some secret. Following her, he orders a Coke with lemon. She asks for a taste of his and offers him a taste of hers. They exchange glasses and sips.

"Good," she smiles, "but I like mine more. How old are you?"

"I'll be fourteen in March," he answers.

"Oh," she answers, not volunteering her age.

The room soon fills with guests, mostly people of his grandmother's age. Terry's mother works at the U.N. and has invited two younger cou-ples "of color," to add both interest to the conversation and an interna-tional air to the gathering. One couple is from the Venezuelan mission and the other from the Nigerian mission.

Terry begins a staccato interrogation of him, relieving him of the need to compose questions that he fears will sound clumsy or naïve.

"Do you like Vermont? What do you do there besides ski? What are your friends like?

What is your girlfriend's name? What grade are you in? Your father's a ski instructor. What else does he do? Do you have to go to church? Is your mother pretty? Is it true there are more cows than people?"

As he answers each question, he senses her waning interest and sees her distracted glances, which make him feel even more inarticu-late. She seems to understand his rising discomfort as he struggles to formulate distinct answers to her rapid-fire questions. But then she asks him yet another question, apparently hoping to find a subject that will put him at ease.

He thinks of the girls at home who are comfortable only in their mutually defended community of girlfriends. They dance with each other, go to the bathroom in pairs, and whisper to one another about their flirtations. He has never met a girl like Terry and wonders if this is what city girls are like.

After an apparently successful digression on his part about skiing the Nose Dive alone at dusk with a full moon rising over Elmore Mountain, Terry abruptly turns away to get another drink, saying she'll be right back. On her way back from the bar, she stops to chat with the African couple, whom she seems already to know.

David is left alone on the edge of the room near the piano and lifts the cover as a way of appearing occupied. Terry's mother, Ruth, clutching a highball cloudy with bluish gin, approaches him and whispers with a wink, "I think she likes you! Watch out." He turns, only to see her swishing back into the crowded center of the room near the fireplace which, though it is cool, is not lit. Three white birch logs lie on the brass andirons.

He takes the opportunity to ease out into the corridor only to find that another couple is being relieved of their coats at the front door by Anna Wiegland, a close friend of Margaret's hired for the evening. David says hello and then excuses himself. When they disappear into the living room, he opens the closed doors to the library and slides into its dark safety. He doesn't turn on any lights; the garish glow of the city washes the room with enough light to see by. He sits down on the couch, then swings his legs up and lies back as he has been taught never to do. He lies there enjoying the quiet dark and the profligacy of his comfort. He can see the occasional landing lights of planes descending over Queens, the red flashing hazard beacons on towers dotting the cityscape and hears sirens chasing through the city streets, the screech of sudden braking and the roar of compression in trucks being suddenly downshifted. He dreams of home.

A swimming hole where he and Annie Foss often go for a dip lies off the Flats Road, well upstream from Ward's Sawmill. Here, just beyond a stand of old hemlocks, the river spills down a long run of exposed ledge, finally cascading several feet into a gravel basin surrounded by mossy boulders. The sun-baked ledge warms the freezing water leaking out of Blodgett Mountain just enough to make a brief dip possible. A profusion of waist-high ferns borders the basin. Few townspeople make the trek to the remote pool since there are more accessible and warmer swimming holes in the valley.

As they stand in the shallows, trying to acclimate themselves to the frigid waters with light splashes, he suddenly dips his thumb into the water and makes the sign of the cross on Annie's forehead and lips and just above her barely evident breasts. "I baptize you in the name of the Father, the Son, and the Holy Ghost." She smiles at him, answering, "Is that what you do in your church?" He nods and looks down at the water, embarrassed at having touched her. She adds, "We baptize, too, but I think the words are different in the Methodist church." Then she yells, "I dare you," and dives into the pool. He follows. The chill takes his breath away. They swim out toward the waterfall and then both emerge into the sun and lie down on the flat warm rock that forms one edge of the basin. In the sunlit water, he can follow the darting shadows of brookies and the occasional flashes of light off their nacreous skin.

As they lie in the sun, he watches Annie discreetly. Her eyes are closed. The sun lights the tiny goose bumps on her tan legs and arms and her quivering blue lips. He tries to envision her body underneath the dark-blue bathing suit. When she is lying down, her breasts all but disappear, making more evident the nipples grown firm in the cold water. His only reference point for the junction of her brown legs is a drawing he discovered in one of his maternal grandfather's sketch books and the nude photos he saw of Georgia O'Keeffe. Neither do much to inform his imagination of Annie without her bathing suit. But the work of imagining leaves him breathless. He doesn't know the act of sex, as his only sexual experience has been solitary. His sins of self-abuse, mumbled weekly in the confessional, approximate the rudimentary sensation of sex. His most graphic definition of the act cost him and some of his friends twenty-five cents which they paid to watch Pudge Roleau stand on a milking stool and attempt sex with a heifer when David was much younger. The cow seemed indifferent as she continued chewing her cud.

"Time to go. I have field hockey practice tonight," Annie says, bouncing upright.

He smiles when he notices that her upright stance restores her breasts. He stands up and together they head up the path surrounded by ferns. That evening under his down quilt, he again sees Annie lying in the sun.

He awakes suddenly, realizing that someone is sitting on one arm of the couch. "Don't get up, just move over," he hears Terry say. She lies down next to him. "It's too crowded in there and there's nobody our age." She is silent for a moment.

"I really should get back. I think I drifted off and my grandmother gave this party to introduce me to her friends."

"Don't flatter yourself. We both know who this party is for. Neither of us will be missed for a minute."

The authority in her voice and her position on the outside of the couch leave him no choice.

"Do you and your girlfriend fuck?" she asks.

"Ah," he stammers, still unsure he heard the question.

"Have you ever?" she persists.

"Well, I ..."

"No, you haven't. It's okay. Don't worry," she answers calmly.

She shifts and kisses him on the mouth.

"I really should go back, and what if ..."

"I locked the doors," she says through the side of her mouth. "Just relax. I'll show you."

She takes his right hand and slides it under her skirt and into her panties. She holds his hand tight, guiding it with occasional admonitions to her own rapid satisfaction, which he experiences as soft groans and a sudden shudder. She brings his hand back to his upper lip and asks if he would like her to reciprocate.

At a loss he stammers, "Yes, but ... we could ... another."

Jumping up, she declares, "Your loss. I give good head. That was fun. Let's do it again sometime."

She straightens her blouse and sweater and pulls her skirt down, then leaves the library. David doesn't understand what Terry has offered him, but understands well enough that under her manual guidance he has done for her what he has so often done for himself. He wonders if his presence made it more exciting for her.

He is alone again. Her scent lingers on his hand and upper lip. It is a new smell. He tries to recall what just happened and will do so many times. He declined her offer so clumsily, and is still trying to understand what she meant. He imagines she must think him a "rube," a term he has often heard at home. He goes to the guest lavatory and washes his hands, but leaves the lingering scent on his upper lip. Then he returns to the party where, as Terry predicted, he was not missed.

Several times during the evening his grandmother notices him by the piano and comes over to introduce one of her friends. Terry seems to be ignoring him, although she winks at him several times from across the room. To his surprise, the couple from the Nigerian Mission, who seemed lost in conversation for some time, walk over to him and introduce themselves. He gives his name and, after asking him where he is from, they follow the question with many others about the condition of farmers and farming in Vermont, a topic to which David can speak. Although their interest seems to focus on the economics of dairy farming, he responds with descriptions of farming methods that seem of considerable interest to them. Mr. Adaloo asks about the arrival of power equipment on the farm and seems especially interested that it that tractors replaced horses rather than water buffalo. He is also intrigued with the idea of harvest and silo storage, acknowledging the complexity that winter introduces to the agrarian calendar. He explains to David that the lack of any significant seasonal change, other than the annual rains, obviates the need for such storage except to prevent rodents and insects from destroying harvests.

The conversation is animated and, for the first time, David feels as if he is part of a discussion in which what he has to say is of interest. The steady stream of questions from both Mr. and Mrs. Adaloo indicate a knowledge of, and curiosity about, farming that surprises David. The self-propelled discussion masks his curiosity about the facial features of the couple. They rise a good foot above him. Mr. Adaloo has on a dark suit and Mrs. Adaloo wears traditional African dress. He has never seen the wide, flat noses that dominate their faces. Mrs. Adaloo's straight hair is sculpted into a lacquered archway that frames her head. Mr Adaloo's hair is short and so curly as to make combing impossible. To be polite and make his curiosity less evident, he looks into their eyes as they speak and only perceives their curious facial characteristics in his peripheral vision.

Mr. Adaloo pursues the question of why farmers don't slaughter their dairy animals while they are younger and suitable as beef, a question David cannot answer. He answers only that cows, to his knowledge, are milked until they die and then are buried or trucked off for "rendering," the meaning of which he doesn't know.

The evening ends suddenly. As soon as the first couple rallies for departure and begins their good-byes, a little after ten, the other guests follow suit. Anna brings in armloads of coats and holds them aloft as guests sort through to find their own. By 10:30 all the guests are gone. He manages an express and somewhat flushed good-bye to Terry and shyly returns her conspiratorial smile. Anna and Margaret bustle about returning platters and trays full of glasses and coasters to the pantry, while the bartender settles for his services with his grandmother and then departs by the service elevator off the kitchen.

His grandmother asks how he enjoyed the party and he thanks her enthusiastically for the evening.

"Ruth said that you and Terry disappeared for a while. Did you have a good talk?"

"We did, we sat in the library and talked. She said she didn't like crowded rooms to talk ..." he answers, looking away at the grandfather clock in the corridor.

"She is a lovely young woman. She goes to Greenwich Academy, you know, a fine school."

"How old is she?" he asks.

"Sixteen, I think, but I would have to ask Ruth. I just sent her a small check for her birthday, but I can't remember whether she turned fifteen or sixteen. Her poor father never amounted to much – 'loves gardens' is about all one could say about him. Good man, though, Scottish by descent."

He kisses his grandmother goodnight and retires to the cool comfort of linen sheets. He lies on his chest with his head on his arms and can see shadows moving in the curtained apartment windows across 71st Street. People seem to be coming and going in a large room behind six windows. He can see the figures moving across all the windows without the delay a door would impose. His grandfather worked for the family who lived in those rooms and owned the Bank of Manhattan. His mother used the term "malefactors of great wealth" and he looked up "malefactors" in the blue American Heritage dictionary his grandfather had given him for an earlier birthday.

The next morning his grandmother sleeps in but he awakens just as light begins to infuse the skyline over Queens. He's in the midst of a dream he cannot recover, but is keenly aware of its sexual nature. After savoring the feeling for a few minutes, he again falls asleep and sleeps deeply until awakened by the sound of his grandmother running a bath in the adjacent bathroom.

The sound of water flowing into water brings back memories of his many times in the tub when his mother sat on the bathroom floor with her arms on the side of the tub humming and splashing water on him to make him laugh and scrubbing him all over with a rough washcloth softened with her scented soap.

Aunt Rose

The remaining days in New York go quickly, with excursions to the Frick, the Met, the Morgan Library, a funeral at the Ethical Cultural Society – one of his grandfather's colleagues – luncheons with friends of his grandmother's he doesn't know, and, on the last day, a solo trip to see his Aunt Rose, now bedridden and in a fugal state, as her meandering mind tries to identify and relate to her few visitors. Rose has outlived her many friends.

David has never been with anyone this frail and has to be prompted by a uniformed nurse to sit close by her bed and listen carefully, as she can only whisper her words. She advises him to respond slowly and clearly, elevating his voice so she can hear. She carries over a ladderback chair and places it next to the night table on which familiar brown vials of medicine stood. He notices that her nurse's uniform resembles the white habit of an order of nuns he saw on a recent visit to Quebec with his Vermont grandmother, Eugénie.

His aunt recognizes him, though slowly, and asks after his mother. She seems to recall his past visits and what they discussed. She asks him to bring her a stack of framed photographs from the crowded table in the corner and to show them to her one by one while she explains to him who they are. Confused, he looks toward the nurse. She smiles and whispers that this is his aunt's favorite pastime now and he should simply comply.

David brings over a small pile of photographs still in their stand-up frames, setting them in her lap. His aunt holds one up at a time so they can both see the subject and she tells him about each photograph. Several of the photographs are familiar to him. The first is a small sepia image in a cheap stamped-metal frame backed with cardboard. It is of grandmother in the bathing suit on the beach; his father is on her right and a young girl is on her left.

"Perhaps my sister did not tell you that you had another aunt. I am, of course your great-aunt and I'm sure you have more like me in Vermont on your father's side. … I mean your stepfather. My sister always makes that distinction. I don't. I've met him only once, but he is one of the loveliest men I have ever met and I have met many, but, of course, not many of the men I've known are really men in the normal sense of the word.

"This little girl is indeed your own aunt, your father's sister. Her name was Louise and she was a lovely girl. Sadly, she lived just outside the halo that surrounded your father. It was much the same in my childhood, though at least we were three girls and our one brother amounted to very little in life. To be honest, he was paid to disappear in Florida … a remittance man we call it today.

"She was a quiet and lovely girl, very much taken by the dance. It is a measure of how little she mattered that my sister never spoke to you of her, but she never liked to speak of the dead as long as I have known her. I used to take Louise to the 48th Street Theater to see Martha Graham in the early days of modern dance. Graham was a student of Ruth St. Denis, but, I believe, took her art to a much higher level. I took her to see Graham's *Chronicle* in 1936. She was 14 and that seemed to change her in some way. She wanted to dance. Like so many children of that period, though, she developed, and soon died of, polio. I spent many of those last months with her. Your father had gone off to school in New Hampshire and your grandfather was immersed in his banking career. It was evident that all hell was about to break loose in Germany and your grandfather was also trying to make contact with all the relatives he could remember. There are so few pictures of your aunt and so many of your father. This is not my favorite. She seems like an afterthought standing there. Your aunt was treated with indifference and died largely unspoken of. I still miss her.

"This picture I know you have not seen. Your father was a handsome boy. You see him here in his emerging manhood. He is having a summer pool party at the farmhouse in Greenwich. It was a lovely place, unpretentious by today's standards. The other boys in the background are school chums. This was about the time when young men started wearing bathing suits that did not cover their chests. You can see why your mother fell for him. She was as beautiful as he was handsome. This would have been the summer before they first met."

"What was my father like?" David asks quietly.

"Oh, like most boys raised in privilege. He could be arrogant sometimes and give one the sense that he thought he knew it all. He was prone to sometimes long and tedious disquisitions on various subjects about things he had just learned, whether it was Tennyson, Steinbeck, or how to prune a hedge. He was very bright, but didn't live long enough to understand the eloquence of modesty. Like most boys growing into men, I expect he was insecure about himself and his place in the world. Of course the war took care of that. I have often thought that, sad as it was, fate may have done him a great favor in the war. His love for your mother at the moment of his death was absolute and never subject to the test to which time subjects all great loves. Your mother, too, would always have that memory. Of course, such a terrible loss does not always serve one well in life.

"Is your mother well?"

"Yes, pretty well," David allows.

"This is a picture of your great-grandfather. You wouldn't have known him although I know you visited Granny in her dotage. I cannot imagine your poor grandfather growing up in that household. It is little wonder he went into banking. Louis began drinking more after his lithography business failed, but who wouldn't, married to your Granny?

"Selma told her coterie of artsy friends that the birth of your grandfather was a "virgin birth." Of course, she never went so far as to say she was intact, but she had some romantic notion that her implied virginity would make her more appealing to the writers, poets and musicians with whom she spent so much of her time.

"After Louis died, your poor grandfather had no choice but to go to work to support his mother's lifestyle. After he finally got up the courage to move his mother into that tiny flat in the Delmonico, she didn't talk to him for three months. When he married my sister without consulting his mother, Granny began seeing him again, but only to invite him over to intimate dinners with the most beautiful and available women she could find. She disliked your grandmother intensely. I don't know why, as she had only met her at the wedding and rarely saw her afterward. She, likewise, paid little or no attention to me either, although she later came to acknowledge our shared love of opera. Granny was a terror, but I did enjoy her, I guess for her flamboyance in what was then largely a world of men."

David listens intently to his great-aunt and then when she goes quiet, he looks over at her and sees she is dozing. He looks up at the nurse. She approaches him and whispers, "You made her so happy. You did very well. She'll sleep for an hour or two. You can go, but do come back. She is ever so fond of you and I've never seen her so animated."

David replaces the chair by the wall, thanks the nurse, and leaves quietly.

A Different Quarry

David and his father agreed that on the way home he should try coach travel. The adjacent seat is vacant, so he lies diagonally across both seats with his head against the window, pillowed on his folded jacket. He falls asleep as soon as he feels the familiar rhythm of the train's motion.

When he awakes, the train is winding slowly north through the White River Valley. Among the trees, he spots the remains of an abandoned marble quarry. The wide-mesh game fence surrounding it has collapsed in several places and is overgrown with vines. His angle of view is such that he can only see the brown and yellow groundwater stains on the marble sides of the quarry. He drifts off again to sleep.

He stood on a similar precipice several times before, once with Stevie Stewart and Jimmy Greaves, who urged him to come along for a dip, knowing full well that David would not "make the jump," occasioning yet another opportunity for them to be admired for their daring and skill.

The overgrown quarry lies high up in the Worcester Range and never sees more than an hour or two of noontime sun. The access road, once heavily trafficked with four-horse drays loaded with cut limestone blocks or smaller stone boats pulled by a single horse, is now overgrown, passable only on foot or by 'dozers and log skidders. Stevie and Jimmy's assurances of safety diminish in credibility as they explain about where to jump and what to avoid. Any courage drains out of David as he stands on the mossy outcrop from which kids jump or dive into the dark water 30 feet below.

Three years later, he brings Annie Foss up fully intending to jump, but his determination again dissolves as they stand together on the brink. He recovers by recounting the stories he's heard of kids drowning or diving headfirst into hidden rock outcrops on the quarry walls and never resurfacing.

In his dream he is alone there now, standing on the quarry's edge looking down at the opaque surface of dark water. He cannot see below the surface, even along the edges of the quarry where the sheer walls are striated with mineral deposits, indicating different water levels. They remind him of the Plimsoll lines on warships he has seen in the book of Steichen's war photographs. The afternoon sunlight is oblique, a splash on the far wall of the quarry.

He has prepared himself to jump. There is no one to watch or to help him should he get hurt. He inhales, raises his right leg and pushes off with his left into the air. As he falls, he scissors his legs together as he was taught in camp and uses his arms for balance. It is a long fall. He feels the sting in his feet and under his arms as he hits the hard surface. The glassy water breaks open around him and he plummets deep into the quarry leaving a wake of bubbles. He opens his legs and arms to slow his descent and his eyes to see how far below the surface the fall has propelled him. Far above, he sees a greenish light from which he tries to calculate his depth. He looks down but sees only pale light attenuating to blackness below. He is in suspension now. He imagines his father's descent into Leyte Gulf.

He has always been able to hold his breath for a long time – 90 seconds once at camp. Buoyancy overcomes his equilibrium and he begins to rise slowly toward the plane of light above. He makes no effort to swim to the surface as he looks around at the water transfused with light. Small dace dart in and out of the shadows. He remembers the exaggerated estimates of the quarry's depth and Pudge Roleau's contention that it was bottomless.

The light's intensity increases and suddenly he breaks the surface with a splash and a gulp of air. Looking up at the rock shelf from which he jumped, he gets his bearings in the confines of the quarry. Now he wishes Annie had seen him jump, though she would have been worried for him. There is no way out of the quarry other than the knotted manila rope hanging from a tree limb on the far side of the quarry. He remembers hearing that some first-time jumpers had been unable to climb out without help, as the algae-covered rope is always slimy from the mists above the water.

Remembering Dougie Cleveland, he sidestrokes slowly toward the rope. Dougie drowned there when some older boys played a joke on him and pulled the rope up after he jumped in and then left, intending to return later that day. Dougie's body was later recovered by divers but the stories of others who drowned and whose bodies were never recovered only added to the mystery and intrigue of swimming above their remains.

David reaches the rope and grapples his way to the top, collapsing on the mossy rock edge and looking up through the crowns of gray birch at the clouds scudding across the sky.

He awakes suddenly, remembering it's autumn again and he'll be leaving, this time next year for his first year away at school. His summer job ended several days before he made the requisite visit to his grandmother's and the remaining days of summer are his own.

Alain is standing on the platform and waves to his son when the train stops in Waterbury. David is relieved to be home and says so. As always, Alain asks with genuine interest about his trip and David tells him of the party at his grandmother's and of his curious conversation with Mr. Adaloo about farming methods in Africa. He recounts his visit with Aunt Rose and her declining state. David and Alain always enjoy joking together about the arcane food David encounters in New York, as Alain has never been there. He must compose his image of the distant city from his son's stories of what he sees and experiences there. Apart from primitive airports in the Middle East and North Africa, Alain's only urban ventures were early sight-seeing excursions to Montreal with his own parents when he was young and later once with Helen and their children when they all stayed in the Queen Elizabeth Hotel, visited Saint Joseph's Oratory, and walked around the old Montreal waterfront.

It's a cloudless morning. WDEV is broadcasting its live Saturday morning regular "Music to Go the Dump by." The two listen as Alain navigates their new Ford station wagon toward home.

"I'm worried about your mother," Alain begins. "I called your Uncle Peter and asked him to stop prescribing all those pills. I don't even know what they're for and I'm not sure he does. He promised to call me back after reviewing her medications, but he hasn't. You're old enough to understand that she doesn't take these pills because she's sick. If anything, they're making her sick. Some days, she doesn't even get out of bed."

"I know," David answers.

"She talks about aches and pains and her need for diet pills to lose weight, but, if anything, she's thinner now than when we first met. I don't want you to worry, but you're old enough to know. Don't say anything to Paul and Juliette."

"Dad, we all know about the pills. We look at the bottles. We've all seen and talked about how certain pills make her to behave in certain ways. It's hardly secret. We don't know why she does it, but we've known for a long time that she's not herself. What does Dr. Phil say?"

"He can't do much other than talk to her. He says many of the pills she's taking are dangerous and she'd need to be in the hospital if she were to stop taking some of them. He said that one of them – I forget the name – is never prescribed to outpatients, but is only used in hospitals during and after surgery. He's also reluctant to confront a colleague in another state. He understands the problem, but doesn't know what to do any more than we do."

David asks, "What does she say when you talk with her about it?"

"I've tried. I can't. She gets very defensive and simply changes the subject. Sometimes she blames me."

"For what?" David asks.

"She wasn't talking sense. I couldn't take her seriously. I think she's afraid that I'll somehow manage to take them away."

They're quiet again. David watches the passing landscape. His excitement at being home is clouded by the topic of their conversation, although he is surprised and relieved that his father is speaking with him as a grown-up. But he is dismayed that he has no suggestions or resources to offer. In this small town, he knows his father cannot discuss his fears about his wife's decline with anyone other than Dr. Phil.

Alain loves his children and has never made David feel any less loved than one of his own. Their conversation only amplifies and emboldens his anger at his mother, especially her suggestion that Alain might somehow be responsible for her descent into the gelid opiates and fervid stimulants.

Alain's eyes are on the road. This affords David the opportunity to look at him discreetly. He sees a sadness he has never seen in his father's eyes. For a moment David sees Helen through the eyes of the man who has become his real father and through them sees not his mother, but the once beautiful woman Alain so loved when she arrived in his small town. He wonders if his dead father still exists in his mother or if the roots of her descent run deeper into her own childhood and upbringing. He cannot yet understand that addictions are an entity unto themselves and need no genesis in one's experience to work their toxic magic.

David does understand how age changes people and relationships, but this cannot explain the slow untethering of his mother's attachment to life and to her family.

They pull into the driveway and the relief David felt at seeing Alain on the platform, waving to him as the train pulled in is subsumed in his fear about his mother. He wonders whom he'll encounter when he goes in to let her know that he's home.

He sets his small suitcase down on the gravel driveway and, to his father's surprise, hugs him wordlessly before picking it up and going into the house.

David looks forward to seeing Paul and Juliette and his friends. Lamoille County Field Days starts the following week and he is anxious to see the new farm equipment and to watch the horse and tractor pulls.

Tina Curlin

David is seventeen when he first meets Tina. She is gorgeous. Farm work has lightly sculpted her tan limbs, endowing her with the subtler curves of muscle and sinew as well as those native to her sex. Her dark blond hair falls long on her shoulders and frames a seductive smile. She discovered her own body at fourteen with an urbane ski instructor from Stowe who spoke with a sexy European accent. At nineteen, her latent sensuality and double-take beauty make it easy to try on possible husbands, but for several months, Tina has not been seen with anyone.

David meets her at Lamoille County Field Days at the horse pulls. Omer Laplante's 3,400-pound team has just moved 9,000 pounds of concrete blocks thirty feet along a dusty paddock to the cheers of several hundred onlookers. The frothing Belgians strain at their traces until the roar of the crowd and Omer's loud "Ho" signals their success. They pause to be released from the evener linking them to the load and then the sweating pair high-steps away, seemingly triumphant at their success. Tina settles on the paddock fence next to him and says simply, "Hello."

He has been away at prep school at the behest of his grandmother, who pays the tuition in the hope that boarding away from home with well-heeled boys his age will offer him a broader perspective and a leg up in society, and inspire in him goals greater than subsistence farming or small-town commerce. In fact, his time away accomplishes the opposite, diminishing his appreciation for the haughty urbanity of his schoolmates. His time in the drab dorms of a New England boarding school only reinforces his enthusiasm for rural life and he can't wait to return home with his new ideas and sensibilities.

Even after becoming reasonably comfortable with his new and mostly privileged classmates, he still thinks of his friends at home, imagining them talking loudly and miming the eccentricities of teachers as they line up for hot lunch. Running through the grass cradling a lacrosse ball and dodging opponents, he imagines himself and Jimmy Greaves shirtless, dripping with sweat and caked in hay dust, stacking bales tightly in Jimmy's father's hayloft, as pigeons perched on the hayfork's iron track high above them coo their approval.

"Omer's got the best team in Vermont," Tina continues.

"Looks that way," David answers, looking straight at her for the first time.

He remembers seeing her on the slopes of Stowe and in the base lodge, each time with a different beau. He recalls her in a succession of stills, the insouciant toss of her hair after removing her woolen headband when coming into the Octagon warming hut at the top of Mount Mansfield, the subtle up-glance and smile at the men watching her from behind as she bends over to close her bindings, the look back at Rosebud, the old chairlift loader who, in spite of repeated warnings, cannot resist an occasional louche comment, lascivious smile, or pinch when assisting a beauty with an oncoming T-bar.

"How do you like that school in New Hampshire?" she continues as she watches the next team prancing into place.

"Well enough," he answers. "I miss my friends here, though."

"Do you ride?"

"Not really, unless you call 'trail riding' riding. I like draft horses."

"We have horses. Call me and we can go riding some time."

Surprised, he turns and looks at her, realizing suddenly that the conversation has changed.

"That would be fun. You live in the Hollow, don't you?"

"Since I was born ... seven of us in that old farmhouse – gets crowded. Makes you want to leave sometimes."

She waits until he looks at her again and then smiles and says, "Call me."

He is alone again and watches as Sissy Tatro's Percherons strain unsuccessfully in their traces. At the start, they jerk the stone boat sideways a few feet, but never move it again as their cleated shoes dig deeper into the paddock dust. The judge dismisses the team and calls for the next one, but no other contestant manages to beat Omer's team.

When David cannot sleep, his thoughts go to the women in his life – not to the girls like Annie Foss, Cecile Collette, his cousin Terry, or Sister Lamoureux – but to the older women like his great-grandmother Selma, his two grandmothers, Tante Colette, his Aunt Rose, and Eugénie.

He remembers when he was eleven and he was left in Eugénie's care for the afternoon while Alain took Helen, Paul, and Juliette to Burlington to buy new school clothes at the outlet store. Eugénie is baking bread. In a large, dark brown ceramic bowl, she kneads a dark dough. She adds a cup of raisins and over-ripe banana pieces and begins kneading again. David is used to seeing her gnarled hands work white dough, then set it out to rise by the stove, knead it once more before shaping it into loaves, pat the loaves into her black sheet metal bread pans, and slide them into a hot oven.

David asks about the color of the loaves. Eugénie explains that this is the day her brother-in-law, Benoit, will come to kill and butcher her three pigs and that the loaves are for the pigs. Confused, David asks why she bakes bread for pigs that are going to die. "All in good time," she answers.

Less than an hour later, Eugénie removes the hot loaves from her gas oven and the room fills with the rich smell of hot molasses. The three loaves cool for a bit on a rack and then she removes them from their pans, setting them side-by-side so they just fill an enamel refrigerator bin. From below her kitchen sink she takes an unopened quart of Nova Scotia screech, a cheap dark rum named for the behavior it induces among those who drink it to excess. She pours the entire bottle onto the three loaves and leaves them to soak up the brown fluid.

Uncle Ben arrives with his truck after lunch and sets up an old cast-iron enamel bathtub on four cinder blocks in the backyard. Underneath he builds a roaring fire of dry pine branches, adding hardwood logs when the fire is going. With a hose from the tap on the side of the house, he fills the tub with water. He hangs a come-along from the garage doorway, lays a maple slab the size of a coffee table across two sawhorses, and arranges a selection of wood-handled knives.

After coffee and doughnuts inside, Eugénie and David bring the three loaves out to the pigpen behind the house. The three eager Berkshires are hungry and Eugénie hands each sow a dripping loaf of her freshly baked molasses bread. David watches in astonishment as each sow snuffles up her loaf in less than a minute and then, after looking at each other to make sure there are no leftovers to tussle over, lies down in the mud to savor and digest her treat. Several minutes later, the three pigs are drooling in the mud and snoring peacefully.

Uncle Ben is soon joined by his son Bruno who is carrying a Remington .30-06 deer rifle. With a nod from Eugénie, who looks away and crosses herself, Bruno lodges two bullets above the snout and between the closed eyes of each sleeping pig. The gunfire does not wake them.

When the pigs cease their twitching and their hind legs quit mimicking an escape, Uncle Ben and Bruno wrestle one of the 250-pound sows over to the water bubbling gently in the bathtub and flop her in, displacing considerable water. After a few minutes of scalding, the men drag the carcass to the come-along, slipping its large hook through the heel tendons and cranking the pig up high enough for to scrape the bristles and begin butchering. The first incision is across the neck and the dark blood spurts out into a stainless steel milking bucket. The blood will be saved to make Eugénie's signature *boudin noir.* Benoit makes another incision from the anus to the neck and scoops out and severs the internal organs, and drops them into another milking bucket for later sorting. Bruno saws the open carcass in half and lays the halves on the maple slab while his father begins with the largest knife to cut it into quarters.

The laborious process is repeated twice and it's dinnertime before the last quarter is wrapped and tied up in butcher paper and loaded onto the truck.

David's father and mother stop by on their way home to pick him up, sparing a few minutes for conversation with Eugénie, Benoit, and Bruno before heading home.

Grand Tour

Late in the summer of his junior year, David and his grandmother reach an arrangement regarding a *grand tour,* which his grandmother has been promoting for several years. When she learns of it, David's mother simply relegates the decision to her son, saying, "You're old enough to make your own decision whether you want to be with your mother or your grandmother." Alain again comes to his aid, telling him after his decision that "a trip to Europe is an opportunity not to be missed. You should take your grandmother up on her offer by all means." He adds in a whisper that he wishes he'd had the opportunity when he was David's age to go overseas. His only trip abroad was when he was four years older than his stepson, flying C-54s in the air transport service force during World War II, shuttling war materiel into Abadan, Iran, and missing the war-torn continent altogether.

Helen has decided that Alain has been won over by her mother-in-law and in the days preceding his departure, goes silent and takes to her room for much of the time.

He is to leave right after graduation, which is attended only by his stepfather and Juliette, as Paul has begun a summer job. His grandmother holds David's arm as the two climb the steep gangplank onto the *Queen Mary*. It is one of the ship's last voyages to Southampton. Like her sister ship, the *Queen Elizabeth*, the *Queen Mary* is showing her age according to his grandmother, who knows, as she has crossed on the *Queens* many times in her seventy-eight years. To his grandmother's great pleasure, the Cunard bursar recognizes her in the crowd and takes time amid the jostling of boarding passengers to usher her and her grandson to their cabin on the B deck.

In her heyday, his grandmother traveled first-class, but now with both assets and former travel companions dwindling, she chooses cabin class for the six-day voyage. She knows as well that the social devoirs of first-class travel will be alien to her grandson and feels they will be more comfortable in cabin class.

As his grandmother puts away her things, carefully laying out cashmere sweaters and lingerie in the drawers of the bureau and hanging long skirts, dresses and an embroidered jacket in the closet, David stares at his open suitcase. Again, his stepfather has helped him pack, after a discreet phone call to his grandmother to determine what he will need on the trip. He remembers his mother's input on being asked the same question earlier, "Ask him, he spends more time in that world than I ever did." Mindful of her increasingly reclusive behavior and her disappointment at his decision to go, he wondered if she would even wish him goodbye when he left. She saw him off but looked away as she offered him a cursory embrace in her bathrobe. He whispered that he loved her and knew she was upset, but she turned without responding and shuffled back to her bedroom.

The six-day crossing is calm and the *Queen*'s decks are resplendent in the bright sunshine. David's grandmother notes sadly on the first night that the first-class dining room is almost empty. The bursar eagerly granted her request to show her grandson the classic elegance of the dining room and first-class parlors so he might see and appreciate the ebbing world in which she has lived much of her life. After landing in Southampton, they take the train to Victoria station and a cab to their hotel.

David is intrigued that cars drove on the left and have their steering wheels on the right. He cannot imagine that it is intuitive to Britons just as it was intuitive to him to drive on the right when he began driving furtively with friends several years before he got his license. He is equally fascinated by the London taxis and comments to his grandmother on the many ways they differ from those in New York. His grandmother seems to take great pleasure in his many observations about life in London and, after dinner that evening, he lies in his twin bed next to his grandmother and listens with interest as she tells him of her first trip to Europe with her father and mother on the inaugural trip of the *Mauretania* in 1907. She describes the Edwardian elegance of the ship with its intricately hand-carved, first-class dining room wall panels and tapestries, as well as her and her sister Rose's excitement at being allowed to travel with their parents on their annual summer trip to the continent. Their father was a prosperous brewer in New Jersey and had recently moved his business to Brooklyn and his family to an elegant town house in mid-Manhattan to better serve the burgeoning influx of thirsty immigrants arriving daily by boat. His grandmother and Aunt Rose would sneak off after the noon buffet while their father rested and their mother read in a deck chair with a plaid coverlet over her knees. They would explore every nook and cranny of the ship not walled off to them, but could only look down from their deck on those traveling in steerage, seeing them sitting on the lowest deck, playing cards, talking and taking in the sea air and sunshine. One day they noticed a ship's officer opening a door to the ship's lower decks that had always been kept locked. They went up and tried the door, but again found it locked and wondered how the officer had managed to open it without pausing or using a key. Rose played with the handle and soon discovered that if the handle were pushed in and turned counter-clockwise, the door miraculously unlocked. They passed furtively into a stairway leading down to where the lower class passengers bunked. Both had heard tales about what could happen in steerage and, after a hushed conference, decided to return to the security of their own travel class. Later on in the voyage, looking down into steerage from the A deck, they saw a small boy juggling apples and wondered to one another where he had learned to do such a thing.

"Children behaved as adults at a much earlier age in those days," his grandmother observes, "We were pretty much left to Mathilde, our German governess, until we learned to leave childhood behind us, me at about six and Rose ... well, I am not sure Rose ever left childhood behind. In my parents' time childhood was seen as a necessary but socially inconvenient aberration perhaps best left to a governess to manage. When Mathilde and later Fraulein Henke succeeded in molding us into young adults, we were welcomed into the society of our parents, but rarely before that time did we join them for meals or social events other than afternoon tea, which I can remember from my earliest days as a little girl. Things are much different now, of course! Parents seem more comfortable with childish behavior and make more time to be with their children and to understand their play. We knew very few other children, and the ones we did know we either met in the park or at formal social events where we were expected to behave as adults. In the country, I suppose, all this doesn't much matter. Did you play with friends much?"

"We did. There is a lot to do in the country and lots of neighborhood kids. We find things to do." He doesn't elaborate, remembering his grandmother's lack of interest in country matters, though this time somehow, with just the two of them, she seems more interested in his upbringing. He is anxious not to trigger an inquiry about his mother so he says he is tired and the two wish each other goodnight. He hears his grandmother snoring quietly several minutes later as he lies there in the pale yellow light of a London street lamp. It is their first night in London and it seems to him that he can still feel the rocking of the ship as sleep overcomes him.

His grandmother has arranged for a driver to take her and her grandson to her favorite places in London. So after breakfast, the concierge introduces them to Harold, a voluble cockney, who is at their disposal for the day. They visit Marble Arch, the National Portrait Gallery, the Tower Bridge, and Buckingham Palace, stopping at Harrods for his grandmother to pick up several canisters of her favorite Ceylon tea.

That evening they dine with an old friend of his grandmother's and David retreats into thoughts of home as his grandmother and Cecily chat gaily about the old days and common friends who have since died or are living out their dotage between New York and London. From time to time, the ladies turn to him, interrupting his reverie to pose a question.

He wonders to himself as he pushes the remnants of uneaten lamb through the grease congealing on his plate if his mother is still angry with him, although she evinced no overt sense of it when he left. He knows it is not her style to be openly angry with him or with anyone, especially if his stepfather is present, but rather to convey her disappointment by silence or averting her eyes, a code she knows he understands.

"How jolly it must be to work on a farm," Cecily blurts out cheerily, "Do you help milk the cows or do they still do that on farms?"

"They do," David says, putting down his fork and looking up at her. "They milk them now mostly by machine, though some do still milk by hand. It's hard work."

"It must be hard on the cows' little titties to be milked by a big machine. I know I shouldn't like that," she chirps, a bit too loud for his grandmother's comfort in the crowded restaurant. His grandmother warned him that Cecily lost much of her hearing and that he will have to look her in the eye and speak up to be understood. Her tendency to compensate by responding too loudly catches the occasional attention of diners at a nearby table.

That evening he has a curious dream in which he is swimming with his stepfather in a broad and slow-moving river. His stepfather taught him to swim as a young boy and to respect the strong currents in the middle of rivers especially in the early spring, and to stay near the shore where his feet can still touch bottom. He remembers the stories of kids swimming in the quiet waters above Wolcott Gorge where the broad river soon widens, becoming very shallow as it roils around massive boulders in its way and then suddenly tumbles out of sight into the steep gorge below where wet, narrow rock walls covered with moss make any escape impossible. Occasionally, swimmers drawn into the swift currents are swept into the gorge below. The few who miss being battered against submerged rocks or held underwater beyond their ability to hold their breath emerge several hundred feet downstream where the waters again widen and pacify.

He and Alain are swimming above the gorge. He is surprised at how far out into the river his stepfather has swum, when suddenly he looks up and notices a naval officer on the other bank of the river sitting in the grass with his knees gathered in his arms. He recognizes the face clearly from the photograph on his desk in his room. He looks for his stepfather who is still swimming alongside him. He stops and tries to plant his feet in the gravel bottom but cannot. He swims next to Alain, wondering if he, too, sees the enigmatic person on the far shore. After several more minutes of swimming his feet feel the river bottom again and he stops and stands waist-deep in the river. Alain is standing and has already begun walking toward the shore. He greets the naval officer as if they have known each other for many years and sits down next to him. David watches from the water. The two men talk quietly to one another for several minutes. Finally, his stepfather stands up and shakes hands with the naval officer. The men pat each other on the shoulder. David's stepfather turns and walks up the riverbank, disappearing over the rise. The naval officer sits back down and appears to be watching David as he stands in the river.

David wakes from the dream, feeling cold. He notices that his sheets are all at the foot of the bed. He hears his grandmother's gentle breathing in the adjacent bed as he pulls the bed covers over himself and lies there thinking about the curious dream. He knows the person on the shore to be his father. He wonders what his stepfather and his father talked about. It seems, when they met, as if they knew each other before this encounter; both served in the war but in theaters at opposite ends of the earth and in different services. He also wonders why he hadn't spoken to his father or why his father had made no effort to speak to him in the dream.

Several days later, he and his grandmother take the boat-train to Paris where again his grandmother has engaged someone to take them around. They spend more time in Paris and his grandmother seems more engaged in their various activities. She seems to take pleasure both in explaining to him the history of the places they visit and in his companionship. They spend a full day in the Louvre walking the endless parquet floors through corridors and galleries. He never imagined that so much art could exist in one place. Jacques-Louis David's jarring painting of Marat stabbed in his bath by Charlotte Corday stays with him for much of the day. He had spent many hours as a child with his Aunt Rose in both the Metropolitan Museum and her beloved Frick, but could never have imagined the sheer immensity of the collection in the Louvre.

The following day, his grandmother has arranged for them to make an early morning stop at Les Halles, where he sees the vast marketplace of vendors in from the farms and fisheries on the outskirts of Paris to sell their produce, animals and fish. He has often wondered how cities feed themselves. In the small farming town where he lives, it is evident how food raised on farms, processed in creameries or bought in stores moves to the tables of the town's few hundred inhabitants. But how does a city of several million get fresh food daily? He is amazed at the sheer size of the market with its overwhelming profusion of smells, shouted orders, and odd-looking fish and eels, unfamiliar vegetables, mushrooms, and endless variety of cheeses and breads of all shapes and sizes. He wanders the stalls staring at the unfamiliar raw materials of the city's diet. Finally, his grandmother gets his attention as he scans the crates of shaved ice displaying a dozen unfamiliar species of fish, eels, and shellfish. He has seen little beyond trout, perch and the occasional land-locked salmon and tries to imagine what all this marine wildlife might look like on a dinner plate. He recalls his trip to Chinatown with his Aunt Rose and the strange fish he saw there.

That evening he and his grandmother eat at a restaurant she was last at with his father when he was David's age. The restaurant is called *La Grenouille* and was highly regarded before the war. His grandmother orders her signature scotch and, to his surprise follows it with a second before the dinner arrives. David has a *faux filet*, which his grandmother explains to him is simply a steak, and she orders *rognons de veau* and *pommes Anna* which she further explains are veal kidneys and buttery potatoes. "Impossible to find at home ... and one of my favorite dishes as a child," she says with a faraway look, "I've had them every year in Paris since I can remember and am never disappointed." He leaves it to his grandmother to order dessert and is not disappointed. He can barely finish the profiterole and watches his grandmother tuck into hers with gusto, though she leaves a good bit on her plate. The waiter brings the bill and his grandmother tenders a large blue 500 franc note, which the waiter takes with a bow. David has just finished mastering the currency equivalents of the English pound when they move on to France and he encounters the franc.

That evening in bed, his grandmother seems especially talkative and uncharacteristically cheerful. After a few minutes of her stifled gig-gling, David asks what is amusing her, worried that he has committed some gaffe in the restaurant. To his surprise, she recalls his Thanks-giving visit the prior year with his roommate Hugh from Exeter. The incident was such a source of embarrassment to his grandmother David never reminded her of it.

Margaret had only just retired and moved back to Germany after 28 years of service. Her hearing had almost entirely failed and she would often stare at his grandmother with a look of incomprehension on her face as her mistress laid out the day's plans. Two years earlier, she lost the hearing in her right ear while sitting on her bed cleaning her left ear with a Q-tip when the phone rang. The damage done by the wooden

Q-tip to the eardrum could not be repaired.

After a staunch farewell at Idlewild Airport, his grandmother began trying out new cooks offered by an agency that made domestic referrals. The first woman sent by the agency came with a compelling tale of need and no record of service. His grandmother had been moved by her story and engaged her provisionally. She soon doubted the wisdom of her empathy when, after several weeks of approving daily grocery orders, she noticed the frequency with which cooking sherry appeared on the list.

David and Hugh had arrived by train the morning of Thanksgiving to find David's grandmother in an agitated state. She had ordered a fresh turkey, but a frozen turkey had arrived the day before and instead of thawing it as she had been told, Mrs. Moffat forgot and left it in the freezer overnight.

The day before, his grandmother had gone over the Thanksgiving menu with great care with her but finally lost patience with the endless stream of repetitive questions about the menu. She wrote out the entire holiday menu on her stationery and nodded to Mrs. Moffat to indicate that she was done. Mrs. Moffat clutched the paper to her substantial bosom and backed out the door nodding wordlessly and leaving a strong odor of perspired alcohol in her mistress's bedroom at ten in the morning.

The anxiety of preparing and serving a holiday dinner must have taken its toll. Unsummoned by the buzzer, Mrs. Moffat burst into the dining room where Hugh, David, and his grandmother were seated at the large Empire table dressed for dinner. The swinging pantry door swung wide, hitting the nearby side table and Mrs. Moffat reeled proudly toward the table bearing a large crystal ashtray with a gelatinous cranberry cylinder that still showed the mold of its tin container. Mrs. Moffat worked earnestly to maintain her footing as each person struggled to detach a piece of the rubbery, wine-colored mass onto their plate. She disappeared again into the kitchen by walking straight into the swinging door, which dislodged the molded cranberry onto the floor. She bent over and grabbed the elusive condiment with both hands and replaced it on the serving ashtray.

After Mrs. Moffat's long absence, David's grandmother rang the buzzer under the table for a good 30 seconds. David and Hugh, sensing disaster, stared ruefully at the cranberry gel on their plates. Finally the swinging door opened tentatively and Mrs. Moffat struggled through the passageway with a huge platter. She tottered toward David's grandmother who gasped when she saw the carnal wreckage of what had once been a turkey balanced precariously in the center. Instead of neat slices of white and dark meat, the carcass looked as though it had been torn apart by feral dogs. The stuffing was mixed in with chunks of meat and bones protruded willy-nilly.

Trying to make the best of it, but wearing an ominous frown, their hostess managed to pull off some dark meat for herself and found bits of stuffing to add to her plate. Hugh and David, taking their cues from David's grandmother, solemnly served themselves. Mrs. Moffat, smiling triumphantly at her success, retreated through the swinging door; then followed a crash from inside the kitchen and the muted sounds of shattering china.

The boys tried to pretend they had not heard the crash and began picking at the meat on their plate. The side dishes on the menu never arrived. It soon became evident to the three that much of the bird was still frozen and what wasn't, was raw. Only the crispy outer skin and outermost part of the breast meat was edible.

With great dignity, David's grandmother rose from the table and said simply. "I will arrange for us to have our dinner at the Westbury. I shall call there and see if they will take us." Nothing more was ever said about Mrs. Moffat, who disappeared, leaving the turkey on the kitchen floor with red and white shards of china glistening through the meat. She evidently slipped in gravy she spilled while milling about the kitchen and left by the service elevator to avoid further recrimination. Oskar later told his grandmother that he saw Mrs. Moffat, "sneaking out through the service entrance with gravy all over her white uniform and smelling like a drunken lord." The incident was closed and David could only imagine his grandmother's anger and embarrassment. David and Hugh managed to contain their laughter until the next day in a taxi headed down Park Avenue to a matinee of Carmen at the Met, for which his grandmother had bought them orchestra seats.

Now a year later, lying in twin beds on the Avenue Foch in Paris, she is looking back on the incident and finding great humor in it, as she retells the story to David, giggling all the while and occasionally expressing opprobrium for Mrs. Moffat's penchant for cooking sherry. It is a side of his grandmother he has never seen, and he wonders whether her own choice of a second scotch has made possible her retrospective amusement at the incident, which at the time so horrified David.

The grand tour continues on to Venice and finally Rome, followed by a long train trip back through France to Southampton where the *Queen* awaits their arrival.

On their last dinner together in England, David's grandmother again indulges herself with a second scotch and she asks David what has pleased him most about their trip. For the first time, David feels comfortable speaking openly about what he has seen. His observations are less about the cultural highlights of the trip, as his grandmother might have hoped, but more about the ways in which practical elements of European city life with which David has become familiar diverge from those at home. He talks at length about the gondola-taxis of Venice and the proliferation of Vespa and Lambretta motor scooters in Rome, the Deux Chevaux cars of Paris and how one would never see those conveyances where he lives. He allows himself to imagine and tell his grandmother what the reactions of his friends at home might be to what he has seen, which says more about his friends and his life in the country than it does about his observations of their voyage. But, unlike earlier times when she has been unwilling to hear about his life in the country, she seems more indulgent of his enthusiastic telling of how what he saw relates to his own world rather than to hers.

David takes this opportunity to broach with his grandmother his decision to take a year off before going to college. Having been away from home for the better part of four years, he is anxious to get some work experience and to earn spending money of his own, as his many friends are doing. His grandmother is at first taken aback by his announcement, perhaps because it is a decision he has made rather than a question he is raising. She knows the risk in his decision, but has lost any further will to oppose her grandson on this issue. His promise to attend college the following year leaves her enough comfort to accede to his change of topic.

On the last night of their voyage home, after dinner, his grandmother suggests they take a stroll on deck. They encounter a strong but warm headwind bearing the scent of the sea as they walk toward the foredeck. The evening is clear and faint stars have begun to appear, while the western sky toward which the three-funneled *Queen* sails is streaked with ominous red light infusing the cloudbank on its horizon. The light reminds him of the Turner paintings he saw at the Tate. He knows the comparison will give his grandmother pleasure and begins to say something when she asks without turning around, "Tell me how your mother is doing" Sensing danger, David answers "Fine; she stays very busy."

"Has she kept in touch with her brother?" his grandmother persists.

"A little ...He does not come up, but they talk," he answers.

There is only the noise of the wind and the engines throbbing below for a while and then his grandmother again takes up the question. "I got a lovely note from Alain saying that she has been in bed for some time, but he did not say why. She isn't sick, is she?"

David senses that his grandmother knows more than she is letting on and resolves not to engage. They walk past a cabin steward aligning deck chairs in the fading light and, after several minutes, his grandmother resumes. "When I was a young woman, I, too, was told by Uncle Leopold, our family doctor, that I was prone to melancholia. He prescribed laudanum drops that I took daily in warm tea. They boosted my spirits somewhat, but I stopped taking them after I married your grandfather. My cousin Emmy, who ended up marrying Stieglitz, also was told she had melancholia by Uncle Lee – he was Alfred's brother, you know, and an eminent physician. Uncle Lee also prescribed laudanum for her but she soon became dependent on it and then, for some reason, it went out of medical fashion and was no longer prescribed. Emmy never did recover really, which is why I always thought Alfred left her for O'Keeffe. She'd been a saturnine child, very plain, too, and then, of course, their poor daughter Kitty spent much of her life in an institution after Alfred took up with O'Keeffe."

They walk in silence until they reach the bow of the ship, but the headwind turns suddenly colder and is too much for his grandmother so they turn back to the warmth of the first-class parlor.

Inside the well-lit room, they sit down on a red plush banquette. David looks at the tapestry hanging just above them. It is a medieval hunt scene and reminds him that deer season will begin soon after he returns home. At a table nearby, several elderly men play cards, smoke, and drink from short-stemmed glasses. A well-dressed woman in a far corner is reading. Otherwise the parlor is empty. His grandmother again notes that, on prior trips, the first-class parlor would have been filled with people until well past midnight.

Suddenly, without looking up at David, she continues, "Your mother was the most beautiful woman I had ever seen and your father was so in love with her he could barely stand the separation the war imposed on them after they married. Your grandfather and I were grateful that she had come into his life. It gave him something to live for and someone to come home to, though, of course ..." Her voice trails off and David sees her inhale an involuntary sob.

After she recovers her composure, she begins again, "Your father had a lot of growing up yet to do when he joined the war effort and he had to grow up so far away from those who loved him, including your mother. He was too young to be a warrior, but then again so were most of the boys who left their families to fight. It was so close to the end, too. Your grandfather never recovered, of course. Uncle Lee prescribed Miltowns, but they didn't seem to make much of a difference. I couldn't bring him back from his grief. Not even your mother, whom he adored, could cheer him, but then of course she was dealing with her own grief and was pregnant with you and all alone in the world and then her own father suddenly died. Her mother, Hilaire, wasn't much of a comfort to her from what I understood from your stepfather.

"Your mother may have told you that your grandfather and O'Keeffe were close ... a little too close for my comfort but I had hoped that their friendship might rekindle in him a will to live on. But that all ended when she moved out west, though they remained friends, as did Georgia and I. We continued to paint together when she came east to visit Alfred at Lake George.

"I had so hoped to be close with your mother, but she seemed to feel my love for you somehow threatened her own. As you must know, each of your visits to the city in the early years was a trial to her. Thank heavens for Alain ... such a fine man. He always managed to find a way for us to be together. I hope someday to see your mother, but I don't think she wants to see me."

"I'm not sure Mom ever got over the loss of my father," David says.

"I now understand why it is so hard for you to read your father's book," his grandmother continues, much to his surprise. He doesn't answer.

"I, too, had great trouble reading it. When I pick it up now, I only read one letter at a time. It's one thing to know a living person, your own flesh and blood, one who bears the continuum of all your ancestors. Your own imperfections become manifest and the parent in you tries both to forgive and correct them. But when the child dies too early and the only artifacts of their prior existence are the letters they wrote you or someone else, you are powerless and their words become a scourge.

"I didn't write your father enough," she continues, "when he was at war. In those days, one didn't easily express love in the written word and I would often run out of news to tell him and it all seemed so banal and repetitive. It hurt me so much to hear later from other war mothers that it was that familiar news that our boys wanted to hear when they were over there."

She paused for a minute to gather herself.

"I don't really understand why your grandfather and I decided to publish his letters. Perhaps it was all we knew to do. There was nothing else left. And now they have become a source of great sadness to me, a reminder of all that I was not."

His grandmother stares at the florid Victorian carpet at her feet, then suddenly looks across the library toward the empty reading tables and the dark portholes interspersed among them. David can see the tears gathering at the corners of her eyes where she dabs at them with a handkerchief drawn from the lace cuff of her evening dress. David gives her time to collect herself. He has never seen his grandmother fighting back tears and he doesn't know how to react, so waits for her to compose herself.

"I'm sorry," she says. "I'm not normally like this, but I've been thinking so much of your father recently. I'm not sure I felt his death when it happened as much as I do today. So many boys were dying and the telegrams just kept coming and coming to friends. It's almost as if I had prepared myself for it and when it came, I was ready. But one is never really ready, you know. I suppose for you it's impossible to miss a father you never knew. In that way you're lucky, and you have a wonderful stepfather who is a fine man. I never met Alain's mother, but she must be a wonderful and strong woman."

"She is." David says, looking at his grandmother for the first time since she started crying.

"I've tried to read my father's book many times, too." David says quietly. "I know I should be more curious, but as I get older it's even harder. It's not what the letters say. The voice in them is not the voice of my father, but of your son. When he wrote these letters, he was only a few years older than I am now. I guess I expected his letters to be the voice of a father I never knew but they are the letters of a nervous kid writing to his parents."

"I know," his grandmother answers softly. "It's late. It's time we went off to bed. We'll be home tomorrow."

Returning to their cabin, David can hear the movement of the sea beneath them, the hum of the massive diesels below deck, and see the bright array of stars above.

The *Queen Mary* steams into New York Harbor, passes Staten Island and the Statue of Liberty and then, after three stentorian blasts from deep within her viscera, is joined by two McCarren Line tugboats named *Phoebe Isabelle* and *Guy Robinson* that nudge her gently into her berth at the West 54th Street pier. In time, gangplanks are lowered and the longshoremen begin carrying off the steamer trunks of the first-class passengers and then the luggage of the cabin class passengers. David doesn't see the departure of those in steerage although he wanted to.

The night before he is scheduled to take the *Montrealer* north, he thinks again of his mother and wonders how she has fared in his absence and what his reception at home will be. He thinks of Alain and remembers the curious dream in which his stepfather meets his father and talks with him.

Island Pond

In deference to his mother, little is made of his return, although in a moment alone, Paul and Juliette ask eagerly what he saw overseas. He shows them the bundle of postcards he collected, narrating the geography and context for each and then gives them the small presents he bought for them, a small guardian angel of Venetian glass for Juliette and a working replica of a French guillotine for Paul. Later in a quiet moment stacking wood, Alain also asks about his journey and his time with his grandmother. Alain knows that his son's time with his grandmother can be fraught, but is steadfast in instilling in his children a respect for family and the obligations it imposes. His mother asks about the trip, but he spares her details, telling her that he learned a lot traveling to the various countries. He doesn't mention his grandmother or their conversations, conveying only her best wishes, as she had asked. His terse report elicits no reaction. Helen simply looks distractedly at her son, who wonders if she had hoped to be his traveling companion even though she'd never been to Europe.

When David pulls down the chain that lowers the hatch-staircase and climbs the stairs into the cool attic space to put away his large suitcase, he sees the Lionel train layout on the floor in the far corner of the attic that his Aunt Rose sent him the Christmas after their visit to F.A.O. Schwarz. While away at school, he had invited Paul and his friends to play with the set.

The layout looks bare now sitting on the unfinished plywood floor with its small oval of three-railed track and the single-siding with its manual switch. The cars and engine sit askew next to the track. Two small wires lead off to the transformer and another heavier cord is plugged into an extension cord that snakes off into a pile of stored boxes.

David remembers the teeming reality of the train layout in New York that he had hoped to replicate on the attic floor. A variety of toy cars and tractors and a station he made from a shoebox augment the set but nothing looks real and everything is out of scale with everything else. The proprietary feeling he had had when he and Paul first set up the sparse train layout didn't last.

That evening, when David brings his mother a tray with the supper Juliette has prepared, she begins talking to him about his father. Not the stepfather he knows and loves, but the man he knows only from photographs, a painting, his book of letters, and a few anecdotes. David is content with the father he has known since he was two and has spent no time trying to understand the boy in the framed photographs handed down to him or the soldier writing letters home from the war in the Pacific.

David has learned to associate his mother's demeanors and behaviors with the contents of her various pill bottles—just as when Alain showed him how to predict weather from the level of mercury in his grandfather's barometer. Dexedrine and amphetamine prescribed for "appetite management" often lead to manic family work projects or adventures, for which no one else had any enthusiasm. Phenobarbital brings on an ice age of implacable coldness; Seconal, anesthetic hibernation. The small brown bottles with red codeine syrup or the large ones with cheap whiskey herald euphoric recall of childhood events, dysthymic ramblings, and occasional tenderness.

He has asked his mother many times when he was young about her sickness and her long periods in bed, but he now understands that the medicines are the sickness and that his own enthusiasm for their life in Vermont is, for his mother, fraught with ambivalence and loss.

"When I was a little girl, I knew my father loved me, but he rationed his affection for me, expressing it only when mother was in Asia. She believed that affection debilitated children and gave rise to a weakened intellect. Any sympathy for the polio she contracted later in life angered her. She'd push away someone trying to help her. I always thought it was how she was raised and, in my better moments, felt sad for her, especially when I first saw the picture of her as a little girl. She was so lonely and sad.

"But because of my father, when love finally came for me, I knew it for what it was, probably because your real father reminded me of my own, and I swore I would never again be without that love."

"Alain is my real father," David says under his breath.

"Yes, yes, I know ...," his mother sighs.

"I suspect your father's childhood was similar. But it was different with boys. Boys were always being celebrated as "little men." I haven't looked at my family albums for years, but when I last did, there were all those photographs of my brother dressed up as Pan or some other Greek god or a Middle Eastern prince or some miniature king. I was always posed naked, either sitting next to him adoringly or looking distractedly at a piece of pottery, except of course for the snake picture. I didn't even know how to be angry or afraid when I was little.

"Funny, how I'm still in my brother's thrall, even in middle age. His pills keep a safe distance between us, just as he did when we were children. It's always been easier for my brother to write a prescription for me than to send a letter or card. I wonder if that's the case with his dying patients. Dr. Phil wouldn't prescribe them.

"My brother was terrified of my mother until the day she died. At least I had painkillers ... in the broader sense. I don't know ... my niece said he drinks more than he should. Maybe that's his way. I haven't seen him or heard from him in years."

David looks at the profusion of vials and dishes at her bedside. Her light is off and in the shadows the jumble reminds him of the Roman ruins he and his grandmother visited outside Rome at Caracalla.

He sits down again on his stepfather's place on the bed. He has never heard his mother talk this way. He wonders what euphoric has induced her reminiscence. He understands that it is his place now to listen and that his anger no longer has purchase.

"Other than my father's love, we never really knew what romantic love was or what it felt like. We just "carried on" as my uncle used to say when he visited."

Helen goes quiet and closes her eyes. David sits quietly, thinking she has again fallen asleep. He gets up quietly to leave.

"Stay," he hears his mother whisper.

"Don't presume to judge your father. You don't know him except in those letters. They were the letters of a spoiled young man, fighting in a war he didn't understand with boys he didn't know. Like so many privileged boys, he was not equipped to fight. Men like him became officers to lessen their chances of dying in combat but they were all too young for war. Old men should fight the wars they start. We were all so starved for love, your father and I clung to each other like shipwreck survivors even though separated by 10,000 miles. Sometimes it's easier that way. The goddess's feet never turn to clay, as mine have. Don't judge from that jumble of childish letters. Your grandparents were selfish to publish them. Like most private letters, they should have been burned."

David stands through a long silence, listening only to the raspy breath coming from the mound of covers. Finally, he hears his mother say, "Your stepfather is a good man. It was easy for you to ignore a father you never knew and who never knew you. Understand it was harder for me.

"I've lived on my brother's pills since I lost your father. I don't blame my brother. I couldn't have lived without them and they're a way for him to feel okay about not having me in his life. It works for us both."

Then his mother falls asleep and David leaves his parent's room.

Shortly after his return, David finds a job working for the state on a survey crew near Island Pond. He and an experienced logger named Ray wield chainsaws and light axes to clear line-of-sight rights-of-way up through the woods for a surveyor and rodman, who accompany them and shoot transit points to the hilltops on which airport hazard beacon towers will be erected. The surveyor sights his transit into the woods and the rodman marks the first tree to appear in the crosshairs. Ray or David cuts it, depending on its size, along with all the trees 25 feet on either side. The surveyor then resets his transit and plumb bob over the stump and shoots to the next tree. The clearings open the way for tower construction and power line crews to follow. The growth in light plane ownership spurs an expansion in the number of single-runway local airports serving the growing civilian aviation industry in New England. The hazard beacons warn incoming pilots of hazardous elevations on or near their approaches.

He and Ray and the surveyors work in the black-fly hell of Island Pond woods for two weeks straight after hauling five-gallon gas cans and forty-pound chainsaws deep into the woods and halfway up a small mountain. Once there, they slowly use up the fuel and chain oil, making the haul-out less of a slog. Because of the time needed to pack in fuel and equipment, the team agreed to work two straight weeks in the woods and then take five days off at home.

At the end of the day, David helps Ray sharpen the saws in a stump-vise Ray has fashioned. Ray always insists on filing the cutters, allowing his apprentice to touch up the rakers with a flat file, as he taught him. Ray keeps an array of rat-tail and flat files and a carborundum stone in an oil-soaked tool pouch in his rucksack. When Ray finishes sharpening the cutters, he passes the saws back to David to tension the chains, leaving just enough so that when he pulls the chain down, it fully exposes one drive link. Ray also teaches him how to touch up the axes, first with a flat file and then with a stone.

Progress is slow, cutting every tree that shows up in the surveyor's transit as well as those on either side. The surveyors often help out, piling slash from the leftover limbing work. Part of the landowner's compensation for the right-of-way is the timber, most of which can be sold for pulp or firewood.

On rare occasions, the transit sight will land on a boulder or rock outcrop rather than a tree trunk and the surveyor and rodman have to go through the elaborate task of either sighting around the boulder with fixed angles unless Ray can blast it out with a few sticks of dynamite. He can set charges and blow a boulder or small ledge in a tenth of the time it takes to sight around it.

Ray befriended David from their first day together after David answered the ad and was hired on the spot. He teases him on occasion about the fancy school in New Hampshire and the occasional unfamiliar words that creep into his speech when he's not paying attention to where he is and with whom, but it seems most often for the benefit of those within hearing distance rather than for his apprentice. Otherwise, Ray makes David feel at home, taking the time to familiarize him with the tools, risks, and legends of logging in a way that suggests both camaraderie and mentorship.

Ray has worked in the woods most of his life. He got into trouble as a youngster in grade school. When confronted by his single mother about the notes he often brought home from school or the failing report cards, he'd answer only that it was hard for him to sit still indoors so long every day. Responding to his mother's tears, he'd try to apply himself, but the endless array of facts, dates, definitions, tables, and formulas would gradually subside into his daydreams of being in the woods during sugaring in March, helping his older brother rebuild the motor in a friend's Ford tractor, or hunting deer in the Worcester Range. Finally, defying his mother's wishes and tearful entreaties, he quit school after eighth grade and got a steady job milking for a farmer in Elmore who broke out in hives when applying tit dip and whose rheumatoid arthritis had reached the stage where he could no longer do daily chores. Over time, Ray became like a son to the wheelchair-bound farmer and, when the farmer died, he left Ray his new McCullough chainsaw.

Chainsaws were a novelty then and Ray fell in love with the device, quickly learning to disassemble and reassemble it without leftover parts. At 18, he hired himself out to local farmers, clear-cutting and pulling stumps to open new fields for cultivation, or thinning sugar works so farmers could get their teams in to collect sap in late winter.

As chainsaws came into ready use, Ray signed on with Burke Lumber in Lyndon as a logger. He learned to drive a team and began to appreciate the role of horses in the woods. The best horses, usually Belgians or the more compact Percherons, could skid a ton of logs from the stump site to a roadside landing half a mile away by themselves, assuming the terrain was not too steep.

Ray's first job was swamping out roads for the horses to follow. This meant clearing a road from the logging area to the landing below. The first time he was left to do it on his own, the crew boss threatened to fire him. He led Ray back along the skid road he'd just spent two days swamping and pointed out the sharp branch ends jutting out on either side of the skid road. After the explosion of French-Canadian expletives subsided and he calmed down, he pointed out to Ray how a horse or team might tear open a front or rear flank hauling their unpredictable loads along the narrow road. The job was done the next day. Every branch on every tree lining the road had been trimmed flush to the tree's trunk with two hits of a razor-sharp cruising axe.

After a grueling apprenticeship during which Ray learned all the peripheral work of logging with horses, the crew boss showed him how to work with and talk to the horses. Using grabs, chains, and an arch, he taught Ray how to tether two or three logs to the horse's trace chains and breast-yoke and then make a clicking noise with his tongue. The horse would lean into the yoke to overcome the load's inertia and follow the skid trail to the landing site where it would be unloaded with pike poles by a trucker and his helper. The horse then returned intuitively to the stump site for another load.

During breaks in the survey work, Ray regales his own apprentice with tales of spring logging, when melting snow greased the skid trails and the logs would overtake the horses, and of having to shoot horses maimed by the runaway logs while still in their traces. Though David has seen teams on neighborhood farms and at horse-pulls at Lamoille County Field Days, his friendship with Ray and the long hours cutting and limbing together gives him an understanding of how integral horses were to logging operations and he dreams of someday having his own team.

Ray's other passion is Western Swing music and he takes every opportunity to regale David with the radio debut of new tunes and bands. His favorites are *Bob Wills and the Texas Playboys, The Skillet Lickers* and Jimmie Rodgers. David often hears him humming to himself during refueling or a coffee break. David asks about the unfamiliar music and Ray explains how, as a young boy, he would sneak late at night into his grandfather's living room and retune his grandfather's Emerson console radio to the border stations in Texas and Mexico and then, with his ear to speaker, listen to the mix of preachers, faith healers, Texas Swing, and Norteños musicians beamed north by the high-power border stations. Bob Wills, Jimmie Rodgers, and then Hank Williams made their appearance on local juke boxes and bars and eventually became a staple on WDEV in Waterbury, but Ray's knowledge of the lesser-known bands greatly surpasses the few staples on local juke boxes.

Once, after a long day, as they bounce along on the bench seat in the back of the surveyor's pickup, Ray asks David what kind of music he likes most. David talks about Crazy Chase and how much he likes the Québécois music he heard in his own family as a kid. He tells Ray about meeting Crazy Chase for the first time and his first visit to the opera with his grandmother, hearing *Aida*. He asks Ray if he's ever heard or seen an opera. Ray says he thought he heard some once when he landed by mistake on a French-speaking station in Quebec City and listened for a minute.

"Did you like it?" David asks tentatively.

"Singer sounded like she got 'er tit caught in a wringer," answers Ray with a scowl.

They often talk of various hits appearing on local juke boxes and the recent debut of Chuck Berry, whose songs Ray often sings aloud, to the surprise of his companions.

Near the end of the current two-week run in the woods, the surveyor groans and signals to Ray to take a look into the transit. The crosshairs center themselves on a wolf pine that Ray estimates at 90 feet. It is mid-afternoon and felling and cleaning the tree will take the rest of the day. To make matters worse the gnarly trunk splits in two ten feet up and calls into question the tree's weight balance. The trunk at the ground is just shy of four feet in diameter. The surveyor and rodman sit down on a tuft of moss and open a dented thermos containing the tepid dregs of that morning's coffee and take turns drinking from the dented screw-on cup, while Ray stares up at the tree's crown.

"I'd say south, southeast," interjects the rodman, looking up from his coffee. Ray is silent as he walks around the trunk of the tree, looking straight up.

"Dunno, could drop due east or north. Where'd ya like it, David?" he asks.

David looks up, surprised to be asked.

"What d'ya mean? Tree that size, not much choice, is there? Seem ideal if we could drop it back here in the space we already cleared so the cleanup'd be easier."

"Sounds good ta me," says Ray picking up his saw. "I'll need ta put on a 28-inch bar and chain for this'n."

The surveyor perks up and says with a smile, "You mean to tell us yer gonna drop that where you want it 'stead 'a where it wants ta go? That tree must weigh three tons and the crown favors a fall inta the woods. Betcha a fiver ya can't drop 'er in the clearing."

"Y'er on," answers Ray. "Might as well take the rest of the day off – it'll take me an hour to drop it once I get the big bar on, and the rest of today for him and me to limb 'er and stack the slash."

"I ain't leaving 'til I got my five bucks," says the surveyor, cocking his head sideways.

"I'm in fer two," added the rodman.

"How'se 'bout you?" Ray asks his helper. "Ya bettin' on 'im er me?"

"I'll go with you," David responds, looking off into the woods.

"Stick wi' me. Ya'll be a rich man someday, like me," Ray says, to the laughter of the three men.

After changing the bar and chain and checking the tension, Ray asks, "Where you wise guys gonna watch from, the woods or the clearin'? Y'ain't only bettin' your wallets on iss one, yer bettin' your lives," he laughs, as he refilled the saw lying on its side.

It's agreed that the surveyors will watch from outside the 75-foot perimeter and that David will stay and spot the fall for Ray as he cuts.

After another long look at the tree from the base with his saw idling in his right hand, Ray jerks the idling saw into position and depresses the trigger, spewing out a flurry of white woodchips as he fashions a deep notch on the clearing side of the trunk. It takes three cuts to create the wide notch. He trims some high limbs away overhead and then begins a felling cut on the back side of the tree. Ray often warns David about bifurcated tree trunks and their unpredictable falls. A tree with two trunks makes it difficult to assess where the weight lies and how it might fall.

David watches the tip of the pine. Ray taught him that the two indicators of a fall are the cracking sound in the cut at the base that is often masked by the whine of the saw or the slow drift of the crown high above that can be deceiving in a high wind. There is neither. Ray turns off the saw and sets it down. The fell-cut is almost half-way through the trunk, above and behind the front notch.

Ray leaves and comes back with his rucksack, out of which he takes two iron wedges. Smoke rises from the burning brown pine needles on which Ray has set the hot saw. He inserts the wedges into the upper cut and begins to drive them in with the flat end of his axe, sinking them halfway into the soft wood as the resinous sap oozes out of the white wound. The woods are silent except for the blows of the axe.

"Any movement up 'ere?" Ray yells to David.

"No, and no wind, either," David answers.

Far off in the woods, they hear the chuckle of the surveyors.

"Shuddup you two, we need to hear this tree break," Ray yells.

"Then the sound 'o yer money leavin' yer wallet," he laughs.

"Keep an eye on that crown and yell when she starts to shift. If'n it starts goin' toward the clearin', yell 'CLEARIN'" and if she goes for the woods yell the direction so's I can hightail it if'n I need ta," Ray orders.

He sinks another wedge into the fell cut and steps back. He taps the earlier wedge and again steps back.

"Still nothing?" he asks.

"Not yet."

"Okay, here we go," Ray says and he reaches out and pushes at the massive trunk with the flat of his hands. "Le'see if I can push 'er over by hand. Show 'em bastards."

David takes his eye off the crown for a second to look at Ray, who looks ridiculous, pushing at the massive trunk. There is a loud crack and David looks up in time to see the crown begin a slow arc toward the clearing.

"Clearing," he yells as loud as he can and runs back in behind the tree where Ray is standing, still leaning against the trunk.

"Mind ya, step back wi' me from the trunk and off to the side. Stay by my side. They sometimes jump back as they settle."

David has seen Ray do this before, but would never have believed that a pine of that size could be a "pushover," as Ray calls them. David is amazed at the elapsed time between the sharp "crack" and the tree's gentle landing in the clearing. The previous six hours of clearing are suddenly filled by the tree. He notices the absence of a thud and shudder felt through the soles of his boots when a large black cherry, butternut, elm or maple hit the ground. The tree simply lies down in a slow arc onto its boughs, lifting the severed trunk skyward as it falls.

The surveyor and rodman enter from the woods, withdrawing the trucker wallets chained to their belts, and surrender their losses.

"W'ouldn'a b'lieved it," mutters the rodman, annoyed at the loss of four hours pay.

As the days in the woods wear on, David begins to notice them shortening visibly. Work ends only when the surveyor can no longer see his objective in the transit and the four of them simply leave their equipment in the woods under a tarpaulin and walk out to the pickup in the field far below. He and Ray ride in the back. Ray pops open a warm beer bottle with the church key on his knife and lies back with his feet stretched out as the truck bounces across the field toward the dirt road and back to the boardinghouse.

That night lying in his iron frame bed, David dreams of the upcoming fairs and field days that mark the end of summer. Even the hot shower before supper doesn't remove the redolence of chain oil that permeates his clothes, skin, and hair. The next morning he notices the chainsaw gouge in his steel-toed boot and vows to be more careful limbing trees.

Lost Keys

Back at home several days later, David is unable to account for the latent sadness he feels. He has another stint in the woods and then summer is over and he'll have to begin the work of applying to colleges, though he can rally no desire to do so.

Before he goes, he has several visits with his mother. Her room has taken on the smell of a "single-room occupancy" welfare residence and the path to his stepfather's side of the bed and adjacent closet are the only spaces left in the room not littered with clothes, food refuse or dishes. He can see from the quilt's horizon that his mother has lost more weight. The profusion of brown pill vials, cough syrup bottles, and *Cadillac Club* whiskey bottles that he and Juliette periodically remove from her side of the room has again begun to proliferate.

"You awake, Mom? I'm back from work and thought I'd say hello and see if you need me to do anything."

There is no response and David knows his mother is in her drug-induced torpor. He picks his way through to her side of the bed to inventory the familiar pharmacopeia. The names are familiar to him, but he cannot connect the Latinate names with any disease or condition. He knows his mother has diabetes, occasional asthma, and periodic insomnia. Depression is not yet a common diagnosis. The only label to mention symptoms is the "Codeine Cough Syrup," suggesting "2 Tsp for persistent cough or at bedtime." All the medicine labels have two identifiers in common: the name of the local pharmacy and the name of her doctor-brother in Greenwich.

David gathers up the food-caked dishes and puts an empty liquor bottle under his arm and leaves the room. Helen's hibernation in the lightless room is now her normal state.

The following morning before he heads outside to help Paul and his stepfather reset the patio flagstones that were badly heaved by the previous winter's frost, he again stops in to see his mother. She is drinking the coffee Juliette has brought her and appears alert as she peruses a Sears catalog.

"You feel any better?" David asks.

"Better than yesterday," she answers, looking up. "Where have you been all this time? Is your job over?"

"Not yet, I have one more and then it's over. It's hard work, but I've learned a lot and I like the guys."

"That always helps," she allows as her eyes again lower to the open catalog in front of her.

"Are you okay, Mom? I never know how sick you are. Can you get up?" David asks, feeling a twinge of unexpected anger.

"Sometimes, it depends on how I feel," she says, without looking up.

"Do you really need all this medicine?" he asks, surprising himself.

"Don't judge me. You've never been sick. You don't even know what it is to be sick. Neither does your grandmother who always 'asks after me,' according to you."

"So you're gonna stay in bed and drink and take your brother's drugs?" he half-shouts.

Knowing he has crossed a line and realizing more with fear than anger that he cannot retract his outburst he turns on his heels and walks out, as the Sears catalog lands behind him at his feet.

Out front he sees Cécile Collette riding by on her two-wheeler and notices for the first time she has outgrown her childhood. Watching her pedal-pump up the hill, he remembers his encounter with Tina Curlin and without a further thought finds her father's number in the phone-book and dials.

"Who's it?" ends the brief succession of rings.

"Tina home?" he asks the female voice.

"Who wants ta know?" comes back the response.

"Tell her David is calling." The phone goes silent and he waits.

"I didn't think you'd call. I thought I'd scared you off."

"No, I was in the woods," he responds.

"With who?" she laughs.

"It's just my summer job."

"Still wanna go riding?" she asks.

"Sure, I've got four days off before I have to go back to work in Island Pond for the last time."

"Come on up tomorrow afternoon. You know where our farm is in the Hollow?"

"I think so. Isn't it the white farmhouse with a big porch below Farnham's Hill with the apple trees on the right?"

"That's it."

"See you around two"

"Wear jeans."

The phone returns a dial tone. He hangs there for a few minutes as the phone buzzes. He sees Tina again leaning against the paddock fence next to him in her jeans with strands of hay still in her hair.

The next day, he heads off in his black VW bug. Through the wid-ening rust holes in the sheet metal floor, he can see the dirt road change to asphalt as he veers onto Route 100 toward Stowe. The Hollow Road leads up into the backcountry at the base of the Worcester Range. A few persistent hill farmers, not yet fallen prey to urban skiers looking for quaint farms or ski clubs looking for cheap accommodation during the season, still eke out a living.

The road winds by the base of Farnham Hill. The disheveled white farmhouse he remembered as the Curlin Farm sits near a grove of ancient unpruned apple trees spiked with water shoots and rich with small apples long since abandoned to the abundant population of deer. Local hunters use the abandoned orchard as an observation point to assess and track bucks for later in the season.

He parks in the yard next to an old Dodge Power Wagon stripped to its frame but with a newish hardwood bed and rusted winch assembly. A few other hulks are settled into the boggy lawn between the porch and Gold Brook, which runs by the house a few yards away. Tina steps out on the sloping porch as he climbs the steps and greets him with a beguiling smile.

"No trouble finding the place?" she asks.

"No, I remembered it from when we used to fish in Gold Brook and from going up to the Marsters' swimming hole when they were away."

"You don't have any riding boots, I guess," she says, looking ruefully at his worn penny loafers.

"These'll have to do," he apologizes. "I told you I don't ride much."

"Well, let's saddle up Becky for you, and Favreau for me."

"Favreau. That's a fancy name for a horse. He or she from France?" he asks, smiling.

"No. He's a gelding named after my Uncle Favreau on my mother's side. That was her maiden name."

"How is your dad?" he asks.

"He's okay when he's not drinking," she answers matter-of-factly.

Tina hands him a western saddle and indicates a chestnut mare with a toss of her head.

David heaves the saddle into place and cinches the sheepskin-lined girths. He then lowers his stirrups and turns to watch Tina do the same. She's wearing dark caramel riding boots, tight jeans and a partially unbuttoned white blouse. The décolletage frames her loosely confined breasts, which shift beneath her blouse as she tosses the saddle onto Favreau's broad back. Tina then leads both horses into the yard and tethers their bridles to the remains of a post-and-rail fence. Becky's mouth fills with white foam as she worries the chrome bit in her mouth. Favreau is motionless. Tina disappears into the house. David hears a baby crying inside. An older woman raises her voice and the crying stops. Tina emerges with a wineskin hanging from her shoulder, runs down the steps, skipping several, untethers both horses, tosses him his reins, and swings herself up onto her horse. David mounts his horse after a couple of trial thrusts with his right leg.

"You'll be fine. Becky's a sweetheart. Just follow me for now until we get up into the hills."

The riders pass through the orchard and begin to climb slowly, zig-zagging up the hill behind the farmhouse as they follow a barely discernible path into an old, sparse stand of sugar maples high above the farm.

"Dad used to sugar here until the bank finally took back the evaporator. He could only make his payments for five months after boiling when he was selling to the ski lodges. It was okay as long as he made double payments to cover the other seven months, but the second year, it warmed up so fast in March that the sap stopped running early and Dad only made about seventy gallons. That meant he could only make his payments for three months. Poor bastard gave all the money to the bank from his sugar sales, even when we needed it. Dad was never any good with money ... always full of ideas ... worked hard but never knew which bills to pay when ... paid whoever yelled loudest and lent money to anyone who asked him."

"How many brothers and sisters do you have?" David asks, hoping the question will detour the conversation away from the family's hardships.

"Three now," she answers, without looking around. "Mom and Dad, bein' raised Catholic, never took to, you know, birth control and God knows couldn't imagine abstinence ... The family just kept growing when I was young ... seemed like there was always one in the oven. One died of that sudden infant death thing right in her crib and another, Johnny, was given to my Aunt to raise over in upstate New York. She couldn't have kids and we couldn't take care of what we had. So now, it's just me, Andy, Jenny and Emma. Andy'll be outta here as fast as she can ... already's got a serious beau chasin' her."

He smiles, remembering the earnest disquisition of Sister Lamoureux in catechism about purity of thought and abstinence. She seemed barely old enough to understand the latter subject herself and yet was the quintessence of the former in her black habit. She was an extraordinary beauty even though her radiant light skin was evident only within the confines of the stiff wimple that framed her face and pressed into her temples. The cognitive dissonance between her strict articulations on moral rectitude in catechism and the sensual beauty of her smile when she led them in prayer with her hands pressed together between her breasts left the girls enraptured, imagining their own saintly virginity and the garrulous boys torn between hope of salvation and their lascivious fantasies about her.

"Mom had the late life surprise when Emma was born last year," Tina continues. As they emerge from the stand of maples, many with rusty taps still in place, they come into a clearing with a small brook running through on their left. The brook has been dammed with fieldstones to create a backwater deep enough to allow animals to drink.

"Let's let the horses drink," Tina says, dismounting in one move and setting the wineskin on the moss.

He follows suit and both lead their horses over to the brook. "No need to tether 'em, they won't wander away," Tina says, sitting down on a mound of moss near the brook and spreading out her long legs.

"Sit down and tell me who you are," she says, taking a shot from the wineskin and handing it to him. "Have some. Nothing fancy."

"I often wonder," he answers, taking the wineskin.

"You grew up in Mo'ville didn't you?"

"Yeah, from the age of two."

"Your dad used to be an instructor at the mountain, I saw Alain on weekends ... handsome guy."

"That's right. Then he settled into his management job in Eden at the asbestos mine. What does your dad do?" he asks.

"Whatever he can. Right now he's a hired hand at the Gale Farm on the Mountain Road and keeps a lot of their equipment runnin'. Won't milk, though – draws the line at pullin' teat. We all worked as soon as we were old enough. Lotta mouths to feed," she answers bluntly. "He's started drinking again, though, and missin' work. I'm not lookin' forward to him losing his job 'cause Mom's sugar's gettin' worse."

"Sorry," David says, lying back and staring up into the crowns of the nearby maple trees. Tina rolls onto her side with her chin cupped in her hand to look at him.

"Bet some of these trees are over a hundred years old," he observes, "That one over there must be a hundred feet. Look at all the old taps still in it. Bitch hitting sugar taps with your chainsaw ... ruin the chain."

"My grandfather used to tap these trees," Tina observes.

"Do you teach or patrol?" he asks.

"Both ... whatever they want," she answers. I'm never sure when I get there for the milk run what I'll be doing that day. My favorite time, though, is dusk. We all trail-sweep after the lift closes and the mountain is empty. Far below, I can see the stream of headlights leaving and winding down through the valley. The sun sets quickly in winter and I feel alone on the mountain. On the last run, I can hear the stillness and the tree limbs creaking as the temperature drops with the sun. By the time I reach the base lodge, it's often dark ... best time of day."

She asks about David's summer job and he tells her about the black flies and how sometimes they run out of fly dope and just rub gas on their arms. How at the end of the day, it would often be an hour or so before they could hear one another without shouting, after the din of the saws stopped ringing in their ears. He tells her about the tall hemlock that fell on Ray when the wind caught it and how, when they finally cleared the brush away and found him, he pretended to be dead, and how angry they all were when he opened his eyes and winked at them.

Through the branches he watches two red-tailed hawks gyre in the sky. One suddenly plummets to the open meadow and, just as suddenly, flies off, pumping its wings with a baby rabbit in its talons. Both hear the shriek of the prey.

She tells David how once they saw from the window in their kitchen in late winter a pack of wild dogs running down an exhausted doe whose sharp hooves penetrated the deep snow, making escape impossible, while the dogs ran on the surface with their spreading paws. And how, after a hard winter, the deer herd is weakened from lack of food

229

and many fall prey to wild dogs.

As he tells her of his hope of one day owning a team of draft horses, she drops her elbow and rolls toward him, kissing him long on the lips. Her lips seek his neck and his chest, and then return to his mouth. He has never been kissed this way. Fear and pleasure rise in him and he doesn't know how to reciprocate.

"Just relax," she whispers. "I'll do all the work. Just enjoy yourself."

"I can't," he mutters.

"Yes, you can," she whispers.

"What if we get pregnant?" he says.

"I can promise you, you won't," she whispers back. "Take it easy, it's fun."

"I have to go," he says.

She rolls onto her back.

"You don't want me?"

"Of course, I do," he answers.

"I'm not pretty?"

"You're beautiful," he stammers.

"Then why are you leaving?"

"I promised I'd be back."

"Promised who?"

"My mother," he answers, embarrassed.

"Is she prettier than me?" she retorts archly.

"It's not that," he allows, embarrassed. "It's just that I've never ...."

"I know. It's all right. It's fun. I'll show you," she urges.

David gets to his feet. "You are the most beautiful person I've ever seen. I would love to, but I can't. I have to go."

And with that he walks down the hill toward the farm, leaving his horse with Tina. Lying back on the moss, she calls after him, "See you soon."

The horse's nibble at the short grass near the brook. Tina hums a Hank Williams tune and watches squirrels chasing one another in the maple branches high above.

Half an hour passes and Tina is drowsing off in the warm sun when she hears David yelling to her from the meadow below.

"Have you seen my car key? I thought I left it in the car, but I must'a put it in my pocket and dropped it. I've been looking all along the path we took. I always leave it in the car."

"Yup," she answers.

"Where is it?" he answers, breathless from the long uphill hike. He squats down next to her. "Did you find it?"

"You're lookin' right at it," she says.

"I don't get it. I really do have to get home."

"I know. But you'll have to find your key first," she says with a beguiling smile.

"I don't understand."

"It's inside me," she smiles softly, "Yours for the taking."

<hr>

As the sun set over the Worcester Range, David and Tina ride down through the glade toward the farm. At the house, Tina puts the horses in the barn while David waits nervously to say goodbye and wonders if he should ask to see her again. He feels weak in the knees.

"Come on inside and meet my youngest sister," she says when she returns from the barn, "I know your Mom is waiting for you, but she can wait another few minutes."

With a hard pull, the warped screen door opens into an expansive kitchen, dominated by a large wood cookstove and an oak dining table with a number of mismatched chairs. An infant sits in a highchair, eating mashed peas and rice with her hands. She is watched over by a girl slightly younger than Tina.

"Meet my younger and nicer sis, Andy. Andy, this is David, he's from Mo'ville. I've just been teaching him to ride. Jenny's still at school. That's Emma in the high chair, she's my newest sister."

Andy is about 17 and shares her sister's beauty, although her features are sharper and her hair considerably darker. A woman well into her fifties ambles in from the living room in men's pants and a man's denim work shirt. A radio drones in the background.

"Say hi to David, Mom. We been ridin' in the high meadow."

"I 'spect you have," she says matter-of-factly. Without looking up, she pours herself some coffee from the dappled enamel coffee pot on the stove. "Wan' some coffee?"

"No, thanks, Mrs. Curlin, I gotta get home and get ready for work up in Island Pond."

"What you do up there?" she asks.

"Work on a chainsaw crew."

"Dangerous work," she mutters, again without looking up. "You best take care."

"I will," he answers.

Emma bangs her cup on the wood tray that confines her in the high chair.

"Got to head out. Nice to meet you all. See you soon," he says to Tina. She follows him out to the car.

"Don't be a stranger. Call me."

"I will when I get back in two weeks," he answers.

"I like you," Tina says, sticking her head inside the VW window with a broad smile.

"Me, too," he answers.

Later that week, while limbing a downed white pine, it occurs to him that Mrs. Curlin is too old to be Emma's mother.

On his next furlough, there is a message from Tina written on the notepad next to the phone. Paul has taken the message. It says only, "Call Tina." Juliette has drawn a small heart next to the message.

He sees Tina a few more times to revel in her sexual reign over him. Under her tutelage he discovers the far corners of his own pleasure and in time discovers hers. He was not prepared for the richness and complexity of physical pleasure. His younger self tried in vain to imagine the naked bodies maturing beneath the shorts and blouses of Annie Foss and Cécile Collette as they grew into young women. His embarrassing encounter with his cousin Terry whetted his appetite for sexual discovery, but did little to inform him of its panoply of pleasure-stimulating movements. He and Tina, however, soon exhaust their few post-coital topics of conversation and each time he leaves her sooner.

His last visit troubles him deeply. Tina's parents are at a barn dance in Huntington and won't be home until the next day. As is often the case, Tina is left in charge of Jenny and Emma. Tina invites David to spend the night. In the middle of the night, a violent thunderstorm blows in from deep within the Worcester Range. The lowering storm clouds go black shortly before dusk. The storm rains torrents of water and bolts lightning down around the farmhouse, rending an old maple in the grove farther up the hill. The lightning strikes light up the mountainous landscape and are followed by pane-rattling claps of thunder. During the storm, Tina's younger sister Jenny has, unbeknownst to either, climbed into bed with them and fallen asleep.

In the predawn hours, David wakes to a gentle probing touch on his penis. He opens his eyes and looks at Tina who is dead to the world and snoring softly. He discovers Jenny between them, sees the quizzical look on her face and realizes that the curious small fingers touching him are not Tina's, but those of her twelve-year old sister. He removes her hand gently, gets up quietly, dresses, and leaves without waking Tina.

Mrs. Roleau and Sylvie

David is again staring at the quilted landscape that is his mother. She lies with her back to him as he stands in the doorway listening to the sudden and irregular inhalations of air symptomatic of the asthma she suffered as a child that has recurred after years of smoking Alpine cigarettes. He's come in to tell her that he's made lunch, but understands, even as he enters, the futility of his invitation. On her bedside table beside the medicine vials is a jumble of dirty dishes from her occasional forays into the kitchen.

He turns to leave when he hears, "You want something?"

"I thought you might want to come in for lunch."

"What made you think that?"

"Bitch day among the medicines?" he asks, taken aback by his own response.

He turns to leave.

"Wait a minute," she whispers.

"I'm going to have lunch with Dad," he answers.

"He's used to eating alone," she whispers hoarsely.

"Since you never cook or eat with us, I suspect he is," David fires back, again surprised by the free rein his anger has taken.

"I know you're furious with me even though you try to hide it."

"You're rarely conscious. When would I have the chance to be angry?"

David hasn't moved from the doorway. With difficulty, his mother turns to face him. He sees the pale blue arteries around her mouth, eyes and forehead and how her brown hair has thinned.

"You okay?" he asks quietly.

"As good as I get," she answers. "My breathing troubles don't help and the medicines don't do much good."

"They must do something or you wouldn't eat them like candy," David hears himself say, now more afraid of his anger than hers. His outburst is answered only by his mother's labored breathing. David stands in the doorway looking at his mother; her eyes don't meet his. He understands that the frail woman lying there and fighting for breath can no longer hurt him.

"You never knew my mother, did you?"

David doesn't answer.

"She was a fiercely intelligent woman, but, in time, her intellect became little more than a weapon. She was a lonely woman, lost in her great knowledge of languages and distant people. I doubt she was ever loved by her parents. Her sex may have been a disappointment to my grandfather, who arranged her marriage to my father. I always suspected my grandfather chose him for a son-in-law because, like grandfather, he'd learned architecture at the Beaux-Arts and my grandfather thought he might someday take over the firm. My grandfather was a

234

well-known builder of bridges and buildings, but by the time my father and mother were married, Papa was more interested in the drawing and painting he learned in Paris than in architecture. My mother knew nothing of how to love or how to be loved. I have only one picture of her as a little girl, and I cry every time I look at it. "

She withdraws a small gilt-framed photo from her bedside table drawer and hands it to David.

The picture is posed. The girl astride a chestnut bay is about twelve.

"She never spoke to me of riding in the way that young girls who love horses do," his mother adds.

David looks at the girl in the picture. His other grandmother is seated on a large mare, a good 16 hands. Her long hair is done up in a single braid like the horse's tail. She seems daunted by the large horse or at least worried that it might move before the picture is taken. She sits side-saddle, wearing a long white pinafore with large lapels.

"Was she afraid of that horse or just of riding?" David asks.

"There's no way to tell. I know enough about riding to know that little girls don't ride horses dressed this way except for show. Even back then young girls wore jodhpurs."

The horse's left eye looks at the camera. The girl is looking down at the horse, perhaps afraid that it might walk out of the picture with her.

In the background, the girl's father stands in a black, wide-lapel suit with his arms akimbo. Lying on the grass at his feet is a Russian wolfhound, looking up at him. Behind him is the red stone house he has designed and built for his wife, son, and daughter. It looks like a fortress, ominous in the weight of its stone. There are turrets in the middle and at each end. It sits alone on a barren shore. There are no other buildings in the camera's view. He appears proud of the house he has designed and had others build. His dog, the horse, and his daughter are the only landscape elements. There are no trees or gardens yet. The house is new and he will soon move his small family into all those rooms. The blades of a windmill rise behind the roofline.

Uncomfortable standing next to his parents' bed, David sits down on his father's side of the bed. He has never heard his mother talk about her childhood. She stops now and he hears only her labored breathing. He realizes she has gone back to her dreams. He stands up and goes into the dining room where a sandwich lunch is in progress.

"Is Mom okay?" his stepfather asks.

"I guess so," David answers. "She told me a story about her mother."

The topic changes to chores of the afternoon and who will mow the lawn.

That night at dinner Alain mentions that Pudge Roleau's been arrested and taken to the State Hospital in Waterbury for evaluation. He doesn't give details of the crime but it's long known in the community that Pudge's sexual attraction to children will eventually lead to trouble. David has heard several stories circulating among the kids in town, but his stepfather's news is the first time he hears an adult confirm the rumors of Pudge's proclivities. Alain says little more than that he's been arrested. Now Mrs. Roleau is alone, as Glenn, her other son, drowned in Lake Elmore.

The news of Pudge's arrest reminds David of the dream he had earlier on the train ride home wherein he saw Mrs. Roleau on the shore flailing her arms and crying loudly to Glenn, the State Police diver finning through the murky depths far below the diving raft and the pale light filtering down through the greenish water with the shadow of the raft bobbing above. He sees again the police diver come suddenly upon Glenn's pale body in the undulating weeds. He remembers how white Glenn's surprised face looked in the dream and the dark blue of his lips and eye sockets. The pallor reminds him of the vitiligo affecting Glenn's brother Pudge, with the pied blotches of unpigmented skin on his arms, hands and face.

He excuses himself and takes an armload of dishes into the kitchen, where he leaves them on the drainboard. It's Paul's night to do dishes.

The late summer light persists now well into the evening and David walks up the hill past Mr. Farr's farm and then past the now empty barn and silos of the Stewart farm. Mrs. Roleau's house lies just beyond, on the edge of one of the Stewarts' fallow hayfields. The Depression-era cottage with its sagging front porch was built by Ned and Lyle Stewart for Pud Roleau when he crossed the border from Venise-en-Québec with his bride to sign on as a hired hand. It was understood that when the immigrant couple gave birth to boys, they, too, would work for the Stewart family and that they might even be able to find a place for a girl, who could help Mabel Stewart with fall canning, candling and packing eggs, and slaughtering chickens. The Roleaus eventually gave birth to two sons and, taking Ned's advice, gave them names that wouldn't carry the "Canuck taint." Glenn was named after the immigration official in St. Albans who had issued the papers enabling their entry, and Pudge was named after his own father who had died not long after his birth. The "ge" was added as he amassed considerable weight during his early teen years.

David climbs the three steps up to the porch, careful to walk near the edge where the sagging boards are still supported by stringers. The rotting sills have long since stopped holding up the house's settling frame and the front screen door no longer closes because of its warped jamb. The inner door is held open by a sad iron. Before he can knock, he hears from inside, "I ain't receivin'."

"It's jus' me," he says.

"Oh, c'min, I'se 'spectin' the law agin."

He enters the small living room. Mrs. Roleau sits in her husband's rocking chair with her favorite hen in her lap. Three other hens perch on the back of the couch. Mrs. Farr had given the hens to Mrs. Roleau so she could have eggs when the Stewarts sold off their animals. They were Mrs. Farr's favorite layers, Orpingtons. The buff-colored hen sits perfectly still in Mrs. Roleau's lap. Mrs. Roleau keeps the bird with her wherever she goes.

"I'm real sorry about Pudge," he starts.

"It's OK, I see'd it comin'," she answers, stroking the hen in her lap. "I tol' the mens I knew they'd be comin' fer 'im. He wan't roight in the head when it come ta 'em li'l girls. His pepère 'uz like 'at, too, but kep' it unner control mostly. Now I'se alone 'cept for Sylvie here. She makes fer comp'ny.

"I'm sorry. Is 'ere anything I can do?" he asks.

"Willard's been good ta me. He's th'overseer o' the poor, don'cha know. Good man. I ain't gonna go 'ungry or nuthin'; 'sides I got all th' eggs I can eat." She smiles and nods toward the three hens perched on the back of the couch.

"Well I jus' wanted to say I'm sorry and to let you know that if you ever need any help here to let me know," David concludes, standing up.

"I be okay, though I can't 'ford no store-bought goods. Gladys checks on me 'casional and brings me butter and jams and some o' their fer-laters."

"I'll check in on you, too." David says, backing out the door onto the porch. As he turns to negotiate the stairs, he hears Mrs. Roleau comment to Sylvie, "Good brought-up boy." He walks home down the gravel road in the dark.

Last Visit

At home, the house is quiet. His mother is in her bedroom and his stepfather is reading the paper on the couch.

"Your grandmother called," he says without looking up, "Wants to talk to you about your postponing college and working for a while. She's not happy. I'm leaving this one to you. You're old enough now to sort it out with her. I've been in the middle for too long ... your turn now. You're almost twenty."

David shakes his head without replying and goes to his room.

His decision to work and postpone college along with his silence about his father's letters, have again emerged as issues between them. David thought their shipboard discussion laid the matter to rest but his grandmother's recent decision to vacate her eighteen-room duplex after

Margaret retired retrieved myriad unresolved memories. Called upon to decide the fate of every object in her vast apartment, earlier resolutions and conclusions are again subject to review.

Alain believes his son must now become a man commensurate with his years and has declared neutrality about the book, college attendance, financial matters and all the issues Dorothy raises on her grandson's behalf.

Several times since his trip with his grandmother, David has taken the book down and tried to read it as one would read a novel, beginning at the beginning and reading through to the end, but, after a few letters, he invariably lays down the book and picks up something else to distract him from the cheerless narrative and condescending tone of the man who was to be his father.

August 15, 1944

I don't know whether I ever mentioned it before, but the reason you couldn't find your toothbrush the morning I left is, because, in the excitement, I swept everything off the bathroom shelf into my briefcase. Your toothbrush is with me now, on the shelf next to me. Glancing at it occasionally fills me with the most maudlin sentimentality. I wonder if possibly I'm not the first warrior in history to take his lady's toothbrush into battle.

Another little item on the lighter side; a sentence in your last letter, No.5, in which you state, "I am sitting under an apple tree and there is not a sole around," comes to mind. Darling, whatever would a sole be doing under an apple tree? In the first place he couldn't breathe out of water. Sole, Puppy, is what you have a filet of. That part of you which is immortal is the soul, (note a "u" is inserted between the "o" and "l", and the final "e" is omitted).

I continue to dream of our future life together, only now, my dreams are less specific. I no longer require a rustic setting and a blue summer sky. Just being with you, Puppy, is a dream enough for ten guys. I'm not that sick and miserable every minute without you. Actually, I've made a pretty good adjustment, but it's an adjustment to a lousy situation, like getting used to having diphtheria.

Hang on to us, darling, and be careful. Don't risk any part of our future unnecessarily. If anything is troubling you, ever, write it to me immediately. I would be a hell of a sight happier knowing that I knew exactly what was going on in your heart, than I would ever be trying to guess what you were sparing me in a cheerful letter ...

The letter ends there. He drops the book on the floor next to his bed and tries to imagine what his grandmother wants of him. He can neither muster nor feign what she feels, reading her son's letters. He wonders if she even remembers their conversation aboard the *Queen*.

Their last call was laden with veiled recriminations about money wasted on prep school and foreign travel, and the importance of a college education in "making a go of it." She tipped an old, and he hoped forgotten, hand, referring to "the risk of David being stuck for the rest of his life in a rural backwater with no prospects of success." He didn't take the bait.

Alain keeps out of it and watches the rift deepen. Dorothy has written to him several times to enlist his parental support. Alain's brief and diplomatic responses acknowledge the importance of college, regretting he never had the opportunity to attend one, but he evades her contention that college must follow boarding school immediately and gently confirms his belief that David is now a man and, as such, must make and live with his own decisions. Privately, he wonders about the impact of inherited wealth on the ability of boys to become men.

David's mother stopped communicating with her mother-in-law when she insisted that David go to boarding school, blaming her for yet another loss.

David regrets not having taken the train. For what may be his last visit to see his grandmother, Eugénie has lent him her rusting Rambler American. She insisted he take it, saying that there were only 5,800 miles on it, she'd had it for eight years, and it needed to be driven more. David slips his valise into the back seat of the Rambler and notices the thermos of coffee Eugénie has left for him on the front seat. It is 4:30 A.M. and he sees the light on in her kitchen. His stepfather's encouragements do little this time to diminish his dread of the trip and the inchoate malaise he feels as he drives south on Route 100 before dawn.

Vermont's longest road winds down through the shadows of the Green Mountains and is said to have more deer crossing it in a day than there are cars anywhere along its 150 miles. He stares at the cones of yellowish light ahead, alert for the familiar stance he has seen so often through the scope of his Uncle Maurice's Mauser. He remembers from an illegal night hunt with Tommy Bates how deer, transfixed by bright light, remain motionless ... "like a deer in the headlights," Tommy says.

It's been five years since he last saw his grandmother, and he remembers how much she seemed to enjoy his company as they made their way through the capitals of Europe. Their recent phone conversations, though less contentious about David's efforts to explain himself and his choices, are now met more with silence than rebuttal. There is too much on which they have disagreed.

He remembers his last voyage on the train – although it is only that in name now – a diesel engine and two coaches running chronically late as it sat on sidings, waiting for more lucrative, long-haul freights to roll by, or slowed to a crawl along the 20-mile-an-hour stretches of track subsiding into the banks of the Winooski and White rivers on the northern stretch. In contrast, he also remembers his first New York visit by train, seeing the stoker's face in the yellow light from the firebox door as the steam engine chuffed past the platform and stopped by the wooden water tower down the tracks.

The warming rays of sun emerging in the southeast make him sleepy as he winds his way through the second-growth woods lining the Taconic Parkway. His drowsiness reminds him of the soporific sound of the train rolling through the countryside and of falling asleep with the moonlit landscape panning by the window in his berth, his only worry waking in time to make his stop. Now, he worries about the folded map sitting on the passenger seat on which his stepfather has carefully traced the route to New York and the page of directions on how to get to his grandmother's new apartment from the end of the Taconic in White Plains. His stepfather's handwriting is crisp, written in block letters rather than the florid script he was taught in convent school.

David enters the city a little after noon. The trip was easier than he anticipated. He gets lost only once, crossing the Willis Avenue Bridge into Manhattan and getting off in Harlem instead of onto the East River Drive. There he remembers moving through the black neighborhoods from the safety of an elevated train and looking down on the street dramas playing out below. Now he is in the street among the inhabitants, stopped by a succession of traffic lights. He reaches across and behind him and pushes the brown lock buttons into their doors. He watches two men in disheveled blue suits mimicking a loose buck and wing with brown bags dangling from their right hands, a young girl skipping rope farther down the block while a dog sniffs at a display of melons and is chased away by a white man in a white apron.

He is jarred by a chorus of car horns behind him and realizes the light has changed. He learns the city's urgency at changing traffic lights, though it is not his own. Just as seven hours earlier he had been alert for deer bounding across the road, he now stares intently at the traffic lights, beginning to creep forward as the opposing light changes to yellow, and then accelerating swiftly when he sees green, all to avoid the wrath of cabbies surrounding him. There are no traffic signals at home – only stop signs.

Alain taught him to drive, instilling in him the goal of driving smoothly, both for the comfort of his passengers and the durability of the drive train. Neither is of any concern in this fast-paced city.

It takes an hour from the end of the Taconic to his grandmother's new apartment on 55th street near the East River. David is no longer distracted by the street activity and finds a place to park quite easily in this wealthier enclave. A maroon awning shades the entrance to 435 East 55th and a young doorman is sorting mail just inside the glass door.

David mentions his grandmother's name and is asked by the doorman, who does not look up, if his grandmother is expecting him. David answers, "Yes." The doorman then asks for her apartment number, which he doesn't know, as he has not yet visited her at her new address. This confirms the doorman's perception, suggested also by the stranger's clothes, that he is from away, so the doorman calls up to the apartment to announce the arrival and to confirm that the young man is expected.

"9D," he is told with a sideways nod toward the single elevator.

He is alone in the electric self-service cab and recalls with a smile his fascination with elevators as the air around him is again disturbed by the cab's ascent. This time, though, he watches the floor numbers scroll by on a mechanical readout rather than on the landings. When the door opens, he steps into a long corridor with seven apartment entrances. He finds 9D at the far end and pushes the black doorbell.

An elderly Asian man answers the door and gestures him in. David says, "Hello," to which the man responded, "I am Ha." David follows Ha down a narrow hallway into a living room where his grandmother is sitting in an upholstered chair. Ha nods toward her and then disappears, walking backward and still smiling.

His grandmother is wearing a long, gold sateen dressing gown that flows from her shoulders down to her matching slippers and around much of the chair, camouflaging the profile her diminished body makes in the chair. She is smiling, but says nothing. She extends a cheek to receive his kiss and nods to an armchair nearby.

"Tell me, how was your trip? Not too long and arduous, I hope?" she whispers. He is unaccustomed to her voice now muted with age.

"It was fine," he answers. "Mom and Dad send their best," he adds, forgetting the former distinction between her son and his stepfather. She seems not to notice.

"You must have left very early," she suggests, looking away.

"It wasn't that bad, since I have to get up at five for work anyway," he responds. "There is very little traffic at that hour and I made good time except when I hit rush hour around Poughkeepsie. I got a bit lost in Harlem."

"Not a very good place to get lost nowadays," she whispers, still looking toward the two windows in the room.

Ha enters the room quietly, carrying a tray with a china tea service and a small plate of shortbread.

"You must be hungry after your long trip," Dorothy says.

"I am," he answers. "How about some chicken livers?" he says in an effort to amuse her, but his effort eludes her.

 Ha pours two cups of steaming pale tea from the large pot whose red and white pattern David remembers from his earlier visits. He adds milk to his tea and helps himself to a biscuit. His grandmother asks if he would like anything else to eat and he asks if she has any fruit. He cannot make out what she says to Ha, but he smiles, bows, and goes out, leaving the tray on the table in front of her.

"Tell me, how is your mother?" she asks. He thinks for a minute, realizing to his surprise that he doesn't know the answer, and says, "She is doing well, thanks. She stays very busy."

"What does she do?" his grandmother responds. He is caught with no answer and says simply, "She reads a lot."

"What does she read?"

"Novels mostly, I think."

"By whom?" she asks, seeming for the first time to be interested in a response.

He realizes that he is caught in a maze and can find no way out.

"I guess I don't know," he answers. "Her bedroom is always filled with books," he lies. His mind's eye sees the array of pill vials, liquor bottles and empty dishes on her bedside table. "I haven't looked at the titles."

His grandmother relents on this line of inquiry, asking after his half-brother and sister, although she has forgotten their names.

He fills the unexpected silence with stories of Paul and Juliette's accomplishments in school, his stepfather's job at the mines, his own jobs working for various farmers and in the woods.

His grandmother looks at him as he speaks, occasionally breaking eye contact to look out the two windows toward the East River. He uses these extended silences to look around the sitting room.

Over a small settee hangs the familiar painting of the blue Madonna cradling the Christ child. The painting fills him with a familiar longing. Elsewhere in the room, he sees other objects from his grandmother's former apartment. The Early American furniture from the dining room and all the large upholstered pieces from the living room are nowhere to be seen. It suddenly dawns on him how much that is familiar to his grandmother and to himself is gone.

Ha comes in with a platter of sliced fruit, two silver forks and two pale green, clear glass plates that he adds to the tray on the table and then leaves.

"Please have some fruit," his grandmother offers. She takes two mango slices and two sections of grapefruit, saying, "This is all I am having. I have so little appetite these days. I used to be such a hearty eater."

David helps himself from what is left, careful to leave some on the plate.

The room is quiet as they eat. Both David and his grandmother are comfortable now with the prolonged silences in their conversation.

"Many of my finer things and personal things of your grandfather's are in storage. The museums have been after me for years for the two pieces in your grandfather's room, especially the tiger-eye maple chest-on-chest. I finally relented and they are gone. There is so little room here. You must promise me you will go visit them someday. They are like nieces and nephews. I don't go out much now or I would accompany you."

"I will," he answers. "Is the piano gone?"

"That, too, was sold ... to a young composer I am told by Fritz at Steinway, who took the matter in hand. I don't miss my things as much as I thought I would when I moved here. I worried so that I would miss the sound of the grandfather clock's movement and its chimes, but I hear so little now. Ha and I communicate more with gestures than words. This apartment is comfortable and Ha is very good to me. I don't taste things much anymore and his native cooking is suitably nourishing, if a bit bland. As you see, he speaks little English, so I am very much alone when it comes to conversation ... so many of my friends have died."

David listens carefully as she aspirates her spare sentences. He follows the expressions on her face that still bears the familiar makeup, though its application now lacks the finesse of her earlier days and appears slightly garish. He notices how her formerly thick, wavy, brown hair, still drawn back severely into a bun, has grayed and thinned. He can see the pink flesh of her scalp. The bones in her jaw and her sturdy septum are more pronounced, and her concave cheeks seem almost translucent in the sunlight streaming in from the south-facing windows. There is moisture at the corners of her mouth.

As they sit there in the afternoon sun, the obligation to converse diminishes. His grandmother seems lost in her own thoughts as she gazes into the light and he is surprised at how his own anxiety has dissipated on seeing her again. He no longer feels the need to observe the amenities he struggled to remember on earlier visits and she doesn't seem to notice or care.

Her eyes close for a moment and he remembers the look in the eyes of his mother's cat, Bagheera, the day he died. The cat had spent most of its last days curled up on the back of the couch where the sun from the picture window exerted its greatest warmth. Occasionally, Bagheera's eyes would open to assess an unfamiliar noise. David had lost his childhood fear of the black cat. The day before he found Bagheera dead, David lay on the couch with the ancient cat splayed out on his chest. The cat had learned to lie there, but always in a crouch, ready to spring away at the slightest disturbance. David gently massaged the nooks and cranial cavities around the face and ears of the old cat. Looking into the faint amber eyes, he saw nothing, a vacancy. He found Bagheera dead in the morning near the fireplace. When he lifted him off the carpet, he was already rigid in death.

His mother cried inconsolably when he brought her news of the cat's death with her morning coffee.

"Are you tired?" his grandmother asks, interrupting the long silence.

"A bit. Are you?" he asks.

"I am accustomed now to taking a nap. Perhaps you would like to go for a walk if you are not too tired. Beekman Place is not far and there is a nice garden there. You may wish to take a book. So many of my books are gone, but there a few left in the hallway. Feel free to take one with you if you wish."

He waits for her suggestion of which book to take, but it never comes.

Their last few days together pass quickly. David sleeps in what appears to be a den and guestroom with a day bed he recognizes as his grandfather's. They take tray meals together in the living room and talk in the morning until Ha brings the mail. His grandmother opens each piece with a stiletto-shaped, ivory letter opener, saves the envelopes in a pile in her lap, carefully reviews each piece, and sorts them into a correspondence pile or another pile for Miss Forshay, who manages her affairs. Letters from absent friends get her immediate attention. He watches her lips move quietly as she reads a letter to herself, occasionally commenting on the news therein, for which David has little or no context.

After the mail is sorted, she answers personal correspondence from her desk, which has survived the move. As she sits writing, he sees above her the collection of Venetian paperweights and the pale blue stacks of letters tied with ribbon. He recalls being in her library with his legs hanging over the edge of the couch, listening to the faint scratch of her fountain pen and wondering what his friends were doing at home.

At lunch, he is surprised to see a small glass of beer with her chicken salad and buttered rye crackers. She reminisces about her days as a young girl on Long Island, where her family had a country home. Her father owned a brewery in Brooklyn and she recalls having beer with her meals from a very young age. She speaks quietly but with enthusiasm about her family's forays to Lake Placid in July, and the many friends and relatives who summered with them there.

On his last day, Ha enters carrying a stack of photo albums. On previous visits, David has seen albums of his grandfather's family, but few, if any of his grandmother's. He immediately recognizes her sister Rose as a young girl and remembers the curious picture of her in what he guessed was Italy or France, eclipsed by the boy on the bicycle and the girl trying to catch him. As his grandmother describes the fun they often had as children, he imagines Rose at play within the Fragonard paintings.

"Come look," she whispers.

He kneels at her side and looks at the photo indicated by her slender finger. "That is all of us except Henry. Henry was not born yet, perhaps he shouldn't have been, given his sad life ... a remittance man for all practical purposes, he lived somewhere in the South. We never saw him."

In the photo there are two girls similar in age and an infant held upright to the camera by the mother. A governess in a candy-stripe nurse's uniform stands behind the mother looking on but not into the camera. The two girls, perhaps eight and ten, are looking at a large picture book. They wear matching dresses with exaggerated lapels and large bows tied in the center front. They have matching bows in their hair. Their lapels, cuffs, and belts are all studded and match one another. The older girl sits on an elaborately carved straight-back chair with no arms and her sister sits on a low footstool. Each holds one side of the book. They are not looking at the camera, but at an image in the book. The open-mouthed infant looks surprised at the proceedings. Perhaps she is caught off guard by the flash of magnesium. She is wearing a long, white infant dress that extends well below her feet. The top of her dress is frilly around the short sleeves and collar. She has no hair yet. The mother sits back in a rocking chair, holding her baby forward for the camera to see. The mother's abundant but short hair is parted in the middle and sports a bow on the left side. Like her two daughters, she wears a frilly white blouse and a long, pin-striped woolen dress that cascades down to the chair's rockers. She seems pleased with her children and the image of them the camera will preserve.

"Do you know which one is me and which one is my sister Rose?" his grandmother asks softly.

"That is you on the stool and Rose in the chair," he answers.

"Right you are," his grandmother answers, smiling. "We enjoyed one another in those days. I often wonder how we drifted so far apart. Perhaps it's because I married and she did not. I wonder ...." Her voice trails off.

David summons the courage to ask her where the portrait of his father is hanging, the one he remembers over the library fireplace in her old apartment.

"I have put it away for you. It is in storage and will be yours when you are ready for it. When I moved here, I put away the painting of your father and the photographs of him and your grandfather. As I have aged, my eyesight has dimmed somewhat and the images of the two men in my life are clearer in memory than in photographs. When I first moved here and Ha was helping me unpack the mover's boxes, I set the photographs over there on the lower bookshelf, but soon realized that they were not the son and husband I had known. Perhaps it was the sadness in their eyes or your father's naval uniform. I don't know. I finally just had Ha to put them away. They're not as I choose to remember them. I see them every day and no longer need or want their photographs."

David walks down First Avenue to the park at Beekman Place. He sits for a moment on a bench so he might confirm for his grandmother that he has followed her suggestion. The small fenced-in park saddens him and he resumes his walk. He comes across an even smaller park at the east end of 57th Street, just off York Avenue. The paved playground is only slightly larger than the width of the cross-town street. It sports five shade trees, each surrounded by heavily painted cast-iron arch-top fencing. He notices a large bronze bear standing erect amid the trees. A tall fence with spear-like uprights curling inland separates the park from the turbid, mocha-colored East River roiling far below.

David sits down next to a woman moving a stroller back and forth, trying to comfort a little girl crying inside. It is still his habit to greet anyone he meets, so he says hello. Then he remembers that greetings are not common among strangers in the city and might even be construed as forward. The woman, however, seems grateful and returns the greeting with a smile.

As he watches the tugs and barges churn their way upstream against the muscular currents in the river, it occurs to him how, at home, the rare cluster of houses that make up a village are an exception to the expansive wilderness that surrounds them. It is the inverse in the city, however, where the mass of high-rise apartments and brownstones are the wilderness and the small man-made vestiges of nature called "parks" are the civilization.

He nods goodbye to the woman on the bench and walks the two blocks to 55th street, remembering that Ha will be bringing out a tea tray when his grandmother wakes from her nap.

At dinner that evening, his grandmother surprises him by saying, "Your stepfather seems like such a kind man. It is a great sadness to me that you lost your own father, but you were very lucky in your mother's choice of a father for you."

He doesn't know how to respond to his grandmother's observation, saying only, "Yes, Alain is a kind man. I am lucky."

"Your own father had a lot of growing to do, but the war played a part in his becoming a man. Those years are lost to us except in his letters, which you will read someday when you are ready."

He could do little more than nod his head in agreement. Dinner over, his grandmother retires early to call her friend Sylvia Sullivan who, after Ed's death, moved to their farm in Connecticut.

In the morning, David has breakfast with his grandmother. Little is said.

As he leaves, he gives her a long hug. It is the first time he has touched her, other than to kiss a proffered cheek. He is surprised by how little of her remains underneath the house dress. He can feel her collarbone, her shoulder joints, and the prominence of her vertebrae beneath the sateen fabric. The robust flesh he remembers seeing in her bathroom when he was young is gone.

He gets on the FDR Drive a few blocks north of his grandmother's apartment. A well-marked exit off the FDR lands him on the Willis Avenue Bridge and he retraces his route to White Plains where he finds the northbound entrance to the Taconic.

As he enters Putnam County and the woods, he relaxes his grip on Eugénie's deteriorating Rambler. Like all her cars, it is meticulously maintained, but no one has been able to halt the bubbling rust eating its way up the thin sheet metal. As he drives north, he thinks about what has not been said – the topics of so many earlier conversations.

"Jew Boy"

On his next visit to see his mother, he senses an ending as he explains to her that Tina is to have his child and, as is expected, he will marry her. When David enters her dark room, he cannot tell if she is asleep or awake as she lies on her left side facing the curtained window by her bed. Helen knows he has been seeing the young woman known in the community for her love of intractable horses and older men, though she never talks about it with her son.

From the sound of her cough, David knows his mother is awake. He says nothing to her of his doubts about his marriage or his waning interest in Tina. He lies instead about his love for her, tells her only that they will marry as soon as the new priest gives them a date.

Alain, Paul, and Juliette sit nervously in the living room, waiting to hear the outcome of David's conversation with his mother. David emerges from his parents' room and says that his mother's only response was that "he's made his bed and now will have to lie in it." He then goes to his room.

Lying on his bed. He wonders what was going through his mother's mind, whether she will leave her bed to attend his wedding, and, if so, whether she can be counted on to be civil. He remembers with a smile his vain excuse at Tina's first seduction ...

"I promised I'd be home,"

"Promised who?"

"My mother,"

"Is she prettier than me?"

He remembers, too, the advice of his Aunt Rose during one of their last conversations together, on the bench in the atrium of the Frick. She asked him if he had a girl friend. Somewhat embarrassed, he tried to describe dispassionately his interest in Annie Foss. Rose turned to him with a smile, and with her usual candor, said, "It's exciting as they say to go to bed with someone and to experience all that physical thrill of discovery, but remember that you will wake up next to that person, and the real test of your love will be in what you find to say to one another in the morning."

❧

Unlike many of their friends who marry right after high school, David and Tina marry in their mid-twenties but for the same reason: they're about to be parents. Other friends marry for what they believe is love, but at this age, the conflation of love, lust, and need cannot be parsed. David likes Tina well enough but would not have chosen her for a wife had she not been bearing his child.

Father LaFramboise explains to David that one can learn to love and that love is a blessing often understood only in retrospect. Tina, too, is Catholic – though Irish, not French. This increases the pressure on them to legitimize their new child in marriage, as well as Tina's "sister," Emma. Like many young brides, she is "showing" at the wedding Mass.

At Doctor Phil's insistence and despite dissuasive pressure from her male colleagues on the ski patrol and ski school, Tina quits working at the mountain. But the newlyweds cannot afford the loss of her income so, after futile efforts to secure a clerking job at Patch's Market, Adrian's Dry Goods, and Morrill's Department Store, Tina is hired for a desk job at Harte's newly formed fuel oil service, fielding calls from customers and dispatching her boss in his new oil delivery truck to refill tanks around town. Many villagers, weary of the task of loading wood and coal furnaces several times a day, have installed new oil furnaces that eliminate the plague of airborne coal dust settling on the doilies and antimacassars in the parlor or the table linens in the dining room; or the earwigs, spiders, and inchworms carried into the house on firewood from the shed.

Meanwhile, David has maintained contact with his friend Ray, who lives in his pickup and gets his messages from Luanne at her diner in Eden Mills. Ray has recently bought a used skidder as a "parts machine" and offers David a job working in the woods with him, although Ray needs several weeks to put his retired Franklin skidder back into running condition. The hauling arch and grapple blade are serviceable, but the winch motor must be rebuilt and needs a new cable. The 152-horsepower Cummins diesel has 4,800 hours on it, but still has good compression and seems to run fine.

Ray planned to sell his team of Belgians to finance the skidder but his Uncle Estey offers him a loan. Since Uncle Estey's emphysema will kill him in three months and he has no surviving kin, it's clear that the loan to his nephew will never be called.

Ray can now buy the 48-inch tires and Canadian ring chains the skidder needs so he can resume work in the woods and take on David, though he is miserly in the pay he can offer.

With time on his hands, David offers to help his friend rebuild the skidder just for the experience. He knows Ray can't afford to pay him until he begins to sell what they cut in the National Forest in the Worcester Range. Ray has secured a federal permit for salvaging "downs" as well as cutting new-growth hardwoods and any softwood.

Tina and David spend each evening after work in the single-bedroom apartment Eugénie found for them above the Rexall Pharmacy. It's just up the street from the small house where, at 87, she now lives alone. Like many third-story railroad flats, it is cheap, hot in the summer, and cold in the winter.

A small living room with two windows overlooks Portland Street from the building's facade. A narrow corridor runs to the back of the building where a perfunctory kitchen overlooks the back alley and fire escape. The windowless sleeping space and cramped bathroom are in between and accessible from the corridor connecting the front and back. One must climb over the plumbing to get into the shower or to bathe, as the claw-foot porcelain tub only fits lengthwise in the narrow space. Two painted iron pipes running between the bathroom and kitchen provide hot and cold running water.

Two iron radiators beneath the two windows in the living room and two in the kitchen ensure that the bedroom and bath in the middle are cold in the winter but Tina and David don't know this yet as it is still early summer. Tina likes to joke that one could "take a leak, brush one's teeth and bathe all at the same time." David jokes less and less.

Emma still lives with Tina's mother in Stowe Hollow and will until Tina gives birth, at which time they will abandon the pretense around Emma's parentage and Emma will move in with David and Tina.

Neither David nor Tina cooks, so their meals are from cans, boxes, or between slices of bread.

After work, David finds more and more reasons not to return home to his sultry apartment and his increasingly sullen wife. He finds the celery-colored walls and peeling plaster on the high ceilings reminiscent of the hospital where he had his tonsils removed when he was eight. The condensation on the cold-water pipe causes rust to bubble out through the layers of paint.

Sometimes, when he sits in the ladder-back oak chair he has moved from the kitchen into the sitting room and leans out the window overlooking Portland Street below, he imagines himself on one of his grandmother's balconies overlooking the two-way traffic eighteen stories below on Park Avenue with its flower-filled median-gardens.

The traffic on Portland Street, however, is intermittent, a mix of pickups, sedans and the occasional tractor or farm flatbed.

Often after work, David and Ray stop at June's for "a cold one." But now they find it more cost-effective to buy and share a six-pack while returning home in Ray's truck. Another decade will pass before it is against the law to drink and drive. Now it is only illegal to drive drunk. The difference is often hard for Officer Messier to ascertain until he arrives at the scene of an accident.

Sometimes, when their conversation about the day's progress on the skidder wanes, Ray will break into one of his favorite Roy Acuff songs, *The Wreck on the Highway.*

Who did you say it was, brother?
Who was it fell by the way?
When whiskey and blood run together
Did you hear anyone pray?

CHORUS
I didn't hear nobody pray, dear brother
I didn't hear nobody pray
I heard the crash on the highway
But I didn't hear nobody pray.

When I heard the crash on the highway
I knew what it was from the start
I went to the scene of destruction
And a picture was stamped on my heart.

There was whiskey and blood all together
Mixed with glass where they lay
Death played her hand in destruction
But I didn't hear nobody pray.

I wish I could change this sad story
That I am now telling you
But there is no way I can change it
For somebody's life is now through.

Their soul has been called by the Master.
They died in a crash on the way
And I heard the groans of the dying
But I didn't hear nobody pray.

David has come to enjoy the euphoric effect of a few beers with Ray; that is, until he stops drinking and goes home, at which point the euphoria fades into silence or a perfunctory and predictable conversation about one another's day. The tang and effervescence of the first cold beer after a hard day's work in the woods decays and the beer leaves a sour residue in his mouth and stomach. David wonders if this is true of his mother and her taste for whiskey.

David has never been in a fistfight and therefore doesn't know the reach of his anger. He remembers roughhousing on the playground at grade school and its escalating once until a playground monitor intervened. He recalls the look of surprise on his adversary's face, his own pleasurable reaction to the adrenaline and the mutual looks of promised revenge soon forgotten.

David and Ray are drinking at June's. Returning from the Worcester Woods where they've amassed sixty cords of pulpwood, waiting to be trucked to the paper mills of Lancaster, New Hampshire, they finish a six-pack and decide to celebrate with a nightcap at June's. Ray introduces David to the "depth charge," a glass pitcher of Carling's Black Label beer with a shot glass of Johnny Walker Black Label scotch dropped into it and consumed as though the pitcher were a stein. Ray finishes his quickly and leaves to sleep off his fatigue on the oil-stained mattress in the back of his pickup. David stays at the bar and nurses his pitcher slowly, increasingly aware of its effect on him.

He remembers his Aunt Rose's full-throated singing of Alfredo's "Trinke liebchen, trinke schnell" aria from *Die Fledermaus,* as she toasted him with a flute of Champagne during a late supper at Lüchow's after seeing the operetta at the old Met. His aunt was flushed with the telling of her own excitement at being introduced as a girl by her uncle to the operettas of Strauss and Lehar in Vienna. She then leaned toward him and whispered "The gazelle is in the garden again," which David had come to understand meant that his aunt needed the ladies' room.

Sitting alone now at June's bar and nursing the last of the beer-whiskey mix, David smiles at the memory of his Aunt Rose's girlish elation as she sang him the aria in the crowded restaurant.

A loud voice behind him calls his name. Recognizing neither the voice nor the alien accent, he turns to see a blond boy, seemingly too young to be in a bar. He turns back to his drink, ignoring the Austrian accent that calls him a "Jew-boy." Austrians hail only from Stowe and are rarely seen in Morrisville, where the populace holds mostly menial jobs at the Mountain, like loading chairlifts, maintaining Sno-cats, grooming trails, or serving hamburgers. Alain was the rare exception in the early days, rising to the rank of instructor in the mostly Austrian ski school. June comes from behind the bar and orders the newcomer to leave.

David ignores the continuing taunts and takes a long draft from the pitcher in his right hand. Suddenly, he feels himself pulled backward off the barstool and finds himself looking up at his attacker from the floor. He gets to his feet and stares at the stranger, trying in vain to place the face and plumb the stranger's rage. He doesn't understand why he's being called a "Jew-boy," since he's been raised in a Catholic family.

David met Jewish boys while away at school and often wondered why they seemed to be trying to hide their ethnic identity by assuming a Protestant mantle. He assumes that Judaism, like his adopted Catholicism, is a matter of religious choice rather than genetic endowment. He never thought of himself as a Jew, though he understands his biological father was from a German-Jewish family mix of Stieglitzes, Schumanns, Obermeyers and Kuhns.

He asks his attacker what he's talking about, when suddenly a clenched fist hits him high on his right cheek just below his eye.

A wave of alien chemicals floods David's nervous system and, before he's aware of it, he is on the blond boy, hitting him in the face and chest. As is customary in bar fights between two people, bystanders do not intervene, knowing it is better to let men and boys fight through their rage until one or the other exhausts it and loses.

They whisper knowing bets to one another about who will win and who will lose, noting who is in the right and who is in the wrong and also who is weaker and who is stronger. They understand that the good guy doesn't always win. As they nurse their beers, they whisper among themselves and watch in case the apparent winner begins to inflict too much damage on the loser, at which point the fight is broken up.

The blond boy has no more fight in him. David has been pulled off him by a large man in bib overalls he has seen around town but does not know by name. The stranger tells David the fight is over; he has won; and to finish his beer and go home.

David leaves his beer and whiskey on the bar, settles with and apologizes to June and walks up Portland Street to the apartment. The adrenaline and cool night air diminish the effect of the alcohol in his system. From the building's entrance, he looks up at the apartment. The lights are off. He climbs the stairs. Few tenants have anything worth stealing, so apartment doors are hardly ever locked, except for those of widows who live alone or of a single mother who, in desperation, locks her child inside and leaves for an errand or the solace of a tryst.

David is still too agitated to imagine sleep so he draws the hardback chair to the window overlooking Portland Street and sits. There are no streetlights. Nor are there any cars or pedestrians at this hour. Working people have gone to bed and almost everyone in this small town must work.

In the morning, Tina wakes him with a loud question, "What the hell happened to you? You've been in a fight."

David feels the effect of the alcohol he has consumed and the dull ache of the bruises that cover his face and right arm. His pillow and sheets are dotted with the dark red dust of dried blood, and the blood that ran from his nose and lip has left a dark stain on the feather pillow. He explains the night's events to Tina.

She answers only, "Klaus, Emma's father. He's crazy."

Aunt Rose among the Cows

David stops in at Eugénie's for a cup of tea before meeting Ray at the diner. Even though there is no longer any reason for her to rise at 4:30, she does so out of habit and her small apartment is usually filled with the smell of fresh coffee and baked goods warming in the oven.

David has cleaned himself up as much as much as possible, but the purple contusion around his right eye and upper jaw betrays the fight the night before.

"Who won?" asks Eugénie, pouring tea into an ironstone mug.

"I didn't even know the guy," answers David, avoiding the previous evening's story for fear of Eugénie's worrying that he might become yet another one of the profligate male drinkers she has endured in her own family. "He's some old friend of Tina's from the Mountain."

"Yes, she had many."

Eugénie sets a plate with three of her sap doughnuts on the table, sits down, and begins to sip her own milky tea from a small, translucent bone china cup. David doesn't look her in the eye.

"I've been meaning to ask after your grandmother and Aunt Rose? I've never met your grandmother but I remember your Aunt Rose fondly from her visit many years ago. If I remember right, she's the only member of your New York family to visit you up here."

"That's right," David answers with a smile, "Rose always liked an adventure. When I'd see her in New York, she'd always ask me where and how we lived, about my school and my life in Vermont. She was always curious. I don't think my other relatives down there would have liked it here as much as she did. "

Eugénie offers David a doughnut, which he breaks in half and dips into his tea, as his Uncle Benoit showed him on the early morning snow-plow run. David realizes suddenly how many people he knew as a boy are gone.

Eugénie chuckles and asks, "Remember Aunt Rose and Mr. Farr's cows?"

David breaks into a broad smile.

"Ooh. That hurt!" David says, rubbing his jaw.

"Good for you to smile," Eugénie says.

"I sure do remember Aunt Rose. She couldn't be convinced that they weren't dying of thirst. Poor Dad talked all through supper that night trying to convince her that they had plenty of water, but she wouldn't hear of it."

"She could've died of a heart attack. She was pretty frail as I remember her. I often wondered if there was anyone in her life to feed her," adds Eugénie.

"Not sure she lived on food," David answers.

His aunt had come up on the train for a four-day visit when David was ten. By the second day she was sure that the Jersey cows grazing on three sides of her grandnephew's family home were "dying of thirst." Unable to convince her amused hosts of the dire situation, she found a galvanized bucket in the mop closet, filled it with water from an outside tap and headed off through the dew-drenched grass in her slippers to water the cows.

Alain was the first to hear the high-pitched shriek and ran out to find her in what looked like a grand mal seizure. He quickly put together the effect of her wet slippers, her left hand holding onto the tin pail full of water, and her right hand trying to lift the electric fence wire high enough to crawl under.

Doctor Phil was called to the house and examined Aunt Rose as she lay panting on the living room couch.

"She's had a shock," he pronounced to the assembled family, making only a slight effort to conceal the twinkle in his eye and a dawning smile.

"Be sure she has plenty of water – and perhaps, to prevent a recurrence, you should leave the bucket of water in Volney's field until she goes home," Dr. Phil advised.

"As I remember it, there was no charge for the house call," Eugénie concludes with a smile.

"I did love Aunt Rose," David whispers. "She died late last year."

Uncharacteristically, Eugénie asks David about his own life and how he and Tina are doing. David speaks freely to his step-grandmother about the hardships in their life together, but gives Eugénie no reason to believe he's given up. She cautions him that the small pleasures of life, like beer and whiskey, can for some become a yoke they can never shake. She talks about her husband, Clovis, and the great love, energy, and humor in him that finally succumbed to his dependence on alcohol and his love of cigars.

"We try and find ways to diminish the sadness and pain in our lives. Your mother has spent so much of her life trying to hide the pain of your own father's death and, from what Alain says, a very sad and lonely childhood. I've found that if one lives through life's hard times, our childhood fear of dying eventually leaves us and, when our time finally comes, we embrace the end like a friend offering relief."

David looks into Eugénie's rheumy eyes and then at the clock over her kitchen sink.

"I have to meet Ray or I'll be late. Thanks for breakfast. Tina and I will stop by for Sunday breakfast after Mass."

"Stay out of trouble," Eugénie calls to him as the door slams shut.

Deer Hunting

David is again among nuns. He learns from the blue brochure in the waiting room that some of the nurses are from the order of Les Hospitalières de Saint-Joseph and that in 1657 the order established the first Canadian hospital in Montreal's Hôtel-Dieu by charter of Louis XIV. A nun bustles in and out of the obstetrics ward waiting room. He remembers Eugénie frowning when her brother-in-law Benoit made jokes to the kids each time she served her signature pastries, calling them by their French name, *les pets de none,* or nun's farts. The nun has something to tell one of the three men waiting there. The oldest man, betraying little emotion, hears her news and leaves.

Like all his grandfathers, David smokes, and, also like them, he knows that cigarettes will eventually deprive him of his ability to breathe and that he will die if he doesn't stop. Alain, too, is a smoker and offered his three children $100 each if they didn't take up the habit until they were 21, remembering the urging of his teen peers that got him started at fifteen. In spite of the offer, David started while at boarding school. His brother Paul tried smoking with his friends but never took up the habit. Juliette will smoke, but hasn't yet. David has taken up smoking Camels. The other man in the waiting room is smoking, as well. Each awaits the birth of a child but there is no camaraderie.

David doesn't understand why the birthing process takes so long. He is exhausted; his mind is adrift. He remembers his mother's accounts when he was little of her own prolonged labor when he was born and of the crescendos of pain that came with increasing frequency and the endless waiting. She told him of her water breaking in their hotel room, the frantic taxi ride with her nurse and the flow of blood that accompanied him into the world and how difficult it had been for the doctor to staunch it after he was born. When she told him this, she had been drinking and had not emerged from her room for several days. David took from her telling that the difficult birth was his fault.

Half-dreaming, he remembers Sister Geneviève's vain effort to explain *transubstantiation* to her fourth-grade catechism class and how confused he had become at the idea that water and wine and a small white wafer would be transformed during the consecration into the "body and blood of Christ" and then consumed by the priest and communicants. He remembers serving Mass and ringing the bell three times at the consecration. Like most children, he understood it literally, not metaphorically.

❧

The three paper cups of tepid, milky coffee he's been nursing have made restful sleep impossible. His thoughts drift into half-conscious dreams. He remembers hunting with Jimmy Greaves and Tommy Bates. They were hiking high on the Worcester Range with their deer rifles. Tommy carried under his arm his father's Remington .30-06 and Jimmy had his own Mossberg .270. Like Tommy, David had a borrowed rifle, an old military Mauser 98 modified for hunting by his Uncle Maurice, Alain's brother. Inadequate for deer hunting, David owned a Winchester single shot .22 Alain gave him when was twelve over the strong objections of Helen. The rifle had been fun for small game and target practice but now was mostly used by Paul for shooting rats at the dump on Saturday afternoons.

The hunters agreed to bring only four loads each. Climbing through a stand of old and peeling paper birches surrounded by blackberries nearing the end of their season, each spotted bear scat in places where the thorny undergrowth was flattened. Tommy indicated a familiar rock outcropping to the west where Blodgett Peak rose above the rest of the range. Its visibility from every point on the slope made it an ideal rendezvous point so they agreed to split up and hunt alone for the next three hours.

Generally reluctant to hunt with friends, Tommy had spent many days alone in these woods sighting-in bucks before opening day. It was only the third day of deer season and he had plenty of days left to track the six-point buck whose cross-haired image he retained even in his sleep.

Sensing they were too high on the mountain for good deer habitat, David walked down into the mixed hardwoods below. Just to the south, a barely penetrable stand of hemlocks looked like a promising deeryard. The dead lower branches protruding from the trees and lying on the forest floor made quiet progress difficult. Tree branches formed a barrier of overlapping, fixed turnstiles. He found a narrow path into the thicket and almost immediately spotted a spike horn looking anxiously at him. Before he could raise his rifle, the small buck bounded off. David was not disappointed, knowing that Tommy would have disdained such a kill. "Sandwich deer," he called them.

Continuing deeper into the thicket, he came upon a doe with two fawns and, farther in, another buck, which he managed to sight-in with his Mauser. The rack was obscured, however, by an evergreen branch. The buck seemed to sense danger but didn't move. David watched him through the scope. He couldn't get a killing shot from his position behind the animal. He watched while the alert buck assessed its options. Then it bounded away, its white tail disappearing among the hemlocks.

From high above near the ridge line, he heard a rifle report echoing off the mountain. It sounded like Jimmy's Mossberg but he couldn't be sure. It was agreed that a third shot would be a "gathering shot," so, after two more shots, he unbolted his rifle and headed toward the base of the cliff.

Jimmy, it turned out, had shot a doe. The least experienced of the three, he had only one previous kill, a deer that his uncle had wounded with the first shot and Jimmy had tracked and finished off. In his excitement this time, he fired without seeing a rack. Tommy, taking the matter quickly in hand, withdrew a knife from his belt and began field-dressing the twitching doe.

He flopped her onto her back and made a shallow cut from just above her genitals up through the sternum, taking care not to disturb the organs. Her legs were in the air and David noticed an occasional twitch in the hind legs. Tommy pulled open the under-belly wound and turned the carcass sideways as the steaming viscera spilled out onto the moss. There was remarkably little blood. Tommy trimmed away the fat near the spine that secured the intestines and released everything back to and including the doe's anus, which he tied off with a piece of string. He took great care not to rupture her bladder or any of her intestines. He trimmed away the thin diaphragm that separated the abdominal cavity from the chest cavity and then, reaching as far up into her chest as possible, severed the esophagus. In one deft move, he pulled out the heart and lungs and with them came the intestines.

"No need to bury all this. It'll be gone by morning," Tommy announced. "Bobcats, coyotes, fox, 'coons, fishers ... they'll clean up."

"Ya sure?" asked Jimmy. "Don' wanna lose my license and get a fine."

"Don't worry. No trace." Tommy answered, kicking dirt around and pocketing the heart and liver.

"Come on. Let's get 'er down. It'll be dark soon. We can bring 'er to my house. Dad'll have her in the freezer by midnight. I wouldn't recommend hangin' 'er in yer front yard. Sterner may notice she ain't got no antenna," he said, eliciting a faint smile from Jimmy.

A nun approaches David. She leans down so her face is right next to his.

"Are you awake? Your wife had a baby girl. You're a father," she says, her smile framed in the starched white wimple. "It was not an easy birth. Your daughter was transverse so, after some effort to realign her, Dr. Phil decided he needed to go in and get her. Tina had a caesarean section." Dr. Phil will explain it all to you. Both mother and daughter are doing fine. She'll be sore for a few weeks and will need plenty of bed rest. In an hour or so, you can come see her and your new daughter. Do you have a name for her?"

David peels his cheek from the clammy Naugahyde and blinks at the nun, understanding for the first time that he is a father and that his wife has undergone surgery.

Curlin Farm

David and Tina are mostly ready for their new daughter, Jeanette. Tina's mother has lent them a crib. The bassinette Tina had also hoped for was sold in a lawn sale several months earlier. Mrs. Curlin has agreed to keep Emma, for the first few months until Tina is comfortable with her new baby. Eugénie gives the new parents a dozen new cotton diapers and a small patchwork quilt that she sewed together from her rag box. Alain bought a $50 U.S. Savings Bond in Jeanette's name and David's mother has asked David to bring her new granddaughter by when he can. Ray has promised her a used chainsaw when's she's fourteen.

Holding his newborn daughter in his arms evokes in David a yearning he can relate only to his own infancy and latent memories of his mother's more maternal days. He knows it will be up to him and Tina to protect her from the casualties that life presents, to make her feel loved, and that children learn by example. The affection parents show for one another is how children learn and understand about love. He wonders if his daughter has any feelings yet other than sensory ones. He is suddenly aware and fearful of his new responsibility as a father. He tries to replay the sequence of events that led him here but is distracted by a question from Tina, who is asking him to make a run to Patch's to get milk, soup, and bread.

Tina recovers rapidly from surgery, as she has always kept her body in good physical shape and partly because she has to. She has managed to keep her job; a phone connected to Harte's number is installed in their apartment. This means that she must remain in the apartment during working hours to answer it and, when it comes time to feed Jeanette, she must juggle her breast-feeding daughter, the telephone receiver, and her note pad. It is rare, though, that the phone rings while she is caring for Jeanette and she manages well enough to keep the flow of money coming in – small as it is. David is now earning money, but sporadically. Ray is not organized to pay him a weekly salary. He simply divvies up the proceeds of his bulk sales of saw timber, pulp, or firewood. Ray keeps two-thirds and gives David a third, which both deem fair, as Ray must buy fuel, maintain the skidder, his truck, and their two saws.

It's harder for Tina, as only rarely can she escape the stifling apartment. On occasion, Eugénie relieves her for an hour so she can run errands or simply be outdoors. But she is uncomfortable leaving for long, even though Eugénie assures her that she will be fine and takes messages when the phone rings.

Tina's mother's untreated diabetes is taking its toll. She has lost one leg, has limited circulation in the other, and her eyesight is diminished by the "sugar." Watching his children disperse and his spouse's health decline, Tina's father drinks every day now.

Tina's anxiety about assuming responsibility for Emma is augmented by her fear of having soon to care for her wheelchair-bound mother in a small house full of narrow stairways and for her increasingly gadabout father.

David and Tina have no phone so Mrs. Curlin uses the Harte Fuel Oil Company number to reach her daughter. The business is growing and Mr. Harte has had to hire a part-time bookkeeper to keep track of billing and credit. If Tina doesn't reach the phone by the second ring, the new bookkeeper has been instructed to pick up the receiver. After several months of fielding a steady flow of anxious calls from Mrs. Curlin, she complains to Mr. Harte, suggesting that his business would be better served by hiring her fulltime to manage both scheduling and billing.

Mr. Harte is sensitive to his first employee's circumstance, however, and decides only to give her a warning. Tina, in turn, warns her mother that she is jeopardizing her only possible job and begs her to stop calling, but her mother's increasingly dire medical straits and absent husband only compound her fears so she keeps calling.

By fall, Tina is without work. It is a relief not to have the phone to worry about, but now David and Tina no longer make enough to cover monthly costs for rent and utilities. David foregoes his share of beers with Ray to save money, so Ray buys them, saying only "fuel ... regular gas, 2-cycle oil, bar and chain oil, diesel for the skidder and beers for the soul."

It occurs to David to write his grandmother if she is still alive and ask her for help, but realizes their distance now could never be bridged. Her fears for him have been realized even though she knows nothing of his circumstances, his marriage and daughter. If she has died, there's no one to let him know other than Ha, who has no idea how to reach him. Nor is there anyone left in New York he knows to call and ask if she is alive.

He imagines a conversation with his grandmother in which she says nothing. He sees her as she was the last time he saw her, sitting in her gold dressing gown in the sunlight, smiling and looking out the sun-filled window. He remembers her telling him that her "head was filled with images of her past and family and that she no longer needed her photograph albums," which she offered to David and he declined.

David occasionally comes home to find Tina and Jeanette gone. There is no note and in the refrigerator is a casserole or bean pot he recognizes as Eugénie's. One night, returning from an early supper with Alain after a three-day stint in the woods in Island Pond, David finds a note from Tina. Having heard from a neighbor that her mother is bedridden and can no longer see, and that her father has again disappeared, Tina has gone home with Jeanette to care for her mother. She also hears that her sister Jenny, now thirteen, is raising Emma. The note does not say "moved" as there are so few possessions in the apartment that there is little for her to move other than her own few clothes, the crib, and Jeanette's baby things. Her note also says that it would be helpful if David were to come by and bring some groceries. David is now alone in an apartment he can no longer afford and doesn't want. He notifies the landlord that he is moving out and goes back to his room at home. He promises Alain that this is temporary, though Alain is happy to help his stepson.

On Friday, he calls Tina and says he'll be up with some food and asks if she needs anything specific. Their conversation is brief. David borrows Alain's car, picks up a few things at Patch's and heads to Stowe Hollow to see his wife and daughter.

Though familiar with abject poverty, he is shaken by what he finds. The poverty he has seen at Mrs. Roleau's and other hardscrabble farmhouses where his school friends live is marked by neatness and basic hygiene. Tina's former home exudes a miasma of putrefaction and death.

Tina is sitting at a kitchen table filled with dirty dishes. She is in tears and nursing Jeanette. Emma is on the floor, playing with a doll that is missing an arm and Jenny is nowhere to be seen. There is a wide gash in the bottom half of the screen door and an unscreened window in the corner is wide open. Two empty bread bags sit next to a dish of rancid, translucent butter covered with flies. An empty bottle of ketchup lies on its side.

David sets the bag of groceries on the table and looks around. Tina doesn't look up at him. In a rare show of tenderness, David sits down in a chair next to her, puts his arm around her and relieves her of Jeanette. He sees the crib in the corner by the woodstove; grabs it with his other hand and takes it out onto the porch. He lays Jeanette in it face down as the nurse taught them and goes back into the kitchen.

Because of his mother's many years in bed, David knows how to wash dishes and clean surfaces, but the filth has permeated the air and the dwelling and he can't imagine the house ever again being habitable. He imagines Eugénie bustling about washing dishes, mopping floors, and removing trash. He smells the ammonia that is the signature of his great-grandmother's housekeeping in her own home. He sees his mother lying in her bedroom like Mrs. Curlin. He sees his grandmother sitting peacefully in her chair with a now vacant smile, and his Aunt Rose in the photograph looking fearfully at the Italian boy and girl in front of her. He tries to imagine himself in one of the many photographs his mother took when he was growing up, but sees only what is in front of him.

Returning from the porch, David asks after Mrs. Curlin.

"I don't know," says Tina, crying openly now. "She doesn't move or talk, but she is breathing."

"I'm going to have Doctor Phil come out and take a look at her when I get back," David says.

"You can't. He can't come out here with the place looking like this. We can't pay him and he'll just call the authorities. I can put this back together," Tina says.

"No, you can't," David responds. "Do you know where your father's gone?"

"No," Tina answers. "It doesn't matter. Now he's drinking again, it'll only make matters worse if he comes back. He'll take money we don't have, eat food we can't spare. 'Sides, when he's drinking, he's useless. At least where he is, his buddies'll take care of him. When we were little, I remember comin' home one day after school and seeing him passed out at the table next to three empty quarts of beer and a dozen empty jars of baby food and a spoon."

"Where's Jenny?" David asks.

"She won't be of any use, she's got a boyfriend. They're probably fucking in the woods."

"You mean the way we did?" David shoots back, immediately regretting his reproachful response.

"Sure, why not? It's all there is out here," Tina answers looking up at him for the first time.

Dr. Phil comes out the following day and, on seeing her condition, loads Mrs. Curlin into the front seat of his Plymouth sedan and drives her straight to the hospital. The only ambulance in town is owned by the Mountain Company and is used only for transporting skiers with broken arms and legs to a local bonesetter who has a monopoly on ski injuries unless they warrant hospitalization. It is illegal to transport the living in a hearse, for reasons obvious to most.

Mrs. Curlin, in diabetic shock, exhibits signs of blood poisoning and incipient gangrene in her remaining foot. In the hospital, Dr. Phil makes a decision only to palliate her, as he can no longer control the rampant infection. She dies three days later.

David cannot take time off from his work with Ray but agrees to come to the farm twice a week to bring food and supplies, and to be there on the weekends. Like many men, he is torn between his desire to be there for his family and the emotional anesthesia afforded by exhausting work.

On learning of Mrs. Curlin's death, Eugénie, now in her late 80s, prepares and drops off casseroles and baked goods at Alain's for David to take with him to the farm. Her cataracts are affecting her eyesight and she no longer drives her aging Rambler beyond the confines of the small town.

Before each foray, David calls Tina from Alain's and asks what she needs. He then gets the supplies and Eugénie's contributions and drives his stepfather's car to Stowe Hollow on Tuesdays and Fridays after work. He spends Tuesday, Friday, and Saturday nights, to help out with "the girls" if his father can spare the family car until Sunday afternoon. David's brother Paul is rebuilding a black VW bug that runs erratically but can usually be pressed into service for quick errands. During the second month of this commuting, the Curlins' phone is disconnected by the phone company, but by then David is familiar with his wife's needs for care and feeding of the children.

Jenny, now fourteen, is self-absorbed and spends much of her time in front of a mirror preening her new pubescent beauty or altering her older sister's hand-me-down clothes to enthrall the hormone-driven suitors orbiting her. She is rarely around and Tina can no longer account for her whereabouts. Tina spends her days and nights caring for Emma and Jeanette. Emma is five and full of elusive energy that exhausts Tina. The tranquil interludes spent nursing her younger daughter offer respite, so Tina is in no rush to wean Jeanette.

During his visits, David sees the claustrophobic desperation in Tina's eyes and she sees the physical exhaustion in his. Though they sleep in the same bed, neither feels any of their former sexual urgency. They know each other now in the stark light of shared experience and have lost the cyclonic energy that drove their earlier desire for one another. David remembers overhearing his Aunt Colette whispering to a friend at her husband's wake that children are the most effective birth control. Experience has imbued with meaning many sayings David overheard in childhood but never understood.

Tina begins to talk of moving off the farm. Her father took the only vehicle that runs and until recently, Tina has had no way to leave, other than with David when he comes and goes with supplies. But David is surprised when he buys a few groceries at Patch's, and stops at Snow's to pick up a dozen ears of fresh corn as an inexpensive treat, to arrive at the farm and find the screen door open and no one there except Jenny, smoking a cigarette and listening to the radio. Jenny tells David that Tina, Emma and Jeanette have gone to live with Tina's father.

In answer to David's urgent questions, Jenny tells him that, after hearing of his wife's death, her father again swore off drink and came home to find solace in his children. Getting little, he left the next day with Tina, who persuaded him to take her, Emma, and Jeanette with him to the ramshackle house he rents in Barton where he's found a day job working with the town road crew replacing culverts. There is no note and it didn't occur to Jenny to ask or write down where her father is living. David knows only that Barton is not far from Island Pond where he and Ray are cutting in the State Forest.

David asks Jenny if she'll be okay alone for a few days. She announces that she is grown up and will be fine alone and that she's very happy to have her own place where she can entertain friends. David gives her ten dollars, promises to check in, and returns home.

Though he can see things unraveling, Alain does not question his stepson about the state of his marriage. David tells him that Tina has left and moved in with her father in Barton. Alain does not press his stepson on the consequences of her move, understanding that men tell each other what they need to know and that his stepson is now a man, if reluctantly.

David returns to work. Nor does Ray ask any questions, sensing only that things have changed in his friend's life and that David will tell him what he wants when he wants.

Aujourd'hui maman est morte

In earlier days, Alain had been an occasional hunter, first taking David to his brother, Maurice's, deer camp when he was eight. It had been just another of the countless foreclosed and abandoned hill farms before Maurice bought it from the bank for twenty cents on the dollar. He got an inexpensive camp surrounded by countless deeryards, while the bank relieved itself of another unsalable hill farm.

Overgrown by burdock, rhubarb, and Queen Anne's lace, the barn and shed had long since collapsed. But over the years, Maurice had maintained the house well enough, replacing the tin roof to keep water out, capping and repointing the brick chimney, digging out and replacing the spring box higher on the hill and replacing the broken panes in the windows. In recent years, though, macular degeneration had so reduced Maurice's vision that he could no longer make sense of the hazy images in his Mauser's scope and the camp had again fallen into disuse, except by occasional couples seeking a private place to have sex.

Alain talks with his brother and Maurice happily offers the camp to David as a place to stay while the future of his marriage plays out. Maurice calls the municipal power office and has the power turned back on. David now has a place of his own and Maurice has someone to look after his property high up in Sterling Valley.

David borrows $200 from Alain and buys a decrepit VW. He then moves the few things he cares about from his childhood home to his new home, mostly books from school, some framed photographs, and a few LPs his Aunt Rose had bequeathed to him of opera and chamber music that he had come to love.

Although he has given up going to Mass, he keeps to his habit of stopping by Eugénie's for Sunday breakfast with Alain, Juliette, and Paul when he's in town. One Sunday after breakfast, he stops by the house to see Juliette, who was not at Eugénie's. He is surprised to see her sitting alone on the couch in the living room. She is a senior now, a good student, but spends little time at home, even on the weekend.

Though she is not crying, it's evident to David that something has happened. Her cheeks are streaked with tears and she only covers her face and shakes her head when David asks her, "What's the matter?"

"It's Mom," she finally says, inclining her head toward the bedroom.

David enters his mother's room. He sees her lying in disarray. She is not breathing, although her startled expression convinces him for a moment that she is. Her eyes and mouth are open as if she is snoring. He pulls the covers over her and watches her intently to see if she is breathing. For some reason, he is loath to touch her and to check either her pulse or her respiration. He looks at the familiar profusion of brown plastic vials and cough medicine bottles on her nightstand several of which are open. He picks up the bedside phone and calls Alain, who is still at Eugénie's having coffee, telling him calmly how he has found Juliette and that Helen has died. Alain arrives fifteen minutes later.

Juliette hugs her father for several minutes, saying only, "I'm sorry, Dad." David does the same and the three of them sit down on the couch.

Juliette characteristically takes matters in hand and cleans up the bedroom before calling Dr. Phil. She gets a brown paper bag from the kitchen and goes into the bedroom alone, emptying all the medicines into the bag and carrying the empty food dishes back into the kitchen to discard. She then pulls the bed together and picks up the scattered clothes while David and his stepfather watch, seemingly lost as to how to help.

"Call Dr. Phil," Juliette says firmly to her father. "David, go down and tell Paul and Eugénie and bring Paul home."

Dr. Phil, familiar both with his unknown Greenwich colleague's prescription of narcotics and stimulants and his own patient's dependence on them, has spoken candidly to Alain about the problem but has no way to stop the flow of prescriptions.

He speaks quietly but firmly to Alain about his decision to list a brain aneurism with a lethal stroke resulting as the "cause of death." Alain doesn't question his longtime friend and family doctor. Nor does he fully understand the import of Dr. Phil's decision, or how, in fact, his wife of 23 years died.

The family endures the community and religious rituals that a death imposes: the open-casket viewing when friends and family come to pay their respects and expose to memory a final image of the dead person, the solemn high Mass with its cursory and ambiguous eulogy by a new priest who never knew Helen, and interment in St. Ann's Cemetery.

At the "viewing," David tries to remember the last time he saw his mother, but recalls instead the sepia photograph of her as a naked girl staring at the black snake traversing her shins, and, later, as the radiant young woman in a wedding gown next to her husband in his white, full-dress naval officer's uniform and sword. He remembers lying with her in her bed in their small apartment when they were new to Vermont before she met Alain.

While looking at the somber faces of his stepfather's many friends, David realizes that he himself is devoid of any feeling. Meursault's opening statement in Camus' *The Stranger* comes to him, "Mother died today or maybe it was yesterday? I can't be sure." He remembers his own startled reaction to the vacancy of the line on first reading it in French class at boarding school, yet it curiously echoes his indifference to the news of his mother's death.

Eugénie stands next to her widowed son in the receiving line at the viewing, sits next to him in the pew at his wife's funeral service and stands with him as the oak coffin is lowered into the hard-pan at St. Ann's Cemetery. She will again prepare weekday evening meals for Alain when he returns from work, as she wished Helen had done.

Eugénie had been welcoming to her son's newly arrived wife, but she would not have been her choice for a daughter-in-law. Eugénie showed Helen the same unremitting love that her son showed for his new wife, but privately she worried about her capacity to endure life in the hardscrabble community of farmers and merchants, given her privileged upbringing. She worried that the beautiful widow to whom her son was so attracted would gradually tire of their quotidian life together. Eugénie had been grateful for her daughter-in-law's decision to convert to the Church before the marriage, but observed with fear her gradual retreat from attendance at Sunday Mass and family events.

Alain understands now that Dr. Phil's decision to specify a natural cause for his wife's death has made possible her interment at St Ann's. Among all the end-of-life rituals, it is the lowering of their mother's casket into the earth that most graphically conveys to David, Paul and Juliette that her life has ended. Paul and Juliette weep openly as the three huddle together beside the hole in the earth.

The family returns to the house to prepare for the onslaught of friends and neighbors. Eugénie goes about the tasks of hospitality, removing wax paper from and arranging the platters dropped off by neighbors and friends, putting flowers in vases and setting them about the house.

Sterling

Several weeks before Christmas, David receives a letter from Tina, post-marked in Barton but with no return address. The letter is a brief list of things that Tina wishes David to know and do. He has never seen anything in writing from his wife other than lists and is surprised by her inability to spell. She has landed a state job in the new county social welfare department that she says pays enough to support the three of them. Her father has managed to keep his job working on the town road crew and is still sober. David is to see Jeanette for a few weeks at Easter and then again in the late summer before school starts. There is no mention of Emma. Nor does she address the future of their marriage, only David's role as Jeanette's father. She does not ask for money, nor does she mention Jenny's whereabouts.

David tries to extract from his wife's broken sentences and mis-spelled words her understanding of the future of their marriage but the letter is merely a list and conveys only what a list conveys. He assumes their relationship is ended but wonders about their marriage. He is unclear about his role as Jeanette's father or as Tina's husband.

He throws himself into his work with Ray, having to spend more and more nights in the woods, an abandoned barn, or the back of Ray's truck, trying to sleep over Ray's snoring. They are both making a good living now, as the price of hardwood has been rising steadily and now the price of saw-timber clear pine is rising as well. Ray and David are cut-ting and selling more wood for lumber and less for pulp and firewood. Townsfolk, switching to oil from coal and wood heat, have pushed down the price for firewood. Although farmers still heat with wood, they cut, split, and season their own.

David and Annie Foss, having maintained a casual friendship over the years, meet again in the hospital where David and Leo Forcier are visiting Marcel Forcier, who has undergone yet another surgery to repair the pelvic damage from his accident. Annie is an LPN with plans to become a registered nurse.

David asks her to the Fourth of July firehouse dance, but she declines, reminding him lightheartedly that he is married. The reminder comes as a surprise.

David and Ray now work Saturdays. "Make hay while the sun shines" is Ray's motto, and David, who has managed to save the lion's share of his rising earnings, agrees. His only expense now is a mechanically well-cared-for but rusty Dodge pickup he bought from a friend of Ray's when his VW died and he gave it to Paul for parts. Before he bought it, David sought Paul's help, offering him ten bucks to check the engine compression and drive train. Paul took his older half-brother's request to heart, checking everything and giving David a green light on the truck.

On Sundays when Alain, Paul, and Juliette arrive to pick up Eugénie for the eight o'clock Mass at Holy Family, she has already set the table, made the coffee, mixed the frozen orange juice, and cooked the bacon and sausage for breakfast. At nine when they return from low Mass it takes her just a few minutes to scramble the eggs, butter warm toast, pour coffee, and bring Sunday breakfast to the table.

David appreciates his time with his family and the news that is exchanged "between bites and chews" as his Aunt Rose used to say. Juliette tells of her successes at school, the wins and losses of her field hockey team, and her aspirations for college. Paul tells of the progress he has made restoring his Volkswagen, his after-school job at Graves Hardware restocking shelves, and his desire to someday own and restore a muscle car. He talks of going to vocational school to learn auto and diesel mechanics. He says nothing of the girl Juliette has seen him with and dismisses his sister's occasional winking allusions to her.

Eugénie says little, busying herself with offerings of seconds and refills. She knows that what matters in the eyes of God is what one does, not what one says, and that it is one's actions that reserves one's place in heaven. She has little patience with her nattering female friends who while away their time together with cards or bingo in the church basement gathering and spreading gossip.

Sunday afternoons are David's only time alone. He leaves for Sterling after helping Juliette dry the chipped china dishes that Eugénie has washed in a sink of hot, soapy water and arranged on the dishtowel-covered enamel drainboard. He kisses Eugénie from behind and Juliette on the cheek and waves goodbye to Alain and Paul.

In Sterling, he often naps in the shade of his favorite tree, a unique and rugged survivor of the disease that has killed off most of the American elms that lined village streets throughout New England and much of the Midwest. It rises from the ground like a fountain under great pressure, spraying its green skyward into the blue, and shades the spring box for his home's water supply. The elm's 30-inch diameter trunk is blanketed on the north side by a deep cushion of moss on which David rests. He can hear the faint trickle of water bubbling up into the spring box nearby.

David dreams now and, as in most of his dreams, he is not apparent to himself except as a consciousness in the room. His father, grandfather and grandmother, great-grandmother Selma, Aunt Rose and mother are now ghosts who people his dreams occasionally or come to mind unexpectedly while he works in the woods.

<hr/>

In this dream his cousin Terry is sitting in an apartment with the same floor plan as the apartment he and Tina have just vacated, but it is well appointed. Terry is sitting in a cushioned window seat reading quietly. The window seat is framed by wood panels from which matching, folded louvers hang. She's wearing a Kelly green cashmere sweater, a below-the-knee crimson skirt, argyle knee socks, and penny loafers. One leg is curled under the other and the whiteness of her right thigh is evident.

She's leaning back against a throw cushion. Her hair cascades over her shoulders and down to the breasts he has touched. She wears narrow tortoise-shell glasses. A book lies open in her lap.

The bench sits next to a small fireplace with a carved marble façade and a cast-iron fire-back with three sporting naiads. Three white birch logs rest on a pair of simple brass andirons. There are no ashes in the fireplace. Neither the fire-back nor the mocha-colored firebrick shows any sign that there has ever been a fire there. Parisian watercolors hang on either side. One shows the *bouquiniste* stalls along the Seine; the other, lovers strolling along the Quai Voltaire. There is a Persian rug on the parquet floor.

He is aroused by this scene of Terry on the banquette. She resumes reading, looking up from the book occasionally and smiling at him, but saying nothing. He is beguiled but trapped in a sensual still life in which, as in all his dreams, he is only an observer.

After he wakes up, he lies there savoring the restiveness his dream has aroused. Aunt Rose is the only person with whom he has shared his experience on the couch in his grandmother's library. He remembers when he told her. They were walking on a cobbled path in Prospect Park near her apartment in Brooklyn.

"Terry had an unusual upbringing. Her mother was an art historian associated with The Modern. Though she had many liaisons, she never married – even after she was smitten in mid-life with her gardener, Angus, a good man but a somewhat feral presence in her life. She bore him a child, Terry, and I know that Terry grew up never far from her parents' relentless passions.

"Your grandmother saw Terry as a way of bringing you home. As you know, my sister was never happy about your mother's remarriage, especially so soon after the loss of your father. It never surfaced in conversation, but was implicit in her communication with Helen. You were the prize. That's why your mother distrusted your grandmother so much and eventually just ignored her. She always felt my sister's disapproval ... of her remarriage and the threat it posed to Dorothy's relationship with you. Once my sister's son and husband were gone, you were all that was left. In his kindness, Alain saw to it that she was not cut off from seeing you, who, for all her misgivings about your mother, loved you both dearly.

"Fear rarely leads to good behavior and as imperious as she seemed, my sister lived in fear. You're old enough now to know that your grandfather could be a stallion at times and carried on affairs with impunity, always imagining that your grandmother had no idea, when, of course, women know these things. Men can be so stupid and arrogant. Your father's death ended all that, though, draining any cupidity or will to live from Howard.

"Terry was the bait. My sister understood the wiles of women and the foibles of men, as she had fallen victim to both. She was a closet reader of D. H. Lawrence and Anais Nin, you know. I always felt sorry for her. Her comfortable circumstance and busy social calendar belied her deep loneliness, even more after she lost her son and her husband, and then you.

"You would never have been happy with Terry, as Terry will never be happy with any man. The thrill of conquest fades after victory and the victor must move on to the next conquest. You'll find someone who loves you as you are and you in turn will love her."

David hears the nearby cooing of a pair of mourning doves. He gets to his feet, his thoughts of Terry still fresh in memory. It will be dark in another two hours and he returns to camp.

Decree Nisi

Late that fall just after deer season, Alain dies under a 1964 Ford *Fairlane.* He's removed the oil plug from the pan to change the oil for a widowed neighbor, Hilda Hartigan. Hilda moved in across the street after the Collettes retired to a trailer park in Florida. She survives on a slurry of junk food and fortified wine, counting on neighbors to rescue her from her various alcoholic misadventures. Alain helps her out periodically, thawing a frozen pipe or changing worn tires or oil. He is waiting for the oil to drain under the jacked-up Ford when she leans on the fender, pushing the car off the scissor jack. The full weight of the rusty Ford's drive train lands on Alain's chest, pinning him to the damp lawn.

Panicked, Hilda fumbles with the scissor jack lying on its side, all the while talking to him, though he can't answer. Long after he stops breathing, she tells him to "wait a bit" while she goes in "to get him a drink and call a neighbor to help her lift the car off him."

As is her way, Eugénie leaves little room for her own grief, taking in hand the funeral arrangements expected by the large community of French-Canadian Catholics. Alain was deeply loved and respected, not only for his industriousness but also for his kindness and generosity. Unable to turn a blind eye to the hardships of many around him, he often hired men down on their luck to do odd jobs at home or at work, thus camouflaging the charity that would have embarrassed them.

Paul, Juliette, and David stand with Eugénie in the receiving line at the open-casket viewing, sit with her in the front pew at Holy Family Church, which is full to overflowing, such that many men and boys must stand outside on the entry steps, leaving pews for wives, children, and elders.

Maurice and his wife Flo return for the service with several of their own children. Maurice delivers a brief eulogy in which he recalls what the cramped congregation already knows about his brother's generosity of spirit and his unwillingness to judge others. Eugénie and her family then go on to at St Ann's Cemetery for the burial of her son.

David is familiar with death, having lost both his mother and father, but he has not yet experienced the deep well of sadness that Alain's death brings forth in him. He hardly ever thinks of his natural father but thinks frequently of his mother and the choices she made in her short life. He understands little of addiction's power to captivate and palliate, and as she drifted further into absence, he would stop in to see her when he was home, find her asleep, and leave. Afterwards, he would remember their times picnicking as a family at Blodgett Falls, swimming at Lake Elmore, or the bedtime rituals of his early childhood. He wonders if the vacancy he feels at her death is anger he fears will overwhelm him as it had done when he turned on Klaus and had to be pulled off him. So whatever loss and sadness he might have felt when Helen swallowed the Tuinal capsules was displaced by his fury at her decision to leave him and her family behind.

David loses control of himself, crying openly at his father's burial. He is unfamiliar with the sadness his father's death has raised in him and surprised at his inability to maintain a detached demeanor.

Paul and Juliette are also at a loss. Close to their father and wholly unprepared for his dying, they again huddle together with David. Eugénie stands nearby with Maurice and Flo and their children. In poor towns, mourning is, of necessity, curtailed by the need to return to work. David takes the week off, but then must head north to rejoin Ray whose productivity in the woods is hobbled without him.

Paul is boarding with his cousin in St. Johnsbury and attending vocational school there, fulfilling his dream to master auto and diesel mechanics. Juliette will be a freshman at St. Lawrence University in the fall. Maurice arranges with his downstate employer to take one of his two vacation weeks to stay on with his mother and his niece and nephew until school starts.

At Eugénie's suggestion, Maurice offers David a long-term lease on his deer camp, since he lives down country and no longer hunts. He is reluctant to sell it, though, in case either of his twin boys should ever choose to leave their lucrative manufacturing jobs and suburban raised ranches in New Jersey and move to Vermont.

David has come to love the old farmhouse, with its yard-long door-step of heavy bluestone. The exterior bears no trace of paint, so he sets to work on Sundays to seal the dried-out wood with creosote. The place looks no different when he's finished, but the coat of clear stain slows the dry rot.

On the inside, David looks only to inhibit decay. Working on Sundays and occasional evenings when he can't sleep, he pulls up the faded linoleum, sands and seals the pumpkin pine floors, and patches and repaints the plaster walls. The electrical wiring, a network of porcelain insulators with cotton-wrapped copper wire running from rotary porcelain switches to cracked porcelain sockets, must be replaced. David decides he only needs electricity in the kitchen to run the refrigerator, a GE toaster given him by Eugénie, and the second-hand Maytag wringer-washer with its cast aluminum agitator, enamel tub and cracked rubber fill and drain hoses that Alain had retired and offered him. A clear bulb in a new white porcelain fixture in the middle of the kitchen ceiling provides light and he later adds another outlet near the sink to power the red heat-tapes wrapped around the incoming water pipe to keep it from freezing where it enters the cast-iron sink from the spring box above.

David knows that in the eyes of the church and the state of Vermont he is married to Tina but he feels alone for the first time in his life. He misses seeing and holding Jeanette, and Easter is a winter away. Though he has lost any desire to be with Tina, he worries about her and, only in retrospect, has come to understand the bitter disappointments in her own life, including himself.

One Friday on the spur of the moment, he leaves work early and drives to nearby Barton to see if he can find and talk with Tina and see and hold his daughter.

From his own last conversations with his mother, he knows that one's feelings may bear no relationship to what has been said, that simple words and gestures often trigger memories that elicit illogical reactions and responses and confound a conversation.

David knows little of his wife's childhood. In their brief time together, their conversations were dictated by exigency more than affection. Most of what David understands about Tina he sees in her eyes. He recalls her look of inchoate desperation the last time they met at the farmhouse, as if, confined in her vocabulary, she could never articulate the accumulation of pain and fear welling up inside her. Tina knows, too, that her young husband is distanced from his own feelings and can offer little beyond the groceries and supplies he brings, and more children to care for.

David tells Ray of his plan and, in spite of Ray's efforts to dissuade him, leaves at three, making the half-hour trip to Barton in time to catch the postmistress. He introduces himself and asks for Tina's address. The postmistress knows all the addresses of the town's 1,840 residents by heart but is, from experience, wary about sharing this information casually, as strangers looking for former spouses might harbor bad intentions. She gives him an address, explaining that it will be of no help, as it is a rural route delivery number, but that it will suffice if he chooses to reach her by mail.

With some embarrassment, David explains his situation and his good intentions toward his wife and child. This meets with apparent success, as Mrs. Delaire then relates the recent developments in Tina's life as though she were her aunt.

Her father has again disappeared and the loss of the second income has made it impossible for Tina to pay rent. Her manager at work has taken an interest in her and she wastes no time in accepting his offer to move in with him, even though his recently divorced wife's things are still evident in the cramped double-wide. Herald Aube is a church-going man and, although he is nearing fifty, Mrs. Delaire assures David that he is a man of good intentions and adequate means to provide for Tina and her two daughters.

David asks where Mr. Aube lives but here the postmistress draws the line, suggesting that he inquire at his former wife's place of employment since she and Mr. Aube are colleagues. David leaves, knowing that he can get Tina's new address from any phone book and, from his permitting transactions at the local forestry office that state offices close at five. He returns to the camp that he and Ray have appropriated for shelter where they were working. When they stumble on deer camps or abandoned farmhouses, they often avail themselves of the shelter to avoid rain, early snow, or, in the spring, black flies. Hunters rarely lock their camps for just this reason.

"How'd it go?" Ray asks.

"She's moved in with someone she met at work. Sounds like he's a lot older. Hope he's not a creep."

"Not a lot you can do about it. At least Tina and the girls have a place to sleep and some food on the table. Sounds like a good outcome to me," Ray offers. "Less, course, you're jealous. How about some supper? I got two cans of Dinty Moore, two Carlings, and some stale bread for dippin'. Game?"

David is confused and says little as he wipes the interior of the stew can with a piece of bread. He is grateful that Tina and the girls have a roof over their heads. He isn't jealous, but is uncomfortable knowing that Mr. Aube is old enough to be Tina's father or Jeanette's grandfather.

After supper, he falls into a deep sleep lying on top of his sleeping bag, as it is unusually warm for a fall night.

When he wakes, it's the middle of the night. He hears mice and chipmunks scurrying about the floors and rafters stowing their tiny harvests of seeds for winter. It has cooled down considerably and he slides his legs and torso into his army surplus mummy bag. Through the frost ferns on the window above him he sees a fingernail moon hanging in the fall sky. Replaying what he has learned, he is again surprised at his lack of feeling. Custom would dictate anger and jealousy, yet he is relieved to learn that his wife is sheltered, even though in a stranger's bed. It's his daughter, not Tina that he is anxious about. He knows Tina can take care of herself, but worries about her ability to take care of Jeanette. After all, when he and Tina met, Emma was in the care of Mrs. Curlin.

The next morning over coffee and stale doughnuts, David tells Ray he is going back to Barton that afternoon to see Jeanette. Ray says he'll fire him if he does ... that he needs an honest day's work out of his helper, especially when mill prices are so high. David acquiesces, knowing this is Ray's way of telling him to leave well enough alone, that finding Tina will only complicate his life.

Work continues through the first snowfall and well into deer season. As usual, Ray gets his buck a few hours after sunrise the first day of the season. This way he doesn't have to miss work. The early kill, however, limits his choice of bucks.

Both men have managed to bank a considerable amount of mill money. The softwood they cut is stacked in 4 x 4 x 24-foot piles until there are enough to order and fill four trucks to haul it to nearby paper mills. The haulers buy the wood outright for cash, trucking it to Ticonderoga, New York, or Lancaster, New Hampshire, whichever mill is paying more. The lumber mills pay by check, so Ray pays taxes only on what he sells for lumber and lives on his "pulp money." David takes a lesson from this.

In March, Tina sues for divorce. David is relieved she's taken the initiative. He reads through her lawyer's letter with Ray looking over his shoulder, looking only for what will happen with Jeanette. Tina is assuming custody, demands $100 a month in child support until she remarries and again offers David Easter weekend and two weeks around Labor Day with his daughter whom he has yet to see since Tina left.

"Boy, did you get off cheap," declares Ray. "My ex wanted twice that and we had no kids. She needed beer and gas money. I told her to go to hell, so she went to work earning it in other men's beds. At least, Tina's being responsible. You got off good."

David doesn't understand what he's reading and there's no one he feels comfortable asking for advice so he simply sends a letter to the return address agreeing to the terms.

Several weeks later he receives a court letter granting a decree nisi, declaring that the marriage, had and solemnized on April 7, 1966, between David Schumann and Tina Curlin be dissolved by reason of an unduly long separation and consequent alienation of affection UNLESS sufficient cause be shown to the court why this decree should not be made absolute within six months of the making hereof.

Based on his own legal experience Ray tells David he'll be free in six months. David tells Juliette and Paul his news. They're relieved for him. He tells Eugénie only after she asks him what will become of his marriage. He is relieved to be able to tell his Catholic grandmother that Tina sued him for divorce. Eugénie gives him a kiss on the forehead and offers to help him when Jeanette is with him, inviting them both to dinner on her first visit now only a few weeks away. "Bring Ray if he's around, but tell him to mind his tongue and his manners at my table," she adds with a smile.

Several weeks later, David sees Annie Foss. He smiles when they meet and she returns his smile, lowering her eyes as if acknowledging their ongoing friendship. At least, this is David's reading of their encounters. David asks Annie for coffee. Her hospital shift has just ended and she accepts.

She leads, asking David how Jeanette is faring. David tells her of their dinner at Eugénie's and their first afternoon alone together in Sterling where he took her for a walk, showing her the abandoned sugarworks and nearby cliffs where he often spotted bobcats in the nooks and caves in the rock face. Later, they gathered fallen butternuts for Eugénie until dark.

Eugénie had sent them home with a bag of waxpaper-wrapped leftovers of pork roast, roast potatoes and carrots, and a loaf of fresh-baked bread. David and Jeanette had a quiet supper together marked only by Jeanette's chatter about a new friend she met where they live and her longing for a tricycle like her friend's. Jeanette is three, going on four.

"Are you in school?" David asks his daughter.

"No, but I want to and I'm going to play school next year," she answers. "I like my friends and, besides, Mommy goes to her work, so I'd rather be at school," she answers. "My older sister, Emma, is in second grade and I want to go like she does. I don't like being at home when she's not there."

Her answer worries David.

"Our neighbor, Mrs. Burritt, stays with me and makes our lunch, but I like it better when Mommy and Daddy are there."

David avoids asking Jeanette about her other "daddy." He is no stranger to the notion of two fathers, having only known his natural father vicariously. He realizes the same is true of Jeanette until now.

Their chatter keeps up through dinner. Then David sees Jeanette rubbing her eyes. He clears the table and leaves the dishes in the iron sink. He wipes the food from Jeanette's small upper lip with a dish rag and helps her extract her nightie from her overnight bag. As she dresses for bed, he brings a chair over to the kitchen sink so she can brush her teeth since he does not yet have a bathroom, though he plans to add one on someday. He has not yet begun to build regular fires in the wood-stove, as the days are still warm. But the evenings are getting cooler so he snuggles into the only bed in the house with his daughter.

"What about our prayers?" Jeanette asks. "Daddy and Mommy always say our prayers before I go to bed."

David is non-plussed, realizing he remembers little more than the a few Latin fragments from the mass, the *Lord's Prayer* and the *Hail Mary*. Jeanette and her father recite the *Lord's Prayer* together and then Jeanette goes on to recite a rhyming prayer with which David is not familiar.

David reads her a chapter from his mother's book, *East of the Sun, West of the Moon* as the two spoon together for warmth. He is holding the book in front of his daughter as he reads so she can see the beautiful illustrations. Half-way through his reading, David realizes his daughter is asleep and he sets the book on the floor. His eyes fill with tears lying with his daughter under the quilt Eugénie made for him. He dreads her departure the following day and knows, too, that there is no practical place in his working life for her yet.

At breakfast the following morning before David must take her back to Barton on his way to work, their conversation ranges widely. Jeanette asks most of the questions, about various things in his house, how they work and what her father does for a living. From her questions, David understands that Mr. Aube keeps a modern home with conventional amenities. Jeanette volunteers nothing more of her stepfather, her mother, or their new life together. Nor does David ask, content that, at least for the time being, his daughter is safe and being cared for.

The following Sunday, Annie smiles as she listens to David talking of his time with his daughter, knowing that it is good for him to be with her. She tells him of her plans at the hospital. The doctor shortage has expanded the spectrum of professional options for nurses and Annie will drive once a week to take night courses at the new UVM College of Nursing in order to qualify as an operating room nurse.

They soon exhaust the news portion of their conversation and both are left sipping coffee from heavy ironstone mugs. This opens space for the question each harbors. Annie again leads, asking after Tina. David tells Annie of his impending divorce and that it will be final in another three months. David then asks Annie if she is seeing anyone. Annie says she accepts occasional invitations for a date but has not met anyone she would choose to see steadily. This clears an opening for a larger conversation that neither knows how to begin. Finally, David asks Annie if she'll come to Sterling for a picnic on Sunday. She smiles and nods her head.

David and Annie

David and Annie live in the woods on the side of Sterling Mountain. Over breakfast, Annie notes that Jeanette will be entering first grade this fall and will turn six next week. Jeanette had come to stay during two long Labor Day weekends and for the requisite Easter holidays but after those visits David is no longer able to make contact with her. His letters to Jeanette and later to Tina and Herald come back unopened. The last letter comes back stamped, "Moved, left no forwarding address."

He and Annie talk of Jeanette and how they might find her. David thinks often of his time with his daughter and how they were coming to know one another. He thinks, too, about his New York grandmother, his Aunt Rose, and Jeanette. He wishes Jeanette could have known his Aunt Rose. Though Annie still holds out hope for a reunion, David is less optimistic about seeing her again.

David sometimes wonders if he and Annie will have children. They have never taken or talked about precautions, although Annie is a nurse. Their lovemaking is usually spontaneous – a combustion of intimacy and desire. Desire occasionally creeps up on them while they are working together outdoors. Annie will be drawn to the tanned musculature she sees in David's back and shoulders as he throws firewood into the old manure spreader he uses as a trailer or David will glance into the armhole of Annie's sleeveless T-shirt and see the gentle rise of contrasting pale skin that only hints at her breast. As David advances, Annie feigns modesty about being seen but there are only birds and animals to watch their lovemaking.

They usually visit Eugénie when they go to town to buy the few grocery or hardware goods they need. Eugénie is stalwart, a fixture in David's life. She's always been there for the family, and unlike many in the community, her deep religious convictions do not provoke her to either judgment or gossip. She has seen the best and the worst in people and, though she holds herself to high standards, she knows it's not her job to judge others. Her calling is to help where and when the need arises, and always in her family.

Maurice's woodlot covers 60 acres and abuts the old Languerand farm with its 115 odd acres of hardwoods. The Languerand widow lets David work her woods in return for fifteen percent of whatever he sells. He culls, cuts, and sells pulpwood in four-foot lengths, firewood in 18- and 22-inch lengths, and lumber in mill lengths. Against Annie's advice and unless she is with him, he works alone, cutting and stacking wood in place and then retrieving it from the woods with his John Deere 510 and the old spreader. He was surprised to find that the ring chains he needs to use the tractor in the winter cost half as much again as his well-used tractor. He has not given up his dream of logging with a team of horses, but the auctioned tractor was both a steal and a necessity.

David is always happy in the woods but looks forward to coming home to Annie, who now works early mornings in the operating room.

Annie, too, is resourceful with wood and works with David on the weekends or sometimes before dusk. She can wield a chainsaw to cut birch and maple whips into biscuit wood for the stove, but she must rely on David to yank the starter cord hard enough to overcome the compression. Even David sometimes has trouble starting the ancient and cranky McCullough. Annie prefers a sharp bucksaw and a sturdy sawbuck. She likes to say she doesn't cut trees down, she cuts 'em up.

Sometimes David lies down in the woods. He recalls Ray's advice in Island Pond to take ten-minute breaks every hour. "Ya git careless wi' the saw and it'll turn on ya 'n' start limbin' ya," he used to say.

In the dead of winter a letter arrives with the raised-letter return address of a New York law firm. The letter is addressed to David at Alain and Helen's even though another family has lived in the house for several years. Mary Sargent, the postmistress, has written the rural route forwarding address in her meticulous copperplate hand. Mary knows where people live or where they've moved to, even those who would prefer their whereabouts be unknown.

The letter is waiting for him next to his dinner plate. Annie and David get very little first-class mail. Annie saves the flyers and catalogs that turn up in their mailbox to start fires in the cookstove. David looks at the envelope and opens it with the butter knife. The letter informs him that his grandmother's last will and testament has been probated by the state of New York, that David is the beneficiary of a share of her estate, and that within three weeks he will be mailed a certified check in the amount of $48,000. The letter is a request for him to sign a release, acknowledging receipt of the letter and his understanding and acceptance of the probate court's action with regard to the final disposition of the assets of Dorothy Schumann.

David is pleased to see that his grandmother has left $5,000 to Ha to help him bring his wife and daughter in Korea to New York and another $5,000 to Margaret for her long service. David scans the short list of beneficiaries in the hopes that his grandmother has left something for Paul and Juliette, but their names do not appear. He doesn't know anyone else on the list. There are several museums, though not the Frick. He decides to give Paul and Juliette some of his inheritance and to discuss the amount with Annie, as they always share the few significant financial decisions they must make.

"My grandmother died in July and this is about her will. She left us

$48,000, but she didn't give anything to Paul and Juliette so I want to, if that's okay."

"It's a fine idea, and your grandmother didn't leave us $48,000. She left it to you, and you should use it or save as you see fit," she answers.

"Maybe Mrs. Languerand is ready to sell her woodlot. She's only asking forty-five hundred dollars for it and we could save the rest," David answers.

"Sounds like a good idea. We'll need a new fridge someday, too, but eat up now and let's go to sleep. I don't know about your day, but mine was long. All our beds are full at the hospital. We had three surgeries this morning and Thelma doesn't move like she did when she was young."

Before they fall asleep, David and Annie fantasize about what they could do with the money. Annie suggests that David start an account for Jeanette even though they don't yet know where she has been taken.

The next afternoon, remembering Ray's advice, David lies on his back and looks up into the canopy of old-growth maple and hickory. He recalls how when he last visited his grandmother she described a performance of *Aida* she attended as a young girl at the ruins of the Baths of Caracalla in Rome, which they visited together. He remembers sitting near her in the living room as she talked about the Baths – their origins in the third century as a place of leisure and learning for Roman citizens. He recalls how her speech became more animated as she described the triumphal march scene, in which Radames returns victorious from his battle with the Ethiopian army, how she closed her eyes and hummed softly the stentorian brass motif heralding the army's arrival, led by three pairs of camels and a pair of elephants and followed by an army of eighty warriors bearing spears and pikes. These, in turn, were followed by a hundred captive Nubians, now enslaved to the Egyptians. The last to arrive on stage was Radames, the conquering hero, resplendent in a golden chariot drawn by four white stallions abreast. She was breathless in her animation as she described to him the splendor of the music and the outdoor spectacle. David imagines Jeanette sitting on the floor next to his grandmother listening to her telling the story of her visit as a little girl.

An Unkind Cut

One late afternoon, David is racing against a cloudbank of lofty, white thunderheads towering over Sterling Mountain. He is anxious to finish limbing the evergreens he has felled to make room for the young maples coming up near his sugarworks. Now that he and Annie can afford the evaporator and arch used to boil the sap down to syrup, David plans to add maple syrup sales to their income.

Three more sixty-foot spruces lie in a row where David has dropped them, waiting to be limbed and cut up into pulp lengths. David has broken his rule of never taking down a second tree until the one on the ground is limbed, cut, and loaded. By dropping the four trees, he has set himself a goal to beat the downpour as he never leaves a fell on the ground unlimbed. He is rushing, and working alone against the advice of all the loggers he has known.

When limbing, David works from the base of the downed tree toward the tip. He usually takes a break every six to eight feet to remove limbs and toss them onto a slash pile nearby. He knows it is unsafe to work where the ground is littered with wood or underbrush, but today he's in a hurry. Winded, he pauses and drops the saw at his side, holding the handle with his right hand. He has done this a thousand times, but in his fatigue he has lowered the saw blade a few inches too far. The unthrottled chain is still moving. It kicks up, catches his jeans, and bites into his thigh well above the knee. He feels the acute pain, kills the saw, and sets it on the ground. Blood is rapidly soaking his shredded jeans. He rips open the jeans and looks at the wound. He knows it's serious and from what he can see through the steady flow of blood, he knows it is only a deep flesh wound and that the blade has missed any tendon or muscle. He needs to stop the bleeding and get to the hospital.

He needs to be with Ann.

He stops briefly at the house to stanch the blood flow with an old sheet that Ann has relegated to the rag pile in the pantry. He remembers arriving at the hospital but no more. When he wakes up he is lying in an examining room in the emergency room. Ann is smiling down at him. A doctor stands behind her, poking through a tray of surgical tools and sutures on a white metal cabinet. David feels nothing.

"You in a rush to get back there?" she asks smiling. "It'll be a few days, you know. The trees'll wait."

"Did I tell you what happened?" David asks.

"You did before the anesthetic kicked in and Dr. Melnor sewed you up. I'm just about to put the bandage on. Take a look. Pretty nice job that saw did on you. It took us long enough to clean all the chain oil and sawdust out of the wound ... nasty stuff."

David tries to bend forward to see the wound on his right thigh. Annie pushes him back down on the examining table and holds up a hand mirror so David can see the fourteen stitches and the expanse of bluing flesh.

"Nice job," Dr. Melnor chimes in, "You had almost fainted as two of our ER guys helped you in. You kept telling them, 'It's not a big deal. It's just a cut. Just go get Ann,' until I finally knocked you out with some Demerol."

David lies still while Ann cleans up and puts things away. He thinks he hears her say that she will take him home after her shift, when the Demerol has worn off. He thinks of his mother and better understands the array of bottles by her bed. Feeling nothing, he falls into a dreamless sleep.

The Unkindest Cut

A thrush trills somewhere above, reminding David that he is again in the woods. He gets up, stomps out a cigarette deep in the moss and goes back to cutting hardwood for next winter's firewood.

He is easily winded now. His fourteen years of chain-smoking Camels have shortened his breath, obstructing it with viscous phlegm that makes him cough and wakes up Ann. She worries he will die as her father did, drowning with short, panic-stricken breaths, unable to oxygenate the blood flowing to his terrified brain.

But he is not Annie's father. Then is not now and he is dying in the woods alone, unable to breathe for another reason – the crushing weight on his shattered ribs and the seizing pain that makes breath impossible.

His right temple is flat against the damp moss. He fell hard on his right side when his steel-toed boot caught in a loop of woody grapevine hidden among dead leaves. It happened fast. He tries to recall the sequence of events. The 50-foot black cherry had pinched the bar on his saw as it began the arc of its fall. He let go of the saw and moved aside but his boot caught fast in the vine. He and the tree fell in the same arc.

In his close field of vision, the forest floor is a landscape of curled wood chips. Some are pale blond and others cinnabar, the mixed colors of black cherry. Farther off, pale green maidenhair fern fronds rise up like a primordial tree and in the distance he can see a mound of dark green moss covering a rock.

He can hear the gurgling of water flowing over rocks in Potash Brook a few yards away, and there is again the sound of a thrush. He is remembering where he is in the woods. He is far from Annie, far from their house, far from anyone. It is early April and trout season is still two weeks away. The kids he often surprises fishing on his woodlot are still in school.

The stabbing pain in his chest is increasingly anesthetized by the body's chemistry of shock. Instinct causes him to inhale, but pain overwhelms the instinct and he relaxes, breathless.

He sees a wild turkey strutting hesitantly toward him, lifting each three-toed foot carefully and planting it firmly before taking another step, always cautious, always guarded. The man lying there is no threat, however. The turkey seems to know this, ambles ever closer, pausing at each step to scratch the groundcover and peck at worms and bugs beneath the bed of leaves. A few feet away, the bird stops, glances at the man but goes on with his feeding. As the bird moves closer, the man notices how the wary tom resembles the bronze meat birds Annie's aunt raises each summer, lacking only the heavy chest and height. The colors are the same.

Gradually, it struts away, all the while disturbing the earth and eating what it finds. It is the closest David has ever been to a wild turkey. He is used to seeing flocks of twenty or thirty foraging in his lower field while the snow is still on the ground. The tom disappears over the knoll that forms the west bank of Potash Brook. David can still hear him scrabbling among the leaves even over the sounds of the brook.

The pale blue two-cycle exhaust that hangs in the air when his chainsaw is whining has dissipated. The resinous smell of wounded wood is everywhere, mingled with the acrid odor of bar and chain oil. The hot saw lies sideways on the ground, stalled and quiet where it fell when released by the tree's fall. Gas-oil mix leaks slowly from the carburetor. David could never get it to idle properly without his hand on the throttle; something about the carburetor mixture he could never get right.

He is exhausted from the pain in his chest. As he tries again to draw breath, a stab of pain from the rib that has pierced his lung again overwhelms his effort. He stares at the fern fronds and listens to the water in the brook. In his mind, he sees the five- and six-inch brookies under the banks undulating slowly to hold their place in the gentle current, an occasional flash of rose-colored light as one drifts into the midstream sun. He closes his eyes to rest and smells the fish in a black iron skillet sizzling in butter over the woodstove at home. Ann is breaking fresh eggs on the other side of the pan. The blue graniteware coffee pot sits on the far right of the woodstove, away from the intense heat of the firebox. It's his favorite breakfast.

His vision is blurring. He is dizzy but not yet confused. When he opens his eyes, the fern fronds now appear like an ancient tree; the moss, a bracken hill in the distance. He himself is tiny. The wood chips are the size of cedar shakes and dominate his short field of vision.

He is suddenly struck by the realization that he never knew his natural parents. His father's death at sea and his mother's rare moments of tender lucidity left him to imagine who they might have been had it not been for the war and his mother's addictions. He is grateful for Alain and Eugénie and the sprawling stepfamily that raised him.

And Annie is always there for him when he needs her, but this time she is unaware that he needs her.

He thinks of her now, but his brain, bereft of oxygen, produces only fleeting evanescent images and sensations from different times in his life: watching Annie knead bread on a bird's-eye maple board with the rich smell of yeasty dough permeating the kitchen; Annie using a hot teacup to draw wasp venom out of his forearm where he had been stung multiple times when a falling tree disturbed a nearby paper nest; helping his nearest neighbor, Eddy Kitonis, split wood to heat the still in his ramshackle cedar oil mill; playing doctor with Ginny Stewart in her stern father's hayloft and first discovering the aching thrill of desire; learning to drive Mr. Farr's tractor. He remembers his great-grandmother and the wisps of white hair surrounding her face. He sees Eugénie stirring a pot on her stove; Mrs. Roleau sitting quietly with her hen Sylvie in her lap; the girl in the swing in the Fragonard; the blue Madonna in the Dali painting. He sees the coin his stepfather made for him on the top of his dresser. He's read all of his father's letters now. He's grateful he and Annie married so she will have his grandmother's money to keep up their place and perhaps help Jeanette. He thinks of his walks with Jeanette and tries to imagine her at nine. The fleeting images of people and places subside.

With great effort, he opens his eyes and sees only light. He hears the purling brook. He thinks about how angry Annie will be to see him lying dead under a tree. He sees his father sinking slowly into Leyte Gulf. Neither father nor son is breathing now. A small runnel of blood appears from his left nostril.